Spain inclu... ...erde...

Andalus: Unlocking ...

Guerra: Living in the Shadow... ... *War;*
Sacred Sierra: A Year on a Spanish ... *and The Spy
with 29 Names.* His Max Cámara series of crime novels
started with *Or the Bull Kills You,* which was longlisted
for the CWA Specsavers Crime Thriller Awards New
Blood Dagger 2011. This was followed by *A Death in
Valencia, The Anarchist Detective* and, most recently,
Blood Med.

ALSO BY JASON WEBSTER

Non-Fiction

Duende: A Journey in Search of Flamenco

Andalus: Unlocking the Secrets of Moorish Spain

Guerra: Living in the Shadows of the Spanish Civil War

Sacred Sierra: A Year on a Spanish Mountain

The Spy with 29 Names: The Story of the Second World War's Most Audacious Double Agent

The Max Cámara novels

Or the Bull Kills You

A Death in Valencia

The Anarchist Detective

Blood Med

JASON WEBSTER

A Body in Barcelona

VINTAGE

1 3 5 7 9 10 8 6 4 2

Vintage
20 Vauxhall Bridge Road,
London SW1V 2SA

Vintage is part of the Penguin Random House group of companies whose
addresses can be found at global.penguinrandomhouse.com

Penguin
Random House
UK

First published in Vintage in 2016
First published in hardback by Chatto & Windus in 2015

penguin.co.uk/vintage

A CIP catalogue record for this book is available from the British Library

ISBN 9780099598268

Printed and bound by Clays Ltd, St Ives Plc

Penguin Random House is committed to a sustainable future for our business,
our readers and our planet. This book is made from Forest Stewardship
Council® certified paper.

For Miles and Ingrid

What is the Truth? was askt of yore.
Reply all object Truth is one
As twain of halves aye makes a whole;
the moral Truth for all is none.
>   Sir Richard Burton, *The Kasidah*

The father ate the bitter olives, and now the son has to
shit them out.
>   Spanish proverb

NOTE

There are several police forces in Spain. Chief Inspector Max Cámara works for the *Policía Nacional*, which deals with major crimes in the larger towns and cities. The *Guardia Civil* is a rural police force, or gendarmerie, covering the countryside and smaller towns and villages. Both the *Policía Nacional* and *Guardia Civil* report to the Interior Ministry, although the *Guardia Civil* is paramilitary and has links with the Defence Ministry.

Some autonomous regions have their own police. The Catalan force is called the *Mossos d'Esquadra*, while the Basque is known as *La Ertzaintza*.

In addition to these national and regional forces, towns and cities tend to have a local police force – the *Policía Local*, sometimes known as the *Policía Municipal*.

PROLOGUE

U home yet?
– *No. Where U?*
In car. Dad pssd off
– *?*
Want Xbox
– *?*
No. Says I got nuff
– *Bstrd*
Hate him
– *Get nothr*
Xbox?
– *Dad, idiot*
;–) want yours. Gives u evrythng
– *Never c him*
2mrrow?
– *No*
– *?*

– Work
Ask for Xbox
– ?
He miss wknd you get Xbox
– :-)
Then giv to me
– No!
;-) I'm ur frend
– Get ur own
Where u now?
– Plza Vrgn
Wtch for benderz
– ?
Behnd cathdrl
– Where?
Want ur arse
– Sicko!!!!!!!
We beat maristas
– 4-0
Coz they shit
– We rule
CSCJ 4 ever!
– U c my goal?
Mine bettr
– Ur goal rank
Curld past keepr
– Keepr already on grnd
No!
– My gol top net!!!
Dik
– Englsh hmwrk
Me too

– My name is Fermín. I have 10 years old
Am 10
– ?
Am 10. Not have 10
– U wrse than Fthr Eugenio
Coz I clever & u stupid
– Dik
U almost home?
– 5 mins
Hungry
– Man fllwng
Tortilla & salad. Always same
– Weirdo
What?
– Bendr after me
Wants ur arse
– Shut up! Gttng closr
Bllx
– Reckn
?
U reckn what?
Fermín
Hey!
Almst home
U there?
Stop shttng me
C u in Englsh
Bye.

ONE

The silver handle of Colonel José Terreros's swordstick was a cast of the eagle of St John, formerly the symbol of Their Most Catholic Majesties King Ferdinand and Queen Isabella, and more recently of the dictatorship that had saved Spain from the great Marxist–Masonic conspiracy. The handle was shiny and smooth, and as he walked to work along Calle Tejero, the colonel gripped it tightly, tapping the bottom of the stick with a strict rhythm on the pavement.

It was a fine morning in Ceuta, with a mild *Poniente* breeze that cleaned and freshened the air. On any other day he might stop at one of the bars along the promenade and have a coffee while gazing out over the strait towards the peninsula, watching the tankers passing lazily between Mediterranean and Atlantic, or the ferries marching more briskly southwards from Algeciras, a vital link between this little Spanish corner of Africa and the Fatherland. But today he felt alive with urgency. He had to press on. There would be time for such pleasures again soon, once a better future had been secured.

His feet took him along his usual route, the Paseo de la Marina Española, first crossing Calle de la Legión and then Calle Millán Astray. He checked every day that the street signs were as they always had been, always should be. Like old friends. Unlike other parts of the country, where tradition was under daily assault, Ceuta still valued the armed forces – institutions that had made the country great. And kept it so.

Over recent years, governments in Madrid had managed to remove some of the more glorious names from Ceuta's streets – there was no longer a sign for Calle General Franco, for example. But Millán Astray, the founder of the Legión, was still honoured. Franco's mentor had played his part in the success of the National Uprising of 1936, but years before that, here in Ceuta, he had created the Legión – the greatest fighting force that the country had ever produced. The original idea for the elite unit might have come from elsewhere, but the French had to fill theirs with foreigners, and the tougher, more rugged Spanish *legionarios* made their Francophone counterparts look like pussycats.

Millán Astray had suffered the wounds of a martyr, sacrificing both an arm and an eye for the nation. A true hero. Let them come, if they dared, and try to remove his name. Let them try to scrub history clean of the great men who had saved the country from the Red scum. Let them pander to the Leftists, the separatists, the Godless and the queers. Let them come here and try to do that. And then they would find themselves learning the true meaning of tradition. And rebellion.

A light gust of wind blowing in from the strait brought

the scent of ship's diesel and salt water from the port and the grey pencil moustache above Terreros's upper lip twitched as the embryo of a smile formed on his mouth: it was the smell of action, of decision.

His offices were near the Cathedral of Our Lady of Africa, a few paces from the main square, down a side street and up a narrow staircase on the second floor. The climb could be difficult at times, but he was still strong, despite his sixty-three years, and had learned to ignore the pain. At the top, a green door with frosted glass led to a small room with an oak desk in a corner. A computer sat on the top; in a drawer, hidden from view, was his 20cm-barrel, ivory-grip .357-calibre Magnum Colt Python, which he liked to polish before lunch every day. On the wall, next to the portrait of Franco and embossed in gold on a wooden plaque, was written the motto of the Legión: *Todo por la Patria*: 'Everything for the Fatherland'.

Within moments of his arrival, there was a rap on the door and a small middle-aged man with a white apron tied around his waist came in bearing a tray.

'*Buenos días, Señor Coronel.*'

'*Buenos días, Paco,*' Terreros answered stiffly.

'You've heard about the latest assault on the border?'

The barman leaned across and placed Terreros's *café cortado* on the edge of the desk with a slight tremble of the hand. It was only half-past eight in the morning, but Paco had been up since five, cleaning and setting up his premises for the early workers stopping off for coffee and brandy before clocking on. Then came the rounds of shops and nearby offices, each with their regular and very specific orders. The steps up to the colonel's office were the worst, and he left it till last, when his tray was that bit less heavy.

7

Days when the wind came from the east – the *Levante* – were the worst, causing his joints to ache. Today was less bad, but he could never reach the green door without panting and breaking into a sweat.

Paco's reward, however, was to allow himself a moment's conversation – never too long; they were both busy men – with the colonel. Terreros was not merely a retired military officer, he was ex-Legión, and no matter what was happening either in Spain or the rest of the world, he had opinions and insights that needed to be listened to. Paco liked to think that the colonel in his turn appreciated the titbits that he brought every so often – rumours, overheard conversations, mere gossip in many cases. But it gave Terreros another ear to the ground. Paco never knew exactly what the colonel did up here. The plaque at the ground-floor entrance described his office as 'La Asociación de Ayuda para Legionarios (the Veteran Legionarios' Welfare Association). But quite what that work entailed he could not say. And despite carrying out occasional favours for the colonel, he never asked.

Today there was something fresh to talk about. The colonel almost certainly knew about the large group – some said as many as a thousand – of sub-Saharan African men who had tried to storm the border between Morocco and Ceuta during the night. Such incidents were becoming more and more frequent, despite the use of razor wire to keep them at bay. Unlike earlier attempts, however, the previous night's break-in had resulted in over twenty deaths: some of the *Guardia Civil* officers on the Spanish side had panicked and started firing rubber bullets, at which point the would-be immigrants had jumped into the sea. But instead of swimming to the First World, many had only made it to the next world instead. Patrol boats had spent the hours since dawn picking bodies out of the water.

Terreros nodded as Paco loitered for a moment in his office, his now-empty tray held at his side.

'It was mentioned on the radio,' Terreros said.

'They reckon it's only the beginning,' said Paco. 'Had some of the *Guardia Civil* men in this morning – finishing after the night shift. Told me all about it. It's just getting worse. One day soon we'll be burying some of our own. It's just a matter of time.'

'You may be right, Paco.' Terreros took a slow sip of his coffee. The barman said nothing. It was the usual routine: the opening comment and then the pause as Paco waited for the colonel's words of wisdom on the matter in hand. Terreros loved it – it was the only reason why he tolerated the man entering the sanctum of his office.

'We are,' he began, 'on the very edge of civilisation here, as you know. The world of Christian values ends only metres away from where we now are. We live with that every day. It has been the role of Spain for centuries to act as the shield and sword of the faith. It is our destiny.'

He placed the coffee glass back on its saucer and stroked a finger and thumb over his moustache. Paco waited, silent.

'The cowards in Madrid are blind to the gravity of the situation,' Terreros continued. 'It may require a sacrifice – the blood of one of our own men – before they can learn to see. God alone can say.'

'Do you think it will come to that?' Paco asked. The tray swung in his hand, his thick black eyebrows almost touching as he tensed his brow.

'It is inevitable,' Terreros said. 'But our little drama here

9

in Ceuta is nothing to the greater struggle that is breaking out on the peninsula, Paco.'

He raised a finger in the barman's face, and a thrilling surge of adrenalin poured into Paco's bloodstream.

'The nation is in peril. You know what I am talking about. The separatists imagine that their time has come, that the sacred unity of Spain – *la España eterna* – can be broken.'

His voice began to rise as he spoke, his face reddening. He got up from his chair and stood close to the barman, staring him hard in the eyes.

'They could not be more wrong. Nothing, repeat nothing, can be allowed to destroy what has been divinely ordained. Spain is, has been and always will be. There is no room for anyone who thinks otherwise. Those who stand in our way will pay the highest price. I swear by the blood of my ancestors that while there is breath in me I will not stop until the menace has been defeated!'

The colonel waved his arm for a final, dramatic flourish, before sitting down at his desk.

Paco understood and made to move: he had got what he came for.

'How right you are, Colonel. How right you are. Now I shall leave you to your important work. Until tomorrow.'

He gave a slight bow, lifted the tray up under his arm and passed through the door, making sure to close it gently but firmly behind him. In a few moments he was downstairs and outside in the street again. The breeze cooled the back of his neck and he felt something like a spring in his step.

Yes, dangerous times were ahead. That was what the colonel had been trying to tell him. Dangerous, and exciting. And he had it on the highest authority. Oh, there would be much to talk about with the lunchtime crowd. Confidentially, of course, and he would never dream of giving away the source of his privileged information, but he would make sure all of his trusted customers were up to date before the end of the day. That was, after all, why they came to his bar in the first place.

Upstairs in his office, Terreros finished his bitter, cold coffee, swore under his breath at Paco, and switched on his computer. After typing in three encrypted passwords to get access to his desktop, he clicked on the file that had been playing on his mind since the moment he had woken up: AGENTS.

There was some cleaning up to do.

TWO

The medal ceremony was about to end. New sons, freshly minted members of the family of heroes, grinned broadly as brightly coloured ribbons were pinned to their crime-fighting chests. Green and white for the *Cruz con distintivo rojo*. He had had one of his own, somewhere, but felt sure he had lost it along the way.

One of the decorated men caught his eye in his moment of glory, the smile on his lips only faltering for the briefest of moments before he looked away. He was among the last three officers to be honoured that afternoon, taking their turn to walk up to the podium and shake hands with the Catalan interior minister. Madrid had sent a representative – the deputy civil governor – but she had been made to stand at the back. On a symbolic level at least, no one was in doubt about who was in charge.

It was his third week in Barcelona. A little over two weeks for the inquiry, and now this – the medal ceremony, delayed so that the men being investigated, and now cleared – could seal their positions as loved and respected members of the policing fraternity. No one had questioned their innocence.

Except him.

The protestor had been taking part in a small but violent demonstration two months before against Catalan moves towards independence. Corralled into the Plaça de Catalunya, the group had started breaking up paving stones to hurl at the riot squad closing in on them. Fights broke out as people tried to force their way through the cordon. Twenty-nine of them needed medical treatment, as well as five of the officers. But there was one mortality: Ignacio Rovira had died that night after being tackled to the ground and held by three members of the riot squad men. One of them had placed his knee across Rovira's throat, crushing the trachea. Despite only being in his late twenties, Rovira had a heart condition, which did not help matters. By the time anyone realised something was wrong it was too late.

There had been a scandal, as was to be expected. The protestors made certain that Ignacio was quickly turned into a martyr for the cause, and in death he became a social media sensation. A photo of his corpse-face being held in the black-gloved hands of a policeman went 'viral' and some supporters even had the image tattooed on their bodies. Newspaper columnists roared in condemnation, while government officials confirmed their faith in the forces of law and order.

But the fact was that in the brief time since 2008 when they had fully taken over policing duties from the *Policía Nacional* and *Guardia Civil*, the Catalan regional police – the *Mossos d'Esquadra* – had already gained a reputation for brutality. Ignacio Rovira's was not the first death that they were linked to. Two other men had died in custody over the previous years; a young woman had committed suicide after a highly questionable conviction for assault on a police officer; immigrants complained of torture and sexual abuse at the hands of the *Mossos*. And it went against the grain: Catalonia liked to view itself as a more liberal, wealthy and culturally advanced corner of the Iberian peninsula – all part of a self-identity that, engineered or not, considered itself separate from the rest of Spain, and increasingly so. That its police force should be universally despised for being violent, unfair and almost a law unto itself was a problem, not least because it carried powerful echoes from the time in recent memory when freedoms had been crushed.

Something had to be done, and so the special commission was formed to investigate the officers implicated in Rovira's death. For extra 'transparency', policemen and -women from across the country were invited to join. And the role of Valencia representative had fallen to Chief Inspector Max Cámara.

Nominally, they all came from different organisations. But they were still police, creating emotional, if invisible, bonds with the men under investigation. If they had joined forces to catch criminals, the team would barely have functioned – each member withholding as much information as possible from the others while trying to shine as the best detective. Yet there was no competition involved where clearing accused colleagues was concerned. One day any one of them might find themselves in the dock, in which case being known for closing ranks would come in useful.

He had not meant to break the bonhomie of their little group – eight senior officers from both the *Policía Nacional*, like himself, and the *Guardia Civil*, along with two members from the *Mossos* and a representative from the *Ertzaintza* – the Basque regional police. He knew that, at times, he had an urge to play the child in the crowd, like a nervous tic, pointing out the emperor's nakedness, and did his best to bring it under control. It was just that he did think there was evidence that undue force had been used against Rovira. Christ, the guy had died while being arrested – was that not doubt enough? And was placing a knee on a person's throat acceptable as a restraining technique?

Even raising the question had caused friction.

In the end, when the votes were cast, he had the impression that someone somewhere was quite pleased that one abstaining voice could be recorded. The outcome had never been questioned – Rovira's medical history, detailing the delicacy of his heart, had given them all the cover they required – but at least there could be no accusations of a whitewash. Perhaps that was why he had been asked to join in the first place.

He had stayed for the medal ceremony out of a sense of duty. Nothing urgent called him back to Valencia and he needed to show that he accepted the commission's decision. As a senior police officer, he was giving the three *Mossos* officers a blessing of sorts by appearing at their official re-baptism. No one was speaking to him, but at least he was making it clear that no bad blood would be coming from his side.

The ostracism was subtle in most cases: the *Guardia Civil* officers kept mostly to themselves in any case, and the medal ceremony only seemed to strengthen their more formal, military style of behaviour. The two *Mossos* members of the commission were the most petty, however, doing everything they could to avoid having to greet him or shake his hand, standing to the side and pointing him out to their colleagues: *He's the one, the traitor, the unbeliever.*

Fuck them. Besides, his ticket for the evening train nestled in his inside jacket pocket and his case was waiting for him at reception. Soon, in a couple of moments, he would be gone, heading away from Barcelona and back to Valencia. He had not seen Alicia at all in those three weeks. He missed her; longed for her.

He drained his glass of cava and looked for a ledge – or a plant pot, anything – where he could dispose of it before leaving. He would have to slip past the small army of wine-waiters and security men before he could get out.

It was time to head home, time to leave the politics, the tensions, the clashing disharmonies, behind.

'I wanted to catch you,' said a voice behind him. 'Before you managed to sneak away.'

He turned and saw a smiling face, a man with a short grey beard wearing a light corduroy jacket, hair slightly long and ruffled – at least for a politician.

'It's Chief Inspector Max Cámara, am I right? I did want to meet you in person.'

He found himself smiling back as the Catalan interior minister shook his hand with a firm yet delicate grip.

'Josep Segundo Pont,' the politician introduced himself. 'I won't keep you for a moment.'

THREE

Segundo Pont placed his fingertips on Cámara's elbow and led him a few paces to the side of the chamber. The *Mossos* had hired the Palau de la Música for the medal ceremony – a grand art nouveau structure in the centre of Barcelona more used to hosting Plácido Domingo or Montserrat Caballé than policemen. But the venue ensured good press coverage for the event, as evidenced by the photographers mingling among the uniforms. Besides, the previous – and now disgraced – Catalan government had been involved in a corruption scandal associated with the building: using it now to celebrate the work of humble civil servants was a way for the new, left-wing, pro-separatist authorities to make a statement.

'I do have a train to catch,' Cámara said.

Segundo Pont squeezed his arm affectionately.

'Of course.'

Like most in the two-month-old Catalan government,

Segundo Pont did not wear a tie, leaving his collar open. It appeared to be the dress code for this younger generation – a suit or a jacket to show that they were serious, but with a touch of informality to say that they were 'ordinary' too. Cámara thought that there was something affected about it, but despite his desire to get away, he was curious about the man, freshly arrived in office. He sensed a still-beating human heart inside Segundo Pont; there was a gentleness about his large, brown eyes. Cámara had the feeling that he was in the presence of a man not afraid of his own emotions – or of those of others.

'I simply wanted to thank you for all your work over the past weeks,' Segundo Pont said; his Catalan accent was noticeable, but mild. 'I know it hasn't been easy.'

Cámara raised an eyebrow.

'Easy?'

'Look,' Segundo Pont said, gripping Cámara's arm even tighter, 'I don't want to make you uncomfortable. What's happened has happened. And all this –' he glanced around the reception room – 'is about drawing a line under things and moving on, as I'm sure you're aware.'

Cámara did not move. What did the man want? In spite of Segundo Pont's rather direct and informal manner, Cámara began to suspect that this was a test. Were his re-actions being gauged?

'No one,' Segundo Pont continued, 'is going to pull the wool over your eyes. That much has been made clear. You're your own man. People appreciate that. They find it scary as well, which is why they avoid you.'

'What . . . ?'

'I've been watching. Everything. It's a habit of mine. But

don't take it amiss. Everyone here respects you. You stood your ground. And that's what's important.'

Cámara focused all his senses, trying to read the politician and his possible intentions, but there was something impenetrable about him, as though he were partly hidden behind a wall.

'What did you want to happen?' Cámara asked. 'Did you really think the outcome was in doubt?'

Segundo Pont frowned.

'We respect the commission's decision without reservations,' he said. 'Which can only be right. But that's not the point. We wanted the best police officers on board for this. It had to be transparent. The situation at the moment, as you know, is delicate. Things are moving very fast in Catalonia right now. We just want to ensure they go in the right direction. There is a possibility – very faint, but a possibility – of social collapse if things go wrong.'

He nodded, as though to confirm what he had just said.

'This commission,' he continued, 'and your part in it, are a fundamental step in safeguarding the reputation of the forces of law and order right now. I can't overstate that, and I wanted to thank you, in the name of the Catalan people, for your role in this.'

It was only now that Segundo Pont released his grip on Cámara's arm. That look in his eye – the caring, considerate expression – had been replaced by something more like concern. Even fear.

'Thank you,' Cámara said, with the slightest hesitation. The truth was that the politician's words were more alarmist than anything he had expected to hear.

'What do you mean that things are moving fast?' he asked.

A nervous smile quivered on Segundo Pont's lips.

'Powerful forces have been unleashed,' he said. 'You're aware of that. The previous government's failures led many to think that a key moment in Catalonia's history had passed. But a Pandora's box has been opened, and certain events now seem inevitable. The elections were a watershed. The former leaders were mere opportunists – ideological separatists are now in power. This time the opportunity won't be missed.'

'Full independence,' Cámara said. 'You think it's achievable? After everything?'

Segundo Pont smiled, but said nothing.

'I haven't said anything,' Segundo Pont whispered, reading the comprehension in Cámara's eyes.

'I get it.'

'It's been a pleasure finally meeting you, Chief Inspector.'

'Hold on a minute.' This time Cámara grabbed the politician's arm. 'You said you wanted the best for this commission.'

'Of course.' Segundo Pont tilted his head slightly to the side.

'So we were hand-picked,' Cámara said. 'You got the team that you wanted. This was set up from the start.'

Segundo Pont held out his hands, as though in prayer.

'I can assure you there was no political interference in the commission. Please, we're not like that. The whole thing had to be transparent, as I say, or it wouldn't have worked.'

'You couldn't have left something so important to chance,' said Cámara. 'You yourself admit it. You wouldn't have allowed this to work on its own, possibly giving the wrong result.'

Segundo Pont shook his head.

'Is this justice?' Cámara asked. 'Does this get us anywhere? Does this help Rovira's family in any way? Their boy is dead, and all that's happened—'

'Chief Inspector, please,' Segundo Pont interrupted him. 'It's not at all as you're imagining. Besides, it's getting late. Are you sure you're going to catch your train?'

Cámara checked the time from a gilt clock hanging on the wall. He had less than fifteen minutes to get to the Sants railway station, on the other side of the city.

'You knew I wouldn't go along just to fit in. There was a case to answer. You needed my abstention – that's what your transparency really boils down to.'

He turned to leave.

'Max.' Segundo Pont leaned forward and held him by the shoulder. 'Please, I want us to part as friends. I want to regard you as my friend – and a friend, a real friend, of Catalonia.'

Cámara looked at him – the human warmth, the use of his first name. Was this man different, or just like the rest?

'Which Catalonia do you mean?' he said.

'Don't think you've gone unnoticed,' Segundo Pont said with a smile. 'Your name is often mentioned.'

Cámara made to step away. A row of taxis was waiting just outside the main doors. He could still make it. Just.

'People are watching you, Max.'

Cámara was already crossing the room.

'We'll be in touch,' he heard Segundo Pont say. 'This country needs men like you now.'

His hands shook as he got into the back of the taxi.

FOUR

The flat felt different.

'Alicia?' Her house keys were not in the bowl by the door: he was alone. He had texted her from the train to say he would be back that night, but with the signal coming and going as he sped southwards it was impossible to say if the message had reached her.

He carried his bag through to the bedroom and set it down on the floor. The bed was unmade, sheets thrown back and tangled. The window was partly open and the smell of car fumes wafted in with the voices of prostitutes and punters negotiating pre-coital deals in the street below.

Pulling out his clothes, he carried them to the washing machine on the covered balcony behind the kitchen. Breadcrumbs lay scattered on the floor; a stick of bread had been cut into and lay in pieces on the table. He leaned over and felt into it: a day, perhaps two days, old.

The washing machine clicked as he turned it on and he

stepped back inside. Again, he had the sense that something had changed. Everything appeared to be normal, and yet the feeling was different, like a new smell.

He continued to move around, reconnecting with his home, as though greeting every room – and whatever spirits might be living in each one.

His grandfather's old bedroom was empty save for the bed, a chair and the wardrobe. There had been surprisingly little to throw out when Hilario died, as though he had been preparing for death, shedding himself of as much as he could before leaving them. Cámara had heard that it took months or even years to sort out the personal effects and paperwork of the deceased, but it was clear that his grandfather had done everything that he could beforehand, even going so far as to close his own bank account. The money he had – not much, just a few hundred euros – was all in cash, kept in a little tin box next to his shoes in the wardrobe. He had been thinking ahead, anxious to be as little burden as possible once he was no longer with them.

Selfless to the last – and yet there had been a cajoling, nagging side to Hilario as well. Perhaps the single most important thing that he taught Cámara was the need never to stop improving. Perfection meant atrophy, and atrophy meant death, so you had to keep refining. Which meant that everything from Cámara's schoolwork as a boy to his police work as a man – and even trivial things such as how he opened a can of soup or tied his shoelaces – came under scrutiny. Life could never be about comfort.

For this reason, Hilario rarely missed a chance to berate his grandson about being a detective. On the surface it was because Hilario was an anarchist and could not tolerate his only living relative being an active member of the forces of law and order. But Cámara realised years before that it was more complicated than that – that the jibing and sarcastic remarks had an effect, nudging and pushing him to improve at his job. It was not police work per se that Hilario minded, it was the intention behind it. Police officers who genuinely worked for the betterment of people and society were to be applauded. Those whose real goal was the strengthening of State power were to be opposed. The problem, for Hilario as for Cámara, was that the organisation of the police itself – with its uniforms and command structures – often led good-natured policemen and -women from the first category to the second. It took great strength of character to remain true to the initial ideal of the work while wading every day into the mud of bureaucracy, power and politics.

Cámara had spent many years with his grandfather – Hilario had taken him in and brought him up after Cámara became orphaned – and much of Hilario's behaviour and way of thinking had now become second nature. In the five months since his death Cámara had often spoken with him, hearing his voice in his mind. The conversations helped him through the choppy, unpredictable seas of mourning. It was more substantial than an accumulated memory of the man: Hilario was still alive in some sense that he had yet to comprehend.

And yet, despite being physically dead, the old bastard still had the ability to annoy him. In his will he had left everything – the flat in Albacete and a few small items – to Alicia. This did not bother Cámara. In fact, he had laughed when he found out: it made perfect sense, bringing him closer to her in some counter-intuitive way, making her part of the Cámara family – or what was left of it. The one legacy that Hilario had passed on to his grandson was a sheet of paper with an essay, written in small, slightly shaky handwriting, on how to make the best paella. He had titled it, rather pompously Cámara thought, *The Paella Manifesto – a distillation of over seventy years' rice cooking*. It contained everything that Cámara was supposed to know about making the Valencian dish, something which, deep down, Cámara liked to think he already made a good job of. Hilario's notes were not general pointers, however, but specifically directed at him:

I've noticed you always put too much salt in paella. Watch yourself, and MAKE SURE YOU PUT IT IN ONLY AT THE SPECIFIED TIME . . .

Don't think that the rice is the most important ingredient. It isn't. It is there as a vehicle for the other flavours. Each element has its role to play, but NEVER ALLOW ONE TO DOMINATE. Paella is nothing if it isn't about HARMONY and UNITY. The one dish must be created from the many ingredients.

The underlining only increased his feeling of being lectured at from beyond the grave. But the one comment that really grated on Cámara was the entry on saffron:

Most saffron available in shops is fake. Don't use it. FIND NATURAL ALTERNATIVES. The colour additive they sell is almost pure tartrazine and will give you cancer. Try turmeric – it's not bad, if not exactly authentic . . .

Cámara himself had exposed the mafia in La Mancha peddling fake saffron, but Hilario could not resist passing the information on as his own.

At first, Cámara had gritted his teeth and smiled when he read the *Manifesto* – everything about it was typical of his grandfather. And he folded it up and placed it in his wallet. Which was where it had stayed ever since.

He stepped away from the bedroom and paced towards the kitchen and back on to the balcony. At the end, beyond the washing machine, was a small hut-like structure made of wood. As he opened the door he was struck by the sharp-sweet smell of a dozen marihuana plants basking in artificial light. They seemed to smile at him and he murmured a low 'Hola' in greeting. He pressed his fingers into the soil of the nearest one: the watering system appeared to be working, while the fan set in the corner kept them well aired. But it was hot and muggy in there: after the briefest of checks he closed the door and went back to the kitchen.

He had not smoked anything since Hilario had died, resisting the temptation to blur the loss in the green furry blanket of his home-grown. Hilario had always taken the most care of them, and even hooked the electricity up to the mains in such a way that they did not have to pay for the expensive lights that simulated sunshine twenty-four hours a day. It could be an expensive hobby otherwise. But surprisingly, in the time that his grandfather had not been with him, the urge had never come. The remains of last year's harvest – dried and ready to smoke – sat in the usual coffee jar in the living room, and this year's crop was steadily maturing. But he did not really care for the plants any more. If he came back one day and found by some miracle that the hut had been dismantled and they were all gone, he would not care, though a curious inertia kept the process going. Perhaps it was a last link to his grandfather: Hilario had always claimed that by providing Cámara with dope he kept him on *his* side of the law. Or at least a toehold of sorts.

In the kitchen, he picked up one of the dry pieces of bread on the table and chewed on it as best he could while he scouted around for dinner ingredients. The fridge was practically empty, with half a carton of semi-skimmed milk, a jar of anchovies and an opened tin of tomato purée with white mould erupting from the top. He would have to go out or go to bed hungry. It was half-past ten – there was still time to find somewhere open.

He was wondering again where Alicia might be when the latch clicked and he heard her come inside. Her keys rattled as she placed them in the bowl by the door. The lights were on and it was clear that he was inside the flat as well, but instead of walking down to the kitchen, he heard her go straight to the bedroom.

'Hi!' he called. No answer.

He pursed his lips and walked to the other end of the flat. Their bedroom door was ajar. He pushed it open.

'Hey,' he said. 'I'm back. How're you doing?'

Alicia was perched on the bed, pulling down her trousers carefully. Tossing them on to a nearby chair, she opened a drawer in her bedside table and pulled out a tube of cream. She squeezed a small amount on to her fingertip, and then started rubbing it on round pink-and-red spots on her thighs.

'Do they hurt?' Cámara asked in a low voice.

She shrugged.

'I . . . er, I thought about popping out to get something to eat,' he said.

She finished rubbing the cream into one sore, then squeezed out some more from the tube and moved on to another. There were seventeen of them; the ones high up, close to her groin, were the worst.

'I'm not hungry,' she said at last. 'And I'm tired.'

She looked at him. Her brown, deer-like eyes, usually so bright and alive, looked clouded and heavy. She tried to smile.

'You sort yourself out. I need to sleep.'

FIVE

It was dark and he no longer felt so hungry.

He had told neighbours that he was a salesman, and the story appeared to work as a cover: the dealers knew not to approach him, but a couple chatting in a doorway greeted him with a nod as he passed. Being known as police was inadvisable. Most of his colleagues preferred to live outside the city, always careful about giving their address for fear of reprisals from criminals they had put away. But he found the satellite towns near Valencia, with their bungalow estates and tennis clubs, dull and uninspiring. He was a city dweller and liked being in the centre. The danger was all part of a need to feel alive.

The street was quiet – it was midweek – but nonetheless the city felt asleep, as though its sparkle were fading. Months before, when the economic crisis had been at its peak, there had been a palpable sense of possibility in the air, that sudden change, revolution even, might come about at any moment. That had now given way to something more lethargic and resigned. Not even the old King's departure – finally, having given in to the inevitable and abdicated in favour of his son – had resurrected it. The new monarch had swiftly and efficiently stepped in, and while he did not enjoy quite the same respect – and could never be the same father-figure to the nation – many at least appeared inclined to give him a chance to establish himself before passing judgement. 'Give the kid a year or two,' the comment went.

In Barcelona, he had noticed, people barely seemed to care about the new head of state; emotionally it was as though they had already separated from the rest of the country: what did events in Madrid matter to them? But inevitably, in much of Spain, the change of king had strengthened the republican movement, and a new, media-friendly but anti-Establishment party had risen meteorically in the polls.

There were still many boarded-up shops in his part of the city – perhaps one or two on every street. Some of them reopened for a few months as a new fad appeared and people tried to cash in: fine beauty parlours offering dodgy laser treatment for body hair had mostly been and gone, as had a handful of iced-yoghurt outlets. Now it was the turn of vapour-cigarette vendors desperately trying to fill a shop window with only half a dozen brightly coloured metal tubes that were, supposedly, the latest thing. The sight of them only sparked an unconscious desire in him, and before he had even realised it, a Ducados was hanging from his lip, smoke pouring out behind him as he walked along.

No, there had been no revolution, but everything felt different, and strangely the same.

A couple across the street were ambling slowly, hand in hand. As the girl talked, the boy leaned in quickly and kissed her on the mouth, cutting her off for a second before she smiled at him and carried on telling her story.

He drew hard on the cigarette, filling his mouth with as much smoke as possible before inhaling it and holding it deep in his lungs. Finally letting it out, he coughed lightly and held the back of his hand to his lip. He did not smoke any more in the flat. After what had happened to Alicia it was the wrong thing to do. She herself had not touched a cigarette since. The doctors had told them that the burn scars would never go away completely. But with time, if she used the creams regularly and avoided the sun for a year or more, they would fade to some degree. Both of them had come to understand, however, that the marks on her skin where the thugs had used her body as an ashtray were but the physical side of something longer-lasting.

At first Cámara had thought that the damage was not too bad. They enjoyed a period of closeness during the first few weeks after she finally left the clinic. Hilario had died not long before and they were united by a mixture of powerful emotions – grief, relief, even joy at the successful conclusion of the case Cámara had been working on, exposing corruption in the local ruling party and sending down the right-wing sadists who had tortured her.

But after a month or so the distance started to open up between them. It was understandable, given what had happened, that Alicia did not want to make love. But at first she had craved him physically, if not sexually. Later, though, she had even refused his embraces, while his tentative moves to rekindle an erotic spark had come to nothing. He did not resent it. But sometimes he caught himself wondering whether they would ever have sex again.

A primitive anxiety had started to eat away at him – that Alicia blamed him for what had happened, for her getting caught up in everything. Not consciously – she was not, ordinarily, the kind of person to hold grudges. But perhaps at some hidden level. She had been trying to help him with the case, to get information, and he had encouraged her. But she had almost died in the process. And the reaction, some kind of delayed shock, had surprised him when it came.

He flicked the cigarette into a nearby drain hole and exhaled. In front of him stood a late-night bar. He could go in, have a couple of glasses of beer, whatever was left to eat, perhaps a glass of brandy or two, and then head home. Or he could go and see his friends. The collective was only a few blocks further on. He had not seen them for weeks.

Pushing his hands deep into his pockets, he carried on walking.

He smelt it before he could see it – the scent of fried garlic, cheap tobacco and human bodies in need of a wash. At the door, drawing on a roll-up, his head bent down slightly and his face hidden behind lumpy dreadlocks, stood a familiar figure.

Dídac smiled broadly when he caught sight of Cámara. '*Tío!* You're back!'

They embraced warmly, Cámara's powerful arms gripping the young man close to him.

'So good to see you,' Dídac said. 'We've been managing,' he grinned. 'Managing without you, but it's always good to have you around.'

Cámara smiled. Dídac was seventeen, and Cámara felt protective towards him. The boy's good humour and innocence made him appear younger than he really was. Cámara was certain that Dídac had never had a girlfriend, although from time to time the boy seemed to have taken a shine to some of the women arriving at their food bank. He was reserved, particularly with new people, despite always wanting to help, and was only ever himself with a handful of friends – with Cámara, with Berto, who owned the place, and with Daniel, his father.

'How's things?' Cámara said, glancing at the door behind. Dídac shrugged.

'We're still here,' he said. 'That's the main thing. They haven't closed us down.'

'Have they tried?'

Dídac frowned. 'Nah, but, you know. The threat's always there. Neighbours complain of the noise sometimes. But they just don't like the idea of free food being handed out. Doesn't fit with the system.'

Cámara smiled at him. 'You're doing a good job, an important job, that's the main thing.'

'Oh, I know that,' Dídac said, punching him on the arm. 'You're not my dad, you know.'

'Sorry, that sounded wrong.'

'It's all right. Come on, let's go in.'

'Good crowd?'

'About the usual. Maybe more, in fact. The media don't report house repossessions and poverty because it's not news any more. But people still need to eat.'

'Restaurants still providing stuff?' Cámara asked.

'Less and less,' said Dídac. 'That's the main problem. Because no one's talking about this any more, people think it's gone away. So some restaurants think we're just scrounging and stop giving us their leftovers. And it doesn't look so good any more. Most were doing it for the publicity in the first place – solidarity with the new poor and all that. Thinking they might win customers with a social conscience. But it doesn't last long.'

He curled his nose and stubbed out his roll-up with his foot.

'But we've still got enough. For the time being.'

He placed his hand on Cámara's arm and led him inside.

'Come on, let's go. Daniel will be pleased to see you. He's got all kinds of new ideas. Big changes. Big plans.'

SIX

Smoking was not allowed inside the food hall. Not because anyone agreed with the ban – that was not their way of doing things – but because if they were caught it would give the authorities the perfect excuse to close them down. Dídac pushed his cigarette stub with his foot towards a small pile on the pavement by the door and they stepped inside.

The first thing that Cámara noticed were posters plastered over the walls; these were new: the place had previously been undecorated. They were mostly coloured red and black, with splashes of purple and yellow. He saw images of raised fists, anguished, hungry faces and dramatic fonts screaming out words like 'RESISTANCE', 'POWER' and 'STRUGGLE'.

The effect was immediate. People of all ages and shades were eating and chatting – many with scruffy, tightly packed bags crammed underneath the long benches where they sat – but the atmosphere had changed. This was no longer simply a food bank offering the homeless and unemployed something to eat; it had become something altogether more politicised. The charity was no longer free: their guests were now expected to absorb some of the ideas of the collective in return for their nourishment.

Berto, the anarchist economist who owned the place, was at the top end of the long rectangular room with a group of volunteers, helping to clean up the used paper plates and plastic cutlery, gathering them up and stuffing them into black bin liners. For a while, at the beginning, they had used real plates, but things got broken and the washing-up rotas became too complicated to manage. Using throwaway alternatives was less environmentally friendly, but worth it, the group had eventually decided, in order to keep things going. Cámara had missed the vote.

After a pause, Berto looked up and caught sight of Cámara in the doorway. He left his helpers and walked over to greet him.

'You've been away too long,' he said with a grin.

'Nice to be back at last,' Cámara smiled back. 'It looks busy.'

Berto nodded. 'Some have already left.' He waved a hand in the direction of the emptier benches. 'But we were packed, yeah. Tell you what, though, we're getting more and more children coming in. Used to be just a handful, but now maybe twenty per cent are kids. Families can't afford to feed them any more.'

He curled his lip.

'From our end there's no sign of things getting any better, despite what they keep saying on the news.'

Cámara liked Berto – he had given them the use of his small, ground-floor premises here when the food bank was forced to abandon the unfinished metro-line station under the city centre. But Cámara could sense that a sermon was about to begin. Looking up, he tried to catch sight of Daniel, spotting him at one of the tables, joking with a group of friends; Dídac had joined them.

'You're absolutely right,' Cámara said to Berto, placing a hand on his shoulder. 'You must fill me in.'

'It's the banks, see—'

'But I just want to go and say hello to Daniel.'

Berto stopped. 'Oh, sure. No problem, Max.'

Cámara dropped his hand and turned to go, but Berto pulled him back.

'Haven't seen Alicia here for a while. She OK?'

'She's got a lot on her mind,' Cámara answered. 'She'll be back.'

Daniel's group – his son and three Latin American men – smiled as Cámara stepped over to them. Daniel was wearing a sleeveless T-shirt – his usual attire, no matter what the weather. He was unshaven these days – an earlier experiment with an over-manicured goatee had thankfully been abandoned and he looked gentler as a result, despite the penetrating shine in his dark green eyes.

Cámara shook the hands of the others, who he did not know, before embracing Daniel.

'Come and join us,' Daniel said. 'There's some food left if you're hungry.'

Before he could answer, Dídac had got up and gone to fetch him some of the remaining leftovers from the counter at the back of the room.

'Thanks,' he said.

'So how are things in Barcelona?' Daniel asked. 'Hotting up, by the looks of it.'

Daniel was from Barcelona himself – Cámara was not sure how long he had been in Valencia. He had given his son a very Catalan name – Dídac was the Catalan version of Diego.

Cámara shrugged.

'It feels . . .' he paused. 'Different. Independence flags are everywhere, and there's a curious, almost manic energy about the place – edgy, nervous, as though something is about to change.'

He grinned. 'But I'm done trying to predict the future. I'll just stick with cleaning up the past.'

The others chuckled and Dídac placed a plate of tortilla and dried strips of *jamón serrano* in front of him.

'Not much left,' he said by way of apology.

'That's fine. Thanks.'

'You ask me,' Daniel said, 'I think independence is inevitable. It gives Catalans something to look forward to, a project they can believe in. Which the rest of Spain is lacking right now. Spain is going nowhere. Catalonia at least has a direction, something to aim for.'

Dídac was nodding enthusiastically.

'The question,' Daniel continued, 'is not whether Catalonia will break away, but when. And then the real question is how the generals and their friends in Madrid will react. That's the real concern here. Will they send the tanks in to keep it part of Spain? It's possible. It's in the Constitution – the justification is right there.'

Cámara shrugged. It seemed there was no way of avoiding political discussions tonight.

'As I say,' he mumbled, 'I've got enough just trying to work out the past.'

'Any interesting cases at the moment?' Dídac asked. He liked it when Cámara told him stories about detective work.

'Leave the man alone,' Daniel said. 'He hasn't come here to talk shop. He needs a rest.'

The two men shared a brief conspiratorial glance.

'Anyway,' Daniel said, 'I'm glad you're here. We're having a meeting afterwards. There's some stuff I want to talk about.'

The diners were already thinning out, many making their way to shelters for the night, or a preferred spot in the old river bed under some trees or a bridge. Within another twenty minutes they had all gone and only the members of the collective remained to finish the clearing-up.

'Right,' said Daniel, sitting at the top of one of the tables with a plastic cup of red wine in his hand. Berto sat down next to him, and the others – three young men and a woman, all in their twenties – gathered round. Dídac swept the floor, while Cámara perched on the table itself, slightly apart from the group.

'I think it's finally time we stepped up,' Daniel began. There was a gentle murmur of approval.

'This food bank's good, but I don't know how long it can last. We're small, we're not connected to any NGOs and we're clearly not part of the system. So sooner or later they'll find a way. And my feeling is we can't keep still. We have to be thinking about what comes next.'

'What about another venue?' the girl said.

'Maybe,' said Daniel. 'But I think we were lucky to get this place anyway. Thanks to Berto.'

Berto lowered his head and smiled.

'I just don't know how easy it would be,' Daniel said. 'Anyone here know of anywhere?'

No one said anything.

'What about distributing food in parks and places?' one of the men said. 'In the river bed, for example.'

'Might work once or twice,' answered Daniel. 'But they'd get wise very quickly. Not sure if it's worth it.'

He paused to see if there were any more ideas before resuming.

'No, you see, I'm thinking more than just giving people something to eat. The point is that it doesn't hurt the people who got us where we are in the first place. And I'm angry, and I want them to know that.'

'We're all angry,' Berto said. 'There just doesn't seem to be enough willingness for change here. People are stuck, just want to go back to the boom years. No one really wants to change anything, deep down.'

Cámara kept out of the conversation, watching.

'That's why,' said Daniel, 'we've got to go more radical. We've been keeping ourselves on the right side of the law. Well, more or less. But the problem is the law – the Establishment – in the first place. There's no respect for ordinary people. Which is why we should show no respect to them. We've got to go in a new direction.'

'What are you suggesting?' the girl asked.

'We go for the bankers themselves,' Daniel said simply. 'They brought this on in the first place. So we demonstrate outside their homes, make a racket, embarrass and annoy them. Make their daily lives as miserable as the ordinary people they left in the lurch.'

There was a moment's pause as the idea sank in.

Daniel had not used the actual word, but Cámara knew precisely what he was talking about: *escraches*, where groups of people would stand around someone's house – often a politician – with placards and whistles in a targeted, almost personalised form of street protest. The Madrid government had already taken measures to stop them.

'What would be the point?' said Berto. 'They've already ruined the country.'

'It's not about a reaction,' said Daniel. 'It's about prevention. I agree, there's no point punishing someone afterwards – you've got to hit them before. What I'm talking about is action to stop them doing any more harm to ordinary people. Because believe me, they can.'

Berto frowned and nodded in agreement. As the group digested Daniel's new 'direction', a few pairs of eyes turned round to look at Cámara.

'Do you think . . .' Berto began, looking at Daniel. 'He's a friend, I know, but he's also . . .'

Daniel looked Cámara in the eye and tilted his head up, as though asking a question.

Cámara sniffed.

'You know that anything that's discussed here stays with me,' he said. 'That's always been the rule and always will be.'

He shuffled on the table, swinging his legs down and turning to face them more squarely.

'But you might want to ask yourselves,' he continued, 'whether you want to talk about potential lawbreaking in front of a policeman. *Ojos que no ven, corazón que no siente.*' What the eyes don't see the heart cannot feel.

From the corner of the room, Dídac smiled. Typical Cámara to use a proverb like that, he thought. He was becoming more like Hilario now that the old anarchist had died.

Daniel paused before his face broke out into a grin.

'You're right,' he said. 'You're absolutely right. Perhaps it's our fault for putting you into too difficult a position.'

Berto nodded.

'You're one of us,' he said to Cámara. 'That's obvious.'

'But it doesn't mean,' Daniel added, 'that he has to know everything we're up to.'

Cámara shrugged. The situation felt tense, even artificially so. He was beginning to feel uncomfortable and would happily walk out.

'I suggest,' Daniel said, 'that we put it to a vote.'

There was a general murmur of assent.

'All those in favour of the chief inspector staying for the rest of the meeting?'

SEVEN

'The situation is getting more and more serious by the day, and no one in Madrid is doing anything about it. Just because the last attempt failed doesn't mean that it can't happen this time. And now that the Left-wingers are in power, things have—'

'The new Catalan government has less room to manoeuvre than it likes to think, we all know that. And Segundo Pont is an influential and stabilising force. He's a man who Madrid can do business with. But apart from that, any unilateral move on their part has already been ruled unlawful by the Constitutional—'

'You don't get it, do you? This is the same language the Madrid government has been using from the start – a purely legalistic approach to the—'

'What other approach is there? Laws are what keep—'

'People on the street are making their opinions known very loudly. Last month, on Catalan National Day, over three million *people marched in support of breaking away. And ultimately legitimacy comes from them.'*

'It's not going to happen. I'm telling you now. Over my dead body. Over the dead bodies of millions of Spaniards will we let Catalonia become—'

'You're not listening. Even the Vatican is moving its pieces in preparation. The Pope has made the Archbishop of Barcelona a cardinal.'

'Forner?'

'Archbishop – soon to be Cardinal – Forner, correct. And Forner has been saying for weeks that the Catalan Bishops' Conference should no longer form a part of the Spanish conference. The fact that the Vatican is making this move is a clear indication—'

Cámara switched off the radio with a sharp prod of his finger, drained the last of his coffee and put on his jacket to leave. Everyone always spoke at once during these political debates, as though the rightness of each pundit's position was measured less by their reasoning than by how loudly they could shout. La Ser was, on the whole, one of the better radio stations, but no one, he was certain, ever changed their minds by listening to it. If anything, the posturing only served to harden positions. An anti-Catalan movement was getting stronger in Spain – it was visible from the graffiti and the comments you overheard. Families of Andalusian and other migrants who lived and worked in Catalonia and who went back to their home village every summer to see relatives were struggling with shifting feelings about regional identity: now rejected as 'Catalans' by their own people, they were joining the separatists in droves, pushing the numbers wanting independence ever higher.

He was fond, if not enamoured, of Catalonia – the pine-covered mountains and valleys near Tarragona were beautiful and some of the wines were delicious – but he had never quite fallen for the charms of Barcelona. Yes, parts of it were attractive, and Gaudí's buildings were eye-catching and iconic, but what had once, very briefly in 1936, been a revolutionary anarchist city now managed to be both grubby and affected at the same time, and suffocated by tourists.

The current developments there were splitting families apart, as could be expected. If enough Catalans wanted to create their own country, he thought, they should be allowed to. The idea that they should be forced to remain part of Spain was anathema to the anarchist in him, although ideally he would prefer them not to bother with the business of statehood at all. Far better to experiment with different, more flexible structures that would resist the inevitable drift towards tyranny that came with any kind of authority. They had done it in the past, if not wholly successfully.

Yet he was disturbed by the aggressive reaction of so many Spaniards to the idea of Catalonia breaking away, acting like a bitter, potentially violent husband, determined not to give a divorce to an unloved wife. No one in Madrid was trying to woo Catalonia back into the marriage bed: at most the couple would be allowed separate rooms, but there would be no talk of allowing her to move out. Central government was behaving according to type, acting the role – centuries old – of the autocratic patriarchal father holding the Spanish family together not through love, but through stubbornness and force.

He poked his head around the door: Alicia was still asleep,

breathing heavily, lying on her front in almost the same position in which he had found her the night before. He wondered about kissing her silently on the cheek, but thought better of it and left. It was time to report back to the office; he had not been there for weeks.

On his motorbike, he could worm his way quickly through the early-morning traffic jams. Someone ahead had double parked, leaving their emergency lights on while they nipped into a nearby office. But it meant that the bus he was trailing could not get past. Unable to squeeze down the side, he mounted the pavement, scooted past a handful of pedestrians, bypassed the obstruction, and was soon on his way again, the sound of the bus's horn behind him echoing down the tall, narrow street.

At the Jefatura, he inched his bike into a space round the back between a Harley-Davidson and a Japanese moped, before going through the main entrance, taking the lift to the first floor and walking down a grey passageway to a door marked '*UCE*'.

'Morning, chief.'

Inspector Torres sat at a small desk next to a grimy window in a corner of their shared, tiny office. He stared at his computer with an absent-minded look on his face, clicking his mouse and not bothering to look up as Cámara walked in.

'Nice to see you've missed me,' Cámara said.

Still looking at his screen, Torres pursed his lips and blew a kiss in his general direction.

'Where's my present from Barcelona?' he asked. 'You haven't brought me anything, have you? Not even a bottle of cava.'

'They're not letting you export it out of Catalonia any

more,' Cámara said, deadpan. 'Hoarding it all for themselves to celebrate when they finally get independence.'

Torres snorted.

'It's all me, me, me with the Catalans,' he said. 'They're so tight I wouldn't be surprised.'

'Becoming another Catalan-hater?' Cámara said.

'I don't have a problem with them,' said Torres. 'Just as long as they don't try to include Valencia in their plans for a Greater Catalonia. But for a bunch of people who are supposedly good with money, they don't seem to have worked out what happens if they do break away. What will they do for cash? Go back to using ducats?'

'Well, at least with gold coins you'd know the worth of things,' said Cámara. 'Still can't get used to bloody euros.'

He sat at his desk and instantly felt the weight of three weeks' catching-up fall upon him like cold wet sand. None of it would be important or have any direct relevance to his work as a detective, but he could already sense the hundreds of memos, emails and directives he would have to wade through over the coming hours before he could lift his head up and get on with police work.

He paused before switching on his computer and exposing himself to the deluge. At times like this his natural inclination was to go out, find a decent bar somewhere and have a long lunch. It was the best way to get things – real things – actually done. But it was only half-past nine, that awkward hour: too late for breakfast and not quite late enough for an *almuerzo* mid-morning snack. Lunch itself was a mere spot on the horizon, barely visible in the fog of morning.

He sat back in his chair and glanced across at Torres.

'Any special crimes to report while I've been away?' The weight on the words 'special crimes' and the innocent, almost singsong lift at the end of the question made his subordinate chuckle, and Torres finally turned away from the screen to look at him.

'You just won't let it rest, will you?'

Four months had passed since they had arrived in their little hole on the first floor. At first their new unit had been identified by a handwritten piece of paper tacked to the door. This was later replaced by a second piece of paper with the initials printed out in bold lettering. Finally they were given a plastic plaque with white lettering on a black background. Neither of them had ordered the changes – in fact they could not say exactly who was responsible. But the reasoning at some higher level appeared to go that the more formal the door to their office looked, the more justified their existence was. '*UCE*' supposedly stood for *Unidad de Crímenes Especiales* – the Special Crimes Unit. Torres had rechristened it the *Unidad de Comidas Especiales* – the Special Eating Unit – for the amount of time they spent out of the office at bars and restaurants trying to work out exactly what they were supposed to be doing.

The idea for the two-man team had come from Commissioner Pardo, their superior and head of the judicial, investigative police. Cámara and Torres had regularly worked together before in the murder squad, where they were something of an unofficial institution – *Estarski and Khutch*, people with memories of the 1970s TV cop show called them behind their backs. But with the economic crisis, cuts had been demanded and the powers at the top of the Jefatura ordered that one of them had to go. Pardo was not about to lose his best detectives, however, and so worked out a plan with the accounts department to take them both out and place them in a new unit instead. That way the numbers could be moulded to make it look as though savings were being made, whereas in fact nothing had really changed. Pardo came up with *UCE* – it was vague enough to cover almost anything, he said. In reality they were meant to be an adjunct of the murder squad on the ground floor – two senior colleagues with bags of experience who could be called upon at any time.

The reality was that Chief Inspector Laura Martín, the new head of *Homicidios*, kept them at arm's length. Her team was doing fine on their own, she would say whenever the question of Cámara and Torres came up. Don't need them.

The first few weeks in *UCE* had been fun, particularly in the wake of their previous murder case, when a fear of losing his job had pitted Torres against Cámara for a while. Their friendship had survived, however, and became strengthened once more as they eased their way into their new 'unit', spending considerable amounts of police time thinking about what they might dedicate themselves to – with the help of an occasional bottle of Ribera del Duero and a paella or two.

As weeks turned into months, however, the mood began to change. A paid, working holiday was fine for a while, but they were both keen policemen who operated best when focused on a case. So far all they had come up with was scouting for potential new methods that criminals might use in the future that the police would need to be aware of. Pardo loved it; it smacked of a research-and-development department in a commercial company, and to some degree Torres was happy to go along with the charade. But Cámara treated it as a mere stopgap, longing for the concrete reality of an actual crime to solve rather than the almost make-believe world of 'what might happen'.

Travelling up to Barcelona, having an actual investigation to deal with – albeit one involving supposed police brutality – had come as a relief. But now, returning to the vagueness of his unit felt all the more frustrating.

He turned back to his desk and reached out for the on button of his computer.

'What are you checking out?' he asked.

Torres swung his screen round for him to see. Cámara saw pictures of what looked like toy helicopters.

'They're called drones,' Torres answered his silent question. 'They're remote controlled. People put cameras on them and fly them around to get aerial video shots.'

Cámara raised his eyebrows with only moderate interest.

'New to me as well,' Torres said. 'But apparently a few have started appearing during recent fiestas. It's just a hobby, but it's making someone nervous.'

He clicked his mouse and a new image appeared of a typewritten note.

'New directive,' he explained. 'Reminding us that all use of such aircraft in public places is illegal.'

Cámara turned back to his desk.

'What are we supposed to do? Shoot them down?'

His in-box almost quaked with new messages to wade through, and he was about to dive in when the phone rang. Torres picked it up, listened and put the receiver back.

'Pardo,' he said. 'Wants us in his office immediately.'

'What's it about?' Cámara asked.

'I don't know. But Laura's in there with him. And I don't think she's very happy.'

EIGHT

They crossed paths with Laura in the corridor, coming the other way as they approached Pardo's office.

'See you downstairs in a few moments,' she said without looking at them.

Torres opened the door and they stepped inside. Pardo had taken off his jacket and was rolling up his sleeves. His eyes and mouth looked small and tight; stress seemed to cling to him like glue.

'Come in. Sit the fuck down,' he said.

Cámara took a seat. After a pause, confused by Cámara's unhesitating compliance with an order, Torres did the same.

Pardo lifted a folder from his desk and tossed it over on to Torres's lap.

'Time for the *UCE* to get cracking,' Pardo said. 'No more time-wasting, fiddling with your balls. This is the kind of thing I created your unit for in the first place.'

Torres glanced down at the papers and gave a low whistle.

'Yeah,' he said. 'Doesn't surprise me. Heard about this one.'

Cámara slung an arm over the back of his chair.

'Is someone going to fill me in?'

'Alfonso Segarra,' Pardo said.

Cámara did not react.

'Do you know who that is?'

'Head of the Horta group,' Cámara answered. 'Supermarket chain. I'm in them almost every day. Only business in the country that hasn't been hit by the economic crisis, by the looks of it. Segarra must be a wealthy man.'

'The fourth richest in Spain, actually,' Torres said.

'Right,' said Pardo. 'Billionaire, churchgoer, personal friend to half a dozen ministers, owner of a local football club. The success of the Horta chain is one of the few things keeping the economy afloat.'

'So what's happened to him?' Cámara asked. 'Is he dead?'

'Not him,' Pardo answered. 'His son. Ten-year-old boy. His body was found two days ago in an abandoned orange grove just north of the city. His neck had been snapped.'

Pardo's breath was quick and shallow.

'Laura's lot were on it originally, of course.'

'But?'

'But given the nature of what we're dealing with – or what we might be dealing with, nothing's clear yet – I want both of you on this case. It's delicate, media-sensitive, and God alone knows where it's going to take you. Personally I wouldn't want to touch the fucking thing with a barge-pole.'

'So you're giving it to us,' Torres said flatly.

'That's right,' Pardo replied without a flicker of sarcasm. 'If ever there was a special crime, this is it. You've both got experience with high-profile cases, and I want the best on this. You're going to have to tread carefully, as I'm sure I don't have to tell you. And believe me, a lot of eyes are going to be watching this – here, and in Madrid.'

Cámara shuffled in his seat.

'Don't rush it,' Pardo continued. 'Not too slow either. But it's important we get everything right on this. Judge Andreu Peris is nominally in charge, but I've spoken to him and he's happy to sit back for a while and let you get on with things before getting involved. We're in luck. Don't want one of those fucking crusader judges on this one, getting in the way all the time.'

Torres passed the folder to Cámara. He glanced down, briefly catching sight of the blue-lipped corpse of the little boy where it had lain among the orange trees. He registered the name 'Fermín' before looking up again.

'Laura's got the details,' Pardo said. 'I've briefed her. She'll cooperate.'

Neither Cámara nor Torres moved.

'Right,' said Pardo. 'Well get on with it, then.'

Cámara stood up. Torres stayed in his seat.

'What is it?'

'One thing,' said Torres. 'You said this kid is Segarra's son.'

'Yes,' said Pardo.

'But Segarra doesn't have a son. He's got three daughters. Everyone knows that.'

Pardo wiped a hand across his forehead.

'I thought I told you,' he said. 'Segarra has a mistress.'

He stared at them as though they were a couple of idiots.

'The kid's illegitimate. Get it? Now come on. Get the fuck out.'

Cámara turned the handle and let Torres out first.

'Oh, Cámara,' Pardo called out. 'Good trip to Barcelona?'

Cámara smiled.

'Interesting,' he said. 'Very interesting.'

'Good,' said Pardo, looking down at some papers on his desk.

'Close the door behind you.'

They walked silently down the corridor towards the lift. Inside, once the doors had closed, Torres spoke.

'Almost the same age as my own boy.'

'How old is Iván now?' Cámara asked. 'Eight?'

'Nine. It's a good age. You can play with them, do fun stuff together. I can't imagine . . .'

The lift clunked down on to the ground floor, the doors opened and they stepped out.

'No,' Cámara said in a low voice. 'Neither can I.'

And within him something flickered, an emotion he had thought long laid to rest; and with it a momentary image of Alicia's body, lying motionless, asleep in their bed, as he had left her earlier that morning. He tried to reach out to touch her, but his hand refused to move.

'You all right?' Torres asked as they arrived at the door of the murder squad.

Cámara shook himself and nodded.

'Yeah. Right,' he said, clapping his hands together. 'Let's get this over with.'

Chief Inspector Laura Martín was leaning over the desk of Inspector Lozano. She quickly glanced up as Torres and Cámara walked in, then carried on talking to her subordinate. Torres stood waiting patiently for her to finish; Cámara sat down in a chair near the door and started chatting to Inspector Albelda, who was tapping out a report on his computer.

'Enjoying things upstairs?' Albelda grunted through his moustache.

Cámara grinned. Albelda's complexion was getting ruddier: he hated to think what state his liver was in.

'Not too bad,' he said. 'But we miss you lot terribly. You should come up and visit some time.'

Albelda kept his eyes fixed on the keyboard.

'I might just do that,' he said.

Laura finished talking to Lozano and took a step closer. Cámara attempted to put on a compassionate face, but it was never easy, this. They had all had cases taken off them at one time or the other – it was like being dumped by a girlfriend, Torres had once remarked. And you tried to think how best to go about it, in case one day in the future it was your turn to wear the boot. But the truth was there was no good or right way of doing it.

'Castro will show you everything,' Laura said simply. And she turned on her heel to pass through to the adjoining office.

'Laura,' Cámara called out. She stopped and gave him a quizzical look. Cámara shrugged apologetically.

'We were doing a fine job of it,' Laura said.

'Of course.'

'And I'm a bloody good detective.'

'You are.'

'But apparently I lack a certain . . . what were the words Pardo used? "Intuitive brilliance". That's it.'

'I'm sorry, Laura.'

'Thoroughness isn't everything, I'm told. Nor a hundred-per-cent clear-up record. But there you have it.'

She walked into the other office and out of view.

'Send us a postcard when you've solved it,' she said. Then slammed the door shut.

Cámara got up from his chair and walked over to the desk of Inspector Castro. Wordlessly she picked up a heap of files from her desk and passed them to him.

'It's mostly on WebPol,' she said. 'But you'll find it all here in case you want hard copies.'

'Thanks,' Cámara said.

Torres stepped over and took them from him.

'Here, I'll take these,' he said.

'Anything you want to add while we're here?' Cámara asked.

Castro shook her head. Cámara glanced around the room, but Lozano was staring at his computer screen, pretending they were not there. Albelda was older – he had seen it plenty of times before. But he kept his eyes fixed on the floor. This was about loyalty. Months before they had all been one – part of the same murder squad. Now they were split in two, and no matter how much time they had spent together in the past, that meant that Cámara and Torres were separate, different – outsiders. This was as far as the cooperation between their two units would go – the handing over of the files. There was nothing more to be said.

Torres was already at the door, making his way out.

'Tell Laura . . .' Cámara hesitated. Castro, Lozano and Albelda all looked at him intently.

'Nothing,' said Cámara. And he left the room.

They paced back down the corridor towards the lift.

'Right,' said Torres. 'Let's see what all this has got to tell us.'

Cámara pulled out a packet of Ducados, stuck a cigarette in his mouth, and made for the front exit.

'I need a smoke first,' he said. 'And a drink. Coming?'

NINE

They did not believe in keeping secrets from him.

Dídac's mother had told him around the time he turned thirteen: she had wanted to abort when she found out that she was pregnant with him. But Daniel had refused, and so out of love for his father she had seen the pregnancy through. And it was the best decision she had ever made: she was the happiest mother in the world.

At least that was what she had told him the last time she had been granted visiting hours. The rules had tightened up since a new justice minister had been appointed. Making life that bit harder for inmates appealed to hardliners. At the Picassent prison they followed the new directive to the letter and now Dídac could only see Isabel for an hour once a month. He would drive over on a borrowed scooter down the Pista de Silla motorway: it was a 50cc and he was meant to ride it on the back roads only, but a mechanic had removed the speed limiter and he could get over 100 kilometres per hour on it with a tailwind. He could get to the gates of the prison within half an hour if he pushed it hard.

There was an antechamber at the side where they had to wait before being taken into the visiting area. It was windowless and bare. But as they were led out, he sometimes caught a quick glimpse of his mother through a small barred window, sitting at her table, waiting for him – a brief moment when he could see her but she could not see him: her hair long and lank, falling over her cheeks, her eyes hollow and dark. By the time he appeared through the main doorway her expression would change: a grin would spread across her face, her arms outstretched to embrace him, a look of insouciance there, as though the experience of incarceration had no effect on her spirit. But he knew better.

And he would take whatever he could to give her. The guards were strict, but chocolates and other foods were allowed. She liked *turrón*, and he would lift two or three packets of the nougat out of his rucksack and hand them over, sliding them across the scratched surface of the table they were supposed to sit on either side of.

She would talk, holding his hands. But mostly she wanted to hear about life outside – what he was doing, about the struggle, the food bank, the collective, their plans for the future. She had been in for five years already – most of the economic crisis had passed her by, and she hated missing the great opportunity that it afforded.

'There's so much I could do. But you're doing a wonderful job, Dídac. I know you are.'

Daniel had visited with him a couple of times at the beginning, but stopped after a while. Isabel never explained. And he never dared asked his father. He had not been aware of any other women, but it would not surprise him if Daniel had made arrangements. Or that his mother sanctioned them. No relationship should be possessive, she had always drilled into him – even from as young as six or seven, before he even knew what 'relationship' meant. Love can only flourish where it is free. Perhaps it hurt them both too much to be forcibly separated like this. Although he felt that secretly Isabel would love nothing more than to see Daniel again. He was a great man, she would tell him, a great anarchist. And although she could not be with him as she would like, he was in good hands. Besides, within just over a year she would probably be able to get out on early release. Then everything would be fine again.

He was seventeen years old, but losing his mother like this aged only twelve had marked him. The arrest, the investigation, the quick harsh sentence (they never judged their own kind so swiftly: corruption cases against politicians or members of the royal family dragged on for years) had been a shock. But she had scared them – really scared them that the whole fragile system might come crashing down on their heads. So they had to act as they did, banging her up for ten years. And all for forging banknotes.

They tried to claim it was an attempt to get rich quick, that Isabel was keeping the money for herself. When that argument fell through the prosecutors argued that it was meant to buy weapons and explosives, that it was part of a subversive plot. Which it was, but not in that way. Simply by flooding the country with huge amounts of perfectly made but fake fifty- and hundred-euro notes, the plan was to devalue the currency and pull the economy down. It was a big scheme: they had printing presses dotted around the country, each one poised to work flat out night and day, pumping out the forgeries. They had the right paper, the watermarks, the metal strip down the middle, the intricate design work down to a T. The whole thing had been master-minded by Isabel and they were ready to go. They reckoned it would take three months, perhaps four, before the effect started to kick in. But then, once it did, the whole paper castle would collapse in a matter of weeks, perhaps even days. And then the chance for real change, once the capitalist system had devoured itself in raging greed, would come and people would finally see that a libertarian future was the best way forward.

Except that they had been betrayed. Someone had squealed. The finger was pointed at Virginia, one of the printers on the job, but she never confessed. Her lighter prison term said it all, however.

Their crime was non-violent, and had never got off the ground once the police raids began. Isabel's lawyer had expected a sentence of around five years. She'd be out in two if things went well. But papers were found that proved – the investigators said – that as well as forging money, the group was also planning to bomb the Holy Grail chapel in Valencia cathedral. The Church was a legitimate target in Isabel's mind, it was true, as it was for most anarchists. The men who ran the Church had wedded themselves to authoritarian power for centuries and were as guilty of oppression as the State. But a bombing campaign had merely been one of many ideas discussed at one time before being ruled out as counterproductive. The prosecution, however, used it to paint his mother as a cruel and dangerous criminal genius. Hence the long sentence. He had never seen Daniel – usually so poised and in control – look so emotional. He shook so badly as the court case ended, shouting and foaming at the mouth, that the guards dragged him away. Isabel had no tissues to wipe away her tears and stared blankly at him through pouring eyes.

It had been a week now since the last visit to Picassent prison. Another three to go before he could return. He thought of her every day, although it was true, perhaps less than before. Sometimes he even caught himself at the end of the day worrying that he had not thought of her, as though he had ignored her and she needed him to think of her just as she was thinking of him, locked away in her cell.

Get a girlfriend, Daniel would say. He had had sex once – or at least he thought he had: the whole thing had been quick and unsatisfactory for both of them. Something had held him back ever since. Many girls – the ones he fancied – felt distant, unapproachable, and if ever one showed an interest in him, she was never right for him and he would turn away. He was weird, he knew. But one day it would sort itself out. He repeated it to himself every night as he lay in bed, like a mantra.

That morning, over breakfast, Daniel had been silent – more so than usual. Until after he showered and dressed and told him they had somewhere to go, something different to do. They climbed into a four-wheel drive – a car Dídac had not seen before – and headed out of the city, up along the coast and then inland for almost an hour, high into the mountains, where the roads grew narrower and twistier, and the orange groves gave way first to terraced fields of carob trees and then to thick forests of pine.

A tarmac road led them away from a small, quiet village, up a long valley, until it turned into a dirt track. They continued for another twenty minutes before arriving in a dusty field. Thick-barked holm-oak trees lined the edges, while a trickle of water from a nearby stream created a tranquil, calming mood.

'This is it,' Daniel said. 'Get out.'

Dídac did as he was told; his father might believe in libertarian freedom for society, but had always been strict with him at home. He was training him, he used to say if ever Dídac complained about the harsh punishments or for pushing him so much. Revolutions only come about through hard work. Once, perhaps twice, late at night he had heard him complain about the others; they were lazy, didn't understand. This training was a secret – only for him.

Dídac skipped out of the car and looked around at the beautiful spot they had come to. Apart from the burble of the stream, there was barely a sound – no birdsong, hardly any sign of animal life. Above, he could make out the peak of a nearby mountain, while two soaring shadows circled gently overhead before sailing on.

'Vultures,' Daniel said simply.

He handed him something wrapped in cloth. It looked heavy.

'Here,' he said. 'Put that on the ground very carefully, then take a look.'

Dídac felt the weight of the thing – it was metal, and already, with a quickening of his pulse, he had a feeling of what it was.

When he unwrapped it he saw a black gun, shaped like the letter T, the barrel forming the cross while the handle and magazine dropped down in the middle. Fear and excitement bristled within him.

'That's a STAR Model Z-84,' Daniel said, crouching down beside him. 'A sub-machine gun. They're very good and very rare.'

He picked it up and nestled it in his arms, his finger on the trigger.

'It's lightweight, waterproof and very accurate.'

His hand slipped down to the bottom of the handle, stroking the magazine jutting out of the bottom.

'This can hold thirty 9-millimetre parabellum rounds. It's a combat weapon, originally made for sub-aquatic operations. Only a thousand were ever manufactured. They're hard to come by. But one or two occasionally come on to the market.'

Questions raced through Dídac's mind: how had his father got hold of it? How much had it cost? Did he have contacts on the black market?

Most of all, however, was the question racing not through his mind but through his blood: was he going to let him try it out?

'I know what you're thinking,' Daniel said. 'I know what you're wondering. The point is, we're at a critical moment, and decisions have to be made.'

He paused before continuing. Dídac felt a quiver in his legs.

'You and I have more important things to do. There's so much more that we can give. The food collective, the bank operations . . . that's small stuff. We can go much, much bigger. But it will mean change, sacrifice. I don't see Valencia as the main battleground these days. A bigger struggle is coming, and it will be played out elsewhere.'

Dídac nodded energetically. Daniel rarely talked to him like this. There was a new strength in his father, new purpose. *I want to follow this man.* The thought registered on some deep, animal level. *I want to be like him.*

'Besides,' Daniel said, 'we don't really know who we can

trust. And in the times that are about to come, loyalty will be the most important quality there is. Do you understand?'

'Yes, yes,' Dídac said.

'I need to know I can count on you one hundred per cent,' said Daniel.

'You can.'

His father looked him in the eye, boring into his mind.

'Good,' he said at last.

He glanced down at the gun.

'Hunters use this place,' he said. 'No one will bother us.'

He held the gun out to Dídac, opening up the foldable shoulder rest and wedging it against his upper arm.

'Take it, feel it, learn to love it,' he said. 'Do this – do it well – and there'll be much, much more I'll be teaching you.'

TEN

POLICIA LOCAL DE VALENCIA
6TH UNIT: EXPOSICIÓ
C/ D'EMILI BARÓ, 91
46020, VLC
WITNESS REPORT
Witness name: Vicente García Sánchez
Sex: Male
Age: 37
Occupation: Carpenter (disabled)
Address: 18, Rosa dels Vents, Carpesa, Valencia
(Horta Nord)
Statement taken at 11.10 hours on 2/10

Witness states that he is in the habit of taking an early-morning walk with his dog, a three-year-old Labrador. Witness is in a wheelchair after car accident suffered when seventeen years old. His usual route takes him out of the village of Carpesa and along tarmac roads into surrounding fields. Usually not out of the house more than twenty minutes – half an hour maximum – before returning home.

On morning in question he left the house at around 07.30, following habitual route east out of Carpesa, before turning north. Tarmac road ends near an abandoned well and witness cannot progress further along dirt track. Dog, however, ran on, in animated state towards a nearby field of orange trees (abandoned) where he started digging with front paws. Witness tried to call him back, but dog insistent. Much barking, very excited. Appeared to be pulling at something with his teeth. Object too far away for witness to identify, but began to get suspicious. After another fifteen minutes, unable to get dog to return to him and dog still barking, witness decided to call a friend who is a *Policía Local* – Agent José Luis Montero, who appeared on the scene some twenty minutes later.

Agent Montero identified the object as a human corpse.

POLICIA LOCAL DE VALENCIA
6TH UNIT: EXPOSICIÓ
C/ D'EMILI BARÓ, 91
46020, VLC
CRIME REPORT
For Attention Of: *Central de Policía Local, Jefatura Superior de la Policía Nacional de Valencia*
Agent J. L. Montero

Date: 2/10
Time: 12.40

In the process of carrying out policing duties on the morning of 2/10 in the locality of Carpesa (Pedanías del Norte) at 08.19 in the area of the abandoned well (NE of the village – road known as Camí del'Alquería del Poço – about 1km from village outskirts) Agent Montero was called by a local inhabitant to investigate a suspicious object in an orange grove beyond the end of the tarmac road. Responding to said call, Agent Montero arrived shortly after and proceeded to the orange grove in question. The object was identified by a dog (golden Labrador) owned by Carpesa inhabitant Vicente García Sánchez. Señor García Sánchez was unable to approach the object himself as he is disabled and confined to a wheelchair.

On approaching the object, Agent Montero was able to ascertain quickly that it corresponded to the remains of a human – possibly that of a child – buried less than a metre below the surface of the ground.

Agent Montero immediately put through a call to the *Comisaría* to report his finding, and other *Policía Local* officers soon arrived on the scene.

The orange grove in question is the property of Antonio Carrasco Hidalgo, 89, resident of Carpesa. It has not been properly tended in some eight-to-ten years and is presently in a state of abandonment.

POLICIA LOCAL DE VALENCIA
6TH UNIT: EXPOSICIÓ
C/ D'EMILI BARÓ, 91
46020, VLC
CRIME REPORT
For Attention Of: *Central de Policía Local, Jefatura Superior de la Policia Nacional de Valencia*
Agent: Sub-Inspector Rojas
Date: 2/10
Time: 14.50

In the process of carrying out policing duties on the morning of 2/10, Sub-Inspector Rojas was called to the village of Carpesa (Pedanías del Norte) following the location of a human corpse in an orange grove near the locality. Arriving at the scene at 11.13 and confirming the report initially made by Agent J. L. Montero that a body – probably that of a youth – had been discovered in a shallow grave, the decision was immediately taken to refer the matter to the *Jefatura Superior de la Policía Nacional.*

Sub-Inspector Rojas remained at the scene until the arrival of detectives from the *Policía Nacional* murder squad, and assisted them with their initial inquiries.

After consultation with the *Policía Nacional* detectives, Sub-Inspector Rojas and Agent J. L. Montero interviewed the proprietor of the orange grove in question, Antonio Carrasco Hidalgo, 89, resident of Carpesa at his home in the village (C/ Ermita San Roque, 12). Señor Carrasco Hidalgo was visibly shocked when informed of what had been discovered on his land. He said that he had stopped tending the orange grove in question some ten years before, around the time that his wife died, and that he rarely visits the field any more due to ill health.

His testimony was corroborated by Señor Carrasco Hidalgo's daughter, María Amparo Carrasco Gómez (63) who lives at the same address. No other residents are recorded as living at the address.

A report on the interview with Señor Carrasco Hidalgo and his daughter was submitted to the *Policía Nacional* murder squad, at which point *Policía Local* involvement in the case officially terminated.

POLICIA NACIONAL, GRUPO DE HOMICIDIOS
Initial report on location of corpse near village of Carpesa (Horta Nord)
Detective: Inspector M. A. Castro
Date: 3/10
Time: 18.30

Following the intervention of officers of the *Policía Local* 6th Unit (see relevant reports), Inspectors Lozano and Castro of the murder squad went to Carpesa to conduct initial investigations.

The corpse was located near the centre of an abandoned orange grove to the north of the village. The nearest inhabited buildings are at least 500 metres away. The grove can be accessed by tarmac road leading away from the village. This turns into a dirt track for approximately 200 metres along the edge of an irrigation channel before ending at the field in question.

The corpse appeared to have been buried in a shallow grave, less than 1 metre deep. An initial inspection suggested that it was the body of a boy between the ages of 8 and 12, 1.4m tall and approx. 30kg in weight. No wounds or injuries were immediately visible. The very light decomposition pointed to a recent time of death, possibly within the previous 24 hours.

The *Policía Local* had cordoned off the area, but already the immediate vicinity of the body had suffered material damage, mainly from the dog that according to reports initially gave the alert of the presence of a body and had proceeded to dig part of it up. Owing to the lack of rainfall over recent weeks, the ground was dry, so the location of any footprints in the area would have been unlikely in any case.

Witness Vicente García Sánchez was the first on the scene. In a verbal statement to *Policía Nacional* detectives he stated that this was his normal route for a daily walk with his dog (Señor García Sánchez is disabled and moves around in a wheelchair), and that he had come to the same spot at a similar time the day before. At no point on this previous occasion did he notice anything suspicious, nor did his dog act in any unusual way. This fact taken with the first evaluation of the light decomposition of the corpse suggested that the body had been buried in the orange grove only hours before, possibly overnight.

Despite the absence of any obvious wounds to the body of the boy, the case was considered suspicious and a murder investigation was officially instigated.

Judge Andreu Peris of Court 2 was called in as the investigating official and the case was placed under his jurisdiction.

Following the removal of the body, Detectives Lozano and Castro consulted the Missing Persons file and a potential match was quickly identified. At 23.05 the previous night Célia Capilla Romero (43), resident at Trinquet de Cavallers 5, 46003 in central Valencia, reported missing her son, Fermín, aged 10. According to information she gave to agents of the *Comisaría de Distrito Centro*, Fermín had been playing in a football match that evening in the old river bed and was expected to walk home in time for dinner. Usually he returned between 20.00 and 20.30, but that evening he had failed to appear. After several calls to his mobile phone failed to locate him, she called friends and the parents of school friends to see if anyone knew the whereabouts of her son. Finally, having failed to locate him and becoming increasingly distressed, she contacted the *Policía Nacional* and filed a Missing Persons report.

Once the corpse of the boy located in Carpesa had been taken to the forensic medicine department and cleaned up, agents of the *Policía Nacional* conducted Célia Capilla Romero to the department where, at 16.30, in the presence of Judge Andreu Peris and Inspectors Lozano and Castro, she positively identified the body as that of her missing son, Fermín.

Célia Capilla Romero was taken to the Nueva Fe hospital shortly afterwards, where she was treated for shock.

FORENSIC MEDICINE DEPT
AUTOPSY REPORT
Medical officer: Dr Rosario Alegre
Subject: Fermín Capilla Romero
Sex: male
Age: 10
Date & time of autopsy: 3/10 09.30

Cause of death: severing of the spinal cord, with severe trauma to the neck and fracturing of vertebrae 5 and 6, causing loss of consciousness. Bruising to the bottom of the chin and contusions in the neck area suggest that this was caused by powerful force being exerted in a simultaneously horizontal and vertical twist designed to cause the specified effect. Death would have been almost instant.

Time of death: lividity and extent of rigor mortis as well as examination of the gut with a last recorded time of consumption at 17.30 (mid-afternoon snack) gives a time between 19.30 and 21.00 on 1/10.

Conclusion: death was deliberately perpetrated by a second party. As such, recommendation that case be considered as homicide.

POLICIA NACIONAL, GRUPO DE HOMICIDIOS
Background and context report on case of Fermín Capilla Romero
Agent: Inspector J. Albelda
Date: 3/10
Time: 15.45

Following the positive identification of the Carpesa body as Fermín Capilla Romero (aged 10), agent

Albelda was tasked with background investigation into the deceased.

Registry records provided the following:
Date of birth: 2/1/2004
Sex: Male
Place of birth: La Clínica Hospital (private), Valencia
ID No.: 90187211 - B
Address: Trinquet de Cavallers, 5, 46002 Valencia
Father: Alfonso Segarra
Mother: Célia Capilla Romero

Fermín was a pupil at the Sagrado Corazón de Jesús School in central Valencia.

Further details on Célia Capilla Romero:
Date of birth: 30/12/1970
Address: as above
Occupation: not given
Marital status: single

Further details on Alfonso Segarra:
Date of birth: 3/4/1957
Address: Alquería del Duc, Benifaraig, 46016 (Horta Nord)
Occupation: businessman
Marital status: widowed
Former spouse: Francisca Grau Escrivá

Señora Grau Escrivá, owner of the Abogados Grau S.A. legal firm, died in Valencia four months ago of pancreatic cancer aged 50 years. She was mother to Alfonso Segarra's three daughters, Francisca (31), Emilia (29), and Julia (21).

Alfonso Segarra is the well-known businessman and owner of the Horta supermarket chain. Until now, the existence of his illegitimate son with Célia Capilla Romero has never been officially acknowledged.

POLICIA NACIONAL, GRUPO DE HOMICIDIOS
Interview with Alfonso Segarra
Conducted by Chief Inspector Laura Martín, head of the *Grupo de Homicidios*
Date: 3/10
Time: 17.10

The Carpesa body was identified as that of Fermín Capilla Romero, illegitimate son of businessman Alfonso Segarra. Following the confirmation that his death was being treated as murder, Chief Inspector Martín went to interview Segarra at his company headquarters in Paterna.

Segarra confirmed that Fermín was his son, as well as the existence of his relationship with Célia Capilla Romero. He stated that he had been in a relationship with her for the past twelve years and paid for her flat on Trinquet de Cavallers, as well as for the upkeep both of herself and the child.

His wife, Francisca Grau, had never known about his other relationship or the boy, he said. Segarra said that he had always wanted a son. He and his wife had three daughters, but he started his affair with Célia Capilla Romero given his desire for a male offspring. At no point, he said, had he considered divorcing his wife and marrying Célia Capilla

Romero. (Presumably this is for religious reasons, although he refused to confirm this.)

Asked whether he believed his wife could have known about his mistress, he denied the very possibility. Everything, he insisted, had been dealt with discreetly and elegantly. But now, with the boy's murder, the whole world knew about his private life.

Asked whether he had received any threats in recent weeks or months that might shed light on the murder of his son, he said that he had never seen anything that might indicate a threat either to himself or his family.

He gave assurances that if anything came to light that might help the investigation he would immediately get in touch with the murder squad.

It was late by the time Cámara and Torres finished reading the reports. Cámara stood up and stretched.

'Segarra's the key here,' he said. 'We need to do some sniffing around.'

Torres grunted from his desk.

'Tomorrow.'

'Of course.'

Torres got up and they both put on their jackets to leave.

'You know, something Albelda left out in his background report —' Torres said.

'What's that?'

Torres opened the door and they stepped out of the office.

'Segarra's a big political donor,' he said. 'Been giving money to the ruling party for years.'

ELEVEN

Torres's ageing Seat coughed white smoke as they drove from the Jefatura, over the landscaped gardens of the old river bed and into the north of the city. The route took them through poorer areas, where apartment blocks built of grey-yellow brick with thin, aluminium-frame windows rose like walls at the sides of every street. On the pavements, Ecuadoreans and Peruvians rubbed shoulders with Pakistanis and sub-Saharan Africans. In the past, the neighbourhood of Torrefiel had been the home of immigrants coming in from Albacete, Teruel and other parts of Spain, looking for work: the area was on the outskirts of the city and offered cheap housing. Today the tradition continued, but with peoples from further afield. Many foreigners had left Spain in recent years, driven out by the lack of work, but in this part of the city, despite a certain flatness in the atmosphere, it appeared that the process of absorption and renewal was still alive.

Descending into an underpass below the ring road, they came up into a different world: the tower blocks stopped, giving way to a flat landscape of well-tended fields and white farmhouses. Beyond, in the far distance, the Sierra Calderona framed the view, scratching its jagged edge against a milky blue sky.

'This is tiger-nut country,' Torres said, looking out over meadows of what looked like thick green grass. 'What they use to make *horchata.*'

Cámara had grown to enjoy the traditional Valencian drink, despite its earthy taste. Cool and sweet, it was ideal after a day at the beach, sitting in a bar with high ceilings and marble tabletops. He was less convinced, however, by the health-giving properties Valencians claimed for it – it was said to cure everything from high cholesterol levels to stress and even a low sex drive.

Beyond the tiger-nut fields, he noticed patches of darker green where orange trees barely taller than himself sprang out of the ground in tight rows. Between each field, water channels lined with brick acted as dividers. He caught sight of a group of men wearing espadrilles and with mattocks in their hands busy irrigating a patch by the side of the road: water flowed out of gaps in the water-channel walls and seeped its way across until every inch of the field had been reached.

'Some of them, like those guys, still do it by hand,' Torres said, glancing over. 'Others use satellite technology now. It has to be perfectly flat for the water to spread to every corner.'

Interspersed among the fields, sometimes standing in small groups, stood two-storey farmhouses – *alquerías* – with terracotta-tiled roofs, often sloping into a central patio area to collect rainwater.

The car overtook a blue-and-red painted cart being pulled by a horse, a man with a straw hat and a thin, ragged cigar sticking out of his mouth, sitting on a bench at the front. Dragging on the road behind, attached to the cart by a chain, was a large tractor tyre with an enormous rock sitting on top.

'To keep the horses strong for pulling ploughs,' Torres explained. 'It's illegal, but everyone turns a blind eye.'

Everywhere were reminders that they were in the modern world: the cars and buses on the road ahead; electricity pylons cutting the sky; an occasional billboard with adverts for shaving foam and whisky; even a plane on the horizon, coming in to land at the airport not a few kilometres distant. But driving into the *huerta* – the horticultural belt to the north of the city – felt in many ways like a journey back twenty or thirty years in time. Cámara glanced over his shoulder – Valencia was there: they had barely left its precinct. Yet here was an agricultural world on its doorstep still getting on with its business as it had for hundreds of years, oblivious almost to the metropolis that had mushroomed in front of it and encroached on its land.

'I'm not sure I've ever been to this area before,' Cámara said.

'Not surprising,' said Torres. 'You mention names of the villages round here to Valencians and they don't know where you're talking about. And yet they're right on the outskirts of the city.'

Carpesa was a small place, made up of barely four or five streets. They drove through a square with squat Judas trees in the centre, past a baroque church with an imposing brick tower topped with a carved stone bell chamber, and down a narrow lane before the houses stopped and the fields resumed again. More tiger-nut plants, waving in the light breeze blowing in off the sea, with orange groves beyond in the middle distance. Torres parked beside a rubbish container. They checked they were on the right street and got out, looking for number 18.

Torres rang the doorbell three times and had waited several minutes before deciding that Vicente García must have gone out. The street seemed deserted, but Cámara spotted an elderly lady sweeping the pavement outside her doorway.

'He's gone,' she answered. 'Staying with relatives in the city. That business about the dead boy.'

She shook her head and carried on sweeping.

'He's had enough tragedy, that man, without this happening to him. First his parents died, then the accident that put him in a wheelchair. He was just beginning to pull through. Then this happened. Hit him hard, seeing that. Dog wasn't the same either. It was a knock for the both of them. *¡Ay!* What kind of a world is it where little children get murdered? I ask you.'

She tutted and stepped back into the shade of her home, leaving Cámara on the pavement.

'The body was found over there, in that direction,' Torres said when he rejoined him.

'Let's walk.'

They headed silently away from the village along a narrow road, past a row of abandoned tractors, rusting and in pieces next to a warehouse with a corrugated roof.

'This is Segarra's territory,' Torres said after a while.

'Meaning?'

'He comes from round here, was born in a village just a few kilometres east. But this is his land, his world. The name of his supermarket – Horta. That's the Valencian for *huerta*.'

'I imagine he owns quite a bit of it,' Cámara said.

'Some, I'm sure,' said Torres. 'I'll check. But this isn't an area of big landowners. Traditionally everyone had their little patch round here and that was practically enough to get by on. It's incredibly rich land – you can get three crops a year out of it if you want.'

They crossed a low bridge over a water channel and into the orange groves. The fruits were still green in October, but in a month or so the first crops would be ripening in time for Christmas. Beneath the trees, low wild flowers grew, creating bright thick carpets that stretched across the landscape.

'Segarra started as a fruit-and-veg seller not far from here,' Torres continued. 'Then the business grew and he turned it into a supermarket – one of the first in the city. But it all began here. They always say about him that he's still a Valencian farmer boy at heart, that the millions haven't gone to his head. That that's the reason for his success.'

They had passed the first orange grove, with its manicured trees, and had reached a scruffier area: a few pieces of rubbish were scattered in patches of long, yellowing grass. The orange trees were clearly not being looked after, sprawling into odd shapes or with dead branches and dried leaves.

'If this land is so fertile,' Cámara said, 'how come so much of it has been abandoned?'

Torres gave a shrug.

'Farming doesn't bring in as much as it once did. Much of this land is owned by elderly guys, and their children don't necessarily want to carry on the family tradition. Too much like hard work for little pay.'

'Still,' Cámara said. 'You'd think they'd do something with it, rather than just leaving it like this.'

At the end of the road they could make out a small brick building with wide cracks in the walls.

'That'll be the well,' said Torres.

Beyond it, fluttering among a dense clutch of vegetation, they could see blue-and-white police tape in another orange grove.

They walked towards it, leaving the road where the tarmac ended and continuing along the dirt track, skipping over a water channel and into the field. Torres walked straight towards the hole in the middle where the tape was attached to some trees, cordoning off the area where Fermín's body had been discovered. Cámara took a different route, crossing diagonally, randomly through the trees, looking down at the debris around his feet – mostly rusting cans of beer and empty food packets – before glancing up. The bell tower of Carpesa was visible several fields away, while in the opposite direction a number of *alquerías* were scattered about. One, that looked larger and whiter and better kept than the others, caught his eye.

Torres was standing still, his hands behind his back, staring at the bottom of Fermín's shallow grave. Both of them had read the *Científica*'s crime-scene report. It had little more information to give than what they already had – the dryness of the soil meant that no footprints had been discernible, while the area was often used by teenagers from nearby villages to drink and smoke late into the night. The quantity of rubbish they left behind made finding anything relating to the crime almost impossible. All the *científicos* could say was that the hole had been dug by a standard spade – not a mattock, which

80

was the usual tool used for digging and working the earth by *huerta* farmers.

Cámara stood silently next to Torres and smelt the air: there were traces of stale urine and worse.

'A shallow grave,' Torres said in a low voice. 'You'd think anyone who knew about snapping someone's neck so cleanly would also understand the basics of burying bodies. I mean, two metres, minimum. Otherwise . . .'

'Someone else took care of the burying?' Cámara said. 'Someone less . . . qualified?'

The word struck the wrong note, but he could not think of an alternative.

'And then doing it here,' Torres continued. 'OK, so it's an abandoned field. But it's commonly used by kids, it's not that far away from where people live. And then the ground is covered with weeds. You dig that up and it's pretty bloody obvious.'

He paused.

'It's almost as if—'

'It's almost as if whoever did this wanted the body to be discovered,' Cámara finished for him.

Torres took a deep breath.

Cámara waited, then spoke.

'That big white *alquería* over there,' he said, pointing over the orange trees. 'Do you know whose it is?'

'That,' said Torres, 'is the Alquería del Duc. That's Alfonso Segarra's house.'

TWELVE

Paterna was a satellite town to the north-west of Valencia. It was here, on an industrial estate not far from the airport, that the Horta headquarters was located. Cámara and Torres drove up to a sprawling complex of buildings, mostly painted white, but unpretentious and functional. It might almost have been a hospital or series of government office blocks. Nothing, apart from the name of the company in large green letters on top of the main structure, declared that this was the home of one of the most successful businesses in the country. Segarra created so much wealth for Spain that his opinions on the economy made headline news, while watching how his company operated and analysing any new measures that it introduced was something of an obsession among financial journalists. Horta had adapted early when the economic crisis began, and as a result had survived and actually increased its profits. In Madrid, politicians were in the habit of saying that the country needed more men like Segarra.

Cámara and Torres signed in at the reception desk and were given visitors' cards. Torres clipped his to his jacket, Cámara put his in a pocket and promptly forgot about it. Both were surprised at the mildness of the security set-up: secretaries and assistants appeared to be the only shields that Segarra employed between himself and the rest of the world, which was unusual for someone so powerful. There was no tinted glass in the windows to hide behind, no surveillance cameras, no men with guns. Cámara felt almost embarrassed to be carrying his standard-issue Heckler & Koch. The place had a church-like calm about it: people spoke in low voices and moved mostly silently and unhurriedly.

'This way, please.'

A woman with shoulder-length brown hair, wearing a dark blue skirt and jacket, led them to the lift, where they ascended wordlessly to the third floor of the five-storey building. They emerged into a simple lobby where a handful of large pot plants made a symbolic attempt at creating an atmosphere of corporate grandeur. Their guide nodded at the woman behind the desk and they passed through to a modest reception room with low, off-white sofas and armchairs arranged in a square around a coffee table with a glass top, on which the day's newspapers were neatly laid out. Everything was there, from the local Valencian daily to the nationals, including those on both Left and Right of the political spectrum.

'You can wait here.'

The woman closed the door behind her. Torres sat down, perched on the edge of one of the armchairs. Cámara glanced around: one wall was made of glass and looked out on to the visitors' car park at the front of the complex where he could make out Torres's Seat. The other walls were decorated with bright, rather sentimental paintings of local scenes, mostly involving the *huerta* with orange trees and fruit and vegetables in abundance. A small wooden cross hung above the door through which they had just entered.

They were not kept waiting for long; after a couple of moments Alfonso Segarra appeared, quietly opening the door, stepping inside and standing before them.

'My apologies,' he said. 'Urgent business.'

He stretched out his hand, indicating one of the seats to Cámara.

'Shall we?'

Although he was only in his late fifties, Segarra had pure white hair, cut short so that it looked like soft felt covering his scalp. His trimmed beard was darker and coarser, drawing attention away from his eyes and down to his chin. Cámara found himself inadvertently staring at the man's mouth for a few moments before examining the rest of his face: his eyes were small and dark, his nose fleshy, and his complexion pale. He was perhaps a centimetre or two shorter than Cámara, and he kept his weight under control – there were no bulges over his belt, while his straight, slightly stiff posture gave him a military air. What was most apparent about him, however, was a calm authority. Here was a man used to being in charge, displaying an unforced and natural superiority.

There was no handshake, no attempt to ingratiate himself: this was not that kind of meeting. But within moments of his arrival an assistant – another woman, younger, one they had not seen before – walked in with a tray carrying small cups and coffee still steaming from a pot.

'Thank you,' Segarra said as she placed the tray down on the table and left.

Segarra poured three cups, then passed one each to his guests. Cámara carefully observed the surface of the black coffee while the cups were still in Segarra's hands: the tremble was barely visible.

'*Cortado?*' Segarra asked, indicating a small jug of milk. Both detectives declined.

Segarra lifted his coffee, blew on it a little, then drank it quickly in two gulps. Cámara lifted his own to his lips: it was still burning hot.

Segarra's cup scarcely made a sound as he placed it back on the table.

'I've been informed,' he said, 'that the best people in Valencia have been tasked with solving my son's murder.'

He looked Cámara in the eye.

'Chief Inspector Max Cámara.' Segarra gave a slight nod before turning to Torres. 'And Inspector Torres of the Special Crimes Unit. I spoke two days ago to your colleague in the murder squad, Chief Inspector Laura Martín. But now the case has been passed on to you.'

It felt almost like a challenge.

'It was felt that, given your . . .' Torres began, but his sentence petered out.

Segarra listened, then patiently turned to Cámara.

'I'm not asking for special treatment,' he said. 'This case should be dealt with just like any other. My son has been murdered. The pain is no greater for me than it is for any other parent in my situation.'

'I understand,' said Cámara. The point was that this case was being treated in a special way, however. And the fact that Segarra knew exactly who they were made it very clear that he had information sources somewhere – probably high up – within the *Policía Nacional*, perhaps even in the interior ministry.

'We spoke to Chief Inspector Martín,' he continued. It was not a complete lie, but Segarra did not have to know about the tensions between the different police departments. 'She told us about her interview with you, but we wanted to talk to you ourselves.'

'Of course,' Segarra said. 'Perfectly understandable. You may find I have nothing more to add, and I really don't want to waste your time. Chief Inspector Martín was clearly working on the theory that someone might have . . .' The pause, the catch in his throat, was so momentary as to go almost unnoticed. 'Have killed Fermín in order to get at me, as it were. It is a sound theory, and one I would entertain myself were I in her – or your – shoes. But the fact is that I cannot think of anyone who would do something like that. There have been no threats, nobody has intimated that they might harm me or my family in any way. And while it is not easy to build something like I have without upsetting some people along the way – enemies come, whether you seek them or not – I cannot think of a single one who might have been driven to such extremes. It is completely unimaginable.'

'We're keeping an open mind,' Cámara said. 'There are no ideas, no hypotheses for the time being. The fact that Fermín was your son might be irrelevant.'

He coughed.

'What I mean to say is that his attacker might not have been aware who Fermín was. Although . . .'

Segarra stayed perfectly still, watching him.

'Although the manner in which he was killed suggests

someone with certain knowledge about techniques for carrying out such an attack.'

Still Segarra did not move, his eyes barely blinking as he looked Cámara in the face.

'Your son's neck was broken,' Cámara said.

'I know,' said Segarra. 'And you're suggesting . . . ?'

'There appears to be no sexual element to the attack, no molestation. Neither was your son – mercifully – made to suffer greatly. Death was instantaneous.'

'Some kind of psychopath,' Segarra said. 'Killing for the sake of it.'

'He may or may not be,' Cámara said. 'What I see, however, is a kill, a simple, quick and efficient kill. And that in itself tells us something about the killer – someone who knew what they were doing and wanted to carry it out cleanly. Apart from the damage to the neck and spinal column, no other violence was carried out against your son.'

After a pause, Segarra spoke.

'And this leads you in the same direction as your colleague,' he said. 'You think his murder has something to do with me.'

'As you yourself said, it's the most likely possibility at the moment based on what we know.'

'But you have no preconceived ideas.'

'It would be very useful to the investigation,' Cámara said, 'for you to think slowly and carefully about this. It could be anything, perhaps something that happened some time ago. It doesn't have to be recent. A comment, perhaps, or something . . .'

'I told you,' Segarra said, 'there's nothing. Believe me, I've done more thinking over the past couple of days than I have ever done before in my life. I have raked over everything, several times in many cases. And I can find nothing, no clue.'

He took a deep breath and linked his fingers together, resting his hands on his lap like a wall.

'My concern is that I am merely wasting your time. Nothing new has come to mind since I spoke to your colleague. Believe me, I would have been in touch if it had. And yet, despite my efforts, I repeat, there's nothing. Nothing at all.'

He unlinked his hands and spread them out, almost in apology, but with his palms upwards, as though indicating that they should stand up.

'And now . . .'

Torres took the cue and got to his feet, as did Cámara a second later.

'Just for the record,' Cámara said, 'and I'm sure this was covered before, but things get mislaid or not recorded properly – where were you at the time?'

'Here, in a meeting,' said Segarra. 'It overran for several hours, as meetings unfortunately often do.'

It was time for them to leave. He shook their hands briefly and escorted them to the door, where the assistant in the blue suit was waiting for them.

'Thank you, gentlemen. Mercedes will show you out.'

And he closed the door.

Torres waited until they were inside the car before speaking.

'Who goes back to work so soon after the death of their ten-year-old son?' he said. 'I've never seen such a composed grieving parent.'

He put the car in gear and they drove out of the Horta complex and back towards the city centre.

'We've got to start digging around,' said Cámara. 'It's going to be hard work. And I've got a feeling that whatever we're looking for is going to be buried very deep.'

He wound down the window, a sudden desire to clean himself with fresh air overcoming him.

It had felt as though Segarra was interviewing them rather than the other way around.

But for what?

THIRTEEN

'The orders are very specific and come from the highest level. Nothing – repeat, nothing – is to be put in motion at this time.'

'Is that why you're here? Came all this way?'

'We need to know that we can rely on you, Colonel. The situation is extremely volatile, as you understand. The feeling is that things could easily escalate. There are very many factors that have to be balanced. Knowing that we can count on your network's support at this time would be one less thing to worry about.'

'Am I a source of worry to you now?'

'That depends entirely on you.'

'I have nothing but the interests of Spain at heart.'

'We are all patriots, Colonel. That goes without saying. What is important right now, however, is that all the forces of order are coordinated. We can't have anyone acting alone or, heaven forbid, improvising. Things could blow up in our faces.'

'I understand how dangerous the situation is. Perfectly. Which is why I find your call for calm, for non-action at this time, curious. Now, more than ever, is the moment to strike. If we wait our enemies will only get stronger. Too much time has been allowed to pass already, they have got away with too much.'

'Colonel—'

'Don't try to shut me up. I was fighting this battle long before you came along. It takes men of action, men with balls, to see the situation clearly. Not desk men from Madrid. You might think that we're out on a limb here. But believe me, everything is much, much clearer from the edges than at the centre of the storm. You are blind to the threat. The proof is that you have allowed it to get so bad in the first place. You cannot reason with these people. They have one thing in mind and they are doing everything in their power to achieve it. And they are laughing at us as they do so. I don't know which is worse.'

'We could shut you down.'

'You don't know what you're talking about, or what you're dealing with.'

'My orders were specific – to get assurances from you, or close the network.'

'Shut me down? Is this supposed to get me on board? An empty threat like that? You wouldn't even know where to begin.'

'Juan Gordillo López in Burgos, Antonio Luis Camacho González in Seville, Sergio Toledo Ruiz in Murcia . . . Does this amuse you, Colonel?'

'That's it?'

'All these men—'

'All those men . . . I'll give you this for free – all those men are out, no longer operative. Whatever information you have on us is out of date. So don't come here trying to bully me. I've seen your type come and go many times before. And you'll end up like the rest of them: burnt out, frustrated and dreaming of the days when you could still call yourself a man.'

'What will it take'

'What will it *take*?'

'We both want the same thing.'

'Do we? I'm beginning to doubt that.'

'The future of Spain is in the balance.'

'It's what I've been saying for years.'

'Colonel, please. By being disunited we are only giving our enemies an advantage. And besides, we know about the killing of the boy.'

'That was never meant to happen. It was a mistake.'

'So you say. But it's set alarm bells ringing in Madrid. And is the real reason why I'm here.'

'I'm listening.'

'Things are in play right now that mean any action on our part might damage our chances of a successful outcome.'

'What things?'

'You know I can't—'

'What things? You want my cooperation, you have to start talking.'

'Our information is that something big is about to happen. We don't know what. But a large stone is about to disturb the waters, and we need to see how the ripples spread out before deciding on the best course of action.'

'Something big.'

'I've said enough already.'

'Bigger than what's already happening?'

'Colonel, I need an assurance. Your network cannot be operating independently right now. It may jeopardise everything.'

'I don't like it.'

'Neither do I. But we cannot allow anarchy to rule. At least not on our side.'

'All right.'

'I have your word?'

'As a gentleman.'

'Thank you, Colonel.'

'I'll expect you to be addressing me by a different title next time.'

'A promotion. Of course. I'll see to it personally.'

'You'd better. And now, if you'll excuse me.'

'One last thing, if you would allow me.'

'Make it quick.'

'The detective, the one we mentioned.'

'In Valencia?'

'Yes.'

'He's a useful fool.'

'Thank you, Colonel.'

'For now.'

Colonel Terreros left the Madrid man to pick up the bar bill and headed out into the square before cutting into the side street and climbing the stairs to his office. After waiting for a few moments to make sure that he had not been followed, he closed the door behind him and sat down at his desk. Switching on his computer, he typed in the day's passwords, ran a security check and opened up a Web browser. Within a few seconds he was looking at a page in English espousing the benefits of legalising drugs, complete with photos of drug-making equipment and recipes about how to make them. The texts had been up for several weeks by now and it would soon be time to change them. Thank God for the instant translation services on the Internet these days, otherwise he would be at a loss – he could barely understand the English himself and the language of Shakespeare was somewhat abused in the process, but it worked.

Clicking on 'Forums', he passed through several pages within the site before finding the relevant link, buried in small letters at the bottom in a body of minuscule text. When the next page opened in a separate window, he saw with some relief that his agent was online at the agreed time.

El Uno: What happened? Those were not the instructions.

El Dos: The situation changed. I had to improvise.

Uno: This complicates things. The intention was to kidnap, not to effect a termination. Repeat: WHAT HAPPENED?

Dos: He struggled, was close to disrupting the whole operation. I had to act quickly.

Uno: You let the situation get out of control. You yourself lost control.

Dos: My apologies. No excuse.

Uno: You are a soldier. You are expected to behave as one.

Dos: Yes.

Uno: We have talked about this before: you lack self-discipline. In other circumstances I might have to bring you in.

Dos: It won't happen again.

Uno: You're lucky. In the end the effect is the same. Your improvisation with the burial went some way to limiting the damage. The message was received. I expect communication within hours.

Dos: What happens now?

Uno: Things are developing fast. I need you to be prepared to move to the next stage at any moment.

Dos: Red and blue?

Uno: Correct.

Dos: Expansion?

Uno: Use your own judgement. You may find it easier to operate in a smaller unit. And you may have to improvise. I cannot guarantee this line of communication for much longer. But you will recognise the sign when it comes. That will be the moment to proceed to the final phase.

Dos: Understood.

Uno: The training has all been for this. Don't mess it up.

Dos: You can count on me.

Uno: We may not get the chance to talk for some time. God be with you.

Dos: And with you.

Colonel Terreros closed the web page and went through the process of turning his computer off, making sure to pull the plug out of his router before he left the office.

Outside, the sun was beginning to set, casting a soothing

golden glow over Ceuta and the mountains behind it. The city felt calmer – the nervousness that had taken over in the wake of the deaths at the border had now eased and people were getting on with things in their usual way.

But within himself, the colonel was troubled. The evenings were often the worst time of day, when the ache from the wound intensified. And deep down, somewhere in the remains of his damaged abdomen, circled the tiniest of doubts about what he was unleashing. The thrill of giving orders, of commanding his best man to proceed, filled him with a vibrant, intense energy and it felt, at one level, like the old days, when his manhood was intact and the rush of blood to his groin had given him power and life. But entirely destroyed by a bullet twenty years before, his organ was now only an excruciating memory, and the erotic thrill of the moment also awakened his sense of incompleteness.

He would walk it off, visit the memorial to his dead brethren of the Legión on the Paseo de Colón before heading back to Paco's for his first drink of the evening. Whisky helped with the pain, and dulled any desire attempting to flicker within him.

And if that failed, he could visit Sandrita. Her rub-downs went some way to easing things. She was delicate with him: he might feel, at least, the body of a woman against his even if he could not satisfy her. Inevitably, towards the end, he would collapse in tears, but it was worth it for the release.

Besides, it was a special occasion. And he might not get another opportunity for some while.

FOURTEEN

'I heard about some foreigners – set up something called the Extreme Paella Club.'

'The what?'

'The idea is you go to the top of a mountain or some place where it's difficult to make a paella . . . and then you make a paella.'

Cámara rolled his eyes.

'Don't tell me, they're Germans.'

'English, actually. But they're all *guiris*.'

'There are certain things that I just can't understand about foreigners. Or that they simply don't get. As though making paella weren't complicated enough as it is.'

'The record holder is some guy who went into the heart of the Namibian desert and made one there.'

The look of incredulity increased on Cámara's face.

'Even took some dried orange peel with him to light the fire with,' Torres continued. 'Nice touch, very authentic.'

'And did he take Valencian water with him all that way as well? You know as well as I do that it doesn't taste the same without it.'

'I don't think so. Dragging ten litres of our tap water all that way would be pretty extreme though.'

'Namibian paella,' Cámara chuckled to himself.

'Probably used elephant meat.'

'Wonder what it tastes like?'

He stared out at the sea for a couple of moments, watching the sunlight caress the ripples on the surface. They had arrived late, and the restaurant was already emptying, which meant they could take a recently vacated table by the window.

'I'm sure it's a lot of fun,' he said, 'making paella in weird, difficult places, but it does rather miss the point.'

Torres smiled.

'You're going to start lecturing me, a Valencian, about how to make paella?' he said.

'What I've noticed,' Cámara continued, ignoring him, 'is that the really good ones, the ones you remember, have an almost alchemical perfection to them. My grandfather was big on this. The ingredients are the same as ever, your timings are pretty much as they always are, and yet occasionally, for reasons that you can't put your finger on, every now and again one comes out that is almost magical, as though it were greater than the sum of its parts, where everything is balanced.'

'Harmonious,' Torres said.

'Yes, harmonious. I've only made two like that in my entire life, and I remember exactly who I was with each time, what we talked about, what the weather was like, all kinds of details about the event surrounding the paella itself, as though the event and the paella were one and the same thing.'

He took a sip of wine. Torres waited.

'It's not easy to describe what I'm talking about, but I'm sure you've experienced it as well.'

Torres nodded silently.

'It's as if . . .' Cámara laughed. 'It's as if the gods have to be on your side for it to work, like a *duende* moment in a flamenco performance – all the ingredients are there, everything is in place, but whether or not the magic spark will be produced is out of your hands, as though other, invisible, factors were at play.'

He glanced out of the window again.

'Like currents under the sea that we can't control, pulling and pushing us along in directions we do not understand.'

Torres stared at him for a moment before speaking.

'Not bad for a Manchego like yourself,' he said. 'I do believe, chief, that you're going native.'

'Become a Valencian?' Cámara sniffed. 'Never. They'd never let me join anyway.'

It was too late for the kitchens to make a paella to order for them, so they took what was left from ones made earlier. The waiter came over with plates piled high with dark yellow rice and placed them on the table before them.

Silently they began – neither had eaten anything since breakfast and they were starving.

After a few mouthfuls they looked at each other and shrugged. It was food, and it was tasty, but it was not paella perfection.

'The gods were not smiling on this kitchen today,' said Torres.

'It's heated up from earlier. We can't expect miracles.'

Torres put his spoon down and finished the wine in his glass before reaching out for the bottle and pouring them both some more.

'Are you talking paella now,' he asked, 'or about this case?'

Cámara kept his head down and carried on eating. He was trying to think about Hilario. And Alicia.

Over a week had passed since their interview with Segarra at the Horta headquarters. Neither of them had ever felt so frustrated with an investigation. Given to them second-hand by the murder squad, it felt like leftovers: they were going through the motions, but so far no luck had run their way.

The latest disappointment had come that morning: having trawled through hundreds of child-abduction and murder cases around the country looking for similarities or patterns, they found only one which appeared to have any potential – the strangling of a twelve-year-old boy in Badajoz two months earlier. His body, like Fermín's, had been dumped in a field, and the killer had not been caught. It was little to go on and they had been talking to the Badajoz murder squad directly, swapping information. But word had reached them that morning that the boy's uncle – who had been one of the suspects – had finally confessed to the murder. And he had been nowhere near Valencia at the time of Fermín's death.

The link had been tenuous, but the fact that the news came as a blow showed how frustrated they were becoming. They had no more clues: Fermín's mother, emotionally destroyed by the death of her son and staying with relatives outside the city, had confirmed – between the barbed, guilt-laden attacks on herself for allowing him to walk home alone – what they already knew. The murder squad themselves had overseen interviews with neighbours and people from the Sagrado Corazón school. So far, Fermín appeared to be a fairly typical ten-year-old who had been returning home from a football match in the old river bed. The last positive sighting had been in the Plaza de la Reina, behind the cathedral, when he branched off in the direction of the Plaza del Arzobispo. A group of boys from the same school, walking a few metres behind, said they thought Fermín had been busy with his phone and had barely looked where he was going. At the Plaza de la Reina they had kept going straight and had lost sight of him.

The phone records were checked, and Fermín's last texts to his friend Rafa was recovered. The references at the end to being followed appeared to confirm that he had been assaulted somewhere before reaching his home. They interviewed Rafa, but the boy was traumatised by what had happened, too frightened to return to school.

'Did Fermín ever mention being followed by a man before?'

'Did he always take the same route home?'

'What did you think when he went silent like that? Had he ever done that before?'

But their gently spoken questions were met by blank staring eyes and a shaking head.

'I didn't mean to swear at him,' the boy had sobbed before they left. 'Am I going to hell?'

Fermín's neighbourhood was generally quieter than the rest of the city centre: elegant, wealthy and religious. The Opus Dei had a church there; there were few bars, little nightlife to speak of. It was not impossible that late on a midweek night very few people would be out on the streets, so an attack, if carried out quickly and efficiently, might not be witnessed by anyone. Especially if the victim failed to raise the alarm. The snapping of Fermín's neck so cleanly would have taken care of that.

And so, from the Plaza de la Reina to the shallow grave in the *huerta* near Carpesa, they were faced with a hole, with only the text messages back and forth with Rafa to shed the tiniest glimmer of light. No more witnesses had come forward, no more evidence had been found, neither in the area where he had disappeared nor around the grave site. Given the nature of his murder and the lack of any sexual molestation, they were assuming that he had been killed quickly before the body was transported out of the city. Traffic cameras had been studied to try to spot a vehicle travelling from Fermín's neighbourhood in the direction of Carpesa – which could theoretically give them a lead – but the scant material available from the handful of cameras in operation had offered them nothing to go on.

The general situation regarding clues was more noticeable for their absence than anything else. And so Cámara and Torres had devoted most of their energies to trying to find a possible motive: who might have wanted to kill Fermín? The obvious way forward was to concentrate on Segarra. They checked the teachers at the Sagrado Corazón and quickly decided that they could rule them out – there was nothing, not even the faintest hint, that any of them might have been capable of this. Stories about priests doing unspeakable things to children were commonplace but no such claims had been made about Fermín's school, at least. And besides, they all had firm alibis for the time of the murder.

No, their instincts had pointed them towards Segarra from the beginning, and there they continued to concentrate.

At least, Cámara told himself, they had managed to build up a picture of Segarra's life: born in Valencia in 1957 to parents from the satellite town of Almàssera, where Segarra was brought up. His father had a small amount of land in the *huerta*, but mostly made his living distributing fruit and vegetables in a truck to nearby towns. His mother was a seamstress: there was an elder brother, but he died of pneumonia at an early age.

Segarra passed through the local school with average grades and did his national service in North Africa before returning to Almàssera and starting to help his father. After a couple of years he set up his own fruit-and-vegetable stall in the markets as they moved from town to town on different days. Three years later he had enough money to set up his own shop. Around this time, when he was twenty-five, he married Francisca Grau, a girl he had known from school. They worked hard and soon Segarra had another shop in the nearby *huerta* town of Vinalesa. It seemed that he might carry on like this, a small-scale fruit-and-veg seller, but he began to have ideas for something bigger – a supermarket. He had heard about such places abroad, and a handful had been established in Spain. Segarra was clever enough to see that this was the future, that housewives would love not to have to traipse around half a dozen places to do the shopping, but find everything they needed under one roof. And so Horta was born and was an instant success. Francisca was not working by this time, having had the first two of their three daughters, but the business soon began to grow. Within a year of the first Horta supermarket opening in his home town, Segarra had established another in a residential neighbourhood in Valencia itself. Within ten years he had twenty more. Now, over thirty years after he had begun there were over 1,500 Horta supermarkets around the country. No one could give the exact number because so many more were opening every week.

As his success grew, so did Segarra's importance: he bought a local football team – the lesser of the two main Valencian clubs – raising its fortunes with his money and bringing it up to the first division. He was courted by politicians – first being befriended by the local variety, later by those operating at a national level. He was a keen tennis player, and commonly shared courts with judges, government ministers, newspaper editors and celebrities.

And yet, for all his wealth, he did a good job of keeping himself out of the public eye. In the wake of the economic troubles, his opinions had become more sought after, as though his achievement of keeping Horta growing through the great recession might be extrapolated to the country as a whole. But you rarely, if ever, saw his face or his name mentioned in the gossip pages. Nor did he make political comments of any kind, despite his friendship with top members of the leading parties.

Frustratingly for Cámara and Torres, scratching around to find something – anything – that might give direction to their investigation, Segarra appeared to be held in high regard by almost anyone.

There were, as was to be expected, those who grumbled about him: union leaders complained that he worked his employees too hard for too little pay, and that he had taken advantage of the economic climate to squeeze them even further. A rival supermarket chain complained that

Horta played unfairly in the battle over providers. Ecology groups accused the company of not doing enough to protect the environment and actually promoting the use of pesticides and herbicides that were banned in other countries.

But there was nothing there that pointed to a possible motive for murdering Fermín. Segarra appeared to have done the impossible and found enormous success without making any serious enemies. Journalists, it now emerged, had known for several years about his affair with Célia Capilla and about the existence of an illegitimate son, but it was as much a testament to his good name as to the lack of salaciousness in most serious newspapers that this had never been reported. Only after Fermín had been killed did the general public discover the double private life of Alfonso Segarra.

A week of work, a week of digging. And they had discovered nothing. No motives, no potential motives, not even the whisper of a motive. And their reaction had been to keep on, to keep circling, scratching away, diving down into whichever cavity appeared, only to re-emerge empty-handed.

A week, and the sense of desperation was beginning to increase – they were both arriving earlier at the office and leaving later. Cámara had barely spoken a word to Alicia. The case was becoming all-consuming, giving them nothing back in return.

Everything was there – the elements, the ingredients – and yet it felt as though nothing had actually started yet. The gods, luck, destiny, the invisible currents, the *duende*, had so far failed to assist them in any way.

They finished the paella in silence, and drank the last of

the wine. It was Cámara's idea – to head out of the office, a change of space, let their minds drift for a while. Sometimes – often, in fact – it helped, particularly when an investigation was stuck like this. But the restaurant had let them down – the food had been edible, nothing more. It felt as though they had wasted their time.

'I'll get it,' Cámara said, waving to the waiter to bring them the bill. Torres did not protest.

Cámara had signed the receipt and was putting on his jacket when his phone rang. The number was withheld.

He pressed the button and lifted the phone to his ear.

'Cámara,' he said.

'My name is Carlos,' came a voice. 'We need to meet.'

Cámara raised a weary eyebrow.

'What's this about?'

'About a trade, Chief Inspector. I can give something to you, and I want something in return.'

'Listen, I'm pretty busy right now.'

He pulled a face at Torres and was about to hang up.

'Believe me, you won't want to lose this opportunity.'

It was rare to receive crank calls – he was careful about who he gave his number to – but a few managed to get through every now and again. Usually it was someone with proof that a new order of Templar Knights was about to stage a coup, or some such rubbish.

'What are you offering?' he asked. He and Torres had reached the doorway and were stepping out into the blinding afternoon sun.

'Information relevant to the murder of Fermín Capilla,' said the voice.

Cámara stopped dead.

'Now about that meeting,' the man continued. 'Listen

carefully and I will give you instructions. You must come alone. Leave Inspector Torres to make his own way back to the Jefatura. I'm sure he'll need an hour or two to digest his lunch. Not always easy on the stomach, a late paella.'

FIFTEEN

'By now you'll have guessed who I work with, so we should clear it up straight away. I'm from the *CNI.*'

Carlos was pushing fifty. He wore a light blue linen suit, a white-and-blue shirt and a dark blue silk tie. He had the body of one who had once been fit, with a bulge around his waist and rounding shoulders, but with a physical memory buried inside there of what it meant to run, to sweat and to fight. Cámara walked at his side as they descended the steps from street level down to the old river bed. Carlos led them off the main pathway, where cyclists and rollerbladers whizzed in and out, and into the shade and privacy of the pine trees.

Cámara had taken in every detail of the man: the short, thinning grey hair; the rimless glasses; the high forehead and the blood pressure. He looked like a fairly ordinary businessman: standing at the agreed spot, his hands in his pockets, relaxed, glancing out at the traffic as it passed. But few people were able to do that these days, to stand motionless in a public space with little to distract them: everyone nervously buried themselves in a portable screen of some kind, as though hiding from the real world. And curiously this difference had made Carlos stand out, which was not necessarily a good thing, Cámara thought, for a spy.

The *Centro Nacional de Inteligencia* – CNI – was the country's low-budget version of an intelligence community, covering both external espionage and internal security. It operated out of Madrid and was made up mostly of military types. In general, relations between it and the *Policía Nacional* were poor – *CNI* men were much happier operating with the paramilitary *Guardia Civil*, who shared a common culture and outlook. The *Policía Nacional* was far too 'civilian' for the spies, and the two organisations avoided each other as much as possible. True, Cámara knew of the *Brigada Operativa de Apoyo* – a small group of his colleagues who could be called on by the *CNI* if ever they needed someone with a police badge to get something done for them – for example, arresting or identifying someone. But there was something of a stigma attached to the idea. The *CNI* and *Policía Nacional* existed in a kind of Cold War, suspicious of each other, occasionally breaking out into open hostility. Cámara had never – to his knowledge – had anything to do with them.

It was not so much a tribal thing with him as the fact that the *CNI* was not held in particularly high regard – either inside our outside the country. The organisation's predecessor, the *CESID*, had been closed down after becoming a national joke – its 'secret' operations had been anything but after confidential papers were stolen and leaked. A former spy chief had been convicted in 1999 of illegal phone tapping – including the mobile of King Juan Carlos – only for the sentence to be quashed by *El Tribunal Constitucional* the following year. And the scandals had continued with the creation of the *CNI* after another director was forced to leave following accusations of spending intelligence money on luxury hunting and fishing holidays and treating *CNI* employees like his personal staff, even getting them to clean his swimming pool.

The organisation was ludicrous on one level. But for Cámara it represented something sinister – State control and unaccountability – that, viscerally, he opposed. The *CNI* was a common factor in the many, labyrinthine entanglements of Spanish politics: every embarrassing leaked document or susprising revelation had a whiff of the spy organisation about it. Officially it focused on North Africa and South America and supposed threats to Spanish security, but the suspicion was that most of the officers' energies were dedicated to stirring up the already murky waters of political power at home. There was no doubt in his mind that the corruption scandal that had brought down the previous Catalan government had been born within the imagination of the *CNI*. The man now next to him was not like some of the policemen who he worked with every day, serving the authoritarian needs of their masters like dogs with an unthinking, almost thuggish, sense of discipline. This man was one of the minds, one of the defenders, of State authority itself, in all its devious tyranny.

Despite introducing himself over the phone earlier, Carlos insisted on repeating his name once they met.

'Carlos,' he repeated, shaking Cámara's hand, as though flagging up that this was a code name. The hairs on Cámara's arms stood on end. He wondered if Carlos made up a new name for each person he met.

Cámara remained silent, but once they reached the pine trees, the *CNI* man began to speak.

'I know you're investigating the murder of Alfonso Segarra's son.'

He kept his eyes ahead and alert, barely glancing at Cámara, a large part of his attention focused on their surroundings and environment.

'And I know that it isn't going as well as you might hope.'

'Have you been spying on me?' Cámara asked.

Carlos grinned.

'It's what I do. But no, as it happens, I haven't been spying on you. Or at least not in the traditional way. You see, I know that you haven't got anywhere with your digging into Segarra himself because I'm the only person who can help you there. And so far I haven't passed on any information to you.'

'If you have any information relating to the case, then it's your duty to help the police investigation.'

Cámara knew such a straightforward approach would not wash, but it was worth spelling out, if only to make his own position clear.

Carlos pulled out a packet of Marlboro Lights, took one for himself and then, in an afterthought, offered one across. Cámara refused.

'Oh, that's right,' Carlos said. 'You smoke Ducados. I almost forgot.'

He lit his cigarette, inhaled deeply and breathed out. Cámara waited.

'The information you need to conclude this case,' Carlos began, 'will be yours. In fact, once I give it to you, you'll realise your investigation has barely begun. And without it you will remain as stuck as you are now. We all want to see little Fermín's killer brought to justice. Believe me, we do our bit, often with enormous difficulties. Don't think we haven't been hit by the crisis as well these past years. Sometimes I'm amazed how we survive. But our job is to make a difference – no matter how small. We're in the same game, essentially, you and I. We're guardians, peacekeepers, shepherds. Which is why I believe we should help each other wherever possible.'

Cámara kept his face expressionless. Carlos was treating him like a machine, attempting to press his buttons and set him in motion, like a child's toy. The deliberate slips meant to demonstrate how well-informed he was; the promise of a panacea for the Fermín investigation; the shared problems; the faux camaraderie; the vision for a better world: it was as though the man were speaking from a prepared speech, perhaps one he had used successfully in the past on others. Cámara imagined that he had four or five like this, one for each perceived psychological 'type'. They were probably buried in the appendices of some spying manual somewhere, the one they gave you when you signed up.

He checked the clock on his mobile phone: his late lunch had taken up a good couple of hours and now his time was being wasted by some shifty intelligence officer with vague promises of help. He should cut things short and get back to the Jefatura before the rest of the day was lost.

'You've got one more sentence,' he said to Carlos, 'to get me interested.'

Carlos stopped and turned to face him.

'The information – hard evidence – that I will give you will lead you directly to the person responsible for Fermín's death. I know, because I've seen it. I know where it is and I know where it's been buried. And I know that without me you will never, ever, find it. Too many people, too many interests, are at stake for a simple detective such as yourself – and I mean that with no disrespect – to find it.'

'What are you talking about?'

'I can't say any more.'

'Listen—'

'You know how this works,' Carlos interrupted. 'We're not idiots here. You can get on your moral high horse and start talking about my duty as a citizen to assist you. But you know perfectly well that things don't work like that. What are you going to do? Get a court order to force me to reveal everything? You wouldn't know which name to put on the paperwork – you don't know who I am. Dig around a bit and you'll even wonder if I exist. But believe me, you need me, you need what I've got to give you. Otherwise this investigation will go absolutely nowhere.'

'I need you,' Cámara repeated.

'That's what I said.'

'Or perhaps you need me?'

Carlos shot him a look.

'You could be useful to us, yes. What I'm offering is a trade. A mutual back-scratching exercise. It's the only way anything in this world ever gets done. You didn't get to chief inspector without learning that, for all your high ideals.'

Cámara could feel blood pulsing in his temples, a pressure building at the back of his head. Almost every part of his being shouted out that he should turn and walk away, that this man, for all his bravado, had nothing to offer him. Or if he had, it would cause problems, lead him down avenues he should avoid. And surely he was a good enough detective to solve Fermín's murder on his own. But the hook was already there – what if Carlos really did have something useful for him? The truth was that he was right – the investigation had stagnated.

'This world, our world, Max, is changing. Look around – every institution that this country is built on is crumbling: the monarchy, the mainstream political parties, the judicial system, the Church. Do you think it can all hold together for much longer? People are angry. The crisis has exposed the rottenness of the whole structure and it's in danger of falling down. Everything. We all want change. But the change has to be ordered, it has to be done properly. I want a fairer world, Max. And so do you. But I'm scared, because when things come crashing down, what comes next isn't always better. In fact, it's usually a lot worse. Right now I'm not sure that Spain as you and I know it will still be around in a few years' time. This country is fragile, always in danger of destroying itself. I don't want to see that happen. And I don't think, for all your avant-garde political ideas, you do either.'

It came out in what felt like a single breath, the words cascading like water from his mouth. It was less prepared than the earlier speech, but Cámara began to smile as Carlos reached the end: realisation crept up and grabbed him, like a hand reaching up from some other, non-thinking part of his brain.

'You want me to spy on the anarchists,' he said simply.

Carlos did not miss a beat.

'I want you to keep me informed about them, yes. We know about your association with them. And in return I will give you everything you need to wrap up the Fermín case in record time.'

The rage moved slowly within him, like molten tar. Anger not so much at the man who had dragged him here so much as at himself for taking so long to see it: the manipulation, the promises, the threats, the sulliedness of it all. He closed his eyes and let out a deep breath, wondering which words to use; which was, in fact, the most correct way of telling a spy to go fuck himself.

When he opened his eyes again, however, Carlos was no longer standing directly in front of him, but had taken a step back and was half-turned, as though ready to leave. He was one move ahead of him. In his hand, held out to Cámara, was a card with a phone number on it.

'In case you change your mind,' he said, and leaned forward to thrust it between Cámara's fingers. Then he spun on his heel and walked briskly away, quickly disappearing from view, up and out of the river bed.

Cámara picked up a stick from the ground, smashed it as hard as he could against the trunk of a tree, brushed himself down and turned to leave.

The cigarette lighter burnt his thumb as he tried to spark it into life.

SIXTEEN

The river bed took him around the edge of the city centre: he could carry on walking as far as the Nuevo Centro shopping centre before cutting left and heading down Fernando el Católico to the Jefatura. At that moment the alternative – grabbing a taxi – did not appeal: he was in no mood to listen to mindless chit-chat about football or the weather.

He walked past gushing fountains and a shallow, litter-strewn lake. At the bottom of an old stone bridge two young men were ignoring a ban on climbing, scaling the sides with their bare hands, their muscles thin and taught like rope.

For a second he had a flashback to Barcelona and the medal ceremony at the Palau de la Música. You haven't gone unnoticed, Segundo Pont had said. Had it been a warning? What did Segundo Pont know?

He was confused. His instincts – usually so reliable – had deserted him. Nothing was clear: for all his tricks, Carlos had achieved one thing – to throw up so many questions and doubts that he felt as though the light that he was always able to follow – his intuition – had been switched off. It was such a fundamental part of him that he was barely conscious of it, but now its sudden absence made him feel as though a limb had been lopped off. He was crippled, incomplete.

Walking, he reasoned, would help: the rhythmic motion would soothe, calm his spirit, perhaps allow him to see again.

But conflicting emotion beat against him like an angry sea. He had been an idiot in so many ways: to allow himself to be drawn in by Carlos in the first place; to think that no one had noticed who his friends were, that he was involved in the food bank – a collective run by anarchists, some of whom were radically inclined and apparently becoming more so. In the end he had left the collective before the vote on whether he should stay to hear about Daniel's new plans – it had seemed the easiest way to deal with the situation. And he thought that by so doing he was drawing clear lines between the different sides of his life. But to think that he was living in a neat little bubble, complete and isolated, made up simply of his life both inside and outside the police, when in fact he was part of a much bigger world, one that was now trying to ensnare him. He had fallen into the trap, like everyone else, of waiting for things to return to normal after the economic crisis. It was the line that so many had been pushing these past months, even *El País*, that once great newspaper, now controlled by the banks who had brought the ruin on the country in the first place. Keep tight everyone, the message was repeated, it's almost over. We'll all be able to come out of our little holes in just a few more minutes. Trust us.

But things never returned to how they had been: it was the universal law. The river flowed ever on, new water replacing the old, only appearing to be the same. And now it had caught him in its flow. He had stayed still for too long.

What would his grandfather say to him now? How would he interpret this, the offer Cámara had just been given to become a government spy?

He searched, trying to listen to Hilario's words, but heard nothing. He was in the dark and alone.

For years he had managed to find a kind of balance; a policeman, an agent of the State and yet also an anarchist of sorts, distrustful of governments and authority. He had managed it somehow, mostly by separating these two, often opposing, sides, reconciling them where and when it suited or was possible, justifying his police work as being carried out in the name of the greater good of society. Or some such bollocks. But banging up murderers brought little in the way of moral grey areas. He did not ascribe to the view held by some anarchists that society itself was the cause of such ills: he had seen too much of the bloody side of human nature to go along with that. Some people were bad in the same way that some people were insane. You had to feel it, to experience it first hand to know the difference. Yes, there were shades and subtleties to it, but no amount of intellectualising could deny the fact. It was something you felt, and once you had tasted it, it could never be forgotten.

And so he had lived in a curious equilibrium, his life partitioned in relatively neat boxes, the contradictions parked, settled, not disturbing each other.

But in an instant everything had changed.

Of course there was no way he was going to spy on his

friends, betray that trust. They knew he was a policeman, but they also knew that nothing they did that was illegal – or on the fringes of legality – would ever be exposed by him. It was the rule they worked by. They were safe, he was safe, the system worked.

And yet . . . Could Carlos really lead him to Fermín's killer? It was much easier to assume that it was a bluff, that the *CNI* man was spinning him along. But what if he was right? What if he really did have evidence – evidence that Cámara himself would never be able to find – that could solve the case? He had a duty to do everything that he could as a detective, but beyond that, he realised that his pride as an investigator was at stake. Pardo had given the case to the Special Crimes Unit, and although their two-man squad was something of a private joke, it meant something to him. Whether or not Fermín's murder was a special crime, it was his obligation to work on it, to bring it to a close. But the only door that had been opened for him – one which he did not know he could trust – merely served to bring his own fragile balancing act crashing down.

It was easy to say no, easy to tell Carlos to fuck off. But . . .

He blinked and saw that he was gripping his phone very tightly in his left hand. He wanted to call Alicia, to tell her about this, to get her thoughts. But he rejected the idea almost as soon as it came into his mind. If Carlos knew so much about him it was reasonable to assume that his phone was being tapped. Besides, he had got Alicia too involved in the previous case, with horrific results. She needed protecting.

He slipped the phone back into his pocket. Inside he felt

Carlos's card. His fingers wrapped around it and he crushed it into a ball. As soon as he found a waste bin he would toss it away.

It was late by now, and dark. Steps led him up from the relative tranquillity of the river bed to street level, where he crossed the road and started heading down Fernando el Católico, with the cacophonic backdrop of a thousand cars and buses and motorbikes charging past like frantic beasts, some people heading home, others coming out, perhaps for dinner. Ahead, in the direction of the Jefatura, he could see blue lights flashing: an imminent arrest, he thought; some operation perhaps about to get under way.

A mood of uncertainty and fraughtness increased as he got closer, however. People on the pavement appeared to be rushing at a greater pace than usual; he saw concerned faces, small groups in corners staring down at mobile phone screens with expressions of alarm. Even the breeze rustling the plane trees by the side of the road had a curious tightness to it.

When he noticed armed policemen on guard at the main doors to the Jefatura, he knew that something serious must have happened. He flashed his badge and went inside: the lobby was a scramble of bodies, dashing in all directions at once.

Avoiding the lift, he climbed the stairs two at a time and dived into his office. Torres was there, his face pinned to his computer screen.

'OK,' said Cámara. 'What's happened?'

'It's Barcelona,' Torres said, looking up.

'Josep Segundo Pont has been assassinated.'

SEVENTEEN

The call was anonymous, short and direct.

Colonel Terreros listened without interruption, then hung up and went to switch on the television in the living room of his flat. The State twenty-four-hour news channel was already reporting the story, showing stock images of the street where it had taken place.

It was still fresh, however, and there were few details to report beyond the attack itself. The newsreaders were only saying that an attempt had been made on Segundo Pont's life, and were unable to confirm whether he was alive or dead. The colonel's source, however, was better informed and had told him categorically that the Catalan interior minister had indeed lost his life.

Terreros felt the thrill of indignation course through his blood. It had already come to this! Political assassinations on the streets of Barcelona. The situation was out of control:

he had waited too long. But there was a chance, now, to act. A chance, still, to restore order.

After a couple of minutes, he switched off the television and went back into the kitchen. His coffee was still warm: he drank it in one gulp, then calmly rinsed the cup in the sink and placed it to dry on the rack. He pushed his chair into its place at the side of the room, made sure that everything was in order, then stepped out into the hallway, where his jacket was hanging on a hook. Putting it on, he checked that he had his keys and his wallet, then patted his groin: no pain – the adrenalin rush was taking care of that.

He opened a drawer and pulled out the small Glock 26 pistol that he kept at home, placing it into the small of his back. From now on he would arm himself at all times. The world had changed: it was his duty as a citizen and a future saviour of Spain to be prepared for any eventuality. The terms of his position as the head of the Veteran Legionarios' Welfare Association stated that he must carry no weapon: his way around it had been to keep one gun at the office and the other at home. But walking the streets at a time like this without any means of defending himself was out of the question. All the rules had changed.

After one final check to make certain that he had everything, he carefully opened the three locks on his door one by one, pulled it open as far as the security chain would allow, checked that there was no danger on the other side, and let himself out of his flat. With his hand behind his back, fingers brushing the Glock, he went lightly down the stairs and out into the street, scanning in both directions before crossing and walking with a steady, unhesitating step towards the city centre.

Within moments of reaching his office and sitting down,

he heard Paco the barman coming up behind him with his tray.

'I saw you walking past, *coronel*,' he said. 'I thought you might appreciate a glass of something. On the house.'

When he had heard about Segundo Pont on the news, Paco had immediately thought of his favourite customer. The colonel would certainly have something to say about this. Moments later he had spotted him walking to his office. It was closing time, and he was tired after a long day, but an opportunity to hear the man's opinions on the traumatic events could not be missed. The assassination confirmed everything that Terreros had been warning about over the past months: a country on the brink, the threat of anarchy and chaos. But the look that Terreros gave him as he stood at the green door made it very clear that his presence was not required.

Paco placed a glass of whisky and ice on the table. Terreros uttered a polite yet curt '*Gracias*' and kept his eyes on clearly very important papers on his desk that required his immediate attention.

'*Hasta luego, Señor Coronel.*' Paco bowed his head a little as he bade him goodbye, then he turned and left, closing the door gently behind him.

It was an honour to serve such men. Men of the kind that Spain needed right now. Paco had heard, just as he was stepping out of the bar, that the Catalan minister had died in hospital. The doctors had tried everything. The poor wife – pregnant as well with their first child. He hoped – prayed – that whoever had done this would be caught and brought to justice. They should bring back the death penalty for such things. The garrotte had served well in the past; it was time they reintroduced it.

But a greater worry beat at his breast: he had heard some say that Segundo Pont was the only politician in Catalonia who could hold back the more radical members of the new Barcelona government. With him gone, the push for independence would only accelerate. This would be the beginning of far worse to come.

Unless . . .

As he walked across the square back towards his bar, he felt a curious mixture of emotion: fear combined with hope, and a sense that in the end everything would be all right. Spain had been close to disaster in the past, but had always managed to come back from the brink. At such times Destiny provided a man who could restore order.

Was everything about to change? Was the world about to be turned upside down? Perhaps. There were forces around him intent on such an outcome. But equally he knew that there were good men, strong men, who would save the country from the disaster that now loomed on the horizon.

And he felt certain that one of those men was the officer from the Legión that he had the honour of serving.

Colonel Terreros would see that the forces of destruction did not prevail. Colonel Terreros would make sure that nothing would change.

One day people would write books about that man. And he would be able to say that he had known him well, considered him a valued friend.

Back in his office, Terreros stared at his computer screen.

It was time.

EIGHTEEN

The window frames shook whenever a lorry passed in the street, despite the flat being on the top floor of the block. During the evening rush hour the noise was so bad it was impossible to sleep, no matter how tired he felt, or how drugged he might be.

The remains of a half-smoked joint grinned at him from the ashtray on the floor at the foot of the mattress, but he ignored it and got up, stepping through to the living room.

'*¿Hola?*'

There was no reply. The flat was dark and empty: his father must have headed out.

As he pissed in the toilet, he looked at himself in the mirror. A couple of spots were forming at the side of his chin – too fresh to squeeze yet: he would wait a day or two before having a go at them. The glass showed the stains where pus had splattered from previous eruptions. He did his best to clean it off – Daniel hated it – but it was not always easy to remove once it had dried a bit. He should get a knife or something to scrape off the bits where it had hardened. It was difficult enough, the two of them living together without his mother. He did his best, but his father was not always easy to please.

After the shooting session in the mountains things had changed for a while. He got the sense – for the first time that he could remember – that Daniel was pleased with him. Dídac was a good shot, 'had a natural instinct', he said. And he felt something that he had failed to recognise at first: a sense that he had done something that his father admired. They had even chatted for a while in the car on the way back to the city: usually it was either silence or political talk, stuff about the collective. But as they passed through a village they had spotted a group of pretty young girls and Daniel had made a joke and started talking about his first girlfriend – someone he had been at school with back in Castelldefels. He had been so nervous and unsure that the girl herself had grabbed his hand while they were kissing and placed it on her breast. 'You're supposed to touch me there.' He made up for it once he got the hang of things.

And Dídac had glowed: first the gun, and now this – his father opening up, telling him the kinds of things that he never talked about, about his life, his past, what he was feeling, not just his plans and ideas.

'You should get yourself a girlfriend,' he said as they approached the city. 'Not gay, are you?'

'No.'

'So what's stopping you?'

And Dídac did not know what to say. The conversation

ended. By the time they got back to the flat the feeling, the glow, had gone.

That had been almost two weeks ago. Since then things had gone back to normal – the work at the food bank, collecting scraps from restaurants, preparing, setting up, clearing up. Today was his day off, and he was resting as best he could. When he was on duty, it took up most of his time and he was happy to do the work, especially for the children. Playing with them after dinner was one of the highlights – they were happy, properly fed for once, alive to the moment, not burdened with the worries of their parents. And they were receiving aid from them, from the right kind of people. In time they would recognise that and follow them, become like them as well. Little by little, drop by drop. And finally the world could be turned into a better place. You just needed to catch people's attention and make them listen. The collective was not just about nutrition for the body, it was food for the mind as well. You attracted them with something to eat, and you fed them ideas at the same time, ideas that would free them from the invisible chains that tied them down and made them poor in the first place. Through their stomachs you could reach their souls: that was why they were doing this.

He had barely seen much of Daniel these past days, they had both been so busy. The radical new direction he had proposed appeared to have been parked for a while, but he had given him the task of printing up some more flyers and leaflets to keep around the collective. Dídac had designed them on the computer, and they used their simple little inkjet printer to do batches of around fifty at a time. But the damn things ran out of ink so quickly – another capitalist trick – and they had drained them dry. Now he would have to pop out to buy some more – there was a guy around the corner who stayed open late and sold bootleg ones for a third of the price if you took back your empties.

He drank a large glass of water, dressed, checked that he had enough money on him and headed out. If he had anything left over from the cartridges he would buy something to eat at on his way back.

But he did not even get to the end of his street.

It was as he was passing the Chinese knick-knack shop that he first overheard something.

'Just the beginning. It's going to get much worse.'

'I feel sorry for his widow.'

'If we're not careful there'll be many more widows in this country soon.'

'I can't believe it.'

'In the middle of the road as well. Shot to the head.'

Outside the lottery shop he stopped and pulled out his phone. After a few seconds, he had managed to open a news app. The assassination of Segundo Pont was the only story.

'Oh my God.'

'That's right, kid.' An elderly man walking past caught the expression on his face. 'I don't want you lot to have to go through what we went through. It needs to be stopped. Someone has to stop it. But I don't know if it's already too late.'

And he shuffled on, mumbling to himself, to no one, to everyone.

Dídac's mind accelerated rapidly, his breath caught in his throat. He knew exactly what he had to do.

He turned and headed back towards the flat. Not running, just walking quickly and with determination. He tried to remember the things that Daniel had taught him. Don't draw attention to yourself: everyone remembers the unusual. If you want to be invisible, be normal.

After a couple of minutes he was skipping up the stairs two steps at a time back to the top floor. The key shook in his hand as he tried to make it fit the lock.

Inside the flat, he shut the door behind him and took a deep breath. If he was going to do this quickly and efficiently he needed to calm himself.

First, the bags they would need to carry their stuff in. He pulled them down from the top of a wardrobe: two large holdalls and a couple of rucksacks. Everything they needed would have to fit in there. The rest of it would be rejected.

And Daniel's words rang in his mind: 'No sentimentality, no emotion – practicality is the watchword. You take only what you need to carry out the job. Anything else is superfluous and could compromise the mission.'

Soon, perhaps within hours, he felt sure they would be leaving this place. And Daniel would be pleased that he had already made a start on packing.

Valencia was over for them. The assassination had changed everything. Daniel would want to go to Barcelona as soon as possible. He felt the certainty of it flow through him like mercury, quickening his thoughts, clarifying everything. He would be sorry to leave the food bank behind, but this was the moment that Daniel had been talking about, the moment when everything would change, the moment for action, not words.

And at the fringes of his mind a new emotion, one that he had never felt before, began to develop within him: soon he would become someone, someone of consequence – someone at the centre of the new beginning.

Quickly stuffing socks into the bottom of a rucksack, he felt thrilled, vibrant and alive.

NINETEEN

Torres went home shortly afterwards, but Cámara stayed and by using the information available on the police intranet and what was coming through on the media, spent much of the night piecing together the events in Barcelona.

Segundo Pont was having an early dinner at Casa Leopoldo. The place was well-known – politicians of all kinds frequented it and it had been one of the favourite restaurants of author Manuel Vázquez Montalbán. Tucked down a side street on the western side of the Ramblas, it existed in a curious grey area of the city between the touristy old quarter of the Barri Gòtic and the scruffier Raval district, where immigrants and drug dealers had only recently begun to give way to an influx of moneyed bohemians and rising gentrification.

Segundo Pont was accompanied by a group of younger members of his party – half a dozen interns and assistants mostly straight out of university who were starting out on their political careers. It was a chance to get to know this leading light, now a member of government, at this exciting time in Catalonia's history. According to their witness statements, Segundo Pont painted a picture of the future for them: soon there would be new challenges to be met, new posts to be filled, and he was looking for new people he could rely on.

They all ordered fish – what Casa Leopoldo was best known for – and before the main course, as they were waiting for drinks to be brought, Segundo Pont nipped outside. None of the youngsters smoked, and so he went on his own. ('Good for you. It's the only vice I allow myself.')

Several moments after he stepped out through the door, they heard the shots. Some thought there were two; others heard three. First outside from the group were Teresa Balaguer and Toni Sants, who found Segundo Pont's bleeding, dying body face down, his legs sprawled over the pavement and his head in the gutter.

Paramedics arrived in less than ten minutes and took the politician to the Hospital Clínic. He had received one shot in the chest and another in the top of the head. Initially, they managed to keep him alive – the bullet in the chest had destroyed much of his right lung but missed his heart and for a while, once they brought the haemorrhaging under control, there was hope that he might make it. But the damage to the brain was more severe than initially suspected; it was as they were preparing to operate that the doctors lost him.

His wife was in there, watching everything.

The *Mossos d'Esquadra* police force was alerted at the same time as the paramedics and the first unit arrived seconds before the ambulance. After talking to the staff and diners at the Casa Leopoldo and knocking on a few doors along the street to interview the neighbours, they concluded that Segundo Pont had been shot near the door of the restaurant by an unknown assailant who had then managed to escape. No one, at this early stage, seemed to have witnessed the actual attack, nor seen anyone trying to get away. A lorry parked on the other side of the street would have blocked the view from the square opposite, while many of the foreign immigrants in the area who might have seen something were reluctant to talk to the police. In addition, it was night-time, and the road was darker than normal on that particular stretch after two of the street lamps had failed. Barcelona, like the rest of Spain, was suffering from the economic crisis, and simple municipal maintenance tasks were taking longer.

The *Mossos* had only one lead – a woman they interviewed in the early hours said she had seen a man on a motorbike driving down the Carrer de l'Aurora around the time of the shooting. She only noticed him because he seemed to be drunk, weaving down the narrow road and knocking the wing mirror off a parked car with his arm as he sped along, holding on to the handlebars with only one hand as he seemed to be stuffing something inside his jacket with the other. She could not remember anything about his motorbike or his appearance except that he was wearing a full-face helmet, possibly with the visor down.

Within an hour the *Mossos* had found the parked car and a few metres further on the remains of the damaged wing mirror. Early analysis by the crime-scene unit suggested that the moped rider might have been wearing a black leather jacket. He would probably have suffered significant damage to his arm smashing off the wing mirror, possibly fracturing the lower section of the humerus.

Beyond that, however, the *Mossos* had nothing, although a very large team was quickly assembled at their headquarters: this was one of the most important cases they had dealt with since they had taken over policing duties across the whole of Catalonia. They were determined to show the world that they were not going to screw it up.

As they were a nominally Spanish law-and-order force, a certain amount of information about the *Mossos* investigations was available on the intranet shared among all the policing bodies in the country. From Madrid an order went out that the *Guardia Civil, Policía Nacional* and other regional forces were to cooperate at all levels with the case. The fact that such a directive was deemed necessary only underlined the lack of coordination and trust between the various groups. The *Guardia Civil* in particular would have liked nothing better than to be able to rub the *Mossos'* noses in a policing failure.

But it became clear that the order was issued more to cover up the fact that the interior ministry in Madrid was trying to turn the Segundo Pont case into a nationwide investigation, coordinated from the top and – more importantly – from the centre, from Madrid itself. The move was immediately halted; Segundo Pont's number two at the Catalan interior ministry was more hard-line and less willing to do deals to soothe political sensibilities. Enric Puig Casals's first act was to issue a statement that night sending clear instructions to the *Mossos*: this was a purely Catalan case that would be solved by Catalan institutions; there was to be no tolerance of any attempted interference from Madrid.

And so within hours of the attack, and with Segundo Pont's body still warm, the bullets that had been fired at his body were turned into more shots in the intensifying political battle between Catalonia and the rest of the country. And soon the hunt for his killer was practically overwhelmed by the wave of emotion that erupted as people reacted to the news.

The assassination in the streets of Barcelona of an admired and prominent politician was bad enough. But two factors served to make it worse. The first was the fact that Segundo Pont was seen as a moderate in a regional government of radical politicians. He had been regarded as a bridge builder, someone who commanded great support within Catalonia itself but who could also negotiate with the national government in Madrid. He was personable, respected and unsullied by any suspicion of corruption beyond the normal, expected level. If anyone could keep the two sides communicating, could prevent the head-on collision that many had been predicting for months, it was Segundo Pont. Now that he had gone, however, no one else was available to play that role. Without him, Barcelona and Madrid would be set on a path of collision.

The second factor was historical, tapping into a collective memory that filled most with dread but a handful of extremists with hot-headed hope: the Spanish Civil War had begun in 1936 after a political murder, that of José Calvo Sotelo. The possibility that everyone denied but secretly feared was that Catalonia's independence moves, and the political violence that now appeared to be breaking out, might be the prelude to something more serious.

TWENTY

It was almost dawn. Alicia would be at home, sleeping. He walked down his street, but rather than stepping to the door of his block of flats and going inside, he carried on. The decision, he knew, had been taken some time before, so why had he even bothered to come this way? He wanted nothing more than to be with her. But despite their living together, despite their sharing of a physical space, they had not truly been a couple now for weeks or even months. And the distance was getting wider.

His feet carried him down narrow, uncomfortable alleyways. The smell of urine got stronger, the expressions in people's eyes more suspicious.

'You looking for something?'

The dealers sent out their feelers, the pimps stared him down.

And he carried on walking: the feel of the place was wrong. Perhaps it was time to move. Again. This part of the city was dark and grubby and had an edge, and he had liked that at the beginning. Not least because it set him apart from other senior police officers, with their delusions of safety in the suburbs and satellite towns. The Barrio Chino was dangerous, and so was being a policeman. It was one of the main attractions of the job, if they could admit it to themselves. Imagining that you could leave that behind, that there was an oasis to escape to, was a fantasy most bought into because they could not cope with the truth.

So vanity more than anything else – a sense that he saw things that other policemen did not – had brought him here. Now he wondered if he would ever find somewhere he could belong. Wondered what belonging meant in the first place.

Everything felt shaken, as though about to crack and collapse around him. And the two pillars that he had relied on in the past to hold him together were no longer there. Hilario had died not only in the physical sense: Cámara could no longer find him within himself. And now Alicia was effectively gone as well.

Was it his fault? Should he go back to the flat now, try to change things, to make another effort to reach out and hold her, to press her damaged body to him until something within her relented, gave way and they could become as one again?

He had tried that before. More than once. It was not so much that Alicia had built walls to hide herself from him. It was more that she simply was not there, had disappeared so far into herself that she was no longer a presence. There were no barriers for him to break down. How do you tend a flower that, above the surface at least, has died? He could not even be certain any more that there were any roots. In his love life, as in his work, his intuition had gone silent.

Everything changed with the assassination. Just as Carlos had predicted – as if he had already known. Fear of social conflict had stalked the country these last months. But a collective memory of the horrors of the past acted as a kind of security. Everyone understood the consequences of political violence. There had been false alarms recently – months before, a local politician in León had been shot dead in the street. And there had been a collective intake of breath, until the murderers – a mother and her daughter – were caught and confessed that personal grievance, not ideology, had made them pull the trigger. The country as a whole had sighed with relief.

Yet now, with Segundo Pont, it felt as though a line had been crossed. Throughout the night, as he learned the details of what had happened in Barcelona, he thought back to the man he met at the medal ceremony. He was impressed and disturbed by him in equal measure: impressed by Segundo Pont's warm, easy way with people; disturbed by what he had tried to propose, what he had known.

'You haven't gone unnoticed, Cámara.'

And neither had he. Had his killer – or killers – already decided that he was to die when Cámara met him? Was he already a marked man? His sin was to be too nice, too moderate, too balanced, perhaps. A time of black and white had descended upon them. No more shades. Anyone who occupied the subtle centre would be got rid of. Were others now in the line of fire?

He found himself in a small park area, with trees and a children's playground. It was deserted now. He sat down on a bench at the far end, placing his arm on the rest and crossing his legs. And he stared out across the street, unseeing.

Political violence. Only months before he had destroyed a gang of right-wing thugs working for the ruling party in the city, the same men who had scarred Alicia, tortured her and come so close to killing both of them. And he had thought at the time that he had done something, made a difference. The Legionaries of Order and Progress, as they called themselves, had murdered and terrorised in order to maintain the status quo, agents of the forces that wanted power to remain with the conservative, big business elite who had had a stranglehold on the city and the region for decades. It was he – Cámara – who had helped to bring them down. And at some level he thought that he had made a better world, removing an ill that had done so much harm.

But now this: the assassination of Segundo Pont and the real sense that the country as a whole – not just his little sphere here in Valencia – might explode. He could easily imagine the talk in some circles: the *Guardia Civil*, the military, the far Right. Holding the country together, defending the unity of Spain, was a particular obsession of theirs. They would be whispering about bringing back order, imposing martial law. Just as they had done countless times before in the past. Did history in other countries, he wondered, repeat itself with such clear regularity?

If ever there had been a time for far-sighted people to be in charge, it was now. Instead the Madrid government was populated with hesitators, people who liked to believe that most problems, in the end, simply blow over. That approach had already brought them this far.

And so there he was, in the cold, dark grey before sunrise,

alone, watching the occasional car drift by, afraid, like the rest of the country, for what might be about to come. And with a case that he was now beginning to feel that he could not solve. Not without some help. Not without a break.

He could sit, and watch, and be swept up in whatever came next. Or he could take a step, be a part of the change, play his part, no matter how small. Stop things, at least, from becoming far worse. Everything would fall out of control, Carlos had said. And then what would happen? He despised Carlos and all that he stood for, but the *CNI* man had offered some kind of a solution. Could Cámara really walk away?

That's right, isn't it? This is the right thing to do? It's about prevention.

But Hilario was still silent.

Alicia. He would do it for Alicia. He had put her through enough already. It was time he did something to protect her. Her, and everyone else.

From inside his pocket, he pulled out Carlos's crumpled card, straightened it and placed it on his knee.

Then he picked up his phone.

TWENTY-ONE

'You look rough.'

'I was just managing to drop off when Berto called me.'

'And you came to say goodbye. I appreciate that.'

The bus terminal was an ugly, charmless place with a perpetual stench of diesel fumes and oil from the slicks on the tarmac. Travellers were scattered around the place, with piles of suitcases or plastic tartan bags waiting for their ride. Most were Moroccans or Sub-Saharan Africans: buses were cheaper than trains and you could carry almost as much luggage as you wanted. It was hot in there, despite being only half-past eight in the morning. If there ever had been any air conditioning in the building it appeared not to be working.

'I had to pop by and see if I could catch you,' Cámara said.

Daniel put an arm around Cámara's shoulders and the two men embraced.

'So that's it? No more Valencia?'

'For the time being,' said Daniel. 'Barcelona's the main battlefield right now, and I don't want to miss it. And besides, I am Catalan, so in a sense I'm going home.'

Cámara nodded.

'You got somewhere to stay up there?'

'We'll be fine.'

'Of course.'

Dídac was standing close by, keeping an eye on their bags, waiting for his father to finish.

'We were going to try one of the car-sharing schemes,' he said when it was his turn to talk. 'It's much the cheapest way of getting around the country these days.'

'Didn't work out?' asked Cámara.

'No one was leaving immediately. Or at least no one with space for all our stuff as well.'

'Looks like you're travelling fairly light to me,' said Cámara.

'Daniel told me to dump half of what I'd packed,' Dídac said. He forced a smile. 'I thought I'd done quite a good job, but . . .'

Cámara squeezed his arm.

'You'll be fine,' he said. 'It's going to be an adventure.'

'I know. I'll just miss everyone here.'

Cámara embraced him.

'We'll see each other again soon. And besides, you'll meet a whole lot of interesting people in Barcelona. It's a city full of surprises.'

'Yeah, I'm excited about it.'

Berto was with them, along with a handful of others from the collective who had come to see them off. After a few minutes an announcement came that the Barcelona bus was about to leave. They all went down to the bay, watched as the bags were hauled into the luggage space, and made their final farewells.

Dídac got on first, and found a seat near the front. Daniel hovered on the steps.

'Thanks for coming,' he said to the small group of friends. 'Nice gesture. For a moment I thought we might manage to slip away unnoticed.'

Berto laughed. Daniel took another step inside the bus.

'Let us know how you get on,' Cámara called out. The bus driver was anxious to get started.

Daniel turned and grinned at him as the doors began to close.

'You trying to keep tabs on me, Mister Policeman?'

TWENTY-TWO

The instructions had been to meet outside the cathedral in the Plaza de la Virgen. Carlos would be dressed as a tourist, with a camera hung around his neck, shorts, sandals and a yellow baseball cap on his head. Cámara was to walk past and Carlos would ask him directions on a map.

On the phone, Cámara thought he was joking. Or perhaps it was the best that the *CNI* man could come up with at that time in the morning – although Cámara was certain that he was already awake when he called. Nonetheless, it seemed like something out of an old spy film, one of the black-and-white ones they showed in the mornings to fill up the schedules.

He had slept on the sofa, telling himself that he did not want to wake Alicia by crawling into bed with her. But the truth was that he could hardly bear to be with himself after making the call. His mind wormed and writhed, wondering whether this was the right thing to do. And he had more or less decided – if 'decided' was the word, clammy as he was with the heat and exhausted with so much churning thought when the sun finally came up – to call the whole thing off, when Berto rang and told him about Daniel leaving for Barcelona.

He had just made it, jumping on his motorbike and speeding to the bus station. And now that they had gone – and the others had left miserably, charged with maintaining the food bank without the help of the man who had set it up – there was less than half an hour before his meeting with Carlos. He was up and awake and a short distance away. The inertia of the moment pushed him along.

He stared at his phone, wondering whether to call home. He had not seen Alicia; he should ring, see if she was all right, just say hello. There had been days recently when communications between them did not even get that far. Talking on the phone might help – a change of format, of medium that could break the pattern they had fallen into. And again he thought that perhaps they could talk about this, about what he was going – or not going – to do. She would know; he trusted her.

But he could not trust his mobile or his landline – the chances that they were both being tapped were too high. Instead, he found a telephone box and dialled Alicia's mobile number. She usually kept it in the living room overnight, plugged into the wall to charge the battery; he thought he had seen it there as he was stepping out the door.

The steady, high-pitched beep of a phone ringing came down the line. Four, five, six times. Then, after a moment, a different tone and an automated message: the other person was not answering. Strange, he thought, that it did not go through to voicemail. Was she up? Perhaps she was in the shower. Or still asleep. She was doing a lot of that lately.

He stepped out of the phone box and back into the blinding sunlight. In the distance he could make out the Miguelete bell tower of the cathedral. In another five or ten minutes Carlos would be there, waiting for him.

He put on his helmet, fired up the bike, and fed into the traffic.

In the end it was simple, felt almost natural: Carlos had clearly done it several times before, quickly acting out the role of someone needing help finding his way around the city, Cámara obliging him and walking away from the cathedral with him in order to show him which way to go. After passing down a side street, they found a discreet café with tables at the back where no one would be able to see them.

Carlos ordered water; Cámara a strong black coffee.

'You understand,' Carlos said once they felt they were able to talk, 'there are no contracts, no formal agreements. You are not – repeat not – an employee of the *El Centro*. If you get into trouble, if there are any difficulties, you're entirely on your own. And you have three priorities . . .' He flicked out a finger with each one. 'Look after yourself, look after yourself, and finally, look after yourself.'

Cámara said nothing. If he had been thinking about looking after himself he would never have agreed to this meeting in the first place. But he was here, it was happening. And he was doing it for Fermín. For Fermín and for Alicia.

He drank the coffee while it was still hot: it burnt his throat. He had no idea how long this was going to take.

'Another thing,' Carlos said. 'This relationship may last for some time, or it may end – quite suddenly and with little or no warning. Just like the police, the centre is subject to the whims and vicissitudes of our elected leaders. One group can leave and another comes in. At which point everything changes. So have no expectations.'

'I don't,' said Cámara sharply.

'Good. Right now,' Carlos continued, 'you're a mess of tension and contradiction. That's fine, it's normal. I've seen it many times before. All the questions about whether or not you want to do this, about whether it's the right thing. Trust me, you've made the right decision. Soon enough you'll see that. And believe it or not, people like you are the best asset the centre has – you're not doing this for ideological reasons, nor for money. You're doing it because it's right, because there are people out there – radicals, extremists, nutcases many of them – who are intent on pushing things to the limit. We belong to the balanced middle, you and I. I know you don't think of yourself as a run-of-the-mill kind of man, but we're more similar than you realise. That's why you're here.'

'You said you could help with the Fermín case.'

'I can and I will,' said Carlos. 'Right here, tucked inside the map we've just been looking at, is an envelope with all the papers you're going to need to break this case.'

The map was on the seat next to him; he lifted a corner of it to reveal a Manila envelope.

'What's in it?' Cámara asked.

'You'll find out when I give it to you. But first . . .' He raised a hand, as though to stop Cámara from reaching out for the papers, but Cámara had not moved a muscle. 'First I need something from you. Information.'

To begin with, he wanted the names of all the people Cámara had associated with at the collective.

'Not the people who eat there, not the immigrants. Just those helping out. It's not the food bank per se. I'm all in favour of that, just as you are. Charity is what makes us human, lifts us above the level of apes. But you know as well as I do that there are other activities planned or already being carried out – more radical activities, perhaps even violent or disruptive ones, not just food handouts.'

'We know each other by our first names.'

'Of course you do. And they are . . . ?'

First names only, he told himself. It was true, if he did know the surnames of some of them. But Carlos did not know that. If he did, why was he asking for names to begin with? Or was it a test?

He listed half a dozen: Berto, Daniel, some of the others. For some reason he did not name Dídac – he was just a kid. Better not to get him involved in any of this.

Carlos listened, not writing any of it down. Cámara wondered for a moment whether he was wearing a wire, recording the conversation, until he realised that he was using a memory trick to remember everything that Cámara was passing on. His lips seemed to move slightly as he ran it all though his mind, perhaps inventing mnemonics on the spot. Was that something else they taught spies?

'And you don't know the surnames of any of them,' Carlos said when Cámara finished.

'No.'

'But you could find them out. You're a policeman.'

Something in him shivered: it was the second time that morning he had been reminded of the fact, as though the whole world could read his inner thoughts, his doubts.

'Possibly.'

'Do it,' said Carlos. 'If you wouldn't mind.'

There was a pause as the implication of what he had said sank in.

'This is not the only meeting we'll be having,' Carlos explained. He glanced down at the map and the hidden envelope.

'Don't worry, there's plenty there. But you'll be wanting more, needing more, believe me. Once you've seen the quality of what I can offer you. Not just for the Fermín case, but for others in the future. And there'll be more. We're living in a curious time – everything that's been hidden is coming out into the open. The corruption, the dirty deals, the scandals that have been secret for so long. What you hear about now is just the tip of the iceberg, and you, as one of the most effective policemen in the city – maybe in the country as a whole – will be leading some of the investigations. Of that I have no doubt. Especially as you're now head of the Special Crimes Unit. There may only be two of you right now, but my bet is you'll be growing fairly soon. You'll have so much on you won't know where to start.'

He drank his water: beads of sweat were beginning to form on his brow.

'But all that is for the future. Not today. Right now we're interested in finding Fermín's killer. But before I hand you this –' he nodded in the direction of the map – 'I need one more piece of information from you.'

Cámara listened.

'The Segundo Pont assassination,' Carlos said. 'You're aware as much as I am that it has changed things, changed them very much for the worse. It's the reason why you're here, am I right? But what I need to know is what the talk has been among your friends about what has happened. Any comments, any reaction of any kind?'

Cámara paused. He had just seen Daniel and Dídac off on the bus to Barcelona, heading north as a direct result of what had happened. The battlefield was going to be up there, Daniel had said. Cámara had thought better than to ask what exactly he intended to do when he arrived. Not least because he knew this meeting was coming shortly afterwards. And what he did not know he could not betray. There was an intense decisiveness about Daniel – there always had been although he seemed even more driven recently. But his setting up of the food bank showed that caring for others was his main concern. His call for carrying out *escraches* outside bankers' homes had come as a surprise, but was harmless in the end – nothing had come of it as far as he knew. Nonetheless, he and Dídac had gone, were at that very moment riding up to Catalonia. It was a reaction to the Segundo Pont murder for certain. But would they be getting involved in anything serious? He could not see it. They might join a few demonstrations, hand out some leaflets – nothing that Carlos needed to know about.

'No,' Cámara said. 'Everyone's in a state of shock, as we all are, I think.'

'No joy, no anger, no emotion of any kind?' Carlos asked.

'Fear,' Cámara said. 'I think it's more fear. And concern. Everything feels very uncertain.'

'You're right there,' Carlos said, almost under his breath.

He picked up the map and moved it closer to Cámara.

'We'll leave it for today,' he said. 'Future contacts will be along these lines. Either I call you or you call me and we arrange to meet. Do not discuss anything sensitive over the phone.'

Cámara nodded.

Carlos lifted the map, letting the envelope fall discreetly out and on to the seat near Cámara's hand.

'There,' he said. 'I'll leave now. Don't get up for another five minutes or so.'

He stood up.

'In the meantime, you can start reading that. I think you'll find it interesting.'

TWENTY-THREE

The entire city was Spanish – technically. But Ceuta was divided. East of the Foso de San Felipe moat, which effectively divided the isthmus from the mainland, was the European quarter: wealthier, better maintained, with the main shops and offices and where trees lined the streets. Most people dressed in Western-style clothes, and it felt like the Spanish mainland, almost like a town on the Costa del Sol, except for the lack of tourists. West of the Foso was a different story. The buildings were cheaper – mostly squat blocks of flats built as quickly as possible some thirty or forty years before. Here, most people dressed in 'Moroccan' clothes – the majority of women wore scarves over their hair; the older men wored jellabas and *taqiyya* skullcaps. Whereas the centre of Ceuta was Christian and relatively affluent, these residential neighbourhoods, closer to the border with Morocco, were Muslim and poor. The grandiose, patriotic names they had been given – the Barrio

Juan Carlos I or El Príncipe – did nothing to take away from the fact that they were a forgotten corner of the country, one that few Spaniards themselves were aware of, or wanted to be reminded of.

Outside, in the streets, with friends and neighbours, she was Selma. She was fifty-two and lived on her own in a flat on the top floor on the Calle Aymat González. Five years earlier her husband had died in an accident at the port; he was a dock worker and during the unloading of a tanker one afternoon, had slipped and fallen between the ship and the quay. His death, they told her, was instantaneous. It was routine in such circumstances to hold an autopsy – all part of the programme to make dock work safer. But it was then that traces of alcohol were discovered in her husband's blood. A small amount – Hicham must have drunk a glass of wine over lunch, perhaps, nothing more. But it was enough for the port authorities to clear themselves of all responsibility, and deny Selma the pension that she should have been entitled to.

She had no children to support her, and most of her family lived on the other side, in Morocco. She had no work or chance of working, part of the problem of living in the poorer area of the city; the latest figures talked of 50 per cent unemployment. She reckoned it was much higher.

After her forty days of mourning had ended, the comments and suggestions began – she should look for another husband, someone who could look after her. Perhaps a widower, someone her own age even. They would start asking around. There was a matchmaker nearby who could help.

But she had refused. Politely, but firmly. She did not want another husband. At least not for the time being. She had loved Hicham very deeply, she said. It would take a while for her to recover from his sudden death. And it would not be fair to any new husband for her to still be mourning in her heart.

She had sold a lot of her furniture and moved out of the flat, finding somewhere smaller a bit closer to the centre. Some said she was mad; others kept silent, wondering at the unusual behaviour of a newly widowed woman no longer in full bloom. If only she had children, something to anchor her, but the doctors had been adamant – there was no chance of her conceiving – and she had borne the tragedy with resilience. This latest blow had destabilised her, however. She started losing her friends; members of her family no longer called her, or they pretended not to notice her if they saw her in the street.

Selma was changing, but more than any of them could guess. In public she was still the same, still dressed in shades of brown and grey, still with a veil over her hair and no make-up. She knew that she was no beauty, and her figure had never been the best. But in private she was creating someone else – a new skin for her to step inside at will, with no one to judge her.

The name Sandrita had popped into her head the moment that her new self revealed itself to her. It was perfect: European sounding, younger, more dangerous. Sexy. Using the timer on her camera she managed to capture a couple of pictures of herself wearing some black-and-orange lingerie she found in a shop off the Calle Real. The colour brought out the tone of her skin, she thought. And within a couple of hours she had posted them on the website Milanuncios.com. *More than just a massage*, she wrote in the text box. *Affectionate, compliant and discreet. Exquisite aromatic oils and candles*. Then she put the number of the new mobile phone she had bought, and as an afterthought, she added, *Special services offered*. And it was done.

Strangely, it was that last line that had brought her in the most work. She was not sure exactly what she had meant by it – it was more a way of making her advert stand out from the others, with their pictures of younger, firmer, whiter-skinned women. But the requests had come in soon enough. Now she regarded many of them as her favourite clients: Joaquín, bound to a wheelchair by cerebral palsy – his father would bring him every couple of months or so, and she would give them a discount, working first with the boy and then the father as Joaquín dozed in a post-coital reverie in the living room. She got seventy-five euros for the two of them, and they were usually finished and gone within the hour. A good rate of pay, and she enjoyed it.

There were others like Joaquín, often physically handicapped in some way, or unable to achieve an erection, perhaps after prostate surgery. The massage did wonders, relaxing them, an overload of sensation for their hungry skin. And she was genuinely kind and caring. That, more than anything else, made them return, she felt. Other women might be better-looking, have beach-brown bodies and no inhibitions. But Sandrita offered something that all men wanted but were lacking: a concentrated dose of affection. Whether they had an orgasm or not – and some of them were physically incapable – was secondary. When they walked out of her door they had a sparkle of joy about them. And that could only help to make the world a better place.

That morning she had José coming. Among the 'specials', as she called them, he was one of the most special. The damage he had suffered might have driven many men to take their own lives. But he survived. There was a driven quality about him, an intensity and passion so that at times he could appear stern, unforgiving. But after a couple of moments with her he relaxed and changed. Now she could see the shift in him the moment he crossed her threshold.

She never asked about her clients' lives, unless they wanted to talk about something. She guessed quite early on that José was military, or ex-military. Something about his bearing, and the wound, looked like something only a man who had seen action in battle might suffer from. The damage to his groin area was comprehensive: deep indents in the skin around the upper thighs and pubic bone, perhaps from shrapnel. She did not ask. And where his penis and testicles should have been, there was nothing but tender, mangled flesh only partially covered by the scant hair he had left. Other clients had a manhood that had ceased to function. With José there was nothing there to function in the first place.

He arrived as usual with a sharp rapping knock on the door. She opened and he stepped in. Only after the door was closed behind her did he lean over and kiss her on both cheeks.

'Wonderful to see you again, José.'

'And you, Sandrita.'

'Everything's ready. I'll get you a drink.'

José liked a glass of sweet red vermouth with ice and a slice of lemon. As he sat down on the sofa, she went into the kitchen, poured him one, checked that everything was in place, and then returned to serve him.

'Thank you,' he said. And he looked at her, smiling. He liked the way that she painted her face, with silver eyeshadow and thick black eyeliner curling up a little at each side: it gave her an exoticism, a promise of voluptuous joy.

She leaned down and stroked his cheek.

'You look like something's troubling you,' she said. 'What's the matter? Tell Sandrita your problem.'

'It's just . . .' he began. 'I may not be able to see you again for some time.'

She frowned. Her sadness was genuine. Almost.

'In fact, there's a chance this may be the last time I'll ever see you.'

'Oh, José,' she said, and she sat down beside him, pressing his face to her breasts. 'How terrible. But why?'

'It's to do with work,' he said, mumbling into her bra. 'I can't say anything more.'

'Of course.'

She pulled his head away and held it in both hands to look at him.

'Events will very soon be taking me away,' he said. 'So I'm afraid that this is almost certainly goodbye.'

She kissed him on the forehead and stood up in front of him.

'Then we shall make it a very special occasion,' she said. 'Wait here and I'll get ready.'

The colonel sat on the sofa drinking his vermouth, staring out of the window over the rooftops of the city. His mind was at rest for one delicious moment, anticipation drowning out for just a few short minutes the many racing thoughts and plans and directions that had been occupying his mind these past days. He closed his eyes, licked the sweet liquid from his lips.

He heard soft footsteps coming out from the bedroom and he opened his eyes again to see Sandrita before him.

She wore a red-and-black corset with stockings and black high heels. Her hair was tied back in a tight ponytail and her expression had changed – no longer soft, but unforgiving.

She leaned down, grabbed his hand and placed it forcibly on to the prosthetic erection strapped to her groin.

'Do you feel that?' she asked. 'Do you remember what it feels like to be a man?'

'Yes,' the colonel nodded, his face blushing.

'Come with me,' said Sandrita. 'I'm going to show you what manhood really means.'

TWENTY-FOUR

Final Report
INVESTIGATION TERMINATED
Sensitivity level: **Maximum**
All inquiries to the Office of the Minister to the President of the Government
NO FURTHER ACTION TO BE TAKEN
This case is now CLOSED

Abogados Grau S.A. – *Hacienda* investigation

Hacienda's tax investigations into Abogados Grau S.A. commenced after attention was drawn by a source in the European Environment Agency (EEA) to the considerable quantities of EU grant monies that were being administered by the law firm. An informal and anonymous tip-off came and after initial inquiries it was decided to launch a full-scale investigation. The suspicion was that Abogados Grau was carrying out tax fraud.

Abogados Grau S.A. had offices on C/ Poeta Querol in Valencia. It was owned and controlled in its entirety by Doña Francisca Grau, graduate from Valencia University and a Doctor in Law since 2003.

The investigation into the finances of the law company confirmed that it regularly received monies in the form of grants from EU funds, principally from the EEA. It acted as an administration company for small farmers in the Valencia area, claiming EU agricultural and environmental grants on their behalf. As a representative agency, ostensibly working for the benefit of farmers to obtain money that they were entitled to under EU law, this was entirely legal.

Over time, Abogados Grau developed a modus operandi whereby they would contact farmers in the Valencia area offering them access to EU funds. In most cases the farmers were elderly (73.1 per cent were officially retired) and were unaware of the grants. A large majority (83.4 per cent) of the land that they owned was no longer profitable as farmland and had been abandoned.

A small percentage (29.3 per cent) of the funds accessed by Abogados Grau were from other EU funds, but the remaining amount (70.7 per cent) came from the Environmental Fund. In 2011 the EU Commission took steps to reduce monoculture agricultural practices around the Union. Monocultures are viewed as a threat to the ecology as they weaken the DNA of the plant strand in question through lack of variety and create a hospitable environment for the development of new plant diseases. The horticultural lands of Valencia, where up to 50 per cent of land is taken up with orange groves, was one of the prime examples cited in the initial studies. The Huerta Development Fund was set up specifically to encourage farmers to change their crops and to diversify agricultural land utilisation.

Abogados Grau appeared to discover a loophole in the EU legislation whereby land in which the monoculture was abandoned – where the production of oranges (in the case of Valencia) ceased – could qualify for the Huerta Development Fund grants without proof being provided that an alternative crop had replaced it. What was more, the law was retroactive, so that orange groves that had been abandoned up to ten years earlier could still be claimed for.

The law firm quickly built up a long list of clients after a small initial publicity campaign. Word of mouth ensured that in less than a year most orange farmers in the Valencia area had learned of the scheme. In many cases it was as profitable for a farmer to abandon his groves and take the EU grant money as it was to continue farming. This increasingly became the case after large supermarket chains began to drive the price of oranges down. In just over two years, Abogados Grau had more than 500 orange farmers on its list of clients and it shut down all other work in order to dedicate itself entirely to the administration and redistribution of the EU grant money.

In the year that the *Hacienda* investigation began, Abogados Grau S.A. received a total of €5,386,911.23 in EU grants – monies that came directly from both the Huerta Development Fund and the Agricultural

Fund. This amount was confirmed by EU finance administration sources, as well as by a *Hacienda* examination of the Abogados Grau accounts.

Over the course of the same year, however, only €2,067,264.82 was distributed by the law company to its clients, leaving a deficit of €3,319,646.41, or 61.62 per cent of the total monies received from the EU funds. In its literature, Abogados Grau claimed to be taking a 15 per cent commission from the monies received for administration costs. This is the maximum allowed by law. Tax documentation presented by the company to *Hacienda* stated clearly that this was the amount of commission that they were charging, showing an annual return of not more than €328,036.70. Yet it was clear that the firm was taking considerably more than the figure officially provided to the tax authorities.

From an initial suspicion of tax fraud, there were indications that the company was also involved in embezzlement. Before passing the case over to the *Policía Nacional* Economic and Fiscal Crime Unit (*UDEF*), however, it was decided to continue the investigation on a wider scale.

From her bank statements, it was observed that Doña Grau made regular trips to Málaga, flying from Valencia airport on the first flight in the morning – usually on a two-monthly basis. From Málaga, Doña Grau would board the helicopter service to the Autonomous City of Ceuta, across the strait – a journey of around fifteen minutes. This was deemed suspicious, and a watch was placed on her.

On or about the allocated time, she repeated her

journey. *Hacienda* operatives observed her catching the plane to Málaga, boarding the helicopter to Ceuta and then arriving at the city's heliport. She had no luggage apart from a tan leather briefcase.

After leaving the heliport, she was observed to take a taxi the short distance to Plaza de Africa in central Ceuta, where she went to a place known as El Bar Paco. She remained there for no more than an hour, ordering a *café con leche*, and then leaving once again for the heliport, where she caught the return flight back to Málaga. After lunching at the airport, she would catch the mid-afternoon flight back to Valencia, arriving at around 17.00. She carried a tan leather briefcase with her the whole time.

Doña Grau was observed making two such journeys and her habits did not change: the same flights, the same briefcase. But this only raised suspicions even more and it was decided to continue surveillance.

Shortly afterwards, however, Doña Grau died. The expectation was that the law firm would close with her death, but observation of the company's accounts for subsequent months showed that the EU grant money was still coming in and that a percentage of it was still being paid out to the farmers. After further investigation, it was discovered that Abogados Grau had been passed over in its entirely to Doña Grau's husband, Alfonso Segarra. At the time it was assumed that Don Segarra would be closing the firm down in due course. Owing to the fact that his wife had recently died, it was decided – for 'humanitarian' reasons – not to pursue the case, but to keep the operations under observation for the following months.

The investigation was unexpectedly reinitiated, however, after a chance sighting of Don Segarra in Ceuta. The *Hacienda* operative in the city had not been tasked with watching the Bar Paco on the day when Doña Grau might have been expected to make her regular visit, but decided to go in his own free time. He saw Don Segarra enter the bar at about the time that Doña Grau would have done. In his hand was a tan leather briefcase. Segarra ordered a *café solo tocado con whisky*, drank it quickly, and left the bar in less than five minutes. He was observed getting into a taxi and asking to be taken to the heliport. Unlike his deceased wife, however, Segarra was not carrying a briefcase with him when he left.

The *Hacienda* operative decided to continue his observations in the Bar Paco – the last place that the briefcase had been seen. After about an hour, he saw the owner of the bar, Don Francisco (known as Paco) Díaz García, leaving the premises with a tan leather briefcase in his hand – the same one that Segarra had brought with him.

The operative followed the bar owner at a safe distance, and saw him walk to a building in an adjacent street and climb the steps to an office on the second floor. A few minutes later, Don Francisco García returned without the briefcase and proceeded to the bar, where he resumed his work.

The only office on the second floor of the building – on C/ Jáudenes – is that belonging to the Veteran Legionarios' Welfare Association.

Shortly after this, the *Hacienda* investigation was closed down on the orders of the Office of the Minister to the President of the Government on the grounds that the target, Doña Francisca Grau, had passed away. All lines of inquiry were subsequently closed and a Cessation Order was placed into effect.

'Where did you get this from?'

Torres stared at Cámara over closed fingertips, his eyebrows pulled high.

Cámara shrugged: Torres got the message.

'What do you reckon?' Cámara asked.

Torres puffed out his cheeks, his hands falling to his desk.

'What do I reckon? I reckon the whole thing's fucking rotten. Alfonso Segarra's wife was running an embezzlement racket nicking millions of EU grant money and all to get farmers round here to abandon their orange groves.'

'And where was Fermín's body found?'

Torres nodded.

'In an abandoned orange grove. You know Segarra's always going on about using local produce, about how Horta supports farmers in the Valencia area. He's a local boy, helping his own. Or supposedly. And yet there's his wife doing everything she can to stop them farming.'

'Possibly in conjunction with Segarra himself,' said Cámara. 'That bit about supermarkets driving down the price of fruit at the same time. I wonder if that's just coincidence.'

'Working like a team,' Torres snorted. 'Nice. I wonder where the oranges I'm buying actually come from, then? It says Valencia on the packaging.'

'Morocco, at a guess. They'll re-label it once it gets here. But we're missing the point.'

'The point?'

'This investigation was closed down just when it was getting interesting.'

'Where did you get . . . ?' Torres began. 'OK, forget it.'

'My feeling is that there's something in this Veteran Legionarios' outfit.'

'The briefcase,' Torres said. 'You think it's stuffed with cash.'

Cámara nodded.

'Francisca Grau makes regular trips down to Ceuta with a lot of money on her in the briefcase, leaves it there and then comes home.'

'But she had the briefcase with her on the return leg each time,' said Torres.

'She had *a* briefcase with her – one that looked exactly the same. But was it?'

Torres grunted.

'OK,' he said. 'I suppose it's possible.'

'And it explains the trips down there in the first place. Why else would you fly all the way to Ceuta every two months? Is the coffee down there really that good?'

Torres smirked. 'You're starting to sound like me,' he said.

'Well, given that today you're not doing a very good job of being you, someone's got to. Anyway,' Cámara continued, 'the thing is that when Segarra went down there himself he forgot to do the switch. It was his first time. He simply left the cash, didn't pick up the identical but empty briefcase, and then headed home. That was his mistake.'

'You're suggesting then,' said Torres, 'that all this money

that Abogados Grau has been embezzling has been going to some welfare fund for retired soldiers?'

Cámara nodded.

'What, millions? For a bunch of veterans?'

'Yes.'

'All right,' Torres said. He could see that Cámara was insistent. 'I suppose we'd better look into it, then, this organisation.'

'I have,' said Cámara. And he handed Torres a piece of paper with a name and a photograph of a man's face on it.

'It's run by him,' he said. 'Colonel José Terreros, former commander of the Legión.'

TWENTY-FIVE

'I know it's probably not a great time to call.'

'That's OK. Are you all right?'

'Yes, I'm fine. I'm at home.'

'Have you put the creams on and everything?'

'Yes. All done. The daily ritual.'

'Good.'

There was a pause. The call was unusual: Alicia knew that it was rarely a good idea to ring him when he was on duty. It was a move towards him, however, a step, and he wanted to welcome it, but he was aware of Torres back in the office working away on their lead. She had caught him in the middle of their breakthrough, throwing his rhythm out, and for a moment it was difficult to change from detective to caring lover.

'Do you—?' he began. He was going to ask her if she needed anything – a problem that he could solve – secretly hoping that the answer would be no: he did not want to break away from the investigation just then. But she interrupted him.

'No, I'm fine. Just wanted to . . . I'm sorry, you're busy.'

'It's OK. I'm glad you rang.'

Which was true, in a complicated sort of way.

'I've been thinking,' she said. 'We haven't really spent much time together recently. I mean, properly. Talking. Communicating.'

'I know.'

'I thought, perhaps, we could do something. Go out, or . . .'

'Of course. I'd love to.'

'When it's a good time, I mean.'

'Yes. No, look,' he said. 'I'm not sure about tonight.'

'No, of course not.'

'But soon. Very soon.'

'OK.'

'We could go somewhere nice. Maybe for dinner.'

'OK.'

'Maybe down to the Albufera lake,' he said. 'Somewhere, I don't know, quiet. Romantic.'

'Sure.'

'OK, wonderful. Leave it with me. I'll sort it out.'

'But only when you've got time.'

'Yes. I'd love to tonight, but it's just . . .' Usually he told her about his cases – they were something he shared. As a journalist, she was interested in his work and often had different, interesting things to say. And he welcomed her comments – had even come to rely on them in the past. But things had changed: he felt guilty – over what had happened to her before, and now over his contact with Carlos, a man from the *CNI*. A man who dealt in secrets. He felt ashamed and sullied, but excited: for the first time since he had taken on the Fermín murder case he had the sense of moving forward. Standing in the corridor outside his office, looking out over the street through dirty white curtains, he was anxious to get back to work. But this – Alicia suddenly and unexpectedly calling, opening up to him after so long – was as important. Two worlds – his private and professional lives – which in the past had often blended into one, were now separate, but both calling for his attention. Should he let them meet, or keep them apart?'

'It's OK,' Alicia said after a pause. 'I understand. But soon, OK? Let's do this as soon as you can.'

'Yes.'

'And you can tell me everything.'

'I will,' he said.

'And I will too.'

He put the phone back in his pocket, momentarily disturbed.

As he stepped back into the office, he saw that Torres was staring at his computer screen and typing, a look of brooding concentration on his face: he had something. Waiting, Cámara picked up the printouts they had made a few minutes before and leaned against a filing cabinet, reading through the material again.

Colonel José Terreros had been born in Málaga in 1951. He joined the army as an officer cadet and transferred to the Spanish Legión as soon as he passed his exams and became an *alférez* – a second lieutenant – in the I Bandera 'Commander Franco' unit, based in the Spanish North African enclave of Melilla, eventually becoming commander of the IV Bandera 'Cristo de Lepanto', in Ceuta. In 1994, then a major, he was part of the Legión's contingent of over a thousand men sent with NATO troops to Bosnia during the Yugoslav wars. While he was there he was wounded in action, receiving a bullet in the lower abdomen. The Legión evacuated him back to Spain, where he received medical attention, but his wounds were severe and he was hospitalised for four months.

Terreros could have taken early retirement and lived off his pension at that point, but true to the legendary fighting spirit of the Legión, he had chosen to continue his military career, taking charge of the training duties at the Ceuta barracks. He had eventually risen to colonel and was effectively the second in command of his unit when eventually, some ten years before, he stepped down from active service. He retained his rank and stayed in Ceuta, where he set up the Veteran Legionarios' Welfare Association, a kind of club for former servicemen to keep in touch, organising events and dinners for veterans of the elite infantry force. The association also controlled a fund to which veterans could apply for financial assistance if they found themselves in difficulties. Terreros was both secretary and manager of the association: the titular president was the Christ of the Good Death, the representation of the crucified Jesus at Málaga cathedral which *legionarios* paraded every Easter. The image of the tortured, dying yet brave Messiah, his loincloth practically falling off his bronze, sculpted flesh, typified, in the hearts of *legionarios*, the idealised, quasi-erotic end to earthly life.

Cámara considered himself fortunate that the Legión had featured little in his life. He remembered a boy at school in Albacete who had done his military service with the force. It was generally considered the worst fate that could befall a young man – for those not of a military bent – and the kid, barely eighteen at the time, had ended up on the barren Chafarinas islands, a tiny Spanish archipelago three and a half kilometres off the Moroccan coast and not far from the border with Algeria. The strict, punitive discipline of the Legión combined with the boredom of his two-year posting had driven him to drugs. Within six months of his discharge he had committed suicide, his mind a tangled mess.

The incident only served to confirm the prejudices Cámara already had against the Legión. It was old Spain: backward, military, religious and conservative. Franco himself had risen from among its ranks and this supposedly elite force had carried out some of the worst atrocities of the Civil War. Now it was operating within a modern, Western army, carrying out so-called peacekeeping operations. But he was less than surprised to see that the *bandera* based in Melilla, where Terreros had first been posted, still bore the name of the former Spanish dictator. Hitler had fought in the German army in the First World War: did his former unit bear his name today? Somehow he thought not. But Spain was Spain, Spain was 'different' as the hackneyed saying went. And the Legión – this supposedly elite unit of morally dubious, often ridiculous men with their aquamarine uniforms, shirts open to the belly, jogging rather than marching in order to demonstrate their superior fitness and manliness – represented so much of a rancid traditionalism of his country.

He had had nothing to do with it. Until now.

The material that Carlos had given him appeared to point towards Terreros, this former Legión colonel, as being involved in the Fermín case in some way. Why else did the *Hacienda* investigation into Segarra's wife end so suddenly as soon as he had been named? The blundering stupidity of such a move had the air of authenticity about it: an alert had gone out, someone higher up had been warned, and the thing was brazenly shut down. No subtlety about it. There could be other reasons why the *Hacienda* inquiry was terminated, and if necessary he could look into it, but right now he had to go with the obvious, what was staring him in the face: Terreros was hot, and no one was allowed to get near him. Which almost certainly meant that there was something more to his story.

One thing looked quite clear already: Segarra's wife, and then Segarra himself, had been taking him large amounts of money on a fairly regular basis. And it looked as though that money had now stopped.

He tossed the printouts on to his desk and looked over at Torres.

'What've you got?' he asked.

Torres bent down and opened a drawer, pulling out a small glass bottle and throwing it across the office. Cámara caught it with expert hands, a look of surprise on his face.

'We celebrating already?'

'Have a drink, chief,' Torres said.

Cámara unscrewed the top of the brandy and took a swig: it felt sweet and warming.

'So?' he said, licking his lips clean.

'I've been digging,' said Torres.

'Good.'

'Looks like there's something we missed.'

'There often is. What is it?'

'About Segarra. He's ex-Legión.'

Cámara smiled. The dots were beginning to join up.

'What?' he said. 'Military service?'

'Yes,' said Torres.

'Which *bandera*?'

'The "Commander Franco" in Melilla.'

'When was he there?'

Torres raised a dark eyebrow.

'Coincides entirely with Terreros being there,' he said. 'So yes, in theory, he could well have served under Terreros.'

'Rank?' asked Cámara.

'He left as a corporal.'

Cámara brought the bottle to his mouth again, took another swig, and grinned.

'Good,' he said. And he stepped over to hand the brandy to Torres. 'You should have some as well.'

Torres drank from the bottle, a dribble of the brandy tricking into his beard.

'So Segarra and Terreros know each other,' said Cámara. 'I think we can work on that assumption. We need to find out more about the colonel, though. What does he have to do with Fermín's murder? If these two men know each other, have served together, why is Segarra's wife – almost certainly on her husband's instructions – taking him so much money over all these years? What's the money for? And what's the connection with Segarra's illegitimate son?'

Torres pressed a button on his computer and across the room the printer kicked back into life.

'I thought you might ask that,' he said as pages began to spew out. 'And I don't know if this is relevant. But as I was sniffing around I saw a reference to this – a report on military tactics Terreros wrote about twenty years ago.'

He walked over to the printer, shuffled the papers together and handed them Cámara.

'Here,' he said. 'What do you think of this?'

TWENTY-SIX

It was late when they arrived. The coach broke down as they were approaching Tarragona and they were forced to wait by the side of the road, sitting in the scant shade of an umbrella pine while a substitute bus came to pick them up. Daniel grew angry, swearing at Dídac to shut up whenever he spoke. By the time they reached Barcelona, they had spent the entire day travelling and it was dark. Dídac was thirsty and tired. When it came to other people, his father was all patience and caring. But never with him.

At the station he dumped his rucksack by a drinks machine and tried to fish in his pockets for some coins to buy an overpriced bottle of water, but Daniel was already on the move.

'Come on. We've lost enough time as it is.'

Dídac scrambled to follow him as he walked out of the station and into the street. Wherever they were headed, they were going on foot.

He had only been to Barcelona a couple of times before – short trips when he was a child. On both occasions he had been with Daniel, his father returning to his native city for meetings and dragging Dídac along because no one else could look after him back in Valencia. There had been no sightseeing; Daniel seemed to have little interest in showing his son his home town. And so the city was practically unknown to him. He had studied maps of it from time to time, whiling away long afternoons by trying to memorise street names and landmarks. Now, the excitement of finally being there was marred by the fatigue of the journey. He wanted nothing more than to stop, have something to eat, and sleep.

Daniel pushed on, four paces ahead of him. After walking what felt like several kilometres, they left the wider boulevards and delved into narrower, darker alleys. Dídac had managed to catch sight of a handful of street signs and guessed that this was the beginning of the old quarter, the Barri Gòtic.

It felt silent and creepy. The shops were closed and mostly boarded up for the night. The occasional light in the distance, as though at the end of a tunnel, indicated the existence of the odd bar or two. But the only other people apart from themselves walking the streets appeared to be tourists, entering the heated labyrinth for a late-night stroll, taking flash-shots with their cameras of one another before heading back to their hotels for the night. It felt quite different from Valencia: more serious, more uptight. Less fun. And he felt the apprehension of a nascent solitude begin to spread its roots within him.

Near the Plaça Reial, Daniel turned left down a narrow street, tall stone buildings walling them in on either side.

He felt cobblestones under his feet, the trickling of sweat down the back of his neck, and a musty smell of dank drains creep into his nostrils. Still Daniel walked on.

At a low archway with the number 2 painted in white above the door, his father stopped, pulled a key out of his pocket, slotted it into the lock and opened. A light inside illuminated stone steps leading up. Dídac followed through and closed the door behind him. The stairwell was so narrow he could barely squeeze in, his rucksack brushing against the stonework on either side as they curled towards the upper floors in a tight, square spiral. On each storey, two small doors hinted at the existence of small, cave-like homes. And he wondered how anyone ever managed to bring any tables or furniture up such a tight entrance. It felt like a prison.

His legs were beginning to tire as Daniel pushed on relentlessly. As they climbed, a young man and woman brushed past, heading down the stairs, and shoved him to one side. The man had a thin black goatee that framed a smirking, knowing grin; the woman's hair was cut short at the sides, hanging long at the back and over her forehead.

'*Hola*,' Dídac creaked, his throat dry.

They barely spared him a glance as they skipped past.

Finally, Dídac and Daniel reached the top floor. His father knocked and was let in by a large man with powerful shoulders and a mop of dark curly hair and a beard. His left arm was held in a white sling.

Daniel shook the man's hand and stepped inside; Dídac followed.

'This is Dídac,' Daniel said.

Dídac put his rucksack down in order to be able to greet the man properly, but when he held out his hand, the man had gone, leading Daniel through the flat to a room filled with books at the far end.

'Make some dinner, will you?' Daniel called back to Dídac. 'We've barely eaten all day,' he added in a lower voice to the man.

'Of course,' came the reply. 'But first, this. We were expecting you much earlier.'

The two men stepped into the end room and closed the door behind them, their voices muffled and unclear.

Dídac pushed his rucksack into a corner, and started looking around. There was a strong smell of tobacco and incense in the flat. The entrance where he was still standing was gloomy, the walls painted in some deep maroon colour. He ran his hand along the wall, feeling his way along, and found a light switch. In an instant, a kitchen, nestling to one side of the hallway, came into view. A work area was covered in plates and cooking implements, all of them needing a wash. Stepping closer, he tried to find something edible among the debris of crumbs, spilt milk, and splashes of grease. At first glance, a crust of bread, hard and with a dubious white growth on the corner, was the only thing visible.

'You look hungry,' said a voice – a girl's – from behind.

He jumped and turned around. The girl was laughing.

'Sorry,' she said. 'Did I frighten you?'

Dídac saw brown eyes smiling at him.

'No. Yes,' he said. 'Sorry.'

'Sorry for what? I'm the one who should be apologising.'

She took a step closer. She was about the same age as him, perhaps a year or so older, he thought. Her straight hair, dyed with dark red and blonde streaks, fell almost to her shoulders, with a fringe cut halfway down her brow. She wore a bright red-and-white striped T-shirt and underneath, he could not help noticing, no bra.

'You look lost,' she said with a smile. 'Haven't seen you here before. You just arrived?'

'Yes,' he said, coughing to clear his throat. 'Just now. We, er, we came up from Valencia. On the bus.'

'Oh,' she said, as though this meant something to her. 'Yes.'

'I just, um . . .' he said, glancing around the kitchen.

'You're hungry,' she said. 'Of course you are. We had dinner with the guys earlier on, but I think there's something left, if we look around.'

He had no idea who 'the guys' were. The couple who had passed him earlier on the stairs? Who, indeed, was she?

'I'm Dídac, by the way,' he said.

'Yes, I gathered that,' said the girl. And she leaned forwards and kissed him on the cheeks.

'Sònia,' she said. 'Here, let me help you. It's not every day we have visitors up from Valencia.'

She squeezed past him in the tiny space of the kitchen, trying to get through to the fridge. He caught her scent as she brushed past: there was something rich about it, like a strange and exotic spice. As she crouched down, the inside of the fridge casting a warm yellow glow on her face, the top of her jeans at the back lowered to reveal the curled V-shape of a red thong grinning up at him.

'There's some cheese,' she said, thrusting her hand in to scout for something edible. 'And some salad. If you want, we could fix those up and fry some eggs. Would that be all right?'

'Yeah. Brilliant.'

'It's not much. Don't think there's any bread left.' She

stood up and poked at the crust on a board that Dídac had noticed earlier. 'Except this wholewheat crap that Ximo insists on buying.'

Dídac swallowed.

'Ximo,' he said. 'Is that . . . ?'

'Haven't you met him?' she asked. 'I thought I heard him open the door to you guys.'

'I don't know. There was a man . . .'

'Lots of black hair? Doesn't bother much with formalities?'

Dídac shrugged.

'Yeah,' said Sònia. 'That's him.'

'And he's, er . . .'

'My dad,' she said. 'It's all right. He won't bite. I'll look after you. This is my flat as much as his.'

'What happened to his arm?' asked Dídac.

'He fell off his motorbike.' She rolled her eyes. 'Idiot.'

The sink was already half-full with dirty plates, but Sònia placed the others on top, making a small tower of washing-up, but clearing just enough space for them to prepare the food. She gave Dídac a knife to cut the cheese up with while she tore lettuce leaves with her fingers and tossed them into a cracked porcelain bowl. From somewhere she managed to find a handful of tomatoes and she passed them to Dídac to chop while she fried the eggs.

'There's some olive oil there in the corner, next to the coffee jar and the salt,' she said. 'Just throw some on. I like soy sauce on salad as well, don't you? So much more interesting than vinegar.'

'Yes,' said Dídac. 'I mean, I've never tried it like that. But I suppose, yes, it must be more interesting.'

She giggled at him.

'It looks like we'll have quite a few things to teach you here, Valencia Boy. Do you play music at all? They always say Valencians make the best musicians. All those street processions.'

'Not really,' Dídac said. 'I did a bit of trumpet at school.'

She stopped and turned from the hob to look at him. Lifting her hands, she brushed her fingertips over his lips.

'Yes,' she said simply, an enigmatic smile flashing in her eyes. Then turned her attention back to the eggs.

'There's knives and forks in the second drawer down,' she said. 'You might want to get them out and put them on the table. They'll be finished soon, I reckon.'

Dídac hesitated.

'Bit further down the corridor,' she explained without looking up. 'There's a table there and some chairs. That's where you can eat.'

Everything happened very smoothly, as though according to a set plan. Dídac found the table, laid out some places and by the time he returned the eggs were ready and being served. Simultaneously, the door at the end of the room opened and out stepped Ximo and Daniel, taking their places at the table while still talking, as though they had rehearsed this scene several times before.

Dídac fetched the salad and cheese and a second later Sònia placed the eggs down in front of them, pulling out a half-full bottle of red wine from under her arm and pouring it into scratched glass tumblers.

'We've already eaten,' she explained to Daniel. 'This is all for you.'

She lifted her glass and clinked it against Dídac's.

'But we'll share a glass of wine and watch while you eat.'

After a few hungry moments, as Dídac gobbled the food,

the conversation began once more. Daniel ate moderately, he noticed, taking his time to cut into the egg and mix lettuce leaves into the yoke with his fork before lifting them to his mouth. All the while, Ximo was talking. It was something political: Dídac barely had the energy to tune in. And he was more interested by Sònia and a kind of fluttering certainty flowing in his blood that he had never felt before. She was watching him as he ate, smiling.

'Is it all right?'

'Yes,' he said, wiping his mouth clean. 'Delicious.'

And she giggled again: she seemed to view him as something curious, a specimen from Valencia to be cared for and examined in detail.

After the wine had finished, and the food was cleared away, Ximo pulled out a bottle of home-made absinthe. He poured a glass for Daniel and himself and placed the bottle on the table, at which point Sònia leaned forwards and poured some into another glass.

'Here,' she said. 'Try some. And don't mind the bits of herbs still floating in it. That's the wormwood, what makes it so strong. You can just spit them out.'

'I thought you were supposed to take it with sugar or something.'

'That's a gimmick. Commercial bollocks. If you make it right you can drink it neat, like this.'

She lifted the glass to her lips and drank it down in one.

'Agh!' she said. 'He makes it stronger every time. Come on, try it.'

She filled the glass and handed it to Dídac. He looked at her, looked at the glass, and then threw it down his throat. It burnt like molten tar, a disgusting bitter taste stinging his tongue.

'I thought you said—' he coughed.

'Good, isn't it?' said Sònia. 'Here, have another one.'

After the third he lost count: the fatigue, the hunger and the dehydration all concentrated the effect of the drink.

All that remained fixed in his mind was the moment some time later when they got up to go to bed. Ximo showed them a messy living room where they could bed down, either on the floor or one of them on the short sofa – if they curled their legs up enough.

With barely a word, Daniel stretched out on the middle of the floor, not even placing a cushion under his head. Ximo disappeared, leaving Dídac to sort out his sleeping arrangements for himself.

And Sònia smiled at him from across the room.

'Come on then, Valencia Boy,' she said, holding out a hand. 'You can come with me.'

Dídac glanced down at the floor, and the figure of Daniel prostrate by his feet, his eyes closed. If his father had heard, he was pretending not to have noticed.

Dídac stepped over him and followed through into Sònia's bedroom.

TWENTY-SEVEN

The Alquería del Duc lay two kilometres to the north of the village of Carpesa. After a series of calls to the Horta group established that Segarra was not at work and not away on business, Cámara and Torres decided to go to the man's home and try their luck there.

The house was reached down a narrow, winding road through the orange groves. With their windows down, the two detectives could hear the tranquil sound of water trickling through the web of irrigation channels. A hoopoe sped out of the trees in front of them in a flash of orange, black and white.

The road came to an end in front of a large, black, solid metal gate. At the side was an intercom system. Torres leaned out and pressed the button. After a few seconds a female voice answered.

'Who is it?'

'Police. From the Special Crimes Unit,' said Torres. 'We want to speak with Señor Segarra. Is he in?'

There was a crackling pause.

'*Un momento,*' said the voice.

They waited in the car. Five minutes went by. It was hot, and they both started to fidget. Torres had banned smoking in his car, despite being a smoker himself. Cámara was reaching for the door handle to get out and light up a Ducados when the gate buzzed loudly, as though a powerful electric current were passing through it, and started to open very slowly. Once they could get past, they drove through a shaded tunnel of mature pine trees. A few metres ahead, painted bright, clean white, was the *alquería*. Beyond it, on one side, lay an open field where two white horses stood motionless in the sunshine; on the other side well-groomed gardens curled around towards the back of the building.

The car pulled up in front of large wooden double doors which shone in the light from the mirror-like varnish on the surface. No other vehicles were visible; presumably they were kept in the large garage a few metres further on.

No one was there to greet them. Cámara and Torres got out of the car and stepped up to the door. Cámara lifted the hand-of-Fatima knocker and rapped it down hard twice. A moment later a young woman in her twenties came and opened the door. She stared at them without saying a word.

'Is Señor Segarra in?' asked Cámara. 'We're on important police business and we want to talk to him.'

'Police,' she said flatly. 'That probably explains it. Elisabeth – the maid. She's under strict orders not to let strangers in. I suppose you've got some ID?'

Cámara smiled at the tone of disdain. I may be young, it said, but I am worldly and wealthy and will not be pushed around. Curiously, experience had taught him that people like her were often the easiest to break.

After seeing their cards, she took a step back and let them enter the artificial cool of the house.

'I'm Julia Segarra,' she said.

They followed her through the large entrance hall towards the back of the house. The walls and floor were tiled with antique Valencian ceramic-work, in bright blue-and-yellow floral and geometric patterns. In one corner, over a metre tall, stood an old-fashioned water purifier, glazed in blue and white, with pastoral scenes painted at the base. The place felt like a museum of traditional life in the Valencia *huerta*.

They walked through a large kitchen. It was modern and well equipped, but on one side the old inglenook fireplace had been kept, although it was no longer used for cooking. The double sink was carved out of a single block of white marble, complete with shiny brass taps.

Passing out on to a covered patio, they walked down terracotta steps into the garden. A fountain played at the centre and in front of them were row after row of beautifully manicured orange trees.

'You'll find my father out there,' said Julia. 'It's a hobby. Helps him to relax after . . .'

She left the sentence unfinished and walked back inside the house.

Cámara and Torres circled the fountain and headed into the private orange grove in search of their prey. They found Segarra with a pair of secateurs in his hand, snipping off green, unripe oranges from the branches of a tree. Cámara noticed his straight, rigid back.

Segarra had a distant, glassy look in his eye, turning to

see who had suddenly appeared in his garden, registering their presence and presumably recognising them, but as though through an old, thick lens.

'Señor Segarra,' said Cámara. 'We need to talk to you.'

Segarra let his secateurs drop to his side and walked towards them.

'Yes, of course,' he said. 'Come with me.'

They followed him back towards the house. On the covered patio he pointed towards a table.

'Please, have a seat. My daughters insist on having air conditioning, but I prefer the natural cool of a shaded spot near running water.' He nodded towards the fountain. 'Our ancestors survived for centuries with this simple, and much more affordable, system.'

Cámara and Torres stood by the table.

'Please, have a seat,' insisted Segarra. 'I'll get us some tea.'

He walked into the kitchen, his voice echoing through the house as he called the maid's name.

'Elisabeth!'

The two detectives sat and waited. After a couple of moments Segarra returned and joined them.

'I like it Moroccan style,' he said. 'Sweet and with lots of fresh mint. Cools the blood. They know a thing or two about such matters, the Arabs.'

He looked at Cámara, almost giving a nod: their visit had caught him off guard, but by playing the host Segarra had reasserted an authority and was now giving him permission to proceed with his business.

'We want to talk to you about Colonel José Terreros of the Legión,' said Cámara, 'and your relationship with him.'

Segarra paused, sniffed, and stared into the distance above Cámara's head.

'Terreros,' he said. 'He was a commander of mine, years back. A long time ago. I was two years in Melilla. One of the happiest periods in my life. Terreros was there. He was already something of a legend.'

'A legend?' asked Torres.

Segarra shrugged.

'For his *legionario* spirit,' he said. 'Then, some years after I left, he was wounded and became even more celebrated among the men.'

He waved a hand towards his groin area.

'They said the bullet took off everything. Most men would probably have shot themselves, or crawled away into a hole somewhere. But Terreros came back, stayed a soldier. He was a *legionario*. The moment he signed up he had married death itself. So there was no other life for him. The Legión was his bride. And she did not care if he were physically complete or not. All that she wanted from him was self-sacrifice. His death.'

'A bit overdramatic,' said Torres.

Segarra's mouth twitched.

'The Legión's creed,' he said. 'It's what makes it the toughest unit in the Spanish armed forces. It's something you have to experience from the inside to understand.'

A Latin American woman wearing a white cotton apron walked out from the kitchen carrying a tray, which she placed on the table before disappearing again.

Segarra leaned forwards, picked up the teapot and started pouring the tea into small, decorated glasses.

'I like to do this bit myself,' he said, lifting the teapot high and expertly directing the flow into the glass in his other hand. 'One of the habits I picked up in Africa. Takes a certain amount of skill.'

He filled three glasses, handing one each to his guests, and then sat back in his chair.

'So why the interest in the colonel?' he said. 'Is that why you've come?'

'We know quite a lot about Terreros,' said Cámara. 'We're interested in your relationship with him.'

'Yes, I've told you. He was my commander back in—'

'Your relationship with him now,' Cámara interrupted.

Segarra looked down at the tea in his hand. He blew on it and took a sip.

'We know about the money,' said Torres. 'The money that your late wife was collecting from EU subsidies, not declaring and then taking down to Ceuta every two months.'

Segarra sipped some more tea.

'And not just Señora Grau,' said Cámara. 'You yourself went down there and took the money for him. That must have been the last payment. Am I right? About three months ago?'

Segarra placed the glass very carefully on the table in front of him.

'I can only assume you've had access to the *Hacienda* report,' he said. 'Congratulations. You must have some powerful – very powerful – contacts.'

Torres sat motionless, but Cámara could sense the tension in him: he had still not revealed to his colleague the source of the tax investigation material on Segarra's wife.

'What was the money for?' Cámara asked.

There was a pause.

'Señor Segarra,' Cámara said. 'We could, if necessary, get

a judge's warrant to take you to the Jefatura for formal questioning. In which case everything – including your wife's involvement – would be recorded. And your presence at the police station would become public news. Everything would be raked over again – Fermín, your relationship with Célia Capilla. I want to make our position very clear. We are not tax officials and are not here to investigate any of your financial affairs. Our remit is strictly limited to the murder of your son. We are both homicide detectives, and finding his killer is our only goal.'

Segarra picked up his glass of tea, took another sip and returned it to its place on the table, never lifting his gaze the entire time.

'What is your relationship now with Colonel Terreros?' Torres said. 'Are you in—?'

'None,' Segarra barked. 'I have no relationship with that man.'

'But you did. Until recently,' said Cámara. 'Your trip to Ceuta. Was that—?'

'Yes,' said Segarra. 'The last time. I was . . .'

He breathed in deeply, closing his eyes. The situation, so under his control until a moment before, was slipping away. Cámara and Torres crept carefully forward, scenting blood.

'What was the money for?'

Segarra waved a hand in the air.

'Terreros has this fund. For veteran *legionarios*.'

'We know about that,' said Cámara. 'But we don't understand why this fund would need so much money. Three million in just one year. And all taken to Ceuta by hand, by yourselves, supposedly under everyone's noses as you performed the briefcase switch at the Bar Paco.'

Segarra sniffed.

'The briefcase switch,' he said under his breath.

'It's what gave you away,' said Torres.

'I'm perfectly aware of the contents of that report,' Segarra said sharply. 'But, look,' he said, holding his hands out to them as though in friendship. 'You're not here on tax business. You said so yourself. And I know, Chief Inspector, that you are a man of your word. You are well known. So, really, if your interest is purely in solving the murder, then I can assure you this has no connection whatsoever. Terreros has nothing to do with any of this.'

'You sound very certain,' said Cámara.

'I am,' said Segarra. And he pushed his chair back as though to get up, trying to draw things to a close.

Cámara stayed where he was.

'There's something,' he said, 'which makes me think that Terreros is very much involved in this.'

'Chief Inspector, please . . .' Segarra began.

The printed papers landed with a slap on the table in front of Segarra.

Segarra was startled for a moment.

'What's this?' he said.

'It's a report,' said Torres. 'Terreros wrote it over twenty years ago. It was an internal Legión communication, part of a review of tactics and procedures with a view to developing new fighting methods. Came out when you were still in Melilla. I'm surprised you don't recognise it.'

Segarra shook his head.

'I was never an officer. It wasn't my business to—'

'We think you'll find it interesting reading,' said Cámara. 'Nonetheless.'

Segarra eyed the document with suspicion from his seat.

'I'll give you a summary,' said Torres. 'It's a manual for kidnapping and extortion. A plan to turn them into legitimate military tactics. It goes into great detail – methods, preparation, materials, the works. But the section on targets is particularly interesting, we think. Terreros recommends the kidnapping of children in order to coerce their parents. All kinds of advantages, apparently – children are smaller, not as strong, eat less and are therefore cheaper to keep alive if the kidnapping period stretches out. And the emotional impact of a person's child being taken away from them is so powerful that they end up doing practically anything to get them back.'

Cámara leaned in closer to Segarra.

'The plan was officially shelved – apparently there were people higher up who found it unacceptable for the armed forces to be turning minors into legitimate military targets. But what we found interesting is this insistence Terreros makes on the young. And then we reckoned that the payment you took down to Ceuta was probably the last one – you knew you were being investigated by the tax authorities, and your wife had died, so it made sense to wind things down, to take the heat off. And, of course, there was the mistake with the briefcase switch.'

'So that was three months ago,' said Torres, taking the baton. 'Which means that Terreros hasn't been receiving his bi-monthly case of cash from you. Cash which, as a former *legionario* and comrade, you were sending down to Ceuta. Perhaps to help retired soldiers, perhaps for other purposes. We don't know because you're not telling us. But then all of a sudden, Fermín, your son, the son of the man who's been taking Terreros the money, disappears.'

'And is found dead,' said Cámara. 'Now that's not the

same as kidnapping, we know. But what if the kidnapping went wrong? It can happen. Perhaps the kidnapper got scared, or carried away. There could be any number of reasons why things turned out as they did.'

'So what we want to know is—' said Torres.

'Did Terreros threaten you?' Cámara finished the sentence for him.

Segarra sat motionless throughout, his hands on his lap, his eyes focused on the ground. After a pause, he lifted his head, sighed heavily, and very suddenly got up, turned away from the table and walked briskly into the house.

Torres was about to follow him, but Cámara put a hand on his arm. Torres hesitated for a moment, half-raised from his chair, before sitting down again.

Cámara gave him a look: just wait.

Torres took his glass of tea and sipped on it nervously, anxious that they had let Segarra out of the trap.

They could hear noises inside the house: footsteps, a few muffled words being exchanged. After a few moments Julia, the daughter, reappeared.

'My father sends his apologies,' she said. 'He's not feeling well. We've called a doctor and he'll be here in a moment.'

'Is he—?' Cámara began.

'It's Fermín,' said Julia. 'It upsets him to talk about it. And I have to ask you to leave.'

Reluctantly, Cámara and Torres got up from their chairs. Julia led them through the house back to the front door and the car outside.

Once they had descended the step and were about to get in, she held out her hand.

'My father asked me to give you this,' she said.

It was a white envelope.

'Do you know—?'

'I have no idea,' she said abruptly.

Cámara took it from her.

'Now please go,' said Julia. 'I have to attend to my father.'

TWENTY-EIGHT

He heard birdsong through the open window. It was first light and most of the city was still sleeping, only its feathered inhabitants and the odd early delivery van breaking the silence. He rolled over, kicking the sheet off his legs, and pulled closer to the waking body beside him. His lips brushed her shoulder and he squeezed closer in, his erection pulsating against her hand lying at his side. She opened her fingers and gripped it gently, murmuring with pleasure, her eyes still closed.

His kisses turned to nibbles, tenderly biting the skin up towards her neck and behind her ear. His hand gently and slowly circled over her chest, caressing small hard nipples, the crevice of her navel and down to the softness below. Her mouth found his and they kissed with force and passion, his arms wrapping powerfully around her, breath and heartbeats quickening in an instant.

'I love you,' he said, his eyes boring into hers. 'I want this.'

But desire and warmth were not reflected back at him. There was pain in her expression, sorrow, distance.

'I'm sorry,' she said, pulling away. 'Not now.'

His fingers stroked her cheek.

'What's wrong?'

'Perhaps later,' she said. 'When we're alone.'

'Alone?'

He looked up. At the end of the bed, sitting with his back straight, turning away as though out of politeness, was Hilario.

'What?'

'Not the best time, I know,' said his grandfather.

'What the hell's going on?'

'Do you know what you're doing, Max?'

Cámara shifted his weight on to his elbows, pulling himself upright and covering himself with the sheet.

'I should hope so. It's not the first time, you know. And what the bloody—?'

Hilario laughed.

'I'm not referring to that, you idiot. Although, now you mention it, I'm sure there's a trick or two I could teach you. If you were to listen, that is.'

'Hold on,' said Cámara.

'Yes, all right. You want an explanation. Always an explanation, a solution. As though the world were made up of mysteries that all had a solution somewhere. And that you can find them.'

Cámara rubbed his eyes.

'Hasn't it ever occurred to you,' Hilario said, 'that sometimes the mystery may *be* the solution? No, of course not. Still black-and-white thinking after all these years, everything that I tried to teach you. Always division, "this or that". Never "and". Never seeing the underlying union.'

He turned to look at him squarely in the face,

'You're caught in the trap, Max. You think that all you have to do is solve this, and the next one and the next one, and then everything will be all right, life will become marvellous and wonderful. Paradise on earth. Believe me, that's not how things work. The problems, the working things out, the having mysteries to solve in the first place, that's the . . .' He sighed. 'Oh, what's the use? If you weren't going to understand before, there's no real reason to think you'll understand now. My patience wears thin with you sometimes. But I was given you. That was – that is – my duty, my task.'

'I'm hearing you,' said Cámara. 'I can hear you again.'

'Well, I should bloody well hope so. Whether or not you're listening is another matter. Probably not, based on previous experience.'

'What . . . ? Just a minute. I was . . .'

'You were about to make love to Alicia. That failed.'

'Because you turned up all of a sudden.'

'No, I did not. I've been here the entire time. It's just that you can't always see.'

Cámara held his head in his hands.

'Too much for you?' said Hilario. 'Stop trying to work things out. It only creates conflict. And that kind of thing makes you ill. Are you eating properly? I bet not. This case is eating you, though. I can see that.'

'The case?'

'The little boy. What was his name? Fermín?'

Cámara nodded.

'Sad, sad business. And I can see why you've gone ahead and done it.'

'Done it?'

'Sold your soul, you idiot. What? You think you could pull that one over my eyes? A crafty old anarchist like me? His only flesh and blood getting into bed with an officer from the secret services? Believe me, the alarm bells have rarely rung so loudly. And they ring pretty loudly with you sometimes. But that? Pfff.'

'I had to.'

'Don't shrug like that. What are you? A victim of the situation? *¡Me cago en Dios!* I shit on God! 'And that's from me, who doesn't even believe in Him. Don't go thinking you can play this Carlos along. Who are you trying to kid?'

'So what the hell was I supposed to do?' Cámara's hands trembled as he held them out, pleading.

'You want me to give you the solution?'

'Yes.'

'After everything I've been saying? About . . .? Oh, forget it.'

He turned and got up.

'No, wait,' Cámara called. 'Don't go.'

'You've got things to think about,' Hilario said over his shoulder, 'but you're so busy worrying about what's not important that you can't see.'

'Hilario!'

'You can't see. Two good eyes, but there's still so much that you can't see.'

He disappeared, and Cámara slumped back into his bed, his hands cold and damp, a sickness in his stomach.

Through the open window he heard the grinding, hissing sound of heavy morning traffic. It was first light and the city was screaming into wakefulness.

And Alicia lay sleeping at his side, her breath leaden and condensed.

The phone purred by his bedside. He threw out a hand and picked it up.

'*¿Sí?*'

'It's time to act.'

He recognised the voice instantly and pulled himself up, pressing the receiver hard against his ear.

'This line is secure,' he said.

'I know,' said the voice.

'What's happened?'

Terreros swung his legs over the side of the bed and sat up straight, glancing at the clock: it was half-past six in the morning.

'The *Hacienda* report,' said the voice. 'A copy was made.'

'As I expected.'

'Things are developing quickly and you have to be ready. Is that understood?'

'Of course.'

'Now listen. Your name, as you know, is in the report and you are now the target. I suggest you start making the necessary arrangements immediately.'

'I'm already prepared.'

'You need to have everything covered. It all depends on what happens now. I cannot stress that enough.'

'Who has the information?' asked Terreros.

'That's classified.'

'It will help.'

'I can only tell you this – the move will come from within the *Policía Nacional*.'

Terreros shook his head and smiled. 'I get it.'

'You can expect a visitor soon from the mainland. Now I need to hang up.'

'Cámara,' Terreros said. 'You're talking about Max Cámara.'

There was a pause; the line vibrated in dull silence.

'*¿Hola?*'

'As you said yourself, Colonel, he's a useful fool.'

And the connection went dead.

TWENTY-NINE

The helicopter for Ceuta left Málaga airport at 09.15. Cámara and Torres had just twenty minutes from their Valencia flight landing to change to the heliport terminal and jump aboard. The pilot knew that they were on police business, but would not be kept waiting too long.

They ran through the vast halls, past souvenir shops selling bottles of sangría and black plastic bulls, walls of sheer smoked glass soaring high above. At check-in desk 2, the young man glanced at their tickets, tutted at their lateness, and beckoned them past. Outside, the blue-and-white helicopter was waiting on the tarmac, engines already running in preparation for take-off.

Within seconds of sitting down and strapping in, they were airborne, lifting into the sky and out over the blue of the Mediterranean. The air was muggy and the visibility low, but in the distance, to their right, Cámara could make out the silhouette of the Rock of Gibraltar and the strait beyond. Just across, on the African side – lower and less dramatic – he could glimpse the beginnings of the peak of Ceuta, Monte Hacho.

The flight took only a few minutes. Next to him, Torres swallowed hard and kept his eyes closed. It was clearly his first time in a helicopter.

Cámara checked his case: the paperwork from Judge Andreu Peris was there, as was a copy of the letter that Segarra had passed on to them. Terreros's threat had been written by hand with an old-fashioned, slightly unsteady lettering. The wording, however, was hard, direct and cold:

> *Funding must resume with immediate effect.*
> *Gravest consequences for non-compliance.*
> *There will be no further warnings.*
> *You know my capabilities and my methods.*

Pardo had given them his blessing.

'I don't know how, but this guy's involved,' he said when they showed him what they had. 'Go get the fucker.'

Ostensibly to question him in connection with Fermín's death. But they had the authority to arrest him if he proved uncooperative. In his head, Cámara could hear the clicking sound of things beginning to fall into place. Soon, quite soon, this case would be tied up.

Alicia had half-woken before he left early that morning – enough to kiss him lightly and wish him luck. She only knew that he was going to Ceuta and would hopefully be back that night if things went all right.

'We'll have that dinner very soon,' he said as he left the flat. 'I promise.'

About his dream – of her, of Hilario – he said nothing.

Moments after he had arrived at the Jefatura to pick up Torres, he was barely certain that it had happened at all. By the time he was on the plane, he had forgotten about it altogether.

It had been difficult to get hold of a photograph of Terreros – there was nothing on the Internet, despite his being named on more than one website as the head of the Veteran Legionarios' Welfare Association. His ID picture, accessed from WebPol, showed a black-and-white image from what must have been an out-of-date passport shot. In the end it was decided to stick with that – it was too risky to get in touch with the defence ministry.

Cámara stared down at someone possibly twenty years younger than the person he was now looking for. His hair was short and combed back over his scalp, his forehead high and intelligent. His eyes were not unkind; if anything they betrayed a certain sentimentality, a softness, even. His mouth was straight, pulling down a little, perhaps, to the left-hand side; lips thin, a little tight, below a pencil moustache. Some of that would have changed over the intervening years, and of course he might have shaved or grown a beard. But certain features – the nose, or the shape of the eyes – developed slowly over time. And the probability was that, as a military man, he would still be in decent shape. He wondered what effect his wound would have. Could it produce a hormonal imbalance and bloat him out?

His ears popping told him that they were already starting to descend. He looked out the window and saw the shape of Ceuta come into focus below, like a crooked finger sticking out of the top of Africa.

Si los tontos volaran, quince años nublado. The proverb popped unbidden into his mind: If idiots could fly the sky would be overcast for fifteen years. They would be back on the ground soon enough. And Torres would be able to open his eyes again.

The helicopter landed with a jolt at the edge of a very short runway jutting out into the sea. The door was opened and they were led out to the terminal building, where a police officer in uniform was waiting for them.

'Sub-Inspector Padilla,' he introduced himself. 'We have a car outside to take you to HQ.'

The squad car drove them past dirty white tower blocks, palm trees lining a sun-drenched beach and the thick, heavy ramparts of the old city walls. They might have been in any Spanish Mediterranean town but for the higher percentage of women wearing veils and the occasional man in a djellaba. Cámara felt his senses crisp and alert, absorbing a myriad of details through his eyes, ears, nose and even his fingertips as he clutched the handle above the door.

'Almost there,' Padilla said. 'Ceuta is a small place. You can get almost anywhere in about five or ten minutes by car. Traffic permitting, of course. It gets worse every year.'

The Police headquarters was a squat art deco building painted in pastel shades of salmon pink and light orange. They parked by the main entrance and Padilla led them upstairs to the office with the biggest plaque on the door.

'Commissioner Vázquez?' asked Cámara. Padilla neither answered nor looked at him, but Cámara thought he saw a flash of complicity from the corner of his eye.

They passed inside. The commissioner was sitting behind a scuffed metal desk wearing full uniform.

'You must be Cámara, from Valencia,' he said, not getting up. 'Take a seat.'

Torres and Cámara sat on the other side, in front of Vázquez. Padilla stood behind them by the door.

'We could of course be more cooperative if we had some idea what this is all about,' said Vázquez. 'It's highly irregular coming here like this without going through the proper channels. You may do things like this in Valencia, but down here we don't appreciate it.'

The commissioner was not from Ceuta: if anything his accent suggested a Galician background. He could barely have been further from home and yet still within Spanish national territory. And what he was really upset about, Cámara thought, was being treated – in his own eyes – as some sort of second-rate police authority. His pride had been wounded.

'Commissioner,' he said, 'I can assure you that everything will be put in order as soon as it possibly can. Inspector Torres here and myself are from the Special Crimes Unit. Our mission here is of the highest sensitivity both in terms of time and security. I'm as much a believer as yourself in the necessity of doing things in the proper fashion.'

At his side, Torres coughed, trying to disguise his laughter.

'But the needs of this particular case,' Cámara continued, 'demand secrecy and swiftness of action.'

Vázquez nodded.

'Until now,' he said. 'Or are you still going to keep us in the dark? I don't need to remind you that I'm the commissioner in charge here. No police action can take place without my permission.'

'Of course,' said Cámara. 'And I'm glad we have this opportunity to clear things up. But I must stress that time is important and we must act quickly.'

'So?'

'We're here to arrest Colonel José Terreros, head of the Legionarios' Welfare Fund,' said Cámara.

'Because?' Vázquez asked.

'In connection with the murder of a young boy in Valencia two and a half weeks ago.'

Vázquez sat back in his chair, placing his fingertips together.

'Yes, all right,' he said at length. 'I understand now. This is still, despite pretences, a largely military city, and a man like Terreros probably has many friends. The need for secrecy is understandable.'

Torres glanced back at Padilla, still standing by the door.

'You can trust Padilla,' said Vázquez. 'He's my best.'

He shifted in his seat, as though coming to a decision.

'And you have my full cooperation, Chief Inspector,' he said to Cámara. 'Just tell me what you need.'

The drive from the Jefatura to the Plaza de España took less than a minute. They parked near the cathedral and walked the remaining few metres towards the office of the Veteran Legionarios' Welfare Association.

Cámara and Torres were accompanied by Padilla and a second officer. Padilla led the way. As they crossed the square, his radio beeped.

'Come in,' he said into the receiver.

'*This is Unit Three,*' said a voice. '*We're at the subject's flat.*'

Simultaneously, on the other side of the city, a unit of four other *Policía Nacional* officers was approaching Terreros's home.

'Progress?' said Padilla.

'*There's no one here. Flat is empty. No sign of subject. Neighbours haven't seen him all day. No sightings of any kind.*'

'OK,' said Padilla. 'Understood. Proceed as normal. We're approaching the office now.'

They turned up the side street, passing through the open front door of the office building and up the narrow flight of stairs to the second floor. At the green door leading to Terreros's office, Torres knocked on the glass and called out.

'Open up! Police!'

They waited for a few seconds, but there was no sound, nor any sign of movement. Then, on Cámara's order, Padilla and the second officer broke the door down with a heavy metal ram. The wood around the lock splintered and they stepped inside.

The first thing they noticed was the smell: there had been a fire in there recently. The smoke had cleared, presumably through the back window which was open, but black streaking scars up one of the walls confirmed what their sense of smell had told them. Torres stepped over to check.

'The bin,' he said, looking at the charred remains inside a small metal container. 'Papers of some sort.'

Padilla was standing by the computer on the desk, which was lying in pieces.

'He's ripped out the hard drive by the looks of things,' he said. 'Probably taken it with him. Or destroyed it.'

Cámara scanned the room, clocking the desk, the shelves with military textbooks, the photo of Franco on the wall and the cross with the pained Christ figure. The extinguished fire, the computer, emptiness, said everything. They were too late. Terreros had fled.

They heard footsteps behind them on the stairs. Cámara turned and saw what looked like a barman standing there with a tray of coffee in his hand.

'Sorry,' Paco said, and turned sharply to leave.

'Wait, come back.'

The second police officer grabbed the barman by the shoulder and pulled him into the office.

'Who are you?' Cámara asked.

The barman's eyes darted uncomfortably around the room.

'Identify yourself,' Padilla barked.

'Francisco Díaz García,' said the man. 'I run the Bar Paco in the square.'

The name was familiar. Cámara turned to look at him more closely.

'What are you doing here?' Padilla said.

'I'm doing my usual round,' said Paco. 'I – I usually bring the colonel his coffee around now.'

'Every day?'

Paco nodded.

'Have you seen the colonel today?' Cámara asked. He lowered his voice a little, to contrast it with Padilla.

'Not in his office,' said Paco. 'I only come this once, around mid-morning.'

'Have you seen him anywhere else?' said Cámara. 'It's important.'

'He was around very early this morning,' said Paco, suddenly concerned. 'I saw him go past the bar, as I was opening up. Doesn't usually come in till a bit later. Not that he's a late starter, like some of them, but I've never seen him that early, I mean.'

'What time was that?'

'Some time after seven, I should think,' said Paco. 'Maybe a bit before.'

'And what was he doing?'

'Just walking past, that's all. I assumed he was coming here. Might have something important to do.'

'Something important?'

Paco looked anxious.

'Well, if he's coming here that early, you just assume, don't you.'

Cámara glanced at Torres, a question in his eyes. Torres frowned.

'OK,' said Cámara. 'You can go.'

Paco turned to leave.

'One other thing, though,' Cámara called out. 'Did you see anyone else coming to this office recently?'

Paco shook his head.

'No one?'

'Just the colonel,' said Paco. 'I never saw anyone else come in here. Till today.'

The four of them stood in silence for a second as they watched Paco walk down the stairs. Then Padilla's radio beeped again.

'Come in,' he said quickly.

'*This is central,*' came a voice. '*Possible sighting of subject.*'

'Where?'

All four of them leaned in to the radio.

'*Tarajal.*'

'We're on our way,' said Padilla.

'The border,' he said, slipping the radio back on to his belt and heading towards the door. 'Terreros is trying to get across to Morocco.'

THIRTY

Within five minutes they were at the border, the siren screeching as they sped along narrow streets and out on to the main avenue hugging the coastline south. It felt as though they had already left Spain and entered Morocco itself: the pavements were populated by young men with short-cropped black hair carrying enormous chequered bags laden with goods to sell on the other side. A beach of grey, uninviting sand was soon hidden behind a high blue wall with caged walkways for pedestrians passing between the two countries, boxing them in like rats.

The radio crackled with almost inaudible updates from the border post: Terreros had been sighted but had disappeared. No one knew where he had gone. The Moroccan authorities had been informed and were requested to stop him if he made it across.

They sped down to a small roundabout just short of the border: cars were backed up in the heat, and despite the best efforts of the officers on duty, it was impossible to drive any further.

Before they came to a halt, Cámara had leapt out and was running along the middle of the road, finding narrow gaps in the logjam, straining with every muscle to get to the border itself in time.

Some stopped to watch what was happening, others carried on with their own affairs. Police operations were not uncommon, but usually they were trying to prevent people from getting in, not from getting out of Spain.

Padilla and Torres were at his side. Reaching the customs building, they could see that the border itself had been closed – no traffic or people were flowing through. An officer of the *Guardia Civil* approached them.

'Sergeant Muñoz,' he said, presenting himself with a salute. 'I'm sorry, sir, we've lost him.'

'What happened?' Torres demanded.

'The alert came through just seconds after he presented his passport,' Muñoz said. 'He managed to get past, but in the confusion we lost him. It's heavy traffic today – the Moroccans have a feast day tomorrow. But we talked to the other side – they insist that he did not pass their checkpoints. He hasn't crossed the border.'

'Are you sure?' Cámara asked.

The sergeant shrugged.

'We have their word,' he said. 'And we have no authority to go over and check.'

'They go through your paperwork pretty thoroughly,' Padilla said. 'It's not quick getting into Morocco. If they say he didn't cross we can probably assume he's still on our side.'

'OK,' said Torres, 'but where the . . . ?'

'He must have slipped back in the flow heading our way,' said Cámara. 'We might have passed him as we were rushing in.'

Silently, he cursed himself: he had been so intent on reaching the border, convinced that Terreros was there, that he had paid no attention to the cars and people coming the other way.

He turned to Padilla.

'Get more men down here. Immediately. Description of Terreros. Arrest on sight.'

Padilla was already barking orders into his radio. Torres started organising the men who were already there: they had to search everywhere – every truck, every car, every possible hideout within a hundred metres. And if that did not work, two hundred metres. Keep going, until they found him.

Cámara turned and looked back towards Ceuta. The road leading to the border was now in chaos: closing the border had built up more traffic and policemen were scampering around the hot and frustrated crowds, checking for signs of their runaway colonel.

He scanned the tops of the small border-post buildings. Could Terreros have scrambled up them? He doubted it: they were too high.

As the search kicked into gear, and the sounds of more squad cars from the city centre were heard in the distance, he closed his eyes and tried to think: what would you do? What would *he* do? Terreros had almost been caught after passing the Spanish passport control, but crossing over to the Moroccan side would be dangerous: they were alerted and would certainly catch him now. But going back to Ceuta was also out of the question: every policeman in the city would be looking for him.

Wherever he was, he would feel trapped, he would almost certainly panic in some way. Which would mean – Cámara hoped – making a mistake.

Cámara started walking slowly through the crowd away from the border. To his left, rubbish and empty boxes lay scattered over a rocky, uninviting slope leading up to brightly painted houses. To his right, Moroccan men loitered, smoking and watching the events unfold like a drama before them. Many of the older ones wore large white skullcaps, while most wore cheap, Western-style clothes. Then there were others in brown or black djellabas, with pointed hoods, almost like monks.

They all noticed him; some looked at him directly and unashamedly. He was their morning's entertainment: what was going to happen now?

But one of them averted his gaze from the Spanish detective, trying to slip behind the others, becoming visible by his attempts to go unnoticed. And his garb made it worse: he was wearing only a white vest with what looked to be modest shorts underneath.

In less than a second Cámara had stepped over and grabbed him by the arm. The man turned and grinned up at him innocently: please, his expression said, no trouble.

'He gave me a hundred euros,' he said apologetically. And he threw up his hands: what else could I have done?

'What were you wearing?' asked Cámara.

The man pointed at one of the others nearby.

'A djellaba?' said Cámara.

The man nodded.

'What colour?'

'Brown. It's brown.'

Cámara let go of the man's arm.

'Which way did he go?'

The man shrugged: he thought he had said enough already. But Cámara's hand soon clenched over his shoulder, gripping him tightly.

'Which way did he go?'

Some of the others fell back. If there was going to be a struggle they did not want to be near an enraged Spanish policeman.

The man's knees seemed to buckle under him. Then he raised his hand and pointed further up the road.

'Back up there?' Cámara asked. The man nodded. He let him go, guiding him gently to the ground and patting him on the arm in thanks. He would be all right.

A squad car was moving closer, pushing its way through the traffic. Cámara leapt over, identified himself and ordered them to put out an alert: Terreros was now disguised as a Moroccan, wearing a brown djellaba, and was last seen heading back towards the city.

Once the message was received, he started jogging along the side of the road, scanning for anyone suspect. But a djellaba was a great disguise: they covered you almost completely and were a common sight here. Only Terreros's footwear might give him away, but with so many people milling around it was not always easy to spot what shoes they were wearing. He ran up to as many as he could, pulling their hoods back from behind to reveal their faces: one, two, three. But none of them was Terreros.

He got to the end of the blue wall and the beach was once more in view. The search seemed hopeless. Terreros could have got anywhere by this point. And what if he had worked out some other way of leaving the enclave?

As he stood at the edge of the road, a police officer came running up.

'Sir!' he called. 'There's a sighting.'

'Where?'

The officer pointed.

'On the beach. Right by the border.'

Cámara jumped over the wall, down on to the sand, the officer close behind. He looked back towards Morocco: at the border itself, a high wall pushed out into the sea to stop people from swimming across. Further obstacles were placed in the way, while a line of small buoys stretching out to sea marked where one country's waters met the other's.

And there, on the sand, was a small pile of brown cloth, and discarded next to it, a walking stick and the biggest revolver that Cámara had ever seen, glinting in the sunlight. To the left, out in the sea already, Terreros's head was bobbing up above the waves: he had finally panicked and was trying to swim to Morocco.

In an instant Cámara was sprinting down the sand. He could see a rubber dinghy being launched from the far side of the border: if Terreros could make it past the wall and over to the buoys, he would be picked up by the Moroccans, having crossed into their territory. And then the process of getting him back to Spain would be lengthy and complicated. Perhaps even impossible, if Terreros had the right friends over there. He must have decided in the end that it was better to make it to Morocco after all, to try his luck.

But not if Cámara could get to him first.

He sprinted, slipping off his jacket, his gun belt and anything else that he could as he sped along the beach. Terreros was an able swimmer and was getting close to the end of the dividing wall. A group of Spanish policemen had emerged from inside the border-control post, but were simply waving their arms and shouting, others trying to launch their own dinghy. No one was thinking about diving into the water itself.

With a skip, Cámara pulled off each shoe and threw himself headlong into the waves, quickly breaking into a crawl as Terreros drew further away. From Morocco, the police boat was moving in fast, while the first buoy – where Spanish jurisdiction ended – was only metres away from Terreros.

Cámara buried his head in the water and powered forwards. After a few seconds, he looked up: Terreros was tiring, and the waves breaking against the wall were proving tricky, lifting him up and almost pushing him backwards. There was just a chance that Cámara could reach him in time. He kicked his legs harder, willing himself on.

But Terreros was not giving up. Pushing off from the bottom of the wall, he flung himself forwards, trying to time the waves in order to get momentum away and out towards the first buoy. And the Moroccan police dinghy floating just beyond.

Cámara forced himself to swim faster than he had ever done in his life and he edged closer and closer. But just as he was about to reach out and grab hold of him, Terreros made a final effort and took hold of the buoy, hurling himself around it and over to the Moroccan side. There he stopped, treading water. Only a few metres away, Cámara halted and looked up: the Moroccan dinghy was already swooping down.

Terreros said nothing, but looked at him with an expression of smug triumph: he was safe.

Cámara watched as the Moroccan policemen approached.

But four or five metres behind Terreros, they stopped, not moving in to pick him up. Terreros barely noticed, enjoying his moment, taking in the face of the man who had almost managed to catch him. And his expression broke into a broad grin.

Cámara looked up at the Moroccan officer in the boat behind, wondering why he was not moving in on Terreros. The man was wearing sunglasses, but at that moment he took them off and looked Cámara in the eye. Then very gently, almost imperceptibly, he gave a nod.

After a quick order, the engine accelerated, the boat turned in a tight corner, and the Moroccan police were speeding back to their own side. Terreros heard them, and turned to watch in horror as his supposed rescuers abandoned him.

Cámara swam over and caught hold of the buoy. Then grabbing Terreros by the wrist, he hauled him back to the Spanish side.

'Colonel Terreros,' he said. 'There are a few questions I'd like to ask you.'

THIRTY-ONE

He wanted to celebrate.

'We'll go to La Sucursal,' he said, putting his bags down as he walked in through the door. 'I can call. It's midweek – I'm sure we can get a table.'

Alicia did not answer.

'Do you fancy that?' he said. 'We'll make a night of it. We deserve it.'

She got up and walked to the sink to pour herself a glass of water.

'No?' he said. 'Something else? We could head out of town if you want.'

She drank in silence.

'Somewhere near the beach? I don't know, what do you fancy?'

She put the glass down and shrugged.

'Come on, it's our night. We haven't done anything like this for ages. We can do anything, go anywhere.'

'I think in the end just something simple,' she said with a frown. 'I don't know, maybe a sandwich and a beer. Something close by.'

'Sure,' he said. 'Anything you want.'

'I like the place on the corner at the bottom of the street,' she said.

'OK. Let's go there.'

While she disappeared into the bedroom, he went to the bathroom and quickly showered and changed his clothes, still riding a wave of elation after successfully arresting Terreros and bringing him to Valencia, where he was sitting in the cells in the Jefatura basement.

When he was ready, Cámara sat on the sofa waiting for Alicia to finish. After twenty minutes, she reappeared looking almost exactly the same as when she had gone in: no make-up, the same clothes as before – jeans and a loose T-shirt. Her hair was brushed and her eyes were red.

'Right,' he said, lifting himself up. 'Let's go!'

He held her hand as they walked the few metres from their block of flats to the *bocatería* at the end of the street. The place was busy and noisy, as it usually was. Many of the more expensive places in the city had closed recently, their clientele reduced to ever smaller numbers, but neighbourhood bars that had managed to hold on during the crisis were doing all right, in general.

They had to wait ten minutes for a table. Cámara ordered a bottle of Mahou for himself; Alicia asked for a glass of red wine. They leaned against the bar, struggling out of the way as people squeezed past to get to the toilets, watching the waiters push their way through the throng with trays laden with hot sandwiches, more drinks, or, in the case of those already on the last course, plates of the bar's celebrated chocolate cake. It was almost worth coming for that alone.

Cámara smiled as the cake sailed past them.

'Yum,' he said, grinning at Alicia. She was staring into space.

Finally they got their table – a tiny steel circle in the corner of the room – and could have a stab, at least, at a conversation over the background noise.

'I'm starving,' he said, picking up the menu and offering it to her. 'I already know what I want. What are you going to have?'

'I don't know,' she said, glancing down at the laminated card. 'Something different.'

He finished his beer and tried to catch the eye of the ruffled-looking waitress standing at the next table.

'I'll have the number seven,' she said, putting the menu down. 'With Roquefort and dates. And another red.'

Her glass was still half-full, but she drained it in one, placing it back on the table in front of him.

'OK.'

After a few minutes' signalling, the waitress made it over to them and they placed their order. And in a moment they were on their own, two people sitting at a restaurant table; it was time to talk. It felt almost like a command.

'So tell me about your trip,' she said, waving a flag of sorts from the other side.

He grabbed at it; it was not what he wanted to talk about. Not now, not to her. But it was all there was for the time being. So he filled her in, telling her about Terreros, about how he had tried to make a run for it, and how they had caught him on the border trying to swim to Morocco.

He mentioned nothing about Carlos and the information that had led him to the colonel.

'Did he kill the boy?' she asked. 'This Terreros character?'

Cámara shook his head.

'I'm convinced he was behind it, that he ordered it. We've got a lot on him, even the handwritten threat that he wrote to Segarra. Tomorrow we start formal interrogations. I'm sure he'll crack, once he sees everything we've got on him.'

'He wrote a threatening letter by hand?' Alicia asked.

'Yes, I know. Some old-fashioned notions, I suppose. Incredible, isn't it?'

'Yes,' she said softly. 'Incredible.'

Their sandwiches came and they ate and drank without speaking much apart from the occasional comment about the food. She nodded when he asked if she wanted a third glass of wine.

He finished first: he was hungry now that the rush of the day's earlier events was beginning to subside. After seeing his arm shoot up, the waitress made it over to their corner again.

He glanced at Alicia. Her mouth was full but she nodded at his implied question.

'Two pieces of chocolate cake,' he said. 'And I'll have a brandy to go with it.'

Alicia finished eating, wiped her mouth and then drank some more wine. It was that moment when he instinctively thought about smoking. Once upon a time, not too long ago, it would have been possible. But he did not feel like forcing his way through the tightly packed diners to join the small crowd on the pavement outside. He would hang on.

She placed her fingertips to her mouth; he tried to smile at her.

'I've been to see a friend,' she said. 'Marga, she's a psychotherapist.'

'Oh,' he said. 'How . . . how's that going?'

Both her hands closed in around her face, hiding her chin.

'I've been four times now,' she said. 'Going back tomorrow.'

He noticed that he was biting the inside of his lip. Quite hard.

'Is it helping?' he said. 'This is about . . . what happened, I take it.'

They did not speak about it; the cigarette burns, the sexual molestation. Yet it was always present, no matter how hard they both tried to ignore it.

'About that,' she said. 'That and other things. Everything.'

'I suppose it's good to get it out,' he said. 'Talk to someone.' He did not know what else to say.

'Marga said I should talk to you,' she said. 'That there were things I needed to tell you.'

He swallowed.

'Tell me?'

'Yes.'

He paused.

'What do you need to tell me?'

'I'm not attracted to you any more, Max,' she said. Tears were pouring from her eyes. 'I can't make love to you any more.'

He reached out to hold her hand, but she pulled it away.

'It's just a matter of time,' he said. 'Really, all this will heal eventually. I love you. We just have to give it—'

'No, Max,' she said. 'It won't heal, it's not healing.'

'It will,' he said softly.

'No, it won't!' she screamed. For a second the noise in the restaurant diminished, before picking up again.

'Maybe we should go home,' he said.

'Stop telling me what to do.'

'I'm not. Oh, look, I'm sorry.'

'Sorry?' she said. 'Sorry? You think that's enough. You think it's enough to fuck around with people and then say sorry. That's your problem. That's the problem we have, right there.'

'What are you talking about?'

'This. You. Do you think sorry can make up for everything? Do you think it can make everything go away? Do you even stop to wonder what I'm going through?'

'Every day.'

'You have no idea!' She slammed her hand on the table; he caught the glass before it hit the floor, but the wine flew across and spattered his trousers.

'How can you possibly know what I suffer?' she said.

'I was there,' he said. 'I saw it all.'

'I know you were there. It was because of you that those bastards got me in the first place.'

He lowered his head.

'It was because of you that they did this to me.'

She placed her hands on her thighs.

'It will never go away, Max. Don't you understand? I will live with this for ever. And no amount of apologies will ever change that.'

'Look, I—'

'Don't!' she said. 'Don't even dream of saying sorry again. Sorry erases nothing. It only makes it worse.'

His stomach was cramped with pain, a wave of his own tears willing themselves up towards his eyes, but he pressed them down.

'What . . .' He coughed. 'What do you want me to do?'

Her crying had stopped now, and there was a harder expression on her face.

'We need to separate,' she said. He felt something in him, an inner core, collapse.

'Separate?'

'For a time. I don't know how long. But I need to be alone.'

'OK,' he said quietly, trying to hide the shuddering inside. 'Whatever you want.'

'It would be better that way,' she said. 'It's what I need.'

'All right.'

He was dizzy, the room was spinning, and he felt an urge to splash his face with water.

'I'll be just a moment.'

There was a queue outside the toilet. He waited with his back to the rest of the bar, not wanting to look back. Once in the privacy of the bathroom, he allowed a sob to pass through his shoulders and up to his face before pressing it down again. The water stung his eyes as he cupped and lifted it with his hands.

Back at the table, there were two plates of chocolate cake. But Alicia had gone.

'She's already paid,' said the waitress, not without some sympathy.

He stepped out into the street; there was no sign of her.

THIRTY-TWO

The feeling was new, as though his skin were no longer a simple film over his flesh, but had sprung into being, become a living, pulsating force that was both a part of him and also, somehow, possessed of a consciousness of its own. He was no virgin. But this experience had been so different that his previous encounter felt like a shadowy dream, as though it had never really taken place at all. This, he told himself, holding Sònia's sleeping body close to his as they lay in bed, was making love. And he was therefore, by logical reasoning, in love with her. At last he understood.

Her head lay heavily on his chest and he stroked a couple of fingers through her hair, bending his face down to plant light kisses on the top of her brow. The room was still gloomy: only the half-light of early morning was penetrating the window. He must have slept for an hour or two at most, convinced that they had carried on well into the night. And he might have expected to fall into deep dreaming afterwards, not least to recover from the intense physical exertion. But now his eyes clicked open almost with a will of their own, as though his body and mind needed to register every second of this moment.

Her breath was warm against his chest and stirred the hairs around his nipple. Below the sheet, his cock twitched unbelievably for more. He wanted to turn her on her side there and then and repeat everything, the desire surging within him with sudden ecstatic force. He placed a hand on the curve of her hip, sliding it round to her buttocks. His breath quickened and he pressed more kisses on her face, lowering down to her nose, her cheek and finally her mouth.

With her eyes still closed, she opened her lips and met his tongue with her own, twisting it around and thrusting it into his mouth. He loved the way that she kissed him, forcefully, penetrating him above as he did her below. Her hands awoke and began sliding down his side, fingertips caressing his ribs before moving down to his belly and delicately starting to stroke. With her mouth she moved away from his lips and nibbled at his neck, the top of his chest, pausing at each nipple before continuing further down. He gave a low groan as her tongue played once more on his sex, pulling away in spasms as the over-sensitised nerves fired pain-pleasure shots towards his brain.

'Gently,' he whispered.

She started to moan, the vibrations of her voice passing through her mouth, into his cock and spreading out into his body.

And he felt the rising within him, the imminent orgasm begin to take hold.

The door slammed open, and before either of them could

register, the sheet that had partially covered them was pulled off, exposing them completely.

Instinctively, Dídac shot back in the bed, covering himself with his hands. Sònia stayed where she was, naked, crouched on all fours.

'What the fuck!' Dídac shouted.

And he looked up to see Daniel standing over him, staring him hard in the eye. Then his father bent down, grabbed some of Dídac's clothes from the pile on the floor and threw them in his face.

'Here,' he said in a calm, direct voice. 'You can either stay here all day wasting your time, or you can come with me and learn what real action is about.'

He turned and walked back towards the door.

'It's time to step up.'

THIRTY-THREE

His mind was heavy. He had to forget the events of the previous evening and leave them behind. It was time to head back to the Jefatura. Time to interrogate Terreros.

As he walked out of the cheap hotel where he had stayed the night, something distracted him: a slim man, perhaps in his late forties, was ambling down the street wearing enormous placards made out of pieces of cardboard and tied around his shoulders with string. He had already passed by and Cámara could only see the message written on his back: *Es la solución del mundo*.

But *what* was the solution to the world's problems? Cámara fell in behind the man, the leadenness of early morning and a sleepless night momentarily shaken off by a curiosity to discover the secret of the street-prophet in front of him. From the drab appearance of his clothes it was clear that he was not wealthy, but the top button of his shirt was done up, his hair was cut short and he was clean-shaven; he might be the kind of person that you saw every day and paid little attention to: ordinary, going about their business, not trying to change anything much in the world. But the confused and amused expressions on the faces of pedestrians coming the opposite way, who could read what was written on the man's front placard, suggested that the gospel he was preaching was eye-catching, perhaps extraordinary.

Cámara followed him for a hundred metres or so, trying to work out what the message might be, not wanting to break out into a run in order to catch a glimpse of the front placard. Finally they reached a crossing; the light was red and the man had to stop. Seconds later, Cámara caught up with him and stood at his side. As soon as the light changed, he dashed out across the road and quickly looked back to read the words, scrawled with black and red marker pen: *Jovenes: Practicar mucho el sexo y procrear CERO*. Youngsters: Have a lot of sex but NO children.

So that was all it took.

Something in him warmed to the idea that ambassadors of free love were still wandering the streets – even incongruous ones. No parents, no families. No break-ups. Sex – at least when it was done right – could make people whole, could turn two bodies, fleetingly, into one.

By the time he reached the Jefatura, he had convinced himself that the stab of pain – of separation – had disappeared.

'Why did you run, Colonel?'

Terreros sat on the other side of the interrogation table, his hands resting on his knees, back straight and eyes focused dead ahead on Cámara. He wore a grey suit that had been collected from his flat before they left Ceuta; it was crumpled and his shirt was creased, yet by his bearing he still managed to convey an air of concentrated energy, unruffled by his sudden downfall.

Amazingly, he had refused his right to legal representation for this formal interview. He would, he said, be looking after himself. God alone would be his judge.

'*Con un par de cojones*,' said Torres with grudging admiration when he heard. 'That macho *legionario* stuff really runs deep. Except for the fact that he doesn't have any balls. Perhaps that's why.'

Every half an hour they had to break for ten minutes because of Terreros's medical condition.

'It's my legal right,' he said. Nobody could come up with a good enough reason to deny him. The entire interrogation time could last no more than ninety minutes in a twenty-four-hour period.

Torres now sat on Cámara's left. With one eye on the clock, Cámara fired off question after question into the hot silence of the room.

'Why did you threaten Segarra?'

'Was it because he was no longer sending you any money?'

'What was the money for?'

'Why did you advocate the kidnapping of children as a legitimate military tactic?'

'Did you order the kidnapping of Segarra's son, Fermín?'

'Did you order him to be murdered?

'Why did you run, Colonel? Why did you run?'

Terreros was silent. He stared.

And finally spoke.

'I don't talk to Reds.'

THIRTY-FOUR

'Don't start getting the wrong idea. You're not the only one she's fucking.'

The bus took them west out of the city centre, from the Passeig de Colom by the sea, through the Eixample district and inland towards the suburbs. Dídac hung on to the rail, trying not to fall against other passengers standing next to him as they turned hard around tight corners. Beside him, his father stood still, seemingly able to balance without any trouble as they rocked from side to side, as though his feet were nailed to the floor.

Daniel kept his gaze on the road, looking over the heads of the other people, but glanced momentarily at Dídac.

'I'm serious,' he said. 'You're a romantic. You think she's the one. After just a few fucks.'

His lip twitched.

'But believe me, things aren't as simple as that.'

Dídac dropped his head, his mouth sharp and hard, his

stomach tightening into a retch as the bus threw him to one side again.

At the next stop a large group of passengers got off and some seats became free. Daniel prodded him in the small of the back, pushing him to go and sit down. He himself remained standing for the rest of the journey.

The bus route terminated in the centre of a drab satellite town: blocks of flats and a handful of shops. Daniel hitched his rucksack higher up his back and set off walking, Dídac following a couple of paces behind.

The joy that had flowed through his body turned into poison. He hated everyone.

He lost track of how long they walked. After what could have been five minutes or half an hour, they struck out beyond the last tower blocks and over dry scrub ground littered with household rubbish. Beyond, in the middle distance, he could make out rows of street lamps arching over a grid system of roads that appeared to lead nowhere.

After a few more minutes they passed a sign announcing that they were entering an industrial complex. Except that – apart from one building – there were no factories or offices in sight.

'Ran out of money,' said Daniel simply. 'Built all this trying to cash in on the boom years, but did it too late, just as the banks collapsed. Infrastructure all there, but no industry.'

He snorted and shook his head.

'Idiots.'

They stepped over a weed-infested pavement to the one building that had been erected: a simple warehouse about the size of half a football pitch. Dídac glanced around, trying to see if there were any cameras: the place might be empty but perhaps even more reason to have a security system set up. But the usual places – the four corners of the building, or over the main door – showed no sign of any.

Daniel had gone around to the back. Dídac skipped along after him, keen to share his discovery.

'We can get in here,' said Daniel, standing by an open door. 'There's no security issues here, but there's no point advertising our presence by going in through the front.'

The door must have been left unlocked, Dídac assumed. They stepped into a gloomy open space with a concrete floor. A small amount of light came in through grimy windows near the top of the building. In one corner two separating walls created a small office area, perhaps designed as some kind of reception. Nearby stood a stack of three giant tractor tyres.

'Gives you an idea of what they were intending the place for,' said Daniel.

Otherwise, there was nothing else in there: it was empty.

Daniel took his rucksack off his shoulders and crouched down on the floor to open it up.

'Come over here.'

Dídac bent down to get a closer look.

'Your eyes adjusted yet to the light?'

He nodded.

'Right,' said Daniel. 'These are your tools. You're going to learn how to make a detonator using a mobile phone.'

One by one he reached into the rucksack and pulled out a battery-powered soldering iron, a Stanley knife, some wire, a relay, a stick of solvent, a 9-volt battery, a small screwdriver, a cheap mobile phone, and some thin metal tubes, about the size of hand-rolled cigarettes.

'Blasting caps,' Daniel explained.

Dídac bent down lower, shifting his weight until he was sitting on his heels.

'You need to be focused for this,' said Daniel. 'No bullshit in your head. I need you concentrated. This is the real thing. Do you understand?'

'Yes.'

'Because if you fuck up with this stuff you'll lose a finger. Or worse. OK?'

'OK.'

Daniel paused, examining him. Then he sniffed and nodded.

'We're making an improvised explosive device – what ordinary people call a home-made bomb. But if we're going to do this properly we use the correct terminology. Got it?'

'Improvised explosive device,' repeated Dídac.

Daniel picked up the phone.

'To set the device off, we need a remote detonator. Anything that can send a signal to initiate an electric charge can be used – a car alarm, a garage door opener, even a remote control for a toy car, for example. But –' he waved the phone close to Dídac's face – 'mobile phones are usually the best because they have a longer range.'

He picked up the screwdriver and started taking the phone apart.

'What we have to do is find the vibration motor,' he said.

After placing the plastic casings carefully on the floor, he held the innards up and pointed at a small metal disc at the bottom corner.

'When the phone rings, that spins,' he said, 'making the phone vibrate.'

He gently pulled it out.

'We don't need it. What we want is access to the contacts underneath.'

Using the soldering iron, he carefully connected two short wires to the phone where the vibration motor had been, attaching the other ends to the small relay. Then he used the knife to cut a hole in the casing for the wires to come out, and put the phone back together. He glued the relay to the back of the phone. Two other wires came out and led to a clip which he snapped on to the battery, which was also then stuck to the phone. A third pair of wires led from the battery.

The process took only a few minutes, during which time Dídac watched closely, absorbing every detail.

Daniel laid the mechanism on the floor.

'Now,' he said, 'when someone calls this number, the current for the vibration motor will pass to the relay, which then passes to the battery, sending a stronger current down these wires.'

With his finger, he lifted the two spare wires leading from the 9-volt battery.

'And these,' he said, picking up a metal tube, 'attach to here.'

'The blasting cap,' said Dídac.

'Good.'

He left it all on the floor and reached over to the rucksack, pulling out a plastic bag. Inside, wrapped in paper, was a small pellet of what looked like an off-white plasticine.

'Composition C-4,' said Daniel. 'Plastic explosive.'

He tossed it to Dídac. His son caught it with a terrified expression on his face.

'It's fine,' Daniel said with a grin. 'You could jump up and down on this stuff and it would never explode. You can even set it alight and nothing would happen. It's a very stable compound.'

Dídac pressed it gently with his thumb: it was pasty and greasy.

'You don't need very much of it – it's a high explosive. A couple of hundred grammes would be enough to destroy that bus we were riding on earlier. And the only thing that will set it off is one of these.'

He held the shiny blasting cap between his fingers.

'And what sets the blasting cap off,' said Dídac, 'is the mobile phone.'

Daniel threw him a look, and something moved inside Dídac: had he managed to impress his father?

Daniel pushed the phone detonator to one side, then reached into his rucksack and pulled out another phone, a relay and more wire.

'Now you do it,' he said. 'I'll watch.'

It was trickier than it looked – not least soldering the small wires into the right places. And it took him much longer. But Daniel said nothing. Dídac knew that if he made a mistake he would find out by the thing not exploding: he was expected to work it out for himself.

Finally, however, after almost gluing his fingers rather than the relay to the back of the phone, he finished, and held his first detonator over for inspection. Daniel simply took it and stuck the end of the blasting cap into the tiny ball of C-4. Then he stood up and walked to the far end of the warehouse.

'You can hide behind that stack of tyres,' he said. 'But your eardrums would probably never be the same again.'

He stepped towards the door. Dídac hesitated.

'A confined space greatly accentuates the explosive power,'

Daniel said, stretching out for the handle. 'Remember that – it's important. The number of deaths from a blast in a closed area – like the bus – is around fifty per cent of people. In fact it's forty-nine per cent. But that figure drops to just eight per cent if the explosion happens in an open space. If you want to kill more people in an open-space environment you need to include shrapnel in the device – bolts, nails, nuts. The blast in itself is often not enough.'

Dídac was motionless, as though the blood had stopped pumping to his legs.

Daniel opened the door, holding his own phone in his hand.

'In a few seconds I'm going to be dialling that number,' he said, nodding back towards the bomb. 'So I suggest you get up now.'

Dídac jumped to his feet.

'And bring all that with you,' said Daniel, indicating the materials on the floor near the rucksack.

Daniel was already walking away from the warehouse when Dídac made it to the door. He ran after his father, who kept his back turned, his head bent down looking at the phone in his hand.

'Watch out for flying glass,' he said.

And he pressed the green call button on the screen.

THIRTY-FIVE

They sat in their office in silence. Torres swivelled on his chair, looking at nothing in particular on his desk, while Cámara stared into space.

A drink? A smoke? The usual crutches that they reached out for had lost their appeal.

'We should get a dartboard in here,' said Torres, mumbling into his beard. 'Something to distract us.'

'We'd only end up throwing the darts at each other,' said Cámara.

'I've never understood that,' said Torres. 'You know how in films there's always a dartboard hanging on the back of a door. So what happens when someone opens it from the other side just as you're launching your dart? Could take someone's eye out. I mean, what a fucking stupid place to hang a dartboard. Never understood that.'

Cámara grunted.

'Can't say I've ever thought about it. The prime location

for a dartboard has, surprisingly, occupied quite a small amount of my concentration over the years. But now I realise this is an important question that deserves serious consideration. Thank you for bringing my attention to it.'

'Fuck off.'

They could feel Terreros's presence in the cells below them, imagining him sitting quietly and calmly on the edge of his bed. Sharp, focused, unperturbed, and enjoying the attention of the guards' frequent visits to escort him to the toilet facilities. Half of their usual arsenal – the long, intense hours of interrogation, the social isolation in the prison, the psychological effect that a simple combination of depriving and pressurising could bring – were denied to them. The colonel was using his medical condition to his full advantage, throwing them off their rhythm.

'It's my fault,' said Cámara. 'I should have foreseen this.'

'How?' asked Torres.

'What?'

'How were you supposed to have foreseen this happening? What, you got some crystal fucking ball hidden away somewhere?'

'Perhaps Laura's right,' said Cámara. 'We moved too soon.'

It had been delicately put, but the remark by the head of the murder squad – who had been given the Fermín murder case originally – had found its target. Many of the difficulties with Terreros, she said, might be overcome if they had more to throw at him. Meaning, of course, that she believed Cámara ought to have gathered more evidence before hauling him in: he had, in her view, swooped down to Ceuta far too soon.

And, Cámara thought, she was probably right. But he had assumed that he had enough, that once Terreros saw what they had on him he would begin to open up, to crack. And he had had that instinctive certainty when they flew down, that sensation he recognised more and more: his intuition, his hunch, flaring back into life suddenly after a prolonged silence. Going to Ceuta had felt a hundred per cent right. And experience had taught him to follow these feelings: the outcomes might not always be predictable, but in the end it always proved to be the correct thing to do.

Now, though, he wondered. Terreros was making fools of them. Not that being made a fool of overly concerned him. He was not impervious to ridicule, and image had to be maintained to a certain degree – as much as anything being perceived as a good, efficient detective helped get things done. But the fact that this investigation had been given to them, the first crowning case of the floundering Special Crimes Unit, made him smart now. After weeks of stagnating, they had made sudden and rapid progress, and it had seemed as though momentum were on their side. But now they had stalled again. Terreros was giving them nothing: all they had, in the end, was his handwritten note, a mere threat: nothing to link him materially to the murder of Fermín.

Commissioner Pardo, Judge Andreu Peris – he could almost feel those above them starting to get nervous.

'I don't suppose . . .' Torres began, but the words petered out.

That's right, thought Cámara. I don't suppose the source that got us so far in the first place might provide us with something more? Get us out of this hole? Torres could wonder, and almost formulate the question himself, but pulled back at the last minute.

Cámara gave it as long as he could, not wanting to appear to be responding to Torres's partly voiced suggestion. At least not too quickly. He stared at his computer screen for a few minutes, shuffled his mouse around for a bit, made a phone call about some administrative matter, and then finally got up, stretching as he did so.

'Might go for a stroll,' he said. 'Get some air.'

Torres grunted, not looking up.

Cámara had his phone between his fingers before he even closed the office door, but he waited until he was out of the building and walking along the Calle Hospital towards the city centre before he finally looked at it. He had memorised Carlos's number, not wanting to record it on the phone itself, pretending to himself that he would never dial it again. But now the digits fell quickly in order under his fingertip. He stared for a moment at the number, wondering. Something for nothing? Would Carlos give him anything unless he could supply some more information on his anarchist friends? The truth was that he had not seen any of them since Dídac and Daniel had left for Barcelona: the Fermín case, the situation with Alicia . . . there was too much else going on. Carlos might demand something from him, however. He would just have to make something up.

He pressed the green call button and held the phone to his ear. After a click, the line beeped as the connection was made and Carlos's phone began to ring. Three, four, five times. But there was no answer.

Cámara cursed; he was an idiot to think that Carlos would respond. He, Cámara, was the one being played in this relationship – *he* worked for Carlos, not the other way around.

He closed his eyes and was about to hit the kill button, when a robotic female voice came on the line inviting him to leave a message. Cámara pulled the phone quickly up to his face again and heard the signal for him to start speaking.

'This is Cámara,' he said. Then he paused.

'I've got something for you. New information.'

He coughed.

'Call me as soon as you can.'

He felt uncomfortable, anxious. There seemed to be no point going back to the Jefatura just to sit in the office in frustration with Torres. But neither could he think of anything else to do. Normally he was a master of distracting himself when faced with a stalemate, waiting for things to happen rather than trying to force them along. There were times to move, and there were times to stop. He likened it sometimes to a dance – sometimes he led and at other times he let events take over.

Now it felt as though there were nothing more that he could do. But what to be getting on with in the meantime? It was as if he had lost some inner compass.

Behind him was the Jefatura, in front lay the city centre, while just a few blocks further on to the left was his flat, a home that was no longer his. He felt trapped and, faced with his own silence, he simply walked over to one of the outside tables of a nearby bar and slumped into a chair shaded by a large red umbrella.

It was hot; he felt sweat forming on the back of his head and start to trickle towards his shoulders. The place was virtually empty and in an instant the waiter was at his side.

Cámara paused. A beer? Brandy? For some reason his

usual choices had no appeal. Sensing the waiter's patience running out, he ordered a bottle of fizzy water, something he never drank. But at least, he tried to convince himself, it might help cool him down. Why was he sitting outside in the first place? Why not go inside and enjoy the soothing embrace of the air conditioning?

With his left hand he placed his phone on the table, staring at it. That was why. He was waiting for the damned thing to ring, or bleep, or make some signal or other. At least acknowledgement by Carlos that he had received the message. He had baited the line with a promise of more information. How could Carlos resist?

And yet something within him knew that Carlos would not be calling. Not today, and perhaps not tomorrow either. In fact the horizon looked empty of any more contact at all with Carlos.

Why?

Because he had only ever been a one-shot. Carlos had needed him for one task only. After that, Cámara was a mere spent casing for him, of no more use, to be discarded.

And what had Carlos needed him for?

To arrest Terreros.

Terreros was in custody. That was enough for Carlos.

He let the thought settle for a moment. Yes, that was right. Carlos had given him enough to get to Terreros and to bring him in. But would give him no more.

But why? Why bring him only so far? It made no sense.

Oyen las voces y no las razones. They hear the voices but not their reasoning. The proverb popping into his head was correct. But what was he not hearing? He was seeing only a small part of the puzzle. What was missing?

He glanced at the phone again. It would never ring. Not

from Carlos. He knew that now, but he left it there all the same, willing it to do something.

The sound of laughter from behind distracted him for a second. He turned his head and caught sight of a small group of people walking up the street: three women. They looked relaxed, happy, enjoying themselves. The women on either side were smiling, listening to the middle one as she talked, spinning out some amusing anecdote. Two of the women were unknown to him, but the third, walking on the left side, was Alicia. His Alicia.

There was a brightness in her eyes, something he had not seen for a long time. And a grin across her face. She was out, having fun, cocooned.

He twitched, ready to stand up and call her name. But instead he relented and fell back into his chair. Better that she did not see him; he wanted to watch, to observe her.

The group walked closer, sauntering slowly along the pedestrianised street. When they came abreast of him, Alicia glanced in the opposite direction from Cámara, her attention momentarily focused on something on the other side.

He barely breathed, his eyes fixed on her. In an instant they had gone past him and he watched their backs as they carried on up the road. The woman in the middle made another joke, and the three of them broke into laughter again, placing their arms around each other.

It took a few seconds for Cámara to realise that the water had been placed on the table. He picked up the bill, left the correct money on the metal saucer, stood up and walked away, leaving the bottle unopened.

THIRTY-SIX

He had control over his urination. The valve in his urethra had been undamaged by the bullet, and so he could hold on or pass water like any other person.

But they did not know that.

At night-time he was provided with a nappy, which he wore to keep up pretences. But during the day the key to his cell clunked open every half-hour to let him out and visit the toilet. For the first few hours they had changed the guard detailed with this unusual task every three or four visits, but today the same man – called Mata – had been coming to his door, swinging it open and escorting him the few metres through the cells to the primitive bathroom at the end of the corridor. Mata was a big and simple-looking man. Doubtless the others had persuaded him to take on this duty for his entire shift. But he was young – probably no more that twenty-five years old – and did not appear to mind too much:

it helped to relieve some of the boredom of being on cell-block duty.

'Hello again,' Mata chirped as he twisted the key for the tenth time.

Terreros got up and stood squarely in the centre of his cell.

'Thank you, Mata,' he said, and stepped out into the corridor.

There were other men in some of the cells; Terreros had calculated that there were three others apart from himself. They were practically invisible as he walked past, however: the bars over the doors were thick, leaving only thin gaps to peer through inside, making it practically impossible to see anything or anyone unless he deliberately stopped to check. But no matter; they were locked up, could do no harm.

Mata fell into his wake as they ambled slowly along, the routine now well established between them: opening his cell, the short trip to the bathroom door – a total of sixteen paces. There Terreros would stop and Mata would lean in from behind to open it for him, sliding the bolt and turning another key. Terreros then stepped inside and Mata would close the door behind him. The first few times he had slid the bolt shut and turned the key as well – the regulation belt-and-braces approach. But Terreros noticed that the last three times he had forgone the lock, merely sliding the bolt across on its own.

Once inside, he would consciously open and close the door of one of the toilet cubicles, making sure that he made enough noise for Mata to hear him. Usually he did not need to pee, and would stretch a little, limbering his arms and shoulders, keeping them as loose as possible. Then he would flush the toilet, wash his hands, perhaps splash his face with water, dry himself, and knock on the door that he was ready to come out.

This time, however, he really did need to urinate. Not wanting to touch the toilet seat with his hands, he flipped it down with his foot, undid his belt, lowered his trousers and squatted. The tiny opening just in front of his anus had acted perfectly well for the past twenty years, the only real disadvantage being that he could not piss standing up any more; he had tried once, but it merely trickled down his leg.

The doctors had talked about the possibility of reconstructive surgery. There was nothing left of his genitals to recover or rebuild, but they could take some flesh from his forearm, they said, and do something with that. With an implant he could even achieve some kind of erection. Many men had gone down that route, they assured him, and lived full and satisfying lives.

And he had laughed at them. At them and their pathetic euphemisms. They could not understand when he refused. Stitch him up, close the wound, make a new hole for bodily functions and he would live with that.

They had insisted: new methods had been developed, they could do incredible things nowadays. But he wanted nothing to do with any of it.

How could they understand? Weak men, with only thoughts of comfort, of 'well-being' in their minds. What use was 'quality of life' if you were already dead? And although they healed the sick, held back physical mortality for so many, he saw them all as dead. Dead in a real, spiritual sense. God himself, he knew, had sent that bullet for him, had cleansed him, purified him through his sacred wound. He did not need to spend his days in an endless quest to satiate lust and desire. The sin of Adam had been erased from him, blotted out. His mutilation was his salvation. How could anyone else possibly understand?

He folded a piece of toilet paper and dabbed his groin dry before standing and hitching up his trousers.

Of course, total purity was impossible to achieve in this world. Only Christ himself was capable of that, and so his occasional visits to Sandrita in Ceuta were necessary, justified, logical. They cleansed him once again, made new his purity, kept him focused. And besides, that stage was finished now. He could forget her; he would not be seeing her again. The new phase had begun.

There was only cold water in the taps. He turned them both on and buried his hands in the stream circling in the basin, looking at his scratchy reflection in the polished metal mirror. The details were unclear, but he knew his own face well, his light brown eyes flecked with small spots of black and yellow.

He stared back, trying to observe himself as though looking at another person. He liked his eyes; they had a decisiveness about them. Action and intelligence.

He turned off the taps and leaned over to hit the button on the dryer on the wall. For a few seconds hot air blasted down on his limp, dripping hands. He finished them off on the sides of his trousers and walked back to the door, rapping on it sharply with the knuckle of his middle finger.

The bolt slid back and the policeman stood before him with a curt nod.

'All right there?'

Terreros stepped out into the corridor, ready to march back to his cell.

'Thank you, Mata,' he said.

THIRTY-SEVEN

There were scuff marks on the floor, the air conditioning rattled loudly and the polyester sheets had ancient cigarette burns in them at the corners. The Pensión Francia was not luxurious, but it was central – just off the Plaza del Ayuntamiento – relatively inexpensive and more importantly had a single room free with an ensuite bathroom. Although that was 'bathroom' in the broadest sense of the term: a sink, toilet and shower basin so small he could barely move in it. Still, it was enough; he could live with it for a while.

He had sworn at the shaking air vent during the night, but he knew that the real reason he had slept so badly was the slow creeping acid corroding his mind, so that by the early hours his body had started jerking in wrought, angry spasms.

Over twenty-four hours, now, of separation. She needed time alone, she said, away from him. And although the idea had cut into him deeply, he had accepted it. Not least because he reasoned that by giving her what she wanted he would have a greater chance of her coming back to him eventually.

But she had appeared so happy, so contented in the street with her friends. So easy and comfortable in herself. Without him. As though a weight had been lifted. She was not suffering without him as he was without her. She was glowing.

A broken, restless shadow of sleep had only come shortly before dawn. Now it was eight o'clock and his eyes opened wide through some will of their own. After five minutes he gave up trying to force them shut and lifted himself from the bed.

His phone was on the table on the other side of the room. His only thought was to give her a ring. Just to say hello, that he missed her. That he loved her. She had asked him not to get in touch, that the only way this would work would be by their having a complete break from each other. And he understood. Yet still he wanted to call. She might like it – a romantic gesture. How could she not?

The knot tightened harder within him.

Have a shower first. At least wake properly before picking up the phone. And in the meantime he could work out exactly what he was going to say. It would be important to get the words right. And it still gave him a chance to change his mind about doing it in the first place. It could work, or it could fuck things up. Even more. Call, or no call? It was barely even a question any more, so confused was his thinking.

He turned on the water and stepped into the shower, steadying himself against the wall, feeling the cool torrent cascade over this shoulders. Soon the clear waters around his feet were joined by the yellow stream of piss as he relaxed his bladder. It was a natural disinfectant, he told himself, calming his guilt as it popped up among the many shouting voices. In a place as grotty as this he should probably have urinated into the shower *before* stepping into it.

Droplets fell from his scalp, through the hair above his forehead and into his eyes before trickling down his cheeks and into his mouth. They tasted salty.

He indulged himself for a few minutes, changing the temperature from hot to cold and back again several times. A poor man's sauna, he liked to think of it as. It helped him to relax a little, a pause, a parenthesis.

Finally, he turned off the taps, slid the plastic panel open and reached for the towel. Inside the room, his phone was ringing.

He slid on wet feet as he jumped out and ran to pick it up. Alicia. He knew it was Alicia. She had had a change of heart. She wanted him back. Everything was going to be all right.

He pressed the button and lifted it to his ear.

'Hello?'

His neck throbbed with a heavy pulse.

'Cámara.' It was a male voice. 'This is Carlos.'

'Carlos?'

'Where the hell are you?'

'I'm . . .' he began. A pool of water was forming beneath him. 'What's going on?'

'Meet me in five minutes at the usual place.'

He registered something in Carlos's voice that he had not heard before: excitement.

'Terreros has escaped from custody,' said Carlos. 'He's on the run.'

THIRTY-EIGHT

Carlos was standing by the main entrance to the cathedral and started strolling away across the square before Cámara reached him. Catch up with me, his body language said. We need to talk away from the main crowd.

Cámara was still trying to call Torres, to find out what he knew, but his number was engaged. He gave up in frustration, put his phone in his pocket and fell in step with Carlos. The *CNI* agent immediately began to speak in a low yet audible voice.

'You managed to get through to anyone?' he asked.

'No,' said Cámara. 'What's going on?'

'It seems that Terreros had help,' he said. 'One of your own. A man named Mata.'

Cámara shook his head: he had never heard of him.

'He was on guard duty down in the cells,' continued Carlos. 'They got friendly. Mata knocked the other guard out cold, then escorted Terreros out to a squad car and drove him away.'

'When did this happen?'

The drama of the situation fuelled Cámara's concentration, sparking him into life: the sleepless night, the angst over Alicia, were gone.

Carlos looked at his watch: it was just after half-past eight.

'Almost two hours ago. But the alarm has only just been raised.'

'I need to get back to the Jefatura.'

This was his case, his suspect. The fact that Terreros had – unbelievably – managed to break out was his concern. He could not remember anyone ever escaping from the police cells. It might even be the first time. The serious crime that his two-man squad was investigating had suddenly become even more serious.

Carlos did not look at him, keeping his eyes ahead as they strolled round towards the side of the cathedral and the archbishop's palace, but now he stopped and stared Cámara in the face.

'No,' he said. Then paused. 'At least not just yet.' A sigh.

'There are things I need to tell you first.'

He started pacing again; Cámara followed. And listened.

'What I'm about to say is top secret,' said Carlos. 'It wasn't necessary for you to know it before, but I believe it is now. And I'm sticking my neck out by telling you, but this isn't a moment for going by the book. We're in a full-scale emergency. And we need you.'

Cámara adjusted his pace so that it mirrored Carlos's exactly, his hands behind his back, just like the spy's.

Carlos took a breath, then continued.

'You'll have guessed by now that Terreros's Veteran Legionarios' Welfare Association was a front for something else. He's concerned about his former comrades all right, but not exactly about protecting their pension rights. Or rather, some of what he does involves that, but behind it there's another secret operation running in parallel.'

He paused as a couple of schoolgirls with bright rucksacks on their backs skipped past on their way to the first class of the morning.

'We know that over the years Terreros has built up a network of ex-*legionarios*,' said Carlos. 'He's running a private secret service, if you like. Paid for by money from Segarra, who's secretly far more right-wing than he publicly lets on. Espionage, security . . .' He sucked on his teeth. 'And sabotage, almost certainly.'

'Terrorism,' said Cámara.

'This isn't the time to start arguing over nomenclature.' Until now Carlos's voice had been low, almost gentle. But for a second he lost his calm. 'You know exactly what I'm talking about.'

At the archbishop's palace they swung left, gravitating towards the quieter side streets where there was less chance of being overheard. Cámara was aware of Carlos breathing deeply, trying to compose himself. And curiously it made him feel calmer by comparison: the *CNI* man seemed disturbed.

'You think Terreros is dangerous,' he said.

'We have to work on that assumption,' said Carlos.

'This network . . .'

'We know little about it.' Carlos laughed drily. 'All we know for certain is that is exists and Terreros is at its head. But we don't know who else is involved, how many operatives he has or what he's planning. Only that he is planning something. And given who he is, his background and a disturbing lack of concern for human suffering, our fears could not be greater.'

'Segarra was involved,' said Cámara. 'Possibly still is.'

'Correct.' Carlos nodded. 'But our information is that he was a paymaster, nothing more. He can't tell us anything.'

The implication was clear: the *CNI* had been monitoring Segarra, probably for some time.

'Alarm bells have been ringing about Terreros for several years,' Carlos continued. 'And we've been trying to get a handle on his organisation, shed light on it in some way. But so far we haven't come up with very much. My superiors would kill me if they could hear me telling you this, but right now I think it's only best if we get things out into the open. There'll be time for finger-pointing and recriminations later.'

'I'm assuming,' said Cámara, 'that his agenda is . . .' He left the sentence for Carlos to finish.

'Terreros is a conservative churchgoer. Unmarried. The Legión is his family. He believes in everything that it stands for – tradition, old-fashioned values, the unity of the Spanish State. You get the picture.'

'So why are you trying to stop him?' asked Cámara. 'Are you trying to tell me these aren't the same ideas that the current government – your superiors – espouse?'

'You're not an idiot, Cámara,' Carlos spat. 'Don't act like one. These things are more complex. Terreros is a loose cannon. We had him under virtual house arrest down in Ceuta. We could control him there. But now he's on the mainland and he's on the run.'

'Do you have any idea where he might be?' said Cámara.

'As you say, best to get everything out in the open. And if I'm going to have a chance of catching him—'

'Five minutes before I called you,' said Carlos, 'I got a message saying the squad car Terreros escaped in had been found north of the city, in Saplaya. You'll find all this out when you get back to the Jefatura. Not least because Mata's body was inside it.'

Cámara's breath caught in his throat.

'He'd been shot in the head,' said Carlos.

They stopped. Cámara coughed and put his hand against a wall.

'Be in no doubt as to how dangerous Terreros is,' said Carlos, glancing to the sides to see if anyone was around before continuing. 'Or how dangerous the situation is.'

Cámara took a breath before they carried on walking.

'Saplaya,' he said. 'Switch cars . . .'

'Get rid of Mata – possibly there was another accomplice there.'

'Someone had to leave a car there for him at least,' said Cámara.

'Exactly.'

'And then . . .' Cámara paused. 'Carry on driving north.'

'It makes sense,' said Carlos.

'To Catalonia.'

'That is our working assumption.' Carlos's face was a picture of tightly controlled emotion. 'Is it falling into place for you now?' he said.

'He's going to—' Cámara started.

'I'm going to share something else with you,' Carlos interrupted him. 'Something I shouldn't but which is necessary given the circumstances.'

Cámara was silent.

'Our understanding,' said Carlos, 'is that the *govern*, the Catalan regional government, is planning a unilateral declaration of independence. The assassination of Segundo Pont has changed the political landscape. There has been a lurch away from his more moderate position. The radicals are in full control now, and they want to seize their opportunity.'

'I've heard talk,' said Cámara.

'Yes, well, the rumours are true. It's totally unconstitutional, of course, but the Catalans are intent on forcing the agenda. Tensions with Madrid have never been higher. And I'm choosing my words carefully.'

'How long till they make their move?' Cámara asked.

'No one can say.'

'And Terreros . . .'

'Terreros,' said Carlos, 'who would rather die than see this country break apart, is almost certainly, as we speak, arriving in Catalonia with a plan of some sort under his arm.'

'A plan for . . . sabotage?' said Cámara.

Terreros suddenly reached out and gripped him by the shoulder.

'You understand now how serious things are?' he said. 'My suggestion – and it is only a suggestion. I'm not giving you orders here, nor am I in a position to – but my suggestion is that you get up to Catalonia quickly. Today. And you do whatever you have to do to find Terreros. And you can count on me. I'll give you whatever you need.'

'The *Mossos d'Esquadra*,' said Cámara. 'Why not use them? It's their territory.'

'Terreros is your suspect,' said Carlos. 'And right now the *Mossos* have got more things on their mind. They're still hunting Segundo Pont's murderers and worried about whose side they'll be on when things get rough in Catalonia. Because believe me, that moment is coming.'

Carlos squeezed his shoulder harder.

'It's you, Cámara,' he said. 'It has to be you.'

Cámara closed his eyes and nodded.

'All right,' he said.

'Good.' Carlos let his arm drop. He looked ready to leave.

For the first time, Cámara became properly aware of where they were, just off the Plaza de Nápoles y Sicilia. He sniffed.

'About here,' he said in a low voice.

'What's that?' asked Carlos.

Cámara swallowed.

'It was about here, we reckon,' he said. 'Where little Fermín was attacked . . . and murdered.'

He nodded at a couple of large rubbish containers.

'Possibly behind there.'

Carlos put his hands in his pockets and leaned in towards him.

'If you don't stop Terreros,' he said, 'Fermín's death is going to look like a drop in a large and very bloody ocean.'

THIRTY-NINE

El Uno: Everything has gone to plan. Presently at Base 2.

El Dos: Understood. Is your position safe?

Uno: El Siete is with me. We eliminated the guard. Everything under control. What is your position?

Dos: As arranged. Everything is in place.

Uno: Good. The accomplice?

Dos: He's ready.

Uno: There can't be any mistakes. Not like last time.

Dos: There won't be.

Uno: Follow the plan to the letter. No improvising. That's an order.

Dos: Yes, sir. What about the detective, sir?

Uno: You don't need to worry about him.

Dos: Understood.

Uno: And relax. Suggest you get some R&R while you still can. I need you sharp and rested on the day.

Dos: Yes, sir.

Uno: But with moderation. The declaration is imminent. Essential you act immediately BEFORE. Will communicate as intelligence comes in regarding timings.

Dos: Understood.

Uno: For the time being, as of now consider this the green light for the final phase.

Dos: Yes, sir.

Uno: You have my blessing.

FORTY

He had not expected to be back so soon.

It was almost ten o'clock by the time he got to Barcelona. The taxi dropped him on a tree-lined street in the Baix Guinardó district, a few blocks up from the Sagrada Familia, Gaudí's strange and soaring landmark basilica. He paid, lifted his bags out from the boot of the car and stepped across to a pool of lamplight at the entrance to an uninspiring grey building with tiny windows. It felt like a prison.

Sotsinspector Ripoll kept him waiting at reception for over twenty minutes before finally appearing. The *Mossos* liaison officer was in full uniform, his cap pressed firmly over his head and shading his eyes from the harsh lighting above.

'Cámara?' he asked, looking down at the seated figure staring out through the glass doors back towards the street.

Cámara stood up.

'Chief Inspector Cámara,' he said, 'of the Valencia Special Crimes Unit.'

Ripoll turned on his heel.

'Follow me.'

Cámara had been relieved when the *Mossos d'Esquadra* station on Carrer de la Marina had accepted his request for temporary assistance. It was large and had the resources he would need, but was distant enough from the central *comissaria*, where, thanks to the inquiry into the death of Ignacio Rovira and his questioning of the assumed innocence of the *Mossos* policemen responsible for his death, Cámara already had a reputation. Back in Valencia, it had seemed the sensible option. Not that sensible options were his forte, but he knew how much damage uncooperative colleagues could do to an investigation.

Now that he was in Barcelona, however, he was having his doubts.

Ripoll carried on walking without a word down a long corridor. At the bottom, he opened a door on the right, holding it open for Cámara to see in.

'Your office,' he said in a flat voice.

Cámara had seen prison cells with more space. A desk was pushed into a corner with a phone and an antediluvian computer so large and heavy it seemed the table might break under its weight. A chair was squeezed in underneath, hemmed in by a short cot bed running the length of the other wall. There was no window and no desk lamp: only a single fluorescent tube suspended from the ceiling.

'The computer's hooked up to the network,' said Ripoll. 'You'll find everything you need there.'

Cámara raised a solitary eyebrow before speaking.

'Thank you,' he said.

So much for his sensible option: it was clear – from Ripoll's body language to the shithole of a visitor's office they had assigned him – that his reputation had spread here as well. Cámara the doubter, Cámara the traitor. He wondered for a moment if he had a single friend in Barcelona.

'All of this could, of course, have waited until tomorrow,' said Ripoll. 'But your boss, Pardo, rang my boss and insisted. So this is all we've got. At this time of night.'

'I see.'

Ripoll looked at him with a mixture of annoyance and amusement, as though he were some strange, unpleasant creature.

'But you obviously decided it was important to come up and start things yourself.'

'That's right,' said Cámara.

'Straight away. Must be embarrassing losing a prisoner like that. I can only imagine.'

Cámara took a step into the room, placing his bags carefully on the small free patch of floor at the side of the bed.

'I'll need to speak with the head of your murder squad,' he said.

'You can,' said Ripoll. 'In the morning. No one's around at the moment.'

Cámara took a step closer towards him.

'I need to impress on you how dangerous the man I'm seeking is. I need and expect full cooperation. Is that clear, *Sotsinspector*?'

Ripoll shook his head.

'You see, that's the thing,' he said. 'What goes around comes around. And we know exactly who you are, Chief Inspector Cámara. So you can expect cooperation from the *Mossos* during your stay here. Just the same amount of cooperation that you yourself showed only a few weeks ago.'

He turned and walked back up the corridor.

'Goodnight,' he said. 'You'll find the bathroom on the other side of the incident room through the double doors on your left.'

His footsteps echoed for a few seconds in the empty police station, before silence fell.

Cámara rubbed his face, checked the office once more, then stepped out and pushed through into the incident room. It was empty apart from a group of four officers sitting at a group of tables near the entrance. They glanced up at him as he walked through, stopping their conversation, and watched as he paced across.

There, scattered on a couple of desks, was the newspaper front page that he had seen on the train heading up, the story that everyone had been talking about all day.

He opened the bathroom door and stepped inside. The cubicles were empty: he was alone. He turned on the tap and put his hands in the water, not wanting to look at himself in the mirror. Torres's last words as he had left Valencia rang in his ears.

'Stay here,' he said. 'You can do as much from here as in Barcelona. There's no love lost for you there. You'll only slow yourself down.'

And he had not listened, insisting that it was the right thing to do.

'And now with this,' Torres had tried one last time. 'They're thinking about other things. No one's going to be interested in a detective from Valencia with a missing prisoner.'

This. It had made them all nervous. The oft-repeated official line was that the armed forces had accepted democracy in Spain. But every year or so signs that a hard authoritarian streak was still alive among the top brass managed to slip out: perhaps a favourable reference to José Antonio Primo de Rivera, the founder of the Falangist party, or some hint at the 'sacredness' of the unity of the country. In the past these comments had usually come from officials low enough for the semblance of normality not to be disturbed – from an elderly colonel or a spokesman for a military organisation. The day before, however, the chief of the defence staff, speaking at a medal ceremony, had referred to Franco as a 'great Spaniard', quoting the former dictator at length and his views about 'National Unity' and 'work' being the best expression of 'popular will'. Franco had made the comments as part of his justification for a totalitarian state.

It was the clearest hint yet that members of the armed forces were contemplating taking action in the face of Catalan – and increasingly Basque as well – moves to break away. A look of deep concern marked everyone's faces: memories of the attempted military coup in 1981 were still alive. They had tried it before; they could try it again. And after the European Union had proved so spineless in Ukraine no one could pretend that Brussels – or anyone else these days – would step in to prevent such an outcome. From the Middle East to the former Soviet Bloc, the old ways were returning: no one wanted to get involved any more. Why should they bother if things blew up on the fringes of Europe?

Cámara tried to imagine the conversation among the officers inside the incident room. Were they already taking sides? Where would the Catalan police stand if the military did get involved?

He did not want to think about it. All he could do was find Terreros as quickly as possible. Before it was too late.

He finished in the bathroom and walked back past the police officers, not looking at them as he pushed through the double doors and into the corridor. The tiny office was on his right. He could go in, settle down, get the computer going and start searching for signs of Terreros. Or he could go out, get some fresh air, perhaps even find a bar for a drink somewhere. Not that this residential quarter of the city seemed the kind of place where that would be easy.

He made sure that the man on reception saw him before stepping out into the night air. He turned left and started meandering along the grid-pattern streets. The place looked deserted, but it would be good to stretch his legs at least.

Terreros. For some reason he knew that searching the *Mossos* records would lead him nowhere. At least not tonight. Something about the *legionario* colonel had been bothering him ever since Carlos had told him that morning about his escape. And it was not so much that he had somehow managed to get clean away from the Jefatura, but about the manner of his arrest in the first place.

Who the hell wrote a threatening letter by hand? And then tried to escape to Morocco? Yes, he had made a good show of it – not least buying the djellaba. But then trying to swim? And the smile on his face when Cámara had caught up with him. Cámara had assumed it was because at that moment Terreros thought he had managed to escape, had crossed the border to the other side. But now he began to wonder. It was almost as if . . . Really? Was he really entertaining this thought? Almost as if Terreros had wanted to be arrested in the first place. Had even orchestrated things to turn out this way.

What had Carlos said? That Terreros was under virtual house arrest in Ceuta. They could control him there. But now he was loose on the mainland. He was free, and far more dangerous. And Cámara himself had helped bring him here, performing his role in what began to feel like a much bigger play.

He stopped in his tracks. This entire time he had been pulled along by the nose, like a donkey being shunted around. What game, exactly, was being played here? And who was playing it?

For a moment he felt as though he were close to grasping the truth, as though a clarity hovered around him, just beyond his reach. But as quickly as the sensation came, it disappeared again.

He was alone, on a dark, unknown street, surrounded by the closed doors of shops and banks and blocks of flats. There was nothing there for him: nowhere for him to go.

He thought of Torres again. Perhaps he should have stayed in Valencia. He felt as though he had abandoned his colleague and friend. But Carlos had got between them, telling him to come to Barcelona, and Cámara had obeyed, his limbs twitching into life like a puppet on a string.

He could not stay, but neither could he bring Torres with him. Common sense said that he had to keep his connection with Carlos secret. And it had suggested a *comissaria* away from the central police hub. Now common sense dictated that he go back to his tiny office and start trawling for signs of Terreros in Catalonia, hunting for a lead of some kind.

But common sense – and the words of others – had got him nowhere. He had never been in control from the start.

He had made mistakes – he could see that clearly now. But it was not too late. He could still fix things. It was time he became who he was, to do things the Cámara way.

He picked up his phone to make a call, but the phone itself seemed to be one step ahead of him. It vibrated in his hand, indicating that he had a new message.

He looked at the screen: it was from Dídac.

FORTY-ONE

'Come on. Let's go for a drink.'

They crossed the Ramblas, away from the Barri Gòtic and towards the Raval area, down dark narrow side streets. On a wall, painted with red spray-paint, was scrawled the word '*màrtir*'.

'That's where Segundo Pont was shot dead,' said Daniel simply as they stepped past. Dídac glanced anxiously at the spot, a sense of dread swirling in his belly. Were those blood spots he could see on the ground? Was there some ghost, some spirit of the awful event, still lingering here? It was as if he could feel it, and the hairs pricked up on the back of his neck.

'Do – does anyone know who did it?' he asked. 'Do you know? Does Ximo know? Was Ximo involved?'

He had barely seen Sònia's father over the past days, but for an instant it was as if he could see him here, gun in hand, driven by intense political rage. Segundo Pont was a stooge, he had overheard him say once at the flat. Catalonia was better off without him.

Daniel carried on walking, not looking across. Dídac understood: no more questions. But he was certain that his father knew.

After another couple of blocks they turned right into a tight alleyway before sidling up to a bar. A couple of large wine barrels had been placed by the door on the pavement and were being used as tables by smokers. Daniel pushed past and made his way to the front, Dídac following close behind.

'What do you want? Lemonade?' asked Daniel.

'No,' said Dídac. 'I'll have a beer.'

Daniel sniggered, then turned to the barman and ordered two *tercios* of lager. The bottles were handed over and he passed one to his son.

'So,' he said. 'Now you're no longer a virgin you're going to start drinking like a man.'

'I wasn't a virgin,' said Dídac.

'OK. Whatever you say.' But Daniel did not believe him.

They walked over to a corner of the bar near the door, standing by a high table recently vacated by a young couple.

'Have you been here before?' Dídac asked. Daniel shrugged.

'These places are all the same,' he said. 'You get a drink, you stand around, then you go. Perhaps somewhere else. Perhaps not.'

Dídac watched as Daniel lifted the beer bottle to drink, holding it near the top between his forefinger and middle finger with delicate, practised ease. And nonchalantly, not wanting to give himself away, he gently slipped his own hand up from the base of his bottle to the neck, trying to arrange his fingers in the same manner. It was difficult: the fresh cool glass sweated in the evening heat.

Daniel stood silently, watching the people in the bar, but he looked fidgety. It's my fault, Dídac thought to himself. I should think of something to say, start a conversation. But nothing came to mind. Sònia? Daniel would mock him. Their preparations? Perhaps. Daniel only really engaged with him when they were working on their new plans. Whatever those plans might be. He still had no idea. There had been a change in Daniel – he seemed harder, tenser even, but the past weeks and days had been among the best he had ever spent with him, learning, training, getting ready for the big action that was doubtless about to come. It was the only time he had felt – fleetingly – that he existed for his father in any real sense. Coming to Barcelona had been the best thing in his life.

He tightened his fingers around the bottleneck, squeezing as hard as he could. Then he checked how Daniel held it. Yes, that was right. Time to give it a go. He still had not drunk anything and the beer would be getting warm soon.

He lifted it to his mouth; the wet bottle squirmed rebelliously between his fingers, but just in time he managed to wedge it against his lips. As he lifted it, the stream of fizzy liquid began to pour into his mouth. He had done it; it was not so difficult after all.

But in congratulating himself on his skilful handling of the bottle, he forgot to swallow. A trickle caught in the back of his throat. He coughed uncontrollably: the beer flew out of his mouth and splattered over Daniel's face; the bottle slipped out of Dídac's fingers and smashed over the hard tiled floor.

Dídac held a hand to his chest, his face turning red as he tried unsuccessfully to dislodge the unwanted moisture in his windpipe. Before he knew what was happening, Daniel had pulled him out of the bar and outside into the street. Holding him from behind, he wrapped his arms around his midriff and squeezed tightly with a hard jerk. Dídac felt the air forced from his lungs, and the beer stuck in his throat was finally expelled with a splutter, dribbling down his chin and falling on the floor near his feet. His eyes were watering and he felt perspiration on his scalp.

Some of the smokers looked on, but turned away when they saw that he was all right. The older, tough-looking guy with the kid seemed to have sorted him out. Inside the bar, a girl had fetched a mop and was doing her best to clean up the spilt beer and broken glass.

Bent double, with his hands on his knees, Dídac was trying to catch his breath, but Daniel looped an arm under his shoulder and pulled him along.

'Come on,' he said. 'You're making a scene.'

Once they got around a corner, out of sight, Daniel threw Dídac against a wall, pressing his hand hard against his throat.

'I should have fucking left you there to die,' he said. 'You fucking piece of shit.'

His grip tightened. Dídac felt the veins thud in his neck and his head as he struggled – less against his father's sudden stranglehold on him and more to understand what was going on.

'S-sorry,' he gasped, barely able to speak.

But Daniel leaned in harder, pressing his weight into Dídac's arm, holding it straight as he pushed.

Dídac saw Daniel's eyes boring into him, black pools of anger. Then bright flashing stars of purple and red.

And nothing.

It was still dark when he woke. He had the sense of returning – from what, he could not say. But it was as if for a moment he had stepped outside of time and back into it. A second, or perhaps hours, could have passed. He was alone, but around the corner he could hear the voices of people still drinking outside at the bar.

Gingerly, he got to his feet and patted himself down, as though needing to feel his own body again, to re-enter and engage with it once more. His throat ached horribly, ascending to a sharp, almost unbearable pain when he swallowed.

The tears came uncontrollably and his stomach spasmed in deep sobs. He needed to leave that place: the street was quiet, but someone sooner or later would start to get curious about the young man with dreadlocks crying on the edge of the pavement.

He wiped his face clean on his sleeve and started to stagger back in the direction of the Ramblas and the Barri Gòtic: there was nowhere else for him to go.

At number 2 he pushed the door open and started to climb the narrow steps, glancing up through the centre of the staircase towards the top floor. It felt like a mountain to climb. And what if Daniel were there? He dreaded the thought, yet hoped desperately to find him.

The key refused to go into the lock for a few seconds, before finally he held it steady with two hands and forced it in. He twisted, pushed the door open and stepped inside.

Silence. No sign of Daniel. Or Ximo. There was one person who he could turn to, however, and the light shining under Sònia's door told him that refuge was only a few metres away. She would understand; she would listen. He needed her now. He loved her. And from the way she had touched him he knew that she loved him too.

He stepped across to her bedroom door and stretched his hand out to push it open, sighing with relief.

Sònia's eyes were closed, but now, as he stepped noisily inside, they snapped open. She was lying in bed, on her back, the sheet loosely covering her. And next to her, with his sleeping head resting on her breast, was the young man with the goatee who had been coming down the stairs the day he had arrived at Ximo's flat.

'Oh,' she said, registering Dídac standing there. 'It's you, Valencia Boy. What do you want?'

He was unable to breathe, as though his very life force were caught in his chest. And his throat began to pound; the feeling of Daniel's hand pressing hard against it, strangling him, sparked back into life.

'Well?' said Sònia. The man lying at her side was stirring now, rubbing his eyes open. And without lifting his head, he stared at Dídac. And grinned.

'I—' Dídac tried to speak. Sònia shook her head at him.

'Look, just fuck off, Dídac,' she said. 'You're weirding me out. Fuck off. Get out of my room.'

He took a step backwards, feeling for the wall, stumbling as he turned to leave. Closing the door behind him, he could hear the other two laughing inside.

His feet barely touched the ground as he sped down the staircase, his own weight pulling him out through the door and back on to the street.

In a nearby alleyway, dark and greasy, the stone doorway of a gloomy building embraced him and he huddled in its corner, arms pulled tightly around his knees.

Wrapped in a blanket of festering, treacherous night, he felt there was only one star shining for him. Faint at first, but as his mind churned it grew stronger for a moment. One person out there, someone he might just be able to turn to now.

He could trust him.

Could he trust him?

He could trust no one.

But there was no one else.

He felt in his pocket for his phone. Should he call? No. Just a text message would do.

He tapped out a single sentence, pressed 'send', and then turned his phone off.

Right now, all he wanted, crouched in his dank corner, was to sleep, to forget.

If he was there, if he could help, Cámara would call back in the morning.

FORTY-TWO

Cámara read the message.

I need help.

He tried Dídac's number, but his call went to voice-mail.

'I'm in Barcelona,' he told the recording machine. 'Ring me when you hear this.'

And he hung up.

The message disturbed him – its brevity, and the fact that Dídac's phone now seemed to be switched off.

He opened the texting app again and stared at the words. Then his fingers began to tap out another reply.

Will be at the Bar Nuria at the top of the Ramblas tomorrow from 9 am. Come and find me there if you can. Max.

The progress bar at the top of the screen shot across, but paused before completing. After waiting what felt like an age, it finally skipped to the finishing line, and the words **Message sent** appeared in its place.

He just hoped that it had been received at the other end.

FORTY-THREE

The shopkeeper stepped over him to open up, rattling the shutters noisily. Dídac rubbed his face and crawled out of his corner, his limbs aching and cold. He steadied himself as he walked a few paces down the street, then at the end he bent double and retched, his empty stomach pushing with insistent force against his ribs. A few moments later the shopkeeper came up and handed him a plastic bottle half-filled with tap water.

'Here,' she said, and thrust it into his hand, a hopeful, uncomfortable smile on her face.

He mumbled a thank-you and drank; the cold trickled down his damaged throat, calming and soothing.

At a nearby bench he sat for a while, sipping gently. His head buzzed as though a thousand voices were shouting at once. And out of the din, bright flashing details of the night before swam in front of him. He kneaded his fingers into his hair and scalp, trying to ease the pressure inside.

After a final slug, he finished the water and tossed the bottle lazily in the direction of a dustbin a couple of metres away. It missed and fell on the floor with a light clatter. For some reason the sound reminded him of his phone: he pulled it out of his pocket and turned it on. A few seconds later it flashed that he had both a text and a voice message. His heart thudded out of sync for a beat as he wondered whether they were from Daniel, perhaps calling to see how he was, where he was. But then he remembered the desperate text he had sent to Cámara just before falling asleep. He wished now he had never written it.

Having listened to Cámara's recorded message, then reading his words, Dídac glanced at the time: it was almost nine o'clock already. In ten or fifteen minutes he could make it to the bar in the Ramblas. He stood up, his legs still slightly shaky: it would be worth going for the chance of some breakfast at least.

He started wending his way through the maze of narrow streets. The first groups of tourists were already appearing, following their guides like swarms of bees in the wake of their queen. He felt their eyes boring into him as he slunk past. They could tell, he knew, that he had slept rough, as though he gave off a peculiar smell, his wretchedness naked and exposed for all to see. If they would just stop looking at him! He tried to cut down smaller and smaller alleyways, to avoid the growing crowds, but everywhere he went the people flocked, as though it were he that they had come to see, not the guidebook monuments.

His chest tightened and he struggled to breathe, sweat clinging to his skin as he tried to walk faster, breaking out into a trot. Crossing the Plaça Nova with his head low, trying to avoid their gaze, he crashed into a waiter serving drinks at a terrace café. The tray tipped out of his hand; the glasses smashed on the ground where they fell. Just like the beer bottle of the night before. And Daniel's eyes, a violent flare within in them, drilled into his mind.

'Watch where you're fucking going!'

He hurried on, not turning back. A hand reached out to grab him, but he slipped away and broke out into a run.

A few shops had opened and people were already filling the street. For some reason he felt safer there, the world of brands and retail offering a buffer of anonymity: products for sale became the focus of attention; other human beings were invisible. At the top of the next street were the Ramblas, where they met the Plaça de Catalunya. Where Cámara would be waiting.

He checked the time: it was a quarter past nine. Already he could sense doubt and hesitation growing within him.

He stepped out into the wide avenue, pushed through the tourists and headed for the trees that lined the central area. The bar was at the far corner, where half a dozen tables were laid out in the hazy, morning-orange sunshine. And there, at the edge of them, he could see Cámara.

Dídac watched him from behind the shelter of a tree trunk: he was no more than six or seven metres away, with his back turned, but sitting at an angle so that Dídac could see his profile. Cámara was holding his phone to his ear, talking in a serious monotone. The words were unclear, but it was clearly police business. It must be. Why else would he be in the city in the first place?

His legs felt heavy, his feet as though they had been welded to the spot where he stood. He could not move, unable to step out, even to call out to the man he had sent his pathetic little SOS to the night before.

What would Daniel say if he could see him now? Perhaps he *could* see him now, was watching him the whole time.

He turned and glanced around with a sudden panic, his eyes darting from side to side. No Daniel. But that did not mean that he was not there. And would he approve if his son now reached out for help from a policeman? Cámara was their friend. Or *had* been their friend. Dídac liked him; Cámara had always been kind to him. But betrayal now stalked him like a hunter, waiting for him to make another mistake, to fall into its trap. Why would Cámara not betray him as well? He was, after all, who he was. He could either be a policeman or an anarchist. Not both. And which was he here, now, sitting at this bar in the centre of Barcelona? Why was he even in the city in the first place?

Dídac watched as Cámara glanced at a newspaper resting on his table, then checked something on his phone. He dialled a number and brought the device to his ear again. At that same moment, the phone in Dídac's pocket broke into song. With a jerking motion, he thrust his hand down and quickly hit the silence button, feeling it vibrate for a few seconds more against his leg before Cámara gave up, and the buzzing stopped. Dídac pulled in tighter behind the tree trunk; he had not been seen, at least not by Cámara.

Sitting at his table, Cámara paused for a moment, staring out into space, seeing but not seeing. A breeze tousled his dark wavy hair, flicking a lock of it over his face, but he did not seem to notice, as though caught in some kind of trance. His shoulders relaxed and he stretched his neck upwards before letting out a long, deep sigh. A moment's pause, stillness, and then he raised his hand to catch the waiter's attention. As he opened his wallet to pay the bill, his police ID card became visible for a split second, with its national coat of arms, the badge of authority.

And repression, thought Dídac.

Instinctively he backed away, skipping to a tree further behind, then to another, watching to make sure that Cámara had not seen him.

But Cámara was walking in the other direction, quickly and with purpose, heading straight for the metro station, where he disappeared from view.

Dídac watched for a few moments, to make certain that he had gone, was not trying to trick him into showing himself. Then he spat hard on the floor and walked away.

Half an hour later, after some rapid and efficient shop-lifting, he stood in a narrow pedestrian street in front of the large glass window of an antique shop. From his pocket he pulled out his newly acquired scissors and with little ceremony began to cut off his dreadlocks one by one, watching their reflection as they fell to his feet. When they were all gone, he rubbed his scalp, feeling the short bristles of his new hair brushing against his palms. He felt lighter, quicker, more invisible already.

He let the scissors fall to the ground and began to take off his clothes, oblivious to the passers-by staring curiously at him. A couple of Japanese youngsters took photos as he undressed, imagining him to be a street artist of some kind. When he was wearing nothing but his underpants, he pulled out the dark grey trousers and white shirt that he had stolen a few minutes before and put them on, buttoning the shirt to the top. His bruised throat rebelled against the pressure, but he embraced the pain: the choking sensation made him feel alive.

Checking himself one last time in the window, he

stroked his hands over his new self, feeling it, absorbing it. Then he turned and walked, barefoot, along the street.

Behind him his old clothes and hair lay in a discarded heap, like a pile of shit.

FORTY-FOUR

Dídac was acting strangely.

Cámara saw him from across the Ramblas as he ambled closer, slowly making his way over. But his body language was different; he seemed to be in pain, his shoulders stiff, his walk slightly disjointed, as though he were uncomfortable within himself. And Cámara could just make out the darker hue of the skin around his throat, curling around in a ring almost from ear to ear. He had been attacked, but if he was coming to Cámara for help, there was also a fear there, as though he did not want to be seen.

Cámara sensed the boy's nervousness and shifted his chair to look the other way; let him come of his own accord, in his own time.

From the reflection in the window of the bar, he could catch glimpses of Dídac scampering behind, jumping from tree to tree as he came closer before stopping, just a few metres away. And then waiting, watching, peering out from behind the trunk as though it were the most natural thing to do in the world. Some passers-by glanced at him curiously before moving on: he looked like an actor; perhaps someone was filming him.

And so Cámara sat passively, staring out into space, his senses awake for any sign that Dídac might come out of his hideout and finally approach him. But the minutes ground on and there was no movement. He began to wonder about turning around, about calling out, letting him know that he knew he was there, but decided against it. As a compromise, he picked up his phone and called Dídac's number. From behind, he heard the trill as it rang once before being killed. Dídac must have hit the silence button.

Cámara closed his eyes for a moment. Dídac was not the only thing on his mind: an article in the newspaper on the table in front of him had stirred something in him. It was a free rag, of the kind that people rarely scanned for more than a few seconds between stops on the bus or metro, and it was already lying on the table when he sat down. He had glanced at it in the usual perfunctory fashion, but one of the articles had caught his eye: an opinion piece on the Catholic Church in Catalonia. Archbishop Forner of Barcelona had now been made a cardinal in Rome and was returning the following day to Catalonia. For weeks he had insisted that he and the other Catalan bishops should leave the Conferencia Episcopal Española – the Church's governing body within Spain – after the other bishops insisted on condemning Catalan independence moves.

There can be no doubt – said the writer – *that this step will be taken with the blessing of the Catalan regional government. The governing left-wing party, never known in the past for its piety, has paradoxically discovered a religious ardour in recent weeks owing to a shared political ideology with Forner. That the Church in Catalonia feels confident enough to contemplate a break with the rest of Spain can only mean one thing: that a unilateral declaration of independence by Barcelona is close, perhaps imminent.*

Tomorrow the ceremony welcoming our new cardinal at the Sagrada Família is taking place. Mere coincidence? I think not. As well as the religious dignitaries invited are also the entire Catalan cabinet. The president is due to make a speech. What better moment and in what better place – a symbol of Catalan national pride and a monument instantly recognisable across the entire globe – to give birth to a new (and ancient) country?

On reading the article, Cámara's initial reaction was to dismiss it as exaggerated. But sitting there, with half an eye out for Dídac, he started to wonder. A declaration of independence was a dangerous move; the sense was that it could happen soon, but as early as the very next day? Yet, as he thought it through, it made sense; better to do it when no one really expected it, or certainly before they had a prepared response. And a declaration within a church, a sacred place, one generally associated with peace . . . How would the centralists in Madrid deal with that? It would be a clever move.

The article was probably right, he thought. The question now, however, was whether Terreros thought the same.

And a comment he had heard recently came back to him, a light and delicate thought of the kind so easily missed. Something about prevention being better than reaction. He had used it himself recently. And almost forgotten where he had heard it first.

He had waited long enough. After another few moments, he called the waiter over and paid for his coffee. He stood up as slowly as he could, giving the boy a final chance to come forward. And he glanced once more at the reflection in the window: Dídac was skipping backwards, moving ever further away.

The entrance to the metro was close by. As Cámara descended on the moving stairway, he looked up at the sky and the heavy dark clouds moving in from the sea.

But it was not thoughts of politicians, declarations or churchmen that populated his mind as he was finally swallowed into the underground. It was the grinning bruise around Dídac's neck.

And the hand that he now suspected had put it there.

FORTY-FIVE

He walked without looking. Eventually one of them would hit, find its mark, and send him on his way. He felt dressed for it now. Just another body, nothing special, nothing even to say who he was. Not even wearing a pair of shoes.

And with luck, he would never be identified.

An anonymous body seeking an anonymous death.

In some corner of awareness he was conscious of swerving cars, screeching brakes, honking horns as he stepped out, eyes fixed ahead, neither seeking it nor trying to avoid it. Letting it come in its own way, in its own time. Only soon, please. Perhaps at the next street crossing.

Would it hurt? A quick, sudden descent into non-existence. Better than being only damaged, partially crushed, left destroyed but not obliterated. Ideally something big and heavy, travelling at a good speed. Like a bus, or a truck. A hard impact, full on. Close his eyes? Yes, that might work, help settle any last-minute fear or doubt. Close his eyes and he would have no idea what would be hitting him at all. Close his eyes now, and it was almost as if he were already dead.

Another kerb. His foot shot out, his eyelids fell, and he stepped down into the road. One, two, three steps . . .

A cold tingling sweat rushed up his spine as it happened, the hairs on his skin reaching out as though to touch the vehicle speeding at him, to press it back, to stop it in its tracks. He could not see it; he did not need to. His eyes might be closed but it was as if he were aware of everything around him, could sense it all through some other means.

And the car – for it was a car, not anything bigger, he was certain – was less than a second away from smashing into him. He stopped and braced himself: it would come in on his right side. A quick and final blow, and then liberation.

The brakes, the screeching, the attempt to avoid what could not be avoided. Did they not know that he himself had accepted this, wanted it, standing there, waiting willingly for it to come?

His heart and brain seemed to fuse together for the briefest of flashes. This was it; this was death. And with a thud, he felt his pulse surge violently within his veins. Counting: one, two, three . . .

No collision, no impact.

As though waking from deep, suffocating sleep, he opened his eyes. The street swirled around him. He heard voices calling out, saw a circle of stationary cars and lorries around him: blue, silver, white, red. Black.

The one nearest to him was larger than the others: a pick-up truck that was almost touching him. From the tyre tracks behind it on the tarmac it had swerved violently to the side only a second before. Its path had been true, its direction straight: this was the car that had been about to snuff out his life. Yet it had failed to do so. Why?

He tried to look through the window into the cabin, but the reflection in the glass obscured his view. Then the door opened and the driver stepped out, walking slowly towards him.

'Is he all right?' someone called from behind.

The driver did not answer. Then he lifted his hand and placed it on Dídac's shoulder.

'Come with me, *hijo mío*,' he said. 'It's time to go.'

It took Daniel a few minutes to get rid of the other cars, convincing everyone that Dídac was all right, that he could look after him now. There had been some problems at home, he explained. The poor kid was not right. He had been lucky to get to him in time.

The incident had caused a traffic jam – never a difficult thing in Barcelona – but eventually things were sorted and they could drive on. Dídac slumped in the passenger seat, pale and drawn.

'Do you need to be sick?' Daniel asked. 'If you need to be sick, let me know and I'll stop. Just don't do it in here.'

'I'm fine,' Dídac groaned. 'I'm fine. His eyes opened and closed. Had he been run over after all? Was this death – being picked up by his father and driven away? How on earth had Daniel been there just then, at the very moment he stepped out into the road? Had he been following him?

He slid further down into his seat. It felt good to let go, let someone else drive him, make the decisions. All he had to do was sit there and be taken along. And a warm, comforting cocoon wrapped its hands around him, soothing and cradling.

He was loved after all.

'Where are we going?' he mumbled sleepily.

'You'll see,' said Daniel.

He glanced over, registering properly the new clothes, the haircut.

'It took me a second to recognise you,' he said. 'You look better like that.'

'I never liked the dreadlocks anyway,' said Dídac.

Daniel smiled, but Dídac did not see: he had already fallen asleep.

He was woken by the car swinging from side to side and a sensation of pressure inside his ears. Opening his eyes, he saw that they had left Barcelona and were climbing a winding road surrounded by forests. A few minutes later they came to a huddle of buildings at the top of a mountain where, at the centre, stood a tall church built of light grey stone. Above, standing on top of a central tower, stood a robed Christ figure, his arms outstretched as though to embrace the faithful.

Daniel parked the vehicle under the shade of a tree, and they walked up towards the church. Beyond, the city lay at their feet, stretching out under a haze towards a barely visible sea in the distance. Dídac could just make out the distinctive shape of the Sagrada Familia, its towers like fingers stretching high above the buildings surrounding it.

Daniel, usually so quick and businesslike, was ambling slowly at his side.

'You OK?' he asked.

'Y-yes,' Dídac said. 'I think so.'

Daniel never asked how he was.

They drew closer to the church, and an entrance built of darker, yellower stone. Above, in bright colours, was a frieze showing some religious scene: Christ again, this time wearing a robe of blood red.

'What is this place?' Dídac asked.

'This is Mount Tibidabo,' said Daniel. He thrust his hands into his pockets, sniffing at the pine-scented air. 'My father used to bring me here when I was little. Take me on the rides. You see that Ferris wheel?'

He pointed towards an amusement park on the other side of the church. Dídac saw the arm of a crane with a large toy plane suspended from it.

'Been there for over a hundred years,' said Daniel. 'We'd come up at weekends, just me and him, spend the afternoon here.'

Dídac felt tired and began to sway on his legs.

'You should sit down,' said Daniel. 'Here.'

They perched on a low wall. Dídac looked out again at the view; it seemed to call to him in some inexplicable way.

'Beautiful, isn't it?' said Daniel. 'It's my favourite place in the world.'

'Your father,' said Dídac, 'my grandfather. You never talk about him. Who . . . who was he?'

Daniel coughed.

'His was name was Daniel,' he said. 'Like me. And he was a soldier.'

Dídac did not move, his eyes fixed on the carpet of trees cascading down from where they sat.

'He died when I was very young,' said Daniel. 'Fighting in the Spanish Sahara, the last real colony this country had.'

'What happened?' Dídac felt something twisting inside him, at once disturbing and reassuring.

Daniel shrugged. 'There was a rebellion, local people

wanting independence. The army was deployed. My father got shot when an attack was launched against a checkpoint.'

He turned and looked down at Dídac, who stared out, not meeting his gaze.

'He was a very religious man,' said Daniel.

For a moment, neither of them spoke; questions bubbled in Dídac's head, but he pressed them down, willing them away.

'This place, then . . .' He wanted to break the silence.

'That,' said Daniel, looking up at the church, 'is the Templo del Sagrado Corazón. The Pope made the man who built it a marquis because he liked it so much.'

'And the name? Tibi . . .'

'Tibidabo,' said Daniel. 'It comes from the Bible. *Et dixit illi haec tibi omnia dabo si cadens adoraveris me.*'

The air seemed to stick in Dídac's throat on hearing his father quoting the words so perfectly.

'It's what the Devil said to Christ when he was in the wilderness,' Daniel explained. '"And he said to him, I will give you all this if you fall down and worship me."'

He swept an arm out indicating the view ahead.

'But Christ resisted the temptation, and turned the Devil away.'

Dídac sat still, breathing heavily through his nose. His jaw was clenched tight, fists wrapped like balls.

'You seem . . .' he said. 'You seem to know a lot about it.'

Daniel stood up slowly, stretching his arms and back as he did so.

'I like it up here,' he said. 'People in Barcelona think that this is where the scene actually took place. But of course –' he grinned down at Dídac – 'it was in the Holy Land.'

He turned and looked out over the city.

'But it's such an amazing spot. You can understand why.'

Dídac began to feel something he had never experienced before: a gentle yet thrilling sensation, like a hand caressing his hair, calming and softening, as though drawing all burdens from his mind and making them vanish before him. The tension in his body of only a few moments before trickled and drained away, and a lightness entered his limbs. It was like the feeling he had had in the car earlier on, in the moment just before falling asleep, only stronger this time, less fleeting, more real. And he reached out to embrace it, the promise that it held of mystery and certainty.

'I think it's lovely up here,' he said, his voice almost breaking as he spoke. 'Thank you for bringing me.'

Daniel held his hand affectionately against Dídac's cheek. And the new feeling inside cemented itself within him finally, securely and for ever.

'And . . .' he said. 'Thank you for earlier. For what happened in the street.'

'Someone has to look out for you,' said Daniel, rubbing his thumb gently on Dídac's temple. 'Besides, you're important. I need you strong and fit.'

Dídac stood up and they began to walk around the outside of the church, taking their time and stopping every so often to look at the world lying passively below, as though a merchant at a bazaar had presented his wares on a richly decorated cloth for them to examine.

'I used to imagine sometimes,' said Daniel, 'that one day I might bring my own son up here, just as my father did me. I'm glad we've finally made it. Today feels like the right day for it, the perfect day, in fact.'

'Today?' asked Dídac.

Daniel looked him in the eye.

'Because tomorrow is a big day. Everything I have been training you for will make sense tomorrow. And we have to be prepared, have to be relaxed and ready.'

Dídac's heart thudded with sudden urgency.

'What's going to happen?'

Daniel kept his gaze fixed on Dídac's face, as though looking deep into him.

'I need to ask you,' he said. 'Sònia. What's the situation?'

'The girl?'

Daniel nodded.

'It's over,' Dídac said with quick emphasis. 'I dumped her.'

'Good. That's important. She wasn't right for you anyway.'

'I know. That's why . . .' But his sentence petered out. 'What about Ximo?'

Daniel shook his head.

'You don't have to worry,' he said.

Dídac glanced nervously at the floor; Daniel took a step away.

'So about tomorrow,' said Dídac.

Daniel leaned against the railings running along the top of the wall, placing his weight on his hands and hunching his shoulders. His eyes were fixed on the distant towers of Barcelona.

'Sometimes,' he said, 'everything has to change in order to remain the same.'

'And which of those do you want?' said Dídac. 'For things to stay the same, or be different?'

Daniel lifted his head up and stared at the sky, then pushed himself off the railings and stood squarely before Dídac.

'When the time for action comes . . . ?' he said.

'I'll be with you,' said Dídac.

Daniel nodded and smiled.

'I think,' he said, 'we should get something for that.' He pointed at the bruising around Dídac's neck.

'It's all right,' said Dídac, the ache in his throat intensifying for a moment. 'The pain makes me feel sharper.'

Daniel reached out and cupped his hands around his face.

'My son,' he said.

Dídac looked up at the church behind.

'Would you like to go inside?' said Daniel.

Dídac nodded.

'It's about helping people, right? The Church? Like our food bank.'

'Yes,' said Daniel. 'It's called Christian charity.'

He put an arm around Dídac's shoulders and led him towards the entrance.

'It's a good place to talk. I need to go through some things with you. After that we'll have lunch. And then we'll go and get something for your feet. Some proper boots this time. Like my father used to wear.'

FORTY-SIX

The street lights were flickering off – one, two, three at a time – as he paced down the Carrer de la Marina away from the police station and down towards the Sagrada Familia. The shops were still closed, but the streets were already busy with cars and motorbikes and buses as the people of Barcelona burst out of sleep into another day, the deep orange rays of a low burning sun reflecting like flames on their skin.

The scent of hot fresh coffee drew him to a bar and a window where he could order while still standing in the street.

'*Un café solo.*'

Within seconds, the cup was thrust before him with a clatter. He picked up the large sachet of sugar and emptied it into the black liquid, then stirred it slowly, the spoon making a barely audible pinging sound as it brushed the sides.

There was a honking sound from behind, and he turned to see a man dressed in overalls skip out of the way and on to the pavement just in time to avoid being hit by an angry rubbish truck. The two men standing nearby greeted him.

'Hey, Pau. You'll get yourself killed!'

'Everyone's crazy this morning,' said the man, drawing closer. 'They're all in a rush.'

'Well, they'll be closing off much of this area soon, what with the ceremony. Everyone's trying to get stuff done before the gridlock sets in.'

'That's right, because the rest of the time there's never any traffic jams, not a single one.'

The group laughed. Cámara knocked back the last of his coffee and turned to leave.

'You should see the amount of police down there,' he overheard one of them say. 'Crawling all over the place.'

'Well, after the assassination . . .'

'They're nervous. That's for sure.'

Cámara nodded a morning greeting to the men as he left, but they stared at him as though he were crazed: Barcelonans rarely did that; he was obviously an outsider. But Cámara ignored them and set off at a slightly quicker pace towards his destination: he had at least another five minutes to go.

There was a certainty about his movements, but he was ruffled by what he now felt certain was going to happen that day. Back in his cramped office, it had taken most of the previous afternoon to find what he was searching for. The computer was as slow as it looked and there were protocols to pass, levels of security, in order to reach the information he wanted, buried in the archives of the defence ministry. Even when he got to the records he was seeking, having finally remembered the special passwords he had access to as a chief inspector, there was no guarantee that the document he wanted would have been digitalised. If it existed at all, it would have been written down in the days when computers were still a rarity in public offices. And if it had been digitalised, there was every chance it was in a modern format that the antique computer he was using could not recognise. He felt trapped between the folds of the technological age – neither old enough nor young enough. But eventually, after much swearing at the screen, he had seen a name – the name he hoped and dreaded he would find. And as it burnt into the backs of his eyes, he almost felt sick.

The Legión, again. Should he have known? How could he have?

Now, as he walked briskly towards the Sagrada Familia, he spotted police barriers stacked at the side of the road, waiting to be set up once the order was given to divert the traffic. A group of policemen were standing in the shade, one of them with a radio pinned to his ear, as though waiting for the word to pounce. Seeing them, the cars accelerated, trying to get past before the flow was cut off.

Cámara clocked them as he walked past: they were simple patrolmen, ordinary police. The more specialised units would also be there, but less visible at ground level.

He turned the corner at the bottom of the street and Gaudí's basilica appeared suddenly before him, a perpendicular mass, like stalagmites slowly erupting towards the heavens. It was impressive, although he could not say whether he liked it. Architecture either moved him or not, acting on a purely emotional level: how it might achieve the effects that it did was largely beyond him. But the sheer size and strangeness of the place could not fail to have an impact. Barcelona, unlike Madrid, had a truly iconic building recognisable throughout the world. Where else could a declaration of independence take place?

As soon as he looked up, he began to see them – small dark dots placed on nearby rooftops. A group of four of them caught his eye, one pair clearly talking the other through: the unmistakable sight of a night detail being relieved by the morning shift. The *Mossos* special operations squad – the *Grup Especial d'Intervenció* – had been there for hours already, clearly distinguished from the ordinary officers by their black, military-style uniforms, the letters *GEI* in white printed on the backs of their bulletproof vests.

Cámara walked around to the rear of the Sagrada Familia, along the Carrer de Provença and down the Carrer de Sardenya to the west entrance – the Door of the Passion. The normal barriers used to herd the tourists along in a queue had been removed and a line of police stood in their way. Already, on the other side of the road in the park area, a crowd was beginning to grow: families, many of them with young children, waving the Catalan flag with its red-and-yellow stripes. Cámara estimated that at least a couple of thousand had already shown up, but more – many more – were starting to join them from the nearby streets. A line of barriers had been placed to hold them back from the traffic still flowing past. He heard singing and laughter: it felt like a festival. Was this their day, the one they had been waiting for for so long?

He heard a chopping sound overhead and glanced up to see a police helicopter hovering above the clustering towers of the basilica. The men at the bar had been right: the police presence for the event was considerable, and so far he had been unable to spot any weakness or hole in their preparations.

Holding out his ID card, he got past the men at the entrance, skipped up the steps and went inside. Coloured light cascaded from stained-glass windows that seemed to grow up the walls like a kind of psychedelic plant life. People were hurrying around in all directions performing last-minute adjustments: a small army of priests – many dressed in black like the gun-toting marksmen outside – making sure that everything was perfect for the big event.

As one rushed past, Cámara stuck out an arm and grabbed him by the elbow, identifying himself as he did so. Father Josep, a thin, wiry man in his fifties with round glasses, was clearly in a rush, but happy to answer the chief inspector's questions.

'Tell me,' said Cámara, 'what's the run of things today?'

'Mass will begin at ten,' said Father Josep, skipping from foot to foot.

'And will go on for . . . ?'

The father shrugged. 'An hour and a half at least. Almost certainly longer. It's a special mass for a special occasion, as you know.'

Cámara smiled. It seemed that everything that day had the word 'special' tagged to it.

'And the mass will be led by Cardinal Forner?' he asked.

'That's right.' Father Josep pointed behind him, towards the entrance on the east side of the building. 'He'll arrive through there, that's the Door of the Nativity. And then when everything's finished he and everyone else will exit through the Door of the Passion, just behind you.'

'Will any of the other doors be open?' asked Cámara.

'No, just those two. The Door of the Glory on the south

side will only be opened on the day the basilica will be finished, which won't be for another ten or fifteen years at least.'

Cámara looked behind him and then across at the Door of the Nativity.

'They're glass,' he said.

'Yes, but they'll both be open throughout the ceremony. The cardinal always insists that he doesn't want the crowds outside to feel they're shut out. Besides, this is a joyous day for everyone and he wants to share that with the people of the city. And the roads will be closed for the duration, so we shan't be disturbed by the noise of traffic.'

'Except the chopper overhead,' said Cámara, but Father Josep looked at him quizzically, not understanding.

'One more thing before you go,' said Cámara. 'I'm assuming the cardinal will be making a speech of some kind during the ceremony?'

'That's right,' said Father Josep.

'But it's not just Church people here. I mean, we're expecting other kinds of dignitaries as well.'

'The entire government will be here,' said the father.

'The Catalan . . .'

'The *Govern*. The entire *Govern*,' he said with a grin.

'Right,' said Cámara. 'And will any of them be speaking as well? Are we expecting anyone apart from the cardinal to talk at all?'

Father Josep gave him a blank stare.

'I don't know what you mean,' he said.

He took a step back.

'Now I have to go.'

And he dashed off.

Cámara stood motionless for a moment, watching him

scuttle away. But he did not have long to wonder about his reticence; seconds later a powerful hand grabbed him by the upper arm.

'Who are you?'

He was forcibly whisked around and came face to face with a man in black uniform, a beret placed at an angle on his freshly clipped scalp.

Cámara whipped out his ID card.

'Come with me,' said the *GEI* man. 'The *jefe de operaciones* wants a word.'

Cámara was led to a side chapel where a group of three men were standing over a table littered with laptops and pieces of paper.

When they saw Cámara, two of them took a step away, leaving only one, who stared at him with open hostility.

'What the fuck is a *Policía Nacional* chief inspector from Valencia doing in my basilica?' barked the man. 'I've got enough to worry about already without crap like this.'

Cámara steeled himself: back at the *Mossos* station, *Sotsinspector* Ripoll, his liaison officer, was supposed to have got the necessary clearance for him to be there. But clearly he had forgotten – or not bothered – to do so. Cámara could either go into long explanations about his case, blaming this on a clear breakdown in protocol procedures, or he could appeal to the man's sense of action, of danger.

'I believe there's going to be an attack of some sort here during the ceremony,' he said as calmly and clearly as he could.

He could see the blood pressure rising in the *jefe de operaciones*'s eyes, his nostrils beginning to flare.

'Do you have clear intelligence on this?' he said. 'What exactly are you talking about?'

Cámara hesitated.

'I've got the entire Catalan government and Church hierarchy coming through that door any minute,' said the *GEI* chief. 'You'd better start giving me some details right now, or I'll throw you out of here on your fucking arse. You got that? Details. Now.'

And he banged his fist hard on the table, the laptops jumping in unison with the impact.

'It's all right, *Sotsinspector*,' said a voice behind Cámara. 'He's with me. I'll vouch for him.'

Cámara turned and saw Carlos stepping into the chapel, a straw hat clutched in his hand. He did not look pleased to see him.

'Cámara is one of mine,' Carlos continued. 'I'll take care of him, and get back to you if there's anything to report.'

The *GEI* man ground his teeth.

'If he's yours, get him out of this operations room. And I don't want to see him again. It's on you, Carlos.'

Carlos smiled at him indulgently, put an arm around Cámara's shoulders, and led him away.

'Come with me,' he said. 'We need to find somewhere we can talk.'

FORTY-SEVEN

'Smoothly done,' Cámara said as Carlos led him away.

'They know who I work for,' said Carlos. 'That's enough.'

They stepped away from the chapel and into the main body of the basilica.

'There's a confessional over there,' said Cámara. 'Might be a quiet place.'

'Are you mad?' Carlos pulled him in the other direction. 'They're all bugged.'

In a corner near the Door of the Nativity, they huddled by the wall, away from the hubbub of policemen and priests.

'This will have to do,' said Carlos. 'First things first – Terreros. What have you got?'

Cámara kept his back to the wall and his eyes focused on the scene in front of him. The bustling intensified suddenly as it appeared that the first dignitaries were soon to arrive.

'We're going to have to move,' said Carlos.

'They're coming in through this door,' said Cámara. 'Let's go across to the other side and find somewhere there.'

The two men hurried across the nave towards the Door of the Passion. There, just before the glass doors, was an anteroom.

'In here,' Cámara said.

Behind them, the guests began to flood in, chatting and taking their seats while an organ played. One of them, a man in a grey suit with closely cropped white hair, caught his attention.

'Alfonso Segarra's here,' he said, throwing Carlos a look.

'He's a very religious man,' said Carlos.

'Did you bring him?'

'I don't have to. Someone like Segarra can go where he pleases.'

'Don't mess me around. It can't be coincidence.'

Carlos lowered his eyelids and frowned.

'I don't believe in coincidences.'

'So why is he here?' said Cámara.

'Señor Segarra gave a speech last night to local businessmen,' said Carlos, 'warning that he would pull out all his operations from Catalonia if it became independent. Went down well with some. Less well with others. We . . . he thought it would be useful to appear here today as well.'

As he spoke, a couple of press photographers took snaps of the supermarket mogul. He looked calm, but tired. As he stepped through the crowds, shaking hands and moving unsmilingly towards the front to take his seat, he seemed to notice that he was being observed, turning his head and catching Cámara's eye. He gave a brief nod, then saw that Cámara was standing next to Carlos and averted his gaze quickly, disguising his discomfort with a smile and focusing his attention on the cross above the altar.

Cámara understood.

'He's working for you.'

Carlos nodded.

'Very good, Cámara,' he said. 'Yes, Segarra is with us now. Terreros was responsible for the death of his kid. That runs deep. Hate, in my experience, is the most powerful reason for someone joining us. Not money or excitement, but wanting to get back at someone you really despise or fear. And we can protect him as well.'

Cámara threw him a look.

'Really?'

'Look, what's going on?' said Carlos. 'What were you doing scaring the *GEI* with talk about an attack?'

'What's the real situation here?' said Cámara.

Carlos glared at him, his grip tightening around his hat.

'It's much more complicated than you could know,' he said. 'Or I can explain.'

'The declaration,' said Cámara. 'Independence. You think it's going to happen here, in a few minutes, right? That's why you brought Segarra – trying to scare them.'

Carlos shook his head.

'We don't know. No one knows except the Catalan president, and he's not giving anything away. Believe me, we're trying everything we can to get that information. It might be today, tomorrow, who knows?'

'But that's why you're here. You wouldn't be bothering to turn up for some religious ceremony otherwise.'

Carlos shrugged.

'As I say, it's a faint possibility. But you're going to tell me what you're doing here. Or I'll make sure the *GEI* throw you out. And they won't be nice about it.'

'Isn't it obvious?' said Cámara.

'Enlighten me.'

'If Terreros is going to make a move it'll be here. Now.' Carlos sneered.

'Here?'

Cámara nodded.

'He wants to act before it's too late,' he said. 'Before the declaration is made.'

Carlos looked at him as though he were mad.

'You haven't grasped how religious Terreros is,' he said. 'He's not going to attack a sacred place like this.'

'But the point about Terreros,' Cámara said, 'is that nothing about his world is as it appears.'

He leaned in towards Carlos.

'And you are a part of that world.'

He realised that he was prodding Carlos in the chest. Reluctantly, he took a step backwards.

'Steady yourself, Chief Inspector.'

From inside the main body of the basilica they could hear the music change and a silence begin to fall on the congregation: Cardinal Forner himself must have arrived, which meant that everyone was now in place and the mass would soon begin.

'Nothing is straight about this,' said Cámara in a lower voice. 'Not you, not Terreros, not anyone.'

'Spare me the sermon,' said Carlos. 'Look, if you're going to ask if I've been using you, the answer is, yes, absolutely. Terreros is a rogue element, one we've only just managed to contain. He's got powerful friends, which means we can't shut him down, so we let him play his little games down in Ceuta, with his dreams of the old days and the old order. He's a dangerous, crippled maniac, wedded to the Legión, who's still blaming Franco for not ensuring the dictatorship continued after his death.'

Carlos paused for breath, the last words shot from his mouth like bullets from a machine gun.

'Now while he was simply collecting money and sitting in his little office,' he continued, 'everything was fine, we had him contained. But then Segarra's kid, Fermín, got killed and the alarm bells went off. It was obvious that Terreros was behind it – Segarra had turned off the taps after the *Hacienda* investigation. He got scared. But the boy's murder was a sign that Terreros was upping the ante, preparing for bigger stuff.'

'So that's why you got me involved,' said Cámara.

'Of course that was why we got you involved,' replied Carlos. 'It was a simple police matter. The investigation was going nowhere, so we gave you a little helping hand, that's all. Then you could do what we couldn't – pick Terreros up and lock him away, neutralise him.'

He gave Cámara a scornful look.

'Or at least that was what was supposed to happen.'

The cardinal's sharp, clear voice started to echo throughout the building from loudspeakers as he began the ceremony.

In nomine Patris, et Filii, et Spiritus Sancti . . .

Overhead, punctuating his words, came the chopping of the helicopter blades in the sky.

'The problem with that,' said Cámara, 'is that it doesn't tell me anything I don't already know. And it's not the whole story.'

Carlos did not move.

'Terreros is one of your informants,' said Cámara. 'Why

would you tolerate him in the first place? There are ways you could shut him down if you really wanted to. But he was useful.'

Carlos held out his hands.

'OK, you're right,' he said. 'I admit it. You're a clever guy, Cámara.'

'Shut up.' Cámara spat the words out. 'I haven't finished. Because like Segarra, Terreros is not just an informant, he's one of your agents.'

Carlos laughed.

'This is silly,' he said. 'You're getting ahead of yourself.'

'Who writes a threatening note by hand?' said Cámara. 'Terreros wanted to be caught, it's obvious. Trying to flee over the border was just part of the pretence. The thing was set up. He knew I was coming. And the only person who could have told him is you.'

He had stepped closer to Carlos again, their faces almost touching. Carlos stared him in the eye, almost challenging him to lash out.

'You wanted him out of Ceuta,' said Cámara. 'You wanted him on the mainland. And you used me to get him here under false pretences.'

Carlos slowly lifted his hands, placed them on Cámara's shoulders and tried to push him away. But Cámara's body did not move.

'We use what we've got,' Carlos said. 'Opportunities come our way, and we take them. Just like in police work. Nothing is as neat as it looks from the outside. Ever. But let me give you some advice. Stick to policing – you're out of your depth.'

'The problem is,' said Cámara, 'you're not bothered that Terreros is on the run. In fact, you were excited the morning you called me about the break-out, not really worried, as you pretended to be. You think he can still be useful for you. Why were you the first person to call me about him escaping? You slipped up, Carlos. That call should have come from one of my own. But how did you know? Because Terreros himself told you. A phone call or a message was got to you somehow. Which was when you called me.'

'Why would I send you up here to catch him if I was happy for him to be loose?' said Carlos. 'There's a bit of a hole in this fantasy of yours.'

'You're keeping up appearances. It's the only thing you've been doing from the start.'

Carlos rolled his eyes.

'Terreros called me a Red,' said Cámara. 'Where did he get that from?'

'Get this straight,' Carlos said. 'We did not pass on any information about you to Terreros. Not. One. Word.'

Cámara stared into his eyes: for the first time he saw conviction there, a straight, unflinching certainty. It was the final confirmation.

'Yes,' he said. 'I believe you. It was the other way around, wasn't it?'

Carlos forced a grin.

'He was the one who gave you information about me in the first place,' said Cámara. 'The reason why you came to me at all. You got him to check me out.'

Their eyes locked in understanding.

'Just like Segundo Pont at the medal ceremony. Did you pass the info to Segundo Pont yourself, Carlos? Was that why he approached me? He was one of yours as well, wasn't he? That was the real reason why I was picked for that investigation, so he could check me out as well. A stabilising influence, people said, someone who Madrid could work with. Why? Because he was a *CNI* agent all along, playing a double game. Was that why he was killed? Did someone find out the truth? One of his own people? No wonder they haven't solved it yet. No one will ever let them know the truth – not you or the Catalans. It's too embarrassing for both of you.'

Carlos snorted.

'Been on the weed again, Cámara?' he said. 'Smoking some of that stash from the back of your flat? Because you're beginning to sound like another drug-crazed, conspiracy-theory lunatic.

'Oh, yes,' he added. 'We know all about—'

'A cog in your creaky, chaotic machine,' said Cámara. 'You never wanted me to spy on the anarchists in Valencia. That was just a power thing, a test. You had all the information on them – and on me – already. From Terreros. But who was feeding it to him in the first place?'

They were barely inches away from each other, Cámara sensing the anger surging through Carlos's blood. With one jerk he could bring his forehead down on Cámara's face. Quickly and smoothly, Cámara took a step back, shaking Carlos's hands free from his shoulders.

'You know who,' said Cámara. 'You've known all along. The same person who murdered Fermín on Terreros's orders.'

He looked towards the door.

'You said Terreros was dangerous,' he said. 'But I don't think you realise quite how dangerous he actually is.'

'What are you talking about?' said Carlos.

Inside the basilica the mass was now well under way, with the hypnotic litany of the church voices. Outside, the crowds were relatively silent as they tried to catch a glimpse of what was going on inside through the open doors. But as Cámara and Carlos stood in the anteroom, Cámara became aware of a new sound from outside: a droning, buzzing noise he had not been conscious of before. And with it, a roaring cheer from the crowd.

His ears pricked up, and every sense in his body with them. Something was not right.

'What is it?' asked Carlos.

'I don't know,' said Cámara. 'And I don't like it.'

FORTY-EIGHT

He had never felt so awake. Every detail, every colour, every face flashing past his window was perceived in high definition and recorded indelibly in his mind. The world – his world, their world – was about to change.

They drove in towards the city centre as the first light of dawn reached out towards the streets and houses. The traffic was building, but Daniel knew his way through back streets and side alleys, and they managed to weave a complex route towards their destination.

In the back of the pickup, a tightly fastened brown tarpaulin kept their cargo from view. 'Don't look round, don't draw attention to it,' Daniel had said. 'If you stare at it, others will to. You make things invisible by ignoring them.'

And so he sat with his eyes on the road, but within him, as he absorbed the feast of stimuli that the city offered, part of his consciousness was also turned on what sat behind him in the truck: what were they going to do with it? What was it for?

They had spent the night sleeping on a couple of mattresses thrown on the floor of a flat in an abandoned, unfinished block on the outskirts of the city. The pickup was four-wheel drive, so they had no difficulty crossing the rough ground in order to get to it: the half-built street had been blocked off by heavy concrete barriers, but they arrived from the back, over the steep cemented banks of a dry river bed. Inside, along with the primitive bedding, was some drinking water and four cans of sardines. The first thing Daniel had shown him was how to dig a hole outside in the hard dry ground with a knife in order to shit in it.

Dídac spent most of the evening in the flat making two mobile-phone detonators while Daniel busied himself with something downstairs in what he referred to as the 'garage' – a simple, covered space on the ground floor with bare concrete pillars that was supposed to be the entrance to the block of flats. Only when Daniel called him did he go down to see what he was doing.

It was almost dark by that point, and on a barren patch of land behind the building Daniel was standing next to what looked like a toy helicopter, except that it was much larger and sturdier.

'This is a drone,' Daniel said.

'I know,' said Dídac. 'You stick a camera on them and take aerial shots.'

Daniel nodded. A tablet computer sat in his hands.

'Here, come closer and watch.'

As the drone rose into the air, the moving image on the screen changed until Dídac was looking at himself far below, on the ground, staring into a tablet screen, watching the drone rise above him, which was filming him.

'Cool,' he said in a low voice.

Daniel passed over the tablet.

'Now you can watch and control it at the same time.'

He pointed to the buttons, explaining what each one did, and within moments Dídac was making the drone fly even higher, above the height of the block of flats, and shifting the camera so that it gazed out towards the horizon. He could see the lights of Barcelona in the distance, winking at him as though sharing the excitement.

'Don't get too carried away,' said Daniel. 'I don't want it to get seen, and we have to preserve the battery life.'

Gently, Dídac brought the machine back down to earth, and it landed smoothly by their feet.

'You seem to have mastered that pretty quickly,' said Daniel. 'You reckon you know how to handle one now?'

Dídac nodded.

'Seems simple enough,' he said, glowing in his father's praise.

'Good, because I've got two and we're going to be using them tomorrow morning. You up for it?'

Which was when the feeling of being alive like never before had first entered his bloodstream.

'Yes,' he said breathlessly. 'Yes.'

'You should go back up, then,' Daniel said. 'I've got some more things to prepare here. I'll be up soon enough. You should get some rest.'

Dídac turned to head back up the stairs, but paused.

'Dad,' he said. It felt strange – he could not remember ever calling him anything but Daniel, but the word slipped out unbidden. Daniel gave him an odd look, one he found difficult to read.

'I was just wondering,' Dídac continued. 'I thought I might give Mum a ring. I haven't spoken to her for a while. They allow evening calls sometimes at the prison.'

He wanted to talk to someone, a friend, to share his feelings in some way. This was turning into the best day of his life. But the expression in Daniel's eyes darkened.

'The lines aren't safe,' he said. 'You should know that by now. I can't allow it.'

And he lifted the drone and started walking towards the pickup.

'Now go back upstairs.'

One black cloud, momentarily blocking out the sun. But it passed soon enough. When Daniel finally came up, Dídac's eyes were closed, but sleep felt like a distant, impossible shore.

Now, as they drove into the city centre, he could sense the presence of the drones in the back of the pickup. Finally, at long last, they were about to act: it felt as though he had been waiting for it for years.

After zigzagging their way across the city, they came to an ordinary-looking street with shops and a few office blocks and people rushing backwards and forwards as they went about their business. Daniel pulled into an open-air car park on the right-hand side, and there, at the far end where two spaces were free, he brought the pickup to a halt, crossing the line into the final space to prevent anyone else from parking there.

Switching off the engine, he got out and went round to the back of the vehicle. Dídac took his cue and followed suit. After untying the fastenings of the tarpaulin, Daniel carefully rolled it back, exposing the two drones, each sitting inside a wooden crate. Dídac saw immediately that they had been modified; they did not look the same as the one he had briefly played with the night before.

'Detonators,' Daniel said simply. It was an order. Dídac skipped back to the cabin, pulled out a rucksack from the footwell and handed it to Daniel, who opened it, checked the contents and then placed it next to the drones in the back of the truck.

'Right,' he said. 'Pull out your phone and programme this number.'

Dídac did as he was told, registering the mobile-phone digits that Daniel repeated from memory.

Daniel checked his watch, pausing for a second.

'We need to get going,' he said.

He pulled out the first drone, lifted it out of its crate and placed it down on the ground in the empty parking space next to them. The pickup partially shielded them from view, but they were surrounded by taller buildings in what felt almost like a canyon. One of them, a square white block, looked institutional, like a prison. Anyone staring out of a window would have a fairly clear view of what they were doing.

But would anyone really object to them flying drones? Only if they saw Daniel's adjustments to the machines. Beneath each one, attached to the main undercarriage next to the camera, was a metal canister and a package wrapped in brown paper.

Daniel picked up the rucksack and placed it on the ground next to the drone. He pulled out one of the detonators that Dídac had made the previous evening and carefully but firmly pressed the blast cap through the brown paper into the soft insides of the package. Then he attached the body of the mobile phone to the other side the drone, strapping it in with duct tape.

He stood up and stepped past Dídac without looking him in the eye, reaching into the cabin of the truck for another bag, which he brought back to the drone. There, he fished out a tablet computer and switched everything on, checking that all was in working order. The screen showed a clear steady image of the ground beneath the still stationary drone, then flicked up and around as the camera was swivelled in its pod until finally resting on an insect's view of their feet.

After a few minutes, Daniel had gone through the same procedure with the second drone, setting it up and switching everything on, before handing the tablet to Dídac.

Then he checked his watch again.

'Remember,' he said, 'have your mobile phone ready, and when I say, you call that number I just gave you. Got it?'

A powerful cocktail of emotional energy surged through him: excitement, pride and cold, cold panic. He could not speak.

Daniel took a step closer and placed his hand on Dídac's shoulder.

'Everything's all right,' he said. 'I promise you, everything will be all right.'

'I . . .'

'Yesterday you told me that when the time came you'd be with me. And I know you meant it, that it came from the heart.'

His hand moved from Dídac's shoulder and up to stroke the side of his head.

'This is it,' he said. 'This is the moment. I need you to be with me.'

And almost as though it had a will of its own, Dídac's head began to nod.

'I'm with you.' The words spilled from his mouth, dribbling down his front as they fell.

Daniel patted his cheek, then pulling his hand slowly away, he bent his arm and brought his straightened fingers up to touch his own temple in a military salute.

And mirroring him, Dídac did the same. Two men like soldiers at a parade.

'It's time to go to work,' said Daniel.

He checked his watch for a final time.

'We need these things in the air in five – four – three . . .'

'What's the target?' said Dídac, staring at the screen in his hand.

'Get it up in the air and above these buildings,' said Daniel. 'Then head east. But be quick. With that extra weight we've only got ten minutes' flying time.'

'Where are we sending them?' Dídac asked, his voice shrill above the buzzing of the propellers as they whizzed violently in tight circles.

'Follow mine,' said Daniel. 'And keep going for seven blocks.'

His drone lifted into the air, rising vertically above them.

'We're going to blow up the Sagrada Família.'

FORTY-NINE

Cámara ran to the doorway of the anteroom and looked out towards the street. Through the open doors he spotted the crowds on the other side of the road: they were looking up at something in the sky and cheering.

Inside the basilica, the ceremony continued, the congregation seemingly oblivious to the growing commotion outside, but the *jefe de operaciones* of the *Mossos* team had noticed the change as well and was speeding across from his temporary headquarters to find out what was going on, pressing his finger against the radio in his ear.

Cámara stepped out into the covered entrance and took a couple of steps down in order to see what the crowds were looking at. He heard the buzzing sound and then saw coloured smoke hanging in the air just a few metres above their heads. Two streams, one yellow, one red – the colours on the Catalan flag.

Another cheer went up as the buzzing became louder and

he cupped his hand over his eyes to shield them from the sun. Then he saw what was causing it: a drone helicopter, no more than a metre across, was passing backwards and forwards along the Carrer de Sardenya with the smoke blowing out of a couple of canisters attached to its under-carriage. And each time it went past, the people squeezed into the square opposite applauded it with nationalistic glee.

Cámara quickly stepped back up towards the basilica to head inside again. The emotional pitch was beginning to rise; the mere sight of two colours – which happened to be the same as the ones on the Spanish national flag, although no one was pointing that out – was sending the crowds into ecstasy. There were more things to be said to Carlos, and he wanted to be on his guard.

It was the expression on the *jefe de operaciones*'s face that made him wonder, however, as he walked back into the cooler shade of the building: he looked worried.

'Shoot them down!' the man started shouting into his radio, looking up towards his marksmen on a nearby roof. 'They're not authorised. Repeat, the drones are not author-ised. Shoot them down!'

And Cámara turned to look back at the flying machine coming closer towards them: there was something else attached to its undercarriage. Not just the gas canisters, but he could not quite make out what it was.

Dídac's hands sweated as he held the tablet; his drone was lagging behind. Daniel had activated the smoke canisters as soon as both drones had begun their approach to the Sagrada Familia. Waiting for Dídac's drone to catch up, he had flown his own over the street a couple of times, trailing smoke in its wake. Through the camera lens Dídac became aware of the crowds outside the basilica cheering and waving with each pass as his drone approached the target.

'I'm going in,' Daniel said. 'Come in after me. Head for the door.'

Dídac glanced back at his father, his eyes breaking away from the screen for the first time since they had launched the drones.

And behind him, from the far end of the car park, he could see a figure approaching: a man dressed in uniform, a blue cap on his head and a gun hanging from a black leather holster on his belt.

'Police,' he hissed, staring hard at Daniel.

'Focus,' spat Daniel. 'Follow me.'

The noise of the cheering crowds was starting to bother Father Josep. The sound system inside the Sagrada Família was good, and Cardinal Forner's voice could clearly be heard by everyone, but he was concerned that the volume was getting too loud in the street, that the solemnity of the occasion was being lost by the more festive atmosphere outside.

Quietly and quickly, without wanting to disturb anyone – or more importantly, be seen by anyone – he got up from his seat and slipped around the back of the congregation towards the Door of the Passion where the hullabaloo seemed to be coming from. The cardinal had insisted that the doors be left open. And he was not about to disobey his orders. But at least one of the doors could be closed. That, at least, might lower the disturbance a sufficient amount to allow the mass to carry on with only a modicum of interference.

He reached the door as the policeman who had questioned him a few moments before the start of the ceremony appeared: the big man with the Manchego accent. He looked disturbed and in a rush, darting past him and into the anteroom at the side, as though looking for someone and not finding him.

Frowning a little, Father Josep reached down to the floor to unhook the lock holding the glass door open, and then gently closed it, holding the metal handle firmly, careful not to make any more noise than was necessary.

But outside the situation now appeared chaotic and confused. Some members of the crowd were still cheering, but others were standing still in what looked like bewilderment or even fear.

He stepped out of the door, trying to see what was going on.

Which was when the first shots began to ring out.

Dídac's hand trembled as he tried to concentrate on the tablet, blotting out the fact that a policeman now appeared to have spotted them and was walking towards them. For a moment he lost control of his drone and wrestled with the tablet, spinning his camera around until it focused, and then pushed the controls on the remote to make it fly straight again.

On the screen, the image of the Sagrada Familia grew larger and larger as the drone flew closer. Daniel's machine was ahead of his and heading down towards the doorway.

But a second before it reached its target, there was a movement: a figure dressed in black appeared at the side, then there was a flash of light. The blackened opening was about to swallow the drone, Daniel was about to get inside, but suddenly the image on Daniel's tablet scrambled, light and dark spinning in a confused staccato.

'What the fuck?'

Less than a second later the image stabilised: an upside-down shot of the porch over the doorway.

'You've crashed,' Dídac said in a low, strained voice.

Daniel was silent, staring in confusion at his computer.

'Someone closed the door!' said Dídac.

Daniel turned and looked round. Dídac did not need to see: he could sense the policeman getting ever closer. There was no time to fix things: it was impossible. One drone was clearly the wrong way up, lying at the entrance to the basilica. There was nothing they could do.

Daniel let the tablet drop from his hands and it fell with a clatter on the ground. Then he reached into his pocket and pulled out his phone. The number was there, already recorded.

Dídac turned his own drone away and flew it quick and high out of harm's way. His fingers were so sweaty they almost slipped on the screen.

Daniel pressed the call button on his phone. There was a pause. Nothing happened.

Then the roar of the blast reached them, like a towering force of energy reaching up into the sky above the city.

FIFTY

The *jefe de operaciones* had guessed what was happening: like Cámara he spotted those other, suspicious attachments to the undercarriage of the drones. But there was so little time to act. By some miracle, a door had been closed at the very instant that the machine tried to fly inside the building, and now it lay upside-down less than three metres from his feet, unable to fly any more.

But what he could now see very clearly taped to the drone confirmed his fears. Not least, the sight of the cheap mobile phone strapped to the side. It was going to go, and he had only seconds to do anything about it.

'Get out!' he screamed, waving his hand madly at the photographers and policemen waiting outside the door.

'Get away!'

The crowd had already been silenced by the two shots fired by his marksmen trying to bring the drone down, but the vision of the *GEI* men was impaired by the coloured smoke, and neither bullet had found its target.

Now, for an eternal second, they all – the crowds, the journalists, the *GEI* agents and the ordinary policemen – watched as the *jefe de operaciones* screamed for everyone to take cover.

And at his side stood a small priest dressed in black robes, a look of confusion on his face as he took a step from inside, wondering what on earth was going on. He looked annoyed, almost, that this special mass ceremony was in danger of being upstaged by the events outside.

But it was the last expression anyone ever saw on his face. In the next instant Father Josep – and the *jefe de operaciones* – ceased to exist.

On the other side of the anteroom, still looking for the missing Carlos, Cámara was knocked sideways by the blast. A hail of glass was blown inwards from the door, showering over the congregation sitting nearby, and a noise so loud it felt as though it might cause his head to crumple boomed throughout the building like a screaming, horrified beast. The whole world shook; for a moment his feet were knocked off the floor and he had the sensation of flying. When he landed, shoulder first, rolling until he crashed into the seating area a few metres beyond, he felt nothing, as though everything were happening to someone else.

He blacked out, perhaps for no more than a second or two, but there was an acute change: the concussed silence in the immediate aftermath of the explosion gave way to wild, uncontrolled and vocal panic. Feet pounded past him and over him as the congregation found their legs and their will to survive and headed en masse for the exits on the south and east sides of the basilica, away from the smoking hole where the Door of the Passion had once stood.

Cámara curled into a tight ball for self-protection as scores of people crashed and tripped over him to make good their escape; beaten down by their urgent feet, he could not stand up.

But then, almost as quickly as they had rushed over his prostrate body, the kicking and jostling stopped. With a gulping, gasping breath, he came up like a drowning man, propping himself against the side of the nearest seat. Something was caught in his throat – an acid, burning smoke – and he coughed it out, leaning over on all fours, almost vomiting with the effort.

Inside the building, the sound of fleeing, panicking people filled the vast space around him. He glanced over: on the floor, a few metres away, was a crushed straw hat with bloodstains spattered on one side. And beyond, the crowds were funnelling through the two open doors trying to get out. But set against their high-pitched wail, he could hear two other sounds.

The first was that of groaning, wounded people. He pulled himself up on to his knees and looked across through the smoky air to where the blast had taken place: scattered bodies were lying over the floor, many of them calling out in dazed, intense pain. Scuttling around, trying to help them, to see which of them might be saved, were a handful of priests. Among them was Cardinal Forner himself, who had cast off his outer robes and was beginning to issue orders to his men, like a military commander.

The second noise inside the basilica made him shoot up

to his feet. He could not see it – the air was still too thick with the aftermath of the explosion – but the sound was exactly the same: the same buzzing he had heard outside just before the blast.

Only now it was inside the building, and it was moving towards the centre.

'Give me your tablet!' Daniel screamed. 'I need more time. Take him out!'

Daniel grabbed the computer and Dídac stared in shocked silence for a second before understanding. The policeman. His father was telling him to hold him back.

He had no weapon, not even anything he could throw or hit him with. And in the heightened, stunned chaos churning inside him, all he was capable of was charging at the man like an enraged bull.

He ducked his head low and sprinted as fast as he could. The last thing he saw before making impact was the policeman's hand reaching down to his holster, but Dídac reached him just in time, the impact sending both of them to the floor.

It was a success; his one idea had worked. But for all the surge in his blood, he was no fighter. The policeman was down, but not out, and now he employed his superior strength and fighting prowess on the young lad who had suddenly and for no apparent reason rushed headlong at him.

Dídac felt the wind kicked out of him as the policeman pushed a fist deep into his abdomen, then a choking sensation as hands gripped around his still bruised throat. With a jerk, his entire body was flung to the side and his head smashed into the tarmac.

For another couple of seconds the hands continued to press and push him, before they began to relax. By the time they had stopped wrestling him and had pulled away from his body, he could barely understand the images now burning into his eyes from where he lay. Warm liquid begin to flow from a cut above his eye and cloud his vision. The last thing he saw was the figure of the policeman standing up and walking away from him, gun in hand, towards Daniel.

The second drone still had a little smoke left in its canisters, streaming yellow and red to mingle with the colourless cloud hanging in the air of the basilica. And as a result, Cámara knew exactly where it was.

The machine came to land in front of the altar, its propellers still whirring.

The first had exploded outside, in the open air. From where he stood he had little idea of the damage it had caused. People were dead – that much was clear. But the Sagrada Família itself was still standing. For some reason that first drone had not made it inside. But this one had. And an explosion inside the building would do immeasurably more harm, almost certainly kill anyone still left inside, and perhaps – depending on how much explosive was strapped to the thing – even bring the basilica itself down.

It had to be stopped; it had to be disarmed.

And the only person who had seen it, who knew where it was and what it was about to do, was him.

His feet took him towards the central aisle. There, he turned left and paced steadily, calmly and inexorably towards the drone. The screaming and the groaning fell away, unheard as he focused everything of himself on this – this one task.

His last task.

Death did not figure: it was all his thought, embracing it like a droplet of water falling into a vast, forgiving ocean.

And he entered a world beyond choice, beyond 'either' and 'or'. There was no question of whether he would get there in time, nor if it would explode before. There was only the bomb, his being, and his non-being, three parts of a whole – a picture that had neither beginning nor end, but simply was and existed of itself.

'You've arrived.'

He heard the voice as clearly as though it had been spoken inside his own body. Hilario, speaking to him, not from outside, not Hilario as he had known him – distinct, separate, another being. But Hilario who was also he himself, with no line between them, no division. Only harmony. Only unity. Not two, but one.

And finally, he understood. No 'or'; only 'and'.

He could see.

Until that moment, he had been living in a world of partition, a world of illusion; now he experienced a world of reality, of no separation, where all things were one – even opposites, or supposed opposites. The shock of the blast, the need of the moment, the nearness of death had brought him awareness. Except that death was always close – only a heartbeat away. He merely drowned out the truth – like everyone else – with so much noise. And now there was silence. There was only this, what he had to do now – only clear vision, like a searing light streaming into his mind.

Terreros was conducting everything, but from afar, hidden somewhere. What was happening around him was being carried out by an agent, a secret member of his private network. Someone who had been living a double life, a man with a dual heart. Except that only one side of him had been visible.

Until now. Everything had changed. Everything was manifest, from the snapping of Fermín's neck, to Segarra's silence, Terreros's escape, the flight to Barcelona and the bruising around Dídac's throat.

The drone sat motionless at Cámara's feet, and he knelt down next to it, as though in prayer.

For a split second Daniel stared down at the dead policeman, blood streaming from the back of his head where the bullet had smashed out of his skull. He pushed the pistol into the back of his trousers and reached for his phone.

There was the number, clearly marked.

He whispered under his breath, '*En el nombre del Padre . . .*'

And pressed the button.

Silence. A pause. And he waited.

But there was no roar.

Cámara kicked the detonator across the floor and watched it clatter before wedging at the foot of the altar. There was a smothered pop as it exploded harmlessly.

Then he lifted the drone and carried it away. A window nearby shone bright yellow and red, the sun streaming in through the stained glass.

He lifted the machine high above his head and threw it with all his strength.

The glass shattered, shards of coloured light flying in all directions.

And from outside he heard the drone crash into the empty street on the other side.

Disabled and disarmed.

FIFTY-ONE

Dídac was woken by the sound of a screaming engine and the harsh squeal of tyres spinning on the road quickly followed by a loud and sustained honking of a car horn.

The small pool of blood made his head almost stick to the ground and he felt dizzy and nauseous. He hauled himself up on to his elbows just in time to see the tail of Daniel's black pickup speeding away from the car park and cutting into the traffic, shooting across the line of vehicles and disappearing from view.

He froze for a second as he tried to understand what was happening, where he was, the events of the past few seconds. Daniel would come back for him, he was sure. Or perhaps expected him to meet him somewhere else close by so that they could make good their escape together.

The drones, the bomb, the policeman, the attack – and now this. Everything flooded simultaneously into his brain. He pulled himself up fully, crouching on his heels, and turned to look back at the spot from where they had launched their flying machines.

Which was when he saw the body. The policeman was on his back, his cap lying a couple of metres beyond. His legs were folded beneath him, one tucked under the other, in what looked like an uncomfortable position. But the policeman was not feeling anything. From the lake of blood oozing from the back of his skull, it was clear that the policeman was very dead.

Dídac reeled to the side, holding himself up with one hand as he tried not to give in to the dizziness now threatening to overpower him.

And for a second he glanced from the body to the exit of the car park and back again, a sense of paralysis beginning to grow.

But the sound of stomping feet coming from the far side shook him into wakefulness, a sharp stab of cold fear reviving his senses.

Daniel had run. Daniel had taken the car and sped away. Daniel – for whatever reason – had abandoned him. But there was no way he was going to sit there and get caught. It was time for him to run as well.

And without thinking or looking, he sprinted to the edge of the car park before they saw him, held his hand out to grip the side wall, and vaulted over.

He was alone, and free.

The sirens grew louder and louder until they reached the outside of the basilica, their voices like a thousand harpies screaming panic, blood, death.

The first paramedics were already arriving, streaming in through the doors where only moments ago the congregation had been fighting to get out. Cámara saw the cardinal with them, telling them what had happened and the situation of the dead and wounded. And in less than a minute the inside of the building began to transform from the shocked, wrecked hull in the aftermath of a bomb attack into a makeshift medical centre, as a swarm of healers set about their tasks.

One body was attracting more attention than most. On the floor, not far from the altar, lay a middle-aged man with closely cropped white hair. Thick dark blood was oozing out of what looked like a head wound. Alfonso Segarra appeared close to death.

There was no sign of the *jefe de operaciones*, and the only policemen visible were prostrate, unable to do anything. Cámara walked to the back of the altar and the chapel where the *GEI* had set up their temporary headquarters. The place was deserted, much of the equipment scattered over the floor where it had been shaken from the table with the blast. But the police radio was still there and blaring away as the police forces in the rest of the city began to respond to the events at the Sagrada Família.

There were a thousand anxious, professional voices, all speaking at once. Calls for backup, progress reports, the current location of units, clarifications and emergency response teams. Back at the *GEI* centre they were desperately trying to find out what had happened to their men at the basilica. The only agents responding were the snipers on the roofs in the surrounding area.

Cámara was about to pick up the radio and report on the absence of the *jefe de operaciones* when a new voice came over – one he recognised. It was *Sotsinspector* Ripoll from the police station on the Carrer de la Marina.

'*Agent down, agent down,*' he said. '*Repeat, agent down. Car park on Carrer de Taxdirt behind the comissaria. We have a sighting of a black pickup truck, last seen heading west. Agent is dead. Confirmed. Agent is dead. Advise pursuit. Call for use of helicopter for tracking.*'

From the *GEI* centre the response was immediate.

'*Related?*'

'*Believe related, affirmative,*' said Ripoll. '*Sighting of drones from this area. Flew in from north west. Suspect seen escaping in black pickup, repeat, black pickup.*'

There was a second's pause before the *GEI* centre responded.

'*Helicopter on its way. Centre to helicopter – report immediately any sighting.*'

Cámara was already heading out of the chapel. He ran across the nave, skipping over broken chairs and pushing past priests and doctors, before leaving through the Door of the Nativity. The air was fresh and clean after the smoke and dirt inside, and he halted, leaning on a column of the porch to take a couple of breaths before carrying on.

Policemen on the other side of the road were doing their best to press people back, pushing them as far away from the basilica as possible. Some were leaving of their own volition in a frightened rush. Others were pushing in the opposite direction, trying to get closer to the drama unfolding at the heart of the city.

Cámara spotted one policeman breaking away from the others to talk into the radio fitted to his motorbike. In an instant Cámara skipped down the steps and out on to the empty street, his police badge already gripped tightly between his fingers.

'Can you pick up the *GEI* traffic on that?' he asked breathlessly.

The policeman nodded. 'Yes, sir.'

'And the helicopter? Can you hear what they're reporting?'

The policeman turned a switch on the receiver and the pilot's voice came over.

'. . . *currently heading north-west, possible sighting ahead.*'

Cámara looked up, trying to spot the helicopter, but it was out of sight.

'We need to follow it, exactly where it's going,' Cámara said, climbing on to the pillion seat of the motorbike. The policeman hesitated.

'What's your name?' Cámara asked.

'Bartomeu, sir.'

'Listen, Bartomeu,' said Cámara. 'You can either ride this with me, or I'll ride it myself. But one way or another I'm going after the man who set off that bomb. Understood?'

Bartomeu was already pulling his helmet on.

'Yes, sir,' he said, climbing on to the bike and firing it into life.

'Just follow the directions from the air,' said Cámara as they sped off.

'Wherever he is, he won't get far,' said Bartomeu. 'The traffic's gridlocked across the city. The only way to get around is on one of these.'

FIFTY-TWO

After squeezing their way through the police barriers at the top of the road, they pushed north before cutting west, zigzagging through the parallel streets of the Eixample. Bartomeu was good, unafraid of mounting the pavement where necessary or whizzing down the narrow corridor between opposite-facing cars sitting at a stand-still in traffic jams. Many drivers had got out of their vehicles and were staring up at the plume of dark grey smoke billowing from the Sagrada Família into the sky. As they heard the motorbike's siren and saw its flashing light, they skipped out of the way, making a path for Cámara and Bartomeu as they pushed on, trying to follow the helicopter's commentary.

'*Ronda del Guinardó, past Alfons Dècim. Sighting. Unconfirmed. Black pickup, heading direction Travessera de Dalt.*'

Bartomeu turned left, then right before speeding the

wrong way up a one-way street, an increased urgency communicating that they were getting close.

At the top of the road, the traffic was totally blocked, cars at a standstill, their engines close to overboiling in the heat of the sun. The motorbike mounted the pavement again, scooting past pedestrians as Bartomeu tried to find a way through the line of vehicles. But they were so tightly squeezed that there was no way through.

Overhead, the helicopter chopped the air and Cámara glanced up to see that it was almost directly above them. Then he looked across the road, and saw.

'*Travessera de Dalt,*' came the pilot's voice. '*Sighting at top of overpass. Vehicle caught in traffic. One police motorbike arriving on the scene.*'

The road ahead was a wide avenue, a flyover with apartment buildings and shops running along either side. Despite being one of the main thoroughfares in the city, it was also a residential district, and there, just at the end of the flyover, backed up against some metal bollards before a long drop down to the trunk road beneath, was a children's playground, with swings and a climbing frame. A group of around a dozen kids were there, running and skipping, while a collection of parents and grandparents sat on the benches at the sides and watched, unaware of the drama that had taken place in the city centre and which was about to burst into their world.

In front of the playground was a communal area with flower beds on either side, and more benches – a kind of mini square. And there, at the edge of it, pulling away from the gridlocked traffic and defiling the sacred pedestrian space with its presence, was the black pickup, positioning itself to face the playground now squarely in front of it, like a bull preparing to charge.

A few angry voices were raised: the behaviour was disturbing. But the old man now approaching the pickup, waving his hand in furious indignation, could only imagine that the driver of the vehicle was trying, in some way, to escape the traffic jam. Not that he had anything more sinister in mind.

Cámara watched from the side of the road, some twenty metres away, as the old man first approached the cabin of the truck and then backed off, his expression rapidly changing from red rage to white fear as the window was wound down.

The driver waited until the glass had slipped completely inside the door before pulling out his Star machine gun. The old man almost fell over himself as he retreated to his bench, collapsing on to it in gaping silence as he obeyed the orders of the man with the gun.

On the other side of the truck, not wanting to draw attention to himself, Cámara slipped off the motorbike – now stuck behind a wall of cars – and motioned for Bartomeu to radio in their position and call for backup. Then crouching low, he slunk along behind the vehicles at right angles, trying to get a little closer.

In the middle of the square, the pickup's engine was beginning to make a loud and powerful noise. Cámara glanced up: the driver was stretching down as though to reach something by his feet, and could not clearly be seen.

Fear started to spread among the people in the square and the parents in the playground. What was this car doing? Why was it revving so aggressively at them?

The old man on the bench was too stunned to speak. He slouched down, trying to point his finger, but no one could understand what he was trying to say.

Cámara pushed through a tiny gap between two cars in the traffic jam, keeping his head low as he steadied himself to sprint across. He could still not see the driver's head properly, but knew that he only had seconds to act. His hand reached for his pistol and after taking a deep breath, he pounced, head down, and ran as fast as he could, jumping over the flower bed and across the square to within three metres of the pickup.

But when he looked up he saw Daniel, and the barrel of his weapon pointing directly at his face through the window of the vehicle.

'Drop the gun, Max,' Daniel said in a slow, shaky voice, raised to make himself heard over the noise of the engine and the helicopter above.

'Drop it now, or I'll shoot.'

FIFTY-THREE

'Daniel . . .' said Cámara, holding out his hand.

'I'm serious, Max.' Despite the quiver as he spoke, Daniel's grip was steady, barely moving as he held his arm straight and stiff.

'There's nothing you can do, Max,' Daniel continued. 'No hero's ending here. You drop the gun and tell your friends out there to do the same. Because I've jammed the accelerator and my foot is on the clutch. This truck is full of C4. Anyone shoots me and it's going right in there.'

He nodded at the playground and the groups of children now starting to huddle around the adults as concern mounted that something serious was happening.

One mother was already heading for the exit, dragging her little girl behind her.

'You'd better tell them to stop, Max,' Daniel said. 'Or I'll shoot them dead before they take another step.' And he flicked the machine gun ever so slightly, his finger pressing on the trigger.

Without taking a step Cámara shouted out towards the playground.

'Halt! Police!' he screamed. 'Stay where you are. Nobody move.'

The mother stood still. Inside the playground the other parents pulled their children closer to them.

'Everything's going to be all right,' Cámara shouted. 'Just don't move. Stay where you are.'

He checked that the message had got through, holding his free hand out with fingers splayed as though to push them back, before turning his attention back to the pickup. The parents and children froze in the playground. Daniel winked at him.

'Nice work,' he said. 'Now drop your gun. I haven't forgotten you're holding it.'

Reluctantly, Cámara let the pistol slide from his fingers and fall to the ground by his feet.

'Hold both hands up near your head,' Daniel said. 'Good. You see, you're right – everything's going to be OK.'

'Is this what they taught you, Daniel?' Cámara said. 'The guns, the weapons, the explosives – how to handle it all.'

He cupped his hands behind his head.

'Is this what being in the Legión was all about? Preparing you for a big moment like this?'

Daniel said nothing, but kept the machine gun trained at Cámara's head.

'I found the file,' Cámara said. 'Yesterday. I should have realised sooner. But there it was – Private Daniel Alemany Llach of the IV Bandera "Cristo de Lepanto" of Ceuta.'

'Very good, Max,' said Daniel.

'Five years' good service,' Cámara continued. 'Commendations, even a medal. And serving under one of the best commanders the Legión has seen for years. Did Colonel Terreros himself ask you to join his secret little network?'

'Network,' Daniel grinned at him. 'Secrets. Did it make your day, Max? More grist for the mill of your radical ideas? The military, the defenders of the nation, quietly and surreptitiously working behind the scenes to make sure that everything stays the same? I bet you came in your pants.'

'The only one having a wet dream here,' Cámara spat, 'is you. Wet with the blood of the people you just killed in the Sagrada Familia. Is this your glory moment, Daniel? Action, violence, killing for – for what? For the sake of the Fatherland, the *Patria*? You pretend to be someone else for seventeen, eighteen years in order to do this? A sleeper, a mole in the ranks of the Reds. Did Terreros ask you to do that, Daniel? Or was it your own idea?'

'Shut up, Max,' Daniel shouted. 'I'm done listening to this.'

'You even slept with anarchists,' Cámara bellowed back. 'Made love to them. Had a child by one of them. How do you do that, Daniel? How do you father a child and bring him up to believe in the very ideas you hate, that you have sworn to fight? Hey? How do you—?'

'By despising the very thing I helped give birth to,' Daniel screamed. 'I despised that kid.'

'Dídac,' said Cámara. 'Say his name. Dídac. He's your son.'

The machine gun began to shake in Daniel's hand.

'He was no son of mine,' he said, his voice lowering suddenly. 'Until—'

'Until what, Daniel? Found out you love him after all, have you? Your own child. You can't hate that. That's real life, not just ideas about how the world should be.'

'Shut up!' The gun waved in Daniel's hand.

'What have you done with him?' Cámara said. 'You almost strangled him, didn't you? Where's Dídac now? Where the hell is he?'

But the expression on Daniel's face cleared, as though he was becoming aware of something for the first time.

'He's fine,' he said, almost to himself. 'I trained him. He's turned out well in the end.'

'Trained him for what?'

'To believe in something real. Not your phantoms and dreams.'

The gun was steady once more.

'You could never know,' said Cámara. 'You were never one of us.'

And Daniel broke into laughter.

'"Us"?' he said. '"Us"? Neither were you, Mister Policeman. You were spying on us. Don't play the sincerity card on me.'

Cámara nodded.

'Terreros told you, did he?' he said. 'Didn't you ever wonder where he got that from, though? How he knew?'

A black look entered Daniel's feral expression. Cámara felt he was on the point of losing him.

'You went too far,' he said, clearly and loudly.

Daniel nodded, his eyes focusing again on Cámara. An unspoken communication, an understanding, passed between them.

'Sometimes people stand in your way,' Daniel said.

'Even ten-year-old boys?'

The gun held steady, but from the corner of his vision, Cámara could see that some of the parents and children were getting restless. The stand-off had been going on for too long: they were getting impatient. And in the distance, several streets away, he thought he could hear sirens as more police moved in on their position. It would not take long before the pickup was surrounded. At which point, any semblance of control that he had over the situation would be lost.

'Was that all that Fermín meant to you, Daniel?' Cámara continued. 'Segarra's son? Just something in your way that you had to remove? You broke his neck like you almost did with Dídac. Perhaps it was Dídac's neck you really wanted to break in the first place. You couldn't handle your feelings for the son you were bringing up but were supposed to reject. Pushing all that emotion down, all that guilt. Was that your pressure valve? Violence? Killing?'

Daniel did not reply.

'It was Terreros's policy,' said Cámara. 'Targeting children. Just like you're doing now. What is it with him? That he could never have kids of his own? Is that where this hate against children comes from, Daniel? Is that why you came here, right here, for this? It's no accident, is it? A playground. What better way to act out your colonel's disturbed fantasies.'

Daniel's face began to redden, his lips tightening over gritted teeth. Behind him, on the other side of the road, away from his line of vision, police marksmen were starting to take up position between the stationary cars. Cámara's eyes stayed focused on Daniel, but he was aware of them on the periphery of his vision.

'But you're not Terreros, are you?' said Cámara. 'You did

father a child, with Isabel, still sitting in Picassent prison for forging those banknotes. It was you who grassed her those years ago, wasn't it? Did you tell Dídac, Daniel? What have you done with him? Have you killed him too? Or has he turned out to be the true son of his father after all?'

Daniel spotted the change. From being concentrated on Cámara and his words, he became aware once more of the world beyond the pickup and saw the parents and children starting to move away from the playground, the darting figures dressed in black behind the cars on either side of the road.

Cámara felt it too, and the sense that everything, quite suddenly, was about to fall apart.

'Where's Terreros?' he said quickly, shouting to make sure his words were heard. 'Daniel, listen to me. Where's Terreros?'

They were at the cusp, the moment of change. Panic was bedding in around them and the policemen were about to make their move.

Daniel glanced around, immediately read the situation, then turned once more to Cámara.

'You'll never find him,' he said with a small shake of the head. 'Don't you get it? No one wants you to find him.'

The breakout began. A group of seven children and parents started their escape from the playground. Daniel spotted them in an instant and, keeping his arm straight, swung the pistol round to shoot them through the windscreen. Cámara dropped to the ground, reaching down for his gun. At that very moment, a shot rang out. Cámara heard a groan from inside the cabin. He stood up: behind him, Bartomeu was holding his pistol with both hands and preparing to take a second shot; inside the truck Daniel was gripping at his side, blood pouring through his fingers and dripping on to the seat.

At the side, the children and parents took their cue and managed to run quickly to the line of cars, where hands lifted them up and away to safety. On the other side of the pickup, a second group was now making good their escape.

Daniel was hurt. Cámara took another step towards him, reaching out to hold on to the door. Daniel looked up at him, his eyes bloodshot and swimming in their sockets. Then his foot left the clutch and the pickup sped off. It crashed through the barriers of the playground, smashing its way past the swings, before careering headlong into the solid iron bollards on the far side.

Daniel's body flew headlong through the windscreen, curving over the bonnet in a jerking motion, before disappearing from view as it fell heavily and definitively on to the road far below.

Cámara hurled himself to the ground, waiting for the promised explosion but there was nothing but silence.

Then the screaming began.

FIFTY-FOUR

'Here, take a look at this, Cámara.'

Pardo slipped over a sheet of paper from the other side of the desk.

'It's the official line. It's the only story about what happened that people are going to hear from us.'

Cámara glanced briefly, uninterested, at the typed words, then looked back at the commissioner.

'The official line?' he said. 'What the hell are you talking about?'

Pardo's office had changed since he had last been there: a couple of new plants, the dust-dirty curtains replaced by fresher, whiter ones that gave the room a cleaner, less depressing air. Money, it seemed, was beginning to trickle slowly back into the police force from somewhere, but reaching no further than the top executive levels. Perhaps, now that the Catalan situation appeared tied up, the purse strings were being loosened, prizes being handed out in a self-congratulatory bonanza.

'You have done an extraordinary job,' Pardo said. 'And the *Cuerpo Nacional de Policía* is extremely proud of you. I've had more than one phone call from Madrid praising my best man.'

Cámara shuffled uncomfortably in his seat.

'That's you, in case I need to spell it out.'

There was a pause, as though Pardo was expecting him to say 'thank you' or something, but Cámara remained silent.

'Right, well,' continued Pardo, 'everyone's very happy with what you did up in Barcelona. Not least of all, me. But the situation is still very complicated. Very fucking complicated. As you're doubtless aware, in the wake of everything that's happened – and the panic – Madrid has suspended Catalan autonomy and effectively taken over. And they've got backing from Brussels as well, talking about Catalonia not being ready for independence. And for the first time in years a lot of Catalans agree. Fucking shit scared – no one wants to see anything like the *ETA* campaign again. We didn't put that lot away just to see another bunch of murderers spring up. Especially now – no jobs, new king, hard Left on the rise, new corruption scandals popping up like toadstools every week. The country's seriously fucked up. Which is why . . .' He nodded at the piece of paper in front of Cámara. Cámara leaned over, picked it up, and then let it fall to the ground.

'If I have to read another memo I'm going to lose the will to live,' he said. 'Just tell me what it says.'

Pardo grinned at him.

'You're tired and a hero,' he said. 'So just this once, I'll indulge you. But don't turn this into a habit.'

Cámara shrugged.

'OK, listen,' said Pardo. 'It all falls on Daniel. He was a radical and dangerous anarchist. We've got plenty on him already from the past. And you can testify to his political beliefs. But he was the one who murdered Fermín. We know this to be true.'

Cámara nodded.

'Yes,' he said. 'He as much as admitted it to me.'

'Exactly,' said Pardo. 'So he murdered Fermín for political reasons – the son of Segarra, one of the richest and most high-profile capitalists in the country. Was he going off the rails? Was he taking the class war to new levels? Maybe. But that's what he did. We don't have to explain the thinking of a madman. But that was just the beginning. Then he went up to Barcelona and planned and launched a major terrorist attack on the Sagrada Familia – a symbol not only of the Church but also the single biggest tourist attraction in the whole of Spain. Gets more visitors than the Alhambra. So it's two in one. Hitting the Church – because he's an anarchist – and also the capitalist economy – again, because he's an anarchist.'

Cámara let his eyes drift to the side, listening, but not concentrating on Pardo's speech. Anarchists – blame the anarchists. As ever. They had been good scapegoats in the past, for both Left and Right. Of course they would be used again. People had heard the same story hundreds of times before, and accepted it for its familiarity. He did not feel angry about it: it was inevitable. And besides, anarchism, for him at least, was not about being a member of a club. It was a way of seeing the world. But he was glad Hilario was not alive to see this.

'And the attack was only partially successful,' Pardo continued, 'thanks to the bravery of Chief Inspector Cámara of the Valencia Jefatura. That's you again, by the way. You saved that fucking cathedral.'

'Basilica,' said Cámara. 'It's not a cathedral, it's a basilica.'

'Same fucking difference. The point is—'

'What about his associates?' Cámara interrupted him. 'Who was Daniel with when he was in Barcelona?'

'The *Mossos* have picked up some anarchist leader called Ximo,' said Pardo. 'And his daughter Sònia. They'll make something stick on them – logistical support, harbouring a terrorist. Except, of course, they're claiming they knew nothing about an attack on the Sagrada Familia.'

'They almost certainly had nothing to do with it.'

Pardo shrugged.

'It's out of our hands. The *Mossos* have got them now.'

Something in Cámara shuddered: such a simple sentence had too many connotations.

'Have we got news on the final death toll?' he said.

'Three,' said Pardo. 'The *GEI* man, the priest . . .' He paused. 'And Segarra.'

'Yes,' said Cámara. 'I heard something.'

'It's big news. You'd think he was the only one killed from the reports.'

Cámara's mind turned for a moment to Célia Capilla. Not only had she lost her son, Fermín, but now her lover as well. And he wondered about Segarra's supermarket empire. Would it be able to survive now that the man who built it from nothing had been killed? He had overheard a comment about Horta employees wearing black armbands in mourning. But they did not know the truth about the man – that he had secretly been funding Terreros's secret, murderous network. The governing party in Madrid had also lost a powerful backer and friend. Segarra's death would

352

leave a big hole at the centre of the political and business worlds.

'All the wounded have mercifully pulled through,' said Pardo. 'But the point is, as I was saying, that without you that number would have been much, much higher. Not to mention the playground. And the Sagrada Familia itself would probably be lying in a heap of rubble instead of suffering only superficial damage. We could have been looking at another Atocha, here. Even worse.'

Cámara's face twitched as the memory of the Madrid train bombings stirred in him. Almost two hundred people had been killed that day in 2004, and it had felt, in the immediate aftermath, as though the country itself had been dealt a near-fatal blow. Change almost never seemed to come in Spain without violence playing a central role, just like now. Patterns of history repeating themselves with almost clockwork precision.

Pardo rapped his knuckles on the desk.

'The bombing's going to set the Sagrada Familia finishing date back by another decade or two,' he said, 'but then these places aren't quick to build in the first place. They've only been at it for well over a hundred years already.'

Cámara picked up the sheet of paper from the ground and placed it on his lap, flicking at the edge with absent-minded aggression.

'There's going to be a medal for you,' Pardo said. 'I can guarantee that now. The interior minister has already given the Police Merit Gold Medal to the Madonna of Montserrat for apparently saving the Sagrada Familia. But then he's Opus Dei, so that kind of mediaeval bullshit's to be expected.'

'I'm not interested in medals,' Cámara said. 'Or medal ceremonies.'

He held the paper up to the light streaming through the window, turning it around as though trying to find something of value there – not the words, but the paper itself, or the patterns that the typed letters made.

'It's not the truth, Pardo,' he said. 'You know that. Not the whole truth, at least.'

He felt too exhausted to get properly angry.

Pardo leaned in on his desk.

'Cámara, listen to me,' he said. 'This is the truth that people can accept and understand. It's the only kind of truth, in the end, that we can deal in.'

Cámara let the piece of paper fall back into his lap and looked at his superior with surprise: it was the most intelligent thing he had ever heard him say.

There was little more to add. He got up to leave, the sheet gripped tight between his fingers.

'Any word on the son?' Pardo asked. 'What was his name? Dídac?'

'No,' Cámara said, shaking his head. 'Or Terreros.'

'They'll show up somewhere,' said Pardo. 'Eventually.'

He smiled when he saw the dartboard hanging from the back of the door. His bags were where he had dumped them the night before on his arrival back in Valencia, and he had slept on a secret camp bed that the people in the *Científica* section kept for emergency kips during night shifts – and assumed that no one else in the building knew about.

A yawn stretched his face open and wide, and he rubbed his hands over his eyes, willing a degree of wakefulness into his body: he felt bruised and dirty – both physically and morally – and wanted nothing more than to sleep in his own bed again.

When he opened his eyes, Torres was standing there before him with two cups of coffee in his hands and a paper bag from the bakery.

'I assumed you wouldn't have had any breakfast yet,' he said. 'So I nipped across the road.'

Cámara relieved him of one of the cups and Torres tossed the bag on to his desk.

'Got you a couple of those croissants,' said Torres. 'The ones that shoot chocolate spread all over you the moment you bite into them. Looks like you could use the sugar.'

'Thanks.'

'No worries, chief.'

Cámara drank half the coffee in one and then started munching on the contents of the paper bag.

'Good to have you back,' said Torres. 'I was almost beginning to miss you.'

Cámara gave him a look.

'I'm serious,' said Torres. 'Everyone's glad to have you back. Look, you've even got a present from Laura Martín.'

Cámara looked to where he was pointing, and, with some suspicion, opened the bottom drawer of his desk. In it, tucked at the bottom, was a half-bottle of brandy. He pulled it out and placed it on top of his desk. A card tied to it with red ribbon said simply '*Congratulations*'.

'I think she's forgiven us for taking over her case,' Torres said.

Cámara opened the bottle, leaned over to pour a slug into Torres's coffee, then added some to his own.

'I should have taken you with me,' said Cámara.

Torres frowned.

'This Daniel was a mate of yours, right?'

Cámara nodded.

'Yeah.'

Torres was about to say something, then thought better of it and went to sit at his desk.

'Oh,' he said, picking up a slip of paper that he had left there. 'Almost forgot. There's a message for you.'

He got up and handed it to Cámara.

'Some guy called Carlos. Said for you to ring him on this number.'

Cámara took it and stared, confused. Then he reached into his jacket pocket and pulled out his mobile phone. It had died at some point over the past few hours: he had forgotten to charge it.

'I wasn't sure if he was dead,' he said. 'He usually calls me on this.' He waved the phone in his hand.

Then he screwed up the slip of paper and tossed it into the bin.

Torres sat back in his chair, but kept his eyes on Cámara.

'So who's this guy, then?' he said. 'This Carlos. He's the one who gave you all those tip-offs, right? About Segarra and the *Hacienda* investigation. What led us to Terreros.'

Cámara raised an eyebrow and looked at his colleague. No secrets: it was what made their partnership work so well.

'Carlos,' he began, 'is the person we've all been working for. You, me, Terreros. Even Daniel.'

He closed his eyes and pressed his fingers together.

'Except that Daniel didn't know it.'

'What are you talking about?' said Torres.

Cámara let out a sigh.

'Carlos is from the *CNI*,' he said, 'and Terreros is one of his agents. He's a source of information. But he does his own thing, has his own network which he keeps at arm's length from the *CNI*. Daniel was one of his men, a sleeper agent, and by the looks of things was passing information on about me, which Terreros then fed on to Carlos.'

'Why?'

'I can't imagine. Perhaps so they could use me, even recruit me. Segundo Pont said something about me being noticed. I thought he was talking as a politician. But actually he was one of Carlos's agents as well.'

'Segundo Pont was working for the *CNI*?' Torres's surprise was genuine.

'Carlos told me as much himself,' said Cámara. 'He was a moderator, Madrid's secret man at the heart of the radical Catalan government. That's why they always said they could do business with him. Because he was theirs in the first place.'

Torres's eyes widened further.

'I think Segundo Pont was sounding me out. Whatever I said must have been good enough for Carlos to approach me later.'

'To give us the stuff on Segarra,' said Torres.

'I imagine that all Terreros's men are ex-Legión,' said Cámara. 'Segarra was part of it, as you know, and was bankrolling things until the *Hacienda* investigation put the wind up him and he pulled out. Which was when Terreros ordered Daniel to . . .'

He pulled on his lip with his fingertips before continuing. It felt like a long time since Pardo had first handed the Fermín murder case to them.

'The way I see it,' he said, 'Carlos was getting nervous about Terreros, perhaps because of Fermín's murder. It should have been a simple kidnapping, but Daniel killed the boy instead. A mistake, perhaps, but – and I never saw this in him, he hid it so well – there was a lot of anger there. Perhaps not surprisingly after pretending to be someone else for so many years. That must really screw with you.'

He shrugged.

'Carlos wanted to bring Terreros under some sort of control,' he continued, 'so he got you and me involved to haul him in. He was never interested in us finding Fermín's murderer – it was all about trying to clamp down on Terreros.'

'But then he escaped,' said Torres.

'Yes, and killed one of ours.'

'I was at Mata's funeral,' said Torres. 'While you were away.'

Cámara raised an eyebrow.

'It was emotional.'

'Yes,' said Cámara. 'I'm sure it was.'

They were both silent for a moment.

'So Carlos was using Daniel as well?' Torres said.

'Carlos is opportunistic,' said Cámara. 'Once Terreros escaped, he was no longer under control, but Carlos could still use him. Daniel thought he was working for Terreros, following his orders to blow up the Sagrada Familia in order to scare Catalans into abandoning independence. Which he was. But that quickly became Carlos's goal as well – at least retrospectively. He thought Terreros would do something, but couldn't imagine the Sagrada Familia was a target.'

'But you did.'

Cámara frowned.

'Daniel said something to me weeks back about the need to act first to prevent things happening. He was talking about something else, but once I began to see . . . What would be the point of a bomb attack after a Catalan declaration of independence? It had to come before if that's what they were trying to stop. So once I suspected an independence move would be made at Fortter's ceremony, it seemed logical to think that the attack would come where and when it did.'

'Not like you to be logical.'

'I have my moments,' said Cámara with a grin.

'But now Carlos has jumped on the whole thing,' said Torres.

'Carlos, the government, the system – whatever you want to call it. A known anarchist attacking a famous Catalan landmark? It's a godsend. And it's worked, by the looks of things. It makes it easier for Madrid to trample over Catalan powers in the role of saviour and peacemaker. No more talk of independence. At least not for now.'

'But Daniel wasn't an anarchist,' said Torres.

'No, he was Terreros's agent. Just pretending. But who knows that? Only you and me. It's so much easier to blame a terrorist act on mad radicals than on former members of the armed forces who are actually – if not consciously – working for the State.'

Torres gave a low whistle.

'You're serious?' he said.

'Yes,' said Cámara. 'That's how it is.'

'We could leak it.'

Cámara nodded.

'To the press,' he said. 'Perhaps. We could . . .' His thoughts turned suddenly to Alicia. 'We might need to think about it.'

'OK.' There was a shine in Torres's eyes, as though he wanted to get on the phone to a journalist there and then, but he saw the expression on Cámara's face and desisted.

'If Carlos wanted Terreros stirring things up in Catalonia,' he said, 'why did he bother sending you up after him?'

Cámara shrugged.

'To keep up pretences.'

Torres snorted.

'It's how he works,' said Cámara. 'The appearance of things, not the reality. That's what's important to people like Carlos.'

'I wonder where Terreros is now,' said Torres.

'I don't know. But I wouldn't be surprised if Carlos has an idea.'

FIFTY-FIVE

They could have him holed up here, on the tiny, fortified island – nothing more than a rock within swimming distance of the Moroccan coast – but Terreros felt freer and happier than he could remember. Seagulls swept in overhead across the waves and he would watch as they flew in any direction that they wanted: towards the land or further out into the Mediterranean in search of food. But he felt no envy, no hunger to get away from what was effectively a prison. His life, his work, his soul – everything glowed with the satisfaction of achievement, of having overcome mountainous obstacles to bring about the final success, the dream of maintaining national unity that had driven him since he had first stepped from boyhood to becoming a man.

He had performed well for his country, and his name would be remembered by patriots for ever. At first only a select few, it was true. But in time, perhaps long after he was dead, the miracle that he had managed to perform, while others simply sat on their hands like a group of schoolgirls, would become known. He would be a national hero, his name taught to generations to come.

The members of his organisation had been released from their duties. The group no longer needed to exist: it had served its purpose, achieved what it had set out to do. Not without loss, but the sacrifice had been worth it. He had lost his best man – Daniel, *El Dos* – but it was the honour of a *legionario* to pay the highest price for the Fatherland. And after living a lie for so long, death would come as a relief. He had been right to pick him out all those years before, when he was still a young soldier. There was a steeliness about him, a thoroughness and violence, but determination and patience as well – attributes that had served him well for the greatest task of his life. There would be a place in heaven for Daniel.

Terreros was provided with enough comforts on this little Spanish possession – a room for his own use, decent food, even a small chapel, conversation with the commander every so often. Controlled exclusively by the military, the Peñón de Alhucemas was mostly forgotten on the mainland, but he knew that they could not keep him there indefinitely. It was a good place to lie low for a while, allow the political situation – now still volatile – to stabilise a little. Then he would return to Ceuta. He enjoyed it there. And life would be that much sweeter in the new Spain he had done so much to forge.

He stood at the window of his room, looking out over the sea, his mind drifting towards future visits to Sandrita, when he heard the distant sound of a helicopter. He pulled out a pair of binoculars that he kept on the table and focused them: it was Spanish, flying over from Melilla. And almost certainly coming to the Peñón.

He turned to the mirror and straightened his already immaculate hair. If there were going to be visitors, he wanted to look his best.

A terrace area next to his room served as a kind of salon. He sat down there in a canvas chair, his eyes staring out at the horizon, and waited. A few minutes after the helicopter engines had stopped, he heard two sets of footsteps behind him.

'Good morning, General,' said a familiar voice.

Terreros got up and turned to see. He saluted and held out his hand to shake.

'Good morning, Carlos,' he said, silently recognising the promotion he had been expecting. 'A very good morning, I believe it to be.'

'Quite right, General,' said Carlos. 'Quite right.'

Carlos did not introduce the other man with him, but Terreros saw from his uniform that he was a sergeant in the Regulares – an infantry unit based in Ceuta made up largely of Moroccan volunteers, and traditional rivals of the Legión. Terreros greeted him, and the man – cleanly shaven, dark-skinned and still in his early twenties – returned the salute.

'I believe this is yours,' said Carlos, holding out a sword-stick. Terreros took it from him and stroked the eagle form of the silver handle lovingly.

'Thank you,' he said in a low voice. 'Very kind of you to remember.'

Carlos bowed his head.

'Have a seat,' Terreros said. Carlos took the other chair. The sergeant remained standing.

'Could I get you some coffee?' Terreros asked. 'I'm sure we could ask for some to be made.'

'Thanks,' said Carlos. 'But we're on a tight schedule.'

'Yes,' said Terreros, a sharpness entering his tone. 'So tell me, to what do I owe the pleasure?'

'There are a few things that need wrapping up,' said Carlos. 'Loose ends.'

'It looks to me,' said Terreros, 'that everything has been a great success. All gone according to plan.'

'My superiors are grateful,' Carlos said with a smile. 'Hence the new rank. It was dangerous, but it looks as though we've got where we wanted to be.'

'Of course it was dangerous!' Terreros barked at him with a harsh military voice. 'But it was absolutely necessary. The country was about to fall apart. Spain – our beloved Fatherland – was about to be destroyed by those atheist Catalan dogs. And we stopped it. We stopped them in their tracks.'

'Yes . . .'

'And do you know why?' Terreros continued. 'Because we have balls. Because we took a risk. But God was on our side. That's the difference. And God favours the brave, Carlos. That's why I did what I did. Because no one else was brave enough to. Sometimes great men have to step up to push back the tide of history.'

'Yes, General.'

'And it worked!' He held up a finger, his eyes flashing bright like headlamps. 'It worked. Once the Catalans saw that their own government was incapable of keeping them safe, of protecting them and their beloved monuments, they quickly turned and fled back to the bosom of the nation. Striking the Sagrada Familia was a stroke of genius.'

He smacked his fist into his hand.

'Always strike the enemy at his weakest point, Carlos. Where his emotions are. That way he's putty in your hands. It's precisely what we did in Barcelona. And look how the cowards abandoned their pathetic dreams of independence and came running back to us in droves. We're a family again. Spain united, as one. As God intended it to be.'

'Thank you, General,' Carlos said, seizing his moment to interrupt. 'We are all – the whole country – indebted to you. Everything has turned out positively.'

Terreros nodded majestically.

'Quite, quite,' he said.

'But there are, as I say,' continued Carlos, 'a couple of issues to deal with.'

'The policeman?' Terreros asked. 'You're talking about the idiot who took me to Valencia? He was useful. I could never have got out of Ceuta otherwise. Although I had to improvise when the fools failed to arrest me at the border. Still, he got me in the end and took me to the mainland, where I could coordinate things. As we planned.'

'He's . . .' Carlos paused. 'Covered,' he said eventually. 'I have enough on him. Some political things, and then a drug issue I can use to shut him up if necessary. Besides, I want to keep him in play.'

'You're better off killing him,' said Terreros. 'Easiest way. No surer method of stopping a man from talking.'

There was a pause.

'Yes,' said Carlos, shifting his weight. He glanced up at the sergeant, who was now standing directly behind Terreros.

'In certain circumstances I agree,' he continued. 'Which brings me to our visit.'

Terreros jumped in his seat, but it was already too late: the sergeant had pulled out a pistol and pressed the barrel into the nape of his neck.

Carlos got up and looked down at Terreros's ashen face. He already looked dead.

'The attack on the Sagrada Família was unauthorised,' said Carlos. 'Your operative was supposed to hit small targets, with minimal loss of life. Bombing the basilica was never the plan. You killed Segarra and you almost killed *me*. Fortunately, however, thanks to that policeman, we managed to avert a bloodbath, liquidate your agent and turn the thing to our advantage. You served your purpose. We got what we wanted. But you are dangerous, a rogue element. And now surplus to requirements.'

He gave him a look of resigned sympathy. Terreros was too stunned to speak.

'The ultimate sacrifice,' he said. 'For the *Patria*. I know you'll understand. You'll be given full honours. *Viva España!*'

Terreros's eyes were hard and red. He tried to lift a trembling arm in fascist salute, but it got no higher than his waist.

Carlos nodded to the sergeant.

'Everything's been arranged,' he said. 'I'll be at the helicopter.'

FIFTY-SIX

Working in the recruitment office was seen by some of his colleagues as a cushy job, but Staff Sergeant Duarte was frankly bored by sitting at a desk all day, sweltering in the absence of any air conditioning and hoping on the off chance that some young man might come in off the street wanting to join the Legión.

The world was a different place from when he had signed up, however: a military life, glory and honour, held little or no appeal for youngsters any more. And now that they were obliged to take women in as well . . . Sometimes it was just better to stick to the old ways. What more evidence did they need than the sight of him there in his office, on his own, with nothing to do all day except stare out at the sea, dreaming of the day, soon, when he could finally draw his pension?

And worst of all, he could not even smoke. Except, he told himself, that getting up from his chair every twenty minutes or so to head outside to light up was at least some form of exercise, and helped to break up the tedium.

The radio blared in the background – more news about the Catalan situation. He was getting bored of it now: always the same old thing, history repeating itself, only changing the details. He barely listened as the newsreader mentioned something about the President of the United States, pressure from Washington, questions over the legality of the Madrid takeover of Catalonia in the wake of the Sagrada Familia attack.

Some terrorist fuck, Duarte thought to himself. The guy – some crazed anarchist radical – had apparently killed himself shortly afterwards when the police got to him. Coward.

He pulled out his packet of cigarettes and got up to walk to the door. Perhaps for the fifteenth time that day. He felt hot, and picked up a plastic cup of water as he strode over, barely hearing the journalist's report about the growing international backlash against the developments in Spain. Some were calling the Madrid move a disguised coup. And if anything, it would inevitably strengthen the Catalan desire for independence. The toing and froing between Madrid and Barcelona – for so long an issue in national politics – looked set to continue, as it had for centuries, and perhaps would for centuries to come.

'History repeating itself,' Duarte mumbled under his breath. 'It always does.'

He stepped out of his office and pulled the lighter up to his cigarette, drawing heavily and watching a trail of smoke get caught in a brief, calming breeze.

From the corner of his eye, something caught his attention. He turned and saw a figure walking towards him: a young man, perhaps seventeen or eighteen. His hair was short and he carried a dirty rucksack on his back. His trousers were scuffed and dirty: he looked as though he had been sleeping for days in what he was wearing.

That's what I'm talking about, Duarte thought to himself, playing out a conversation with some invisible acquaintance about the problems of the young. No self-respect, no goal, no ambition. What are we supposed to do if that's our raw material?

The young man was wearing military-style boots, but dragging his feet as he walked on the other side of the road. Glancing up, he caught sight of Duarte's uniform and crossed the street to speak to him.

'Is this the Legión?' he asked. His face was drawn, tired. And his eyes had an expression that Duarte had not seen for some time: haunted, looking for shelter, a place to escape.

Duarte drew on his cigarette.

'It is,' he said.

'I'm looking for the recruitment office,' said the man.

Duarte stared at him, then threw the cigarette on to the ground and turned on his heel.

'Follow me,' he said.

They walked into the office. Duarte sat down behind his desk. The young man let his bag drop to the floor and stood in front of him.

'You want to join the Legión?' asked Duarte.

'Yes,' said the man. 'I mean, yes, sir. Sorry.'

'There'll be plenty of time for that later,' said Duarte with a sigh. This one would not last five minutes. But who was he to turn people away? The commander would be delighted to hear they had someone new.

Duarte pulled out a pile of forms from a drawer and placed them down in front of him to start writing.

'You're Spanish?'

Yes,' said the young man. And he pulled out his ID card from a back pocket.

Duarte took it and read the details.

'What kind of name's that?' he asked.

'It's Catalan,' said the man. 'Dídac. It's the Catalan for Diego.'

'All right,' Duarte grunted.

'But I want to be called Diego from now on,' he said. 'If that's possible.'

Duarte grinned at him.

'Yes, that sounds better,' he said. 'You're doing the right thing, son. You're doing the right thing.'

He gave him a salute, which was immediately returned in kind.

'Welcome to the Legión.'

FIFTY-SEVEN

He wondered about calling, but his feet had a volition of their own, walking directly and with certainty to his flat. He glanced up at the windows, as if searching for a sign of life – perhaps her face at the window, waiting for him to return. But there was nothing.

He climbed the steps to the first floor, his feet heavy on the stone steps as he ascended. Go now, a part of him was saying, go now before it's too late.

But he carried on.

At the door, he thought he could hear someone inside. The sound of footsteps? Was she there? Was she alone?

His key slipped easily into the lock; he turned it and let himself in.

Alicia was in the kitchen, frying some chicken, rabbit, beans, tomato and paprika. Paella. The unmistakable smell reached him where he stood in the doorway.

It took a few moments for her to notice him. She stopped,

put the spoon down, and glanced up: sunlight was shining in from the open door behind him. He looked like a ghost. Or an angel.

'Hello,' he said.

ACKNOWLEDGEMENTS

Thanks to Esther, Sebas and Rafa for keeping me informed about Spanish police matters; Jenny Uglow, Mary Chamberlain and everyone at Random House involved in the Max Cámara series; Peter Robinson for always smiling; Mike for his hospitality; Rob for being a sounding board; Father Richard Meyer, Heather McCaughey, Pep Noguér and Marga Ripoll for details about the Catholic Church; and Salud, Arturo and Gabi for so much else.

dead good

*For all of you who find
a crime story irresistible.*

Discover the very best crime and thriller books on our
dedicated website – hand-picked by our editorial team
so you have tailored recommendations to help you
choose what to read next.

We'll introduce you to our favourite authors and the
brightest new talent. Read exclusive interviews and
specially commissioned features on everything from the
best classic crime to our top ten TV detectives, join live
webchats and speak to authors directly.

Plus our monthly book competition offers you the
chance to win the latest crime fiction, and there are
DVD box sets and digital devices to be won too.

Sign up for our newsletter at
www.deadgoodbooks.co.uk/signup

Join the conversation on:

penguin.co.uk/vintage